INDELIBLE INK

FIONA McGREGOR

Atlantic Books

LONDON

First published in trade paperback in Great Britain in 2012 by
Atlantic Books, an imprint of Atlantic Books Ltd.

First published in Australia in 2010 by Scribe Publications Pty Ltd.

Epigraph taken from A Magic Mountain by Czesław Miłosz © Czesław
Miłosz Royalties Inc. 1975. Used by kind permission of HarperCollins
Publishers Inc.

Parts of this book, in slightly different form, previously appeared in HEAT,
Griffith Review, The Best Australian Stories 2006 and Meanjin.

1 2 3 4 5 6 7 8 9

A CIP catalogue record for this book is available from the British Library.

Trade Paperback ISBN: 978 085789 412 0

E-book ISBN: 978 085789 413 7

Printed in Great Britain by the MPG Books Group

Atlantic Books
An Imprint of Atlantic Books Ltd
Ormond House
26–27 Boswell Street
London
WC1N 3JZ

www.atlanticbooks.com

In memory of my mother, Gwenda

*Thou shalt not make any cuttings in thy flesh on account of the dead
or tattoo any marks upon you: I am the Lord.*
— Leviticus 19:28

*Please Doctor, I feel a pain.
Not here. No, not here. Even I don't know.*
— Czesław Miłosz, 'I Sleep A Lot'

INK

FOR THE FIRST TIME IN YEARS, the children were all at Sirius Cove for their mother's birthday. A westerly had been blowing since morning, depositing grit on the deck as the family brought out food and fired up the barbecue. Leon, who hadn't been in Sydney for over a year, was struck by the effects of the drought on the city and the emptiness of the house since his parents' divorce. Ross had taken his most valuable furniture and artworks with him, and Marie as lone inhabitant seemed to have shrunk and the house to have grown. Passing the cabbage tree palm that grew close to the deck, Leon leant out to touch the bark, thick and hard as an elephant's hide. An old habit that comforted him.

Clark moved the seedling that Leon had given their mother away from the heat of the barbecue. It was sinuous and elegant with narrow delicate leaves. 'What's this?'

'*Agonis flexuosa.*' Leon broke a leaf off and crushed it near Clark's face, releasing a sharp peppery smell. 'It needs to be planted soon.'

'We can look after it for you, Mum,' said Blanche.

Clark placed chicken on the griddle. 'Yes, please,' he said to Hugh, who was pouring wine.

Marie was walking back to the kitchen. 'I might have a spot for it down near the banksia,' she said over her shoulder.

Blanche sent Leon a look, which he ignored. She was wearing a hat with a wide floppy brim so her mouth, full and always painted red, was the only thing visible. It was smiling wryly.

The children sat down to eat.

'Where's the wine?' Their mother's vexed voice travelled out. 'Where's my glass?'

'Here, Mum.'

'I've poured you a glass, Mrs King,' Hugh said.

'But I had one in here.' The wine she'd had in the kitchen was in a bigger glass, and the last of the Queen Adelaide Riesling, which Marie was convinced didn't sit on her breath as heavily as the Taylors Chardonnay that Blanche and Hugh had brought.

'Mum. Will you come and sit down, before it gets cold?'

There it was, stashed behind the toaster. Marie returned to the deck, flushed and happy, with her Riesling. 'This is the first outdoor meal of the season,' she announced. 'I think we should drink a toast.'

'The weather's beautiful,' said Hugh.

'I think it's sinister,' said Clark. 'It's the last day of August and it feels like summer.'

Dense blue harbour pushed against the canopy of trees below. The flapping of sails from yachts going about was close enough to have come from next door. They had moved the table against the glass doors for maximum shelter, and pinned the napkins down with cutlery.

'It feels so weird without Pat Hammet,' Leon said ruefully.

'She stayed in that house on her own for nearly ten years after Judge Hammet died, you know,' said Marie.

'Yeah, and left the place totally run-down,' said Blanche.

'I liked it run-down,' said Clark. 'I liked Pat. That house was amazing.'

The new neighbours, the Hendersons, had pulled down the Hammets' one-hundred-year-old Gothic pile shortly before the Kings' divorce. They had rebuilt so close to the fence that Marie's winter light was almost gone, and in place of the front garden was a four-car garage for Rupert Henderson's fleet of vintage Jaguars. There were surveillance cameras on the front wall, and the back garden, facing the harbour, would soon be a swimming pool.

'Pat's still around,' said Marie. 'I see her up at the Junction sometimes. Salt of the earth.' She pushed out her chair.

'Where are you going, Mum?'

'To get more wine.'

'You're not supposed to be moving,' said Hugh. 'I'll go.'

'No, no, I know where it is.'

'It's like this entire city has obsessive-compulsive disorder,' Clark went on. 'Nothing's allowed to be more than ten years old. There's no *patina*. It's so philistine.'

'Remember the Hammets' before Pat moved out?' said Blanche. 'The flagging down the bottom was caving in. I went over there to give her some Christmas cake, and there was this giant bush rat dead in the middle of the path —'

'Apparently that house could have been heritage listed. It could have been saved.'

'— it was so foul.'

'It's about history, our need to destroy our history.'

'A lot of the interior timber was cheap and poor quality,' Hugh said to him.

'It couldn't have been.' Clark spoke with his shoulders hunched, bracing for a sneeze. Bloody cat must have been sleeping on the chairs again. He looked around the room but couldn't see Mopoke anywhere. He glared at Hugh instead. 'It wouldn't have lasted.'

'I'm afraid it was,' Hugh said with an insider's authority. 'I think we're often so desperate to look historical that we make these decisions on sentiment, and it's nonsense.'

'I was meaning in a bigger sense.'

'It's bricks and mortar. It needs to last. Architects in the past weren't necessarily better. If someone built Gothic in Mosman now, there'd be an outcry.'

Leon lowered his voice and inclined his head to his siblings, subtly avoiding Hugh. 'I was thinking how much Mum is the house. You know, Dad was all the *stuff*, and now that's gone you don't feel his presence much. It's really just her.'

'She should replace the furniture before the house goes on the market,' said Blanche. With the chaise longue and armchairs gone, the bookshelf had become the prominent marker on this side of the room, and most of the books looked tatty.

'Why buy new things when you're about to move to a smaller place?' said Clark.

'Because it looks like shit?'

'Why don't you wait until *she* says she wants to sell,' said Leon.

Marie returned with another bottle of wine. She handed it to Hugh, then held out her glass.

'Might help to get a bit more furniture in here,' Hugh said.

'I mean, I actually like it with less furniture,' said Blanche. 'I like the sense of space. Like what Leon was saying ... I mean re*place*.'

'So do *I*,' Marie agreed. 'Do you want more chicken, Hugh?'

'Thanks. That'd be great.'

Marie spooned extra sauce on. Poor Hugh. After all these years the boys still hated him. Even Blanche was embarrassed by him. Marie also thought Hugh was an oaf, but as her children thought she was a drunken fool, she often found herself siding with him, out of guilt as well. She thought that family get-togethers would be better without Ross, but his legacy of carping remained. Even little Nell, if here, would probably be making snide remarks. The physical elements of heredity were inexorable, but the gestures and tones seeding generation after generation seemed more like psychological afflictions that she, as mother, should have thwarted. Then again, as at least half the afflictions had come from her, there wasn't much she could do apart from sit back and watch them replicate. Yes, actually, Hugh, as oafish as he was, being free of the King afflictions was a relief. Marie never expected Blanche would marry this man with his thinning, colourless hair, his thick rugby neck, yet she liked Hugh for the same reason that she disliked him — his dreary predictability — and assumed her daughter felt similarly. It was also a relief finding things to agree on with Blanche.

Clark offered the wine around.

Blanche shook her head. 'I'm driving.'

'Why don't you come east, Mum? I think you'd like it. It's less Henderson, more Hammet.'

'I've never lived on that side of the bridge, Clark.'

'You could actually get more value for money in Kirribilli,' said Blanche.

Marie sighed. 'I don't want to talk about this today, thanks.'

'We'll put you on to the people who renovated our kitchen and bathroom,' said Hugh eagerly. 'They did an excellent job.'

'You could get them done for as little as seventy K, Mum.'

'That's such a con,' said Clark. 'When I was house hunting you'd see these ads saying *Just renovated* and it'd be a slap of paint or a bit of Ikea and they'd double the price. Even a mug like me could see through it.'

'We're not talking about Ikea, Clark.'

Marie thought of putting ice in the wine, the crack it would make like her arthritic big toe escaping its shoe at the end of the day. The chill emanating from the cubes through the surrounding alcohol to frost the glass, and persuade her she wasn't drinking as much as she really was. But she was aware of how often she had already left the table, so for distraction she unwrapped her remaining presents. Clark had given her a book. Marie read every book she was given. She liked Graham Greene, Inga Clendinnen and Angela Carter. She didn't like Bryce Courtenay or Paul Auster. Clark gave her crime and local history; she drank the latter down oblivious to style, interested only in content. But her favourite books were her gardening ones, the most significant shelf taken up by eight volumes of *The Encyclopedia of Australian Plants*. Today's birthday present was about first contact. She thanked Clark. Blanche and Hugh had given her a bottle of Issey Miyake. 'Oh,' she said, '*perfect*. I've just run out.'

'If you don't like it, I'll get you something else. And I'll have that. Honestly.'

'Thank you!' Marie tilted her head and angled the perfume at her clavicle. Most of it sprayed over her shoulder, in Hugh's direction. Hugh's neck was flushed and dimpled like the skin of a blood orange. He laughed then refilled their glasses.

Blanche dipped her head and Leon guessed she was grimacing. He got up to help her clear.

Clark walked down to the bottom of the garden, a magical place of mysterious plants whose names he mostly didn't know. Pale green spiky heads weighing on thick stems. Low, fleshy things, one of which sprouted a pink flower like a studded club. Magnolia, hibiscus, red grevillea. Tree ferns, palms, their nuts like pebbles strewn across the path, which grew more indistinct the further down he went. He roared out a sneeze, nearly slipping on the dry leaf cover. Some of the compost slopped out of the bucket he was carrying. Righting himself, he saw Leon arrive and sit beneath the orange tree. He emptied the compost, wiped his hands on the grass, then trudged back up the path to sit next to his brother.

'Blanche told me you got the sack,' Leon said.

'More or less. Restructuring. That's what they call it these days.'

'*Collateral damage.*' Leon used an American accent. 'What are you going to do?'

'I don't know.' Clark shredded a twig to a point, then began picking his teeth with it. His teeth veered at odd angles, as though trying to avoid whatever he was taking in.

'Have you applied for any jobs?'

'There's no work out there if you haven't done postgrad. They advertised lots of other positions too. Even for the guides they got about a hundred applications, four of them PhDs.'

Leon felt sorry for his brother, bowed over his shoe, but he wasn't sure how to talk to him. He was wary of Clark lashing out. Nearly forty, divorced, now the sack. Not that anyone was sorry to see the back of uptight Janice. The fact that his own business was failing didn't strike Leon as a point of solidarity, let alone something to talk about, probably because it was his own fault. 'That's terrible. I thought you were one of their best guides.'

'I wasn't a guide.' Leon had never come to the museum. 'I worked in publications and archives.'

'Well, I hope it works out, mate.'

They sat in silence beneath the tree. Tricked by the heat, the jacaranda had begun flowering. The bark on the angophora was growing coarse. Leon recorded the browning of the rhapis and Blanche's totem magnolia. The sickness, the thirst. He reflected how different it would be working in Sydney in this weather. He would be drought-proofing one garden after another, or creating false economies for clients in Mosman and Woollahra. He would be learning about a whole new biosphere. They didn't anticipate this in college fifteen years ago. The whole horticulture industry was scrambling. Meanwhile, the so-called dabblers like his mother were getting by on common sense. The xanthorrhea she planted as his totem when Leon was born looked robust as a bush native. He could have described its circumference with his arms outstretched. It was a lot to give up, a garden like this. The thought of somebody coming in and destroying it was unbearable.

'So you think Mum should sell as well,' Leon said.

'Yeah. I think the upkeep on a place like this is too much and she needs a fresh start.'

'Sure. But it's *such* a big deal. She created this. You reckon Hugh wants to take on the sale?'

'Of course. A house like this'd pay a massive commission.'

'Maybe he's not so bad, as far as real-estate agents go.'

Blanche was calling from the top of the path. 'We're about to have the cake, guys.'

'Didn't Blanche just get a promotion?'

'Yep. Creative Director. Way into six figures.'

Leon whistled. 'Hugh always seems so genial, kinda harmless, you know? We can at least keep the bastard honest. Can't we?'

'Don't count on me to oversee financial anything.'

'Are you coming?' Blanche crunched down the path towards them.

Leon stood and brushed himself down. His voice lowered. 'D'you think Blanche will?'

'Who knows? She doesn't have to be *dis*honest to benefit very nicely. Does she?'

'We should all get a commission of the commission.'

Blanche stopped a few metres away. 'Mum said there might be ticks down here now.'

Clark jumped up and shook himself.

'I can see one in your ear.'

'Where? Where?'

'There.'

Terrified, Clark began to burrow into his ear canal.

'Oh. It's crawled out the other ear now. Must've gone through your brain.'

'*Blood-suckin' freaks*,' Leon said in another accent, half American, half something else.

He walked up to the house laughing. Clark and Blanche dawdled behind.

'I can't believe he gave her a *tree*,' Blanche said. 'Of all things. At this time.'

'I thought it was a shrub.'

'It's a swamp gum, Clark. They're quite beautiful actually. But, like, couldn't he give her an orchid or something in a pot?'

'He's sentimental about the place too. Why are you guys insisting she renovate?'

'You make out like we've got some kind of great power. *Insisting*. God,' Blanche groaned as the path steepened, 'I'm ex*hausted*.'

'Working too hard?'

'We didn't sleep. Our neighbour's fighting with his wife.'

'That loud?'

'Their bedroom window's adjacent to ours. It goes on all night. And if we shut the window, we get completely roasted. Hot-blooded Venezuelans.'

Blanche had arrived that day with red eyes and Clark had wanted to interpret them as a sign of marital conflict, a career crisis, something, anything, to make her seem vulnerable. He couldn't help but be disappointed to hear it was someone else's problems. He sharpened at the word *Venezuelan*, waiting for a racial clanger.

'Have you looked in the kitchen?' Blanche went on. 'The grout coming off near the sink and that burn mark next to the stove? Those little things. It can make a real difference.'

'I hadn't even noticed.'

'I wonder what her friends think. Susan, for example.'

Beneath the deck now, they could hear Hugh and Marie singing along to the Ronettes. Blanche glanced sheepishly at her brother. She couldn't imagine being with Hugh at her mother's age, nor could she imagine being alone. She had always assumed these two outcomes but the future cataclysm they implied had never been so clear. She considered her mother's solitary rudderless state, and her elder brother's, and a feeling of dread washed over her.

'God,' Clark said. 'That woman. Mum's so submissive with her or something. You know, Susan buys a yellow straw hat, Mum buys a yellow straw hat.'

'Mum didn't get a mobile though. And Susan *lives* on hers.'

'Yes, she did. She just never uses it.'

'*Did* she? She never told me. And I've been hassling her to and everything. Did she give you her number?'

'Yep.' Clark stepped ahead of her as the path narrowed. Blanche fell silent.

Clark said in a low voice, 'Mum just wants to please everyone. Including us. You know that.'

The next Saturday after lunch at Mario's, Susan suggested they go to the new homewares shop on Macleay Street. They went in Susan's car as Marie had had most of the two bottles they'd ordered at lunch. Marie rode with her hand in her bag, palming her wallet. She hummed with excitement. Who knew what she might find out there? All those things waiting for her to give them a home and bring them to life. She remembered her pile of unpaid bills, but she owned a house in Sirius Cove and it was her birthday and spending while in debt had an extra frisson. The casual signature below a sum that could have fed her for months. To be that free and reckless.

She followed Susan into the shop. An assistant at the back noticed them immediately. Marie always liked walking into places with Susan, a tall good-looking blonde with long tanned legs and ankles so tautly defined as to have been carved from wood. Marie was the cute curvaceous side of the partnership, the entry point, and Susan the lure. They browsed with their heads together.

'Why don't you get a lounge suite?' said Susan.

'I thought I'd just get a new chair and a lamp or something.'

'You should start with a lounge suite, then work your way down. If you start with the small things, it just ends up higgledy piggledy and nothing matches.'

Marie barked her shin on a chair and stumbled against Susan, who tipped forward then righted herself on the back of a couch. They giggled tipsily. 'Not this ugly thing,' Marie hissed at the couch.

'Out of my way!' Susan gave the next couch a little whack.

They forged on.

'What about these?' Marie stopped before a pair of Chinese vases.

'Oh no, you don't want those.'

'Why not?'

'Ross has a pair just like them.'

They continued towards the centre of the shop. Something sour released in Marie at the mention of Ross's name.

'Furniture traps memories like odours, Marie. It's bad feng shui for you to hang on to that couch of yours. Isn't this a lovely shop? You have to get something here. Gina's managing Mosmania now, you know, and I can tell you there's absolutely nothing in there. *No-thing.*'

The svelte, bearded assistant approached. 'Can I help you?'

'Yes,' said Susan. 'We're interested in lounge suites. For my friend here. Let's have a look at those.' She set sail across the floor towards some lumps the colour of ice. 'I like that one, Marie. It's timeless. Versatile.'

'Excellent choice.' The assistant nodded. 'It also comes in navy, slate, jade and coral. The covers are washable.'

Susan sat on one of the couches and looked over at Marie, eyes bright. 'It's comfortable, you know. And *I'll* get you a lamp, to go with this, for your birthday.'

Marie could feel acid rising up the back of her throat. She sat obediently next to Susan. Interesting to see the revisitation of styles in the light-filled, glass-fronted shop. Off to one side stepped the functional elegance of Scandinavian couches, with their narrow wooden arms and slim cushions. Ross had had some couches like that taken to the tip less than a decade after buying them. And now they sold for thousands of dollars.

Marie bounced up and down, testing it out. The couch *was* comfortable. She could have lain down and fallen asleep.

'How do you like it?' said the assistant.

'It's very comfortable but I'm not sure about the colour.'

A man in beige chinos sat on the other icy lump, hands flat

either side. He moved around, smiling at the woman standing over him, urging her to join him. She had a fringe that dipped in a melancholy curve below her brow. 'I still prefer the one on eBay,' she said, pouting.

'But you can't *sit* on your eBay couch, sweetheart.' He patted the cushion beside him. 'It could be Sag City and you won't know till you get it. Come on. Try this out.'

She sat next to him, expressionless, staring straight ahead.

'You might change your mind, but the best things will go,' Susan said into Marie's ear. 'Everybody thinks there's an endless supply just because it's furniture. But you wait, they will go!'

Marie looked at the colour chart. Navy and slate would be too dark. Coral reminded her of the 1970s. 'Is there any jade in stock?' she asked the assistant.

'I'll go and check.'

'Don't you think jade looks drab?' said Susan. 'It always ends up looking grey.'

Jade. Chinese. Marie's mind wandered as Susan answered her mobile. She couldn't remember Ross's Chinese vases. What shocked her after he had left with his things wasn't so much the loss as how quickly her mind papered it over. Where is this? What happened to that? her children would say. Marie would have no idea what they were talking about. Oh, *Dad*, they would answer themselves. She worried about the holes beneath this paper, the day it would give way and she would fall through into the dark abyss of reality. No such thing as a free lunch, Marie thought, in her fug, on the glacial lounge suite. Around her wheeled the endless cycle of acquisition and rejection, the costly stink of yesterday's garbage. She slid through it like a stain.

Susan was braying into her phone, 'Hal-lo! No, I'm out. Yes, you must!'

Marie straightened her spine, thought of her wallet and felt a power enter her. It seemed to come from her posture and her credit. These things emanated into the room, alchemised, then returned as this strange and thrilling power. Susan was snapping her phone shut with a clatter of bracelets, filing it into her jacket pocket. Marie turned to her, shoulders thrust back. 'What's his new house like?'

'You can imagine.' Susan rolled her eyes. 'Full of clutter. He's gone completely Chinese, which is why I warned you off those vases. He doesn't have very good taste, you know.' She drew in her chin and looked Marie in the eye.

'Do you and Jonesy go there very often?'

'No.'

The man in beige chinos and his partner moved over to the dining section.

Marie looked straight ahead, confused. So the vases were new. So much for her amnesia. Or were they there already? She pulled the tag around to look at the price of the lounge suite. Nine thousand dollars. She could have got a rainwater tank for that.

'Why do you have to torture yourself, Marie? You should be *treating* yourself.'

'What's she like? She's young, isn't she?' Marie could hear the belligerence in her tone. She didn't like the sound of herself after a few glasses of wine. Her voice emerged louder than she intended, with the exaggerated enunciation of a person for whom clear speech was difficult: a stroke victim, a deaf mute. A drunk.

Susan's irritation was evident. She stood and straightened her skirt. 'Okay, she's plump and plain. An interior designer. Not that you'd know it, looking at all that *clutter*. She fusses over him.'

A little bark of amusement from Marie. 'Short and blonde? Big tits?'

'There's nothing I can say when you're like this. Listen, why don't I buy you a lamp. Let's go and get a lamp to go with the lounge suite.'

'He's got himself another me. I suppose I should be flattered!'

'I didn't mean it like that.'

Susan moved away; Marie followed her. They ebbed towards an uninhabited corner of the shop, bright with scores of lights. They had entered during the last hour of daylight and the street outside was growing dark. Again Marie recognised items from her past — a mushroom-shaped lamp with orange head and white stalk; others on stands sprouting lights at intervals, like lilies. One of those would come in handy. She was again confused by similarities with furniture from the history of her home, as though her home had only ever been a retail outlet. The air became progressively still and muggy. Susan began to fan herself with a catalogue. The catalogue whirred louder and louder, inside Marie's ears a giddy thrumming, then she was tripping over an electrical cord, grabbing on to a lamp, on her hands and knees, skirt up her thighs and Susan was saying, 'Oh god, Marie, oh god,' and the assistant was rushing towards them as Marie vomited her lunch of Pinot Grigio and scampi linguine across the floor.

When she looked up, she saw Susan scarlet-faced, tearing tissues from a small packet. Marie struggled to her feet and wiped her face, clouded with shame. But in the distance glimmered a feeling of levity, even exultation. The man in beige chinos looked at her in horror then left the shop, steering his woman in front of him. The assistant was frozen, hand over mouth. Desire for the lounge suite slaked Marie: she couldn't imagine leaving the shop without it. Her house would be empty, bereft, and she would have nowhere to rest.

Susan fluttered some tissues over the winey vomit. 'Don't worry about the lamp,' she was saying to the assistant. 'I'll pay for the lamp.'

Marie got out her Visa card and walked towards him determinedly. 'I'll sign for that lounge suite now.'

'And then,' Susan whispered, 'I'm putting you straight into a taxi.'

It was Saturday night out there. She was fifty-nine, divorced, with money in her wallet, and she had never been out alone on a Saturday night. She told the taxi driver to head back up to the Cross instead of over the bridge. She had gone to a bar there years ago, on top of a building, with a view across the city and harbour. She was angry, bored, and her mouth was dry. Marie needed a drink.

Halfway up William Street, the traffic slowed to a crawl and Marie looked out the window, fascinated by the gaudy scene. A woman as big as a man stood near a building's entrance like a fruit vendor, offering her enormous breasts to the passing cars.

A prostitute half her age and size teetered past in spike heels to a companion propped against a pylon, head lolling. They leant against one another, slivers of cardboard with fluff for hair, trying not to blow over in the wind. Part of the road had been torn up and construction barriers lined each block. A group of English boys lurched down the footpath, shouting drunken songs. All of this had to be endured like a thicket of lantana grown across the path. The taxi struggled onwards. The rawness of the street, not two blocks from that sumptuous bar with deep chocolate lounges and tinkling piano, amazed Marie. As the taxi paused at a red light, some Aborigines sauntered up from Woolloomooloo screaming with laughter, then stopped to stare directly through the window at her.

Inside the bar, safely seated before the million-dollar view, Marie ordered a glass of Cape Mentelle. It was hours since her last drink. She swallowed the wine quickly and ordered another, then noticed a man at the bar staring at her. Tall and slim with thick grey hair, he was picking peanuts out of a dish and tossing them into his mouth with languid precision. Marie sat facing the window, watching his reflection in the glass. She turned to catch the waiter's eye, meeting those of the man at the bar in the elegant suit.

He turned away to exchange a word with the barman. She hoped he was ordering another drink; he could have been paying for hers. She was the only single woman over here; a party of loud shiny Americans and Australians spread across the couches beside her. She uncrossed and recrossed her legs around the cut she had sustained in the homewares shop. Checked the angle of her face in the glass, sucking in her cheeks for more bone structure as she ordered her wine.

Oh, we love coming here, said one of the Americans. *It's so beautiful, and the people are so friendly.*

Marie moved into their meeting, the first touch of his hand, the shape of him seated in the chair opposite, as the waiter gave her order to the barman. She went into the first months, the initial electric offering of bodies, discovery, compromise. They argued and reconciled, settling into companionable silence by the time her wine arrived, thinking so far into their life together that she only noticed at the last minute the man paying his bill then leaving, shattering an ancient intimacy. She sat there humiliated, sipping her wine, staring at the city lights.

Have you been to Bondi? said one of the Australians. *Oh yeah,* came the reply. *It's beautiful.*

Why would he have been looking at her anyway? The homage of glances she had once known had been withdrawn. Menopause seemed to have hit overnight, dragging down her comely jowls. Marie couldn't avoid the sight of herself in the lift mirrors, repeated in nightmare triptych. Her navy skirt and linen jacket, lipstick cracking off dry lips. She wasn't exactly dressed for a night on the town. How much could she have improved this body anyway? These sagging breasts, this broadened arse, hands cracked with fish emulsion and years of confinement inside the hardened pigskin of gardening gloves. She exited onto Darlinghurst Road.

So here she was, on the street, an object of scrutiny just like those she had scrutinised an hour before. She stood on the corner waiting for the lights to change, a snake of cars sliding past. A finned red Pontiac paused before her, engine throbbing. Inside were four swarthy youths, a screen hanging over the front seat. None of them was paying much attention to the movie. They were looking out at her, smirking. One of them wound down the window, just as Marie realised the movie was a close-up of frantic copulation. The car took off and a yell hung in the air. *Faggot!*

Next to Marie, waiting to cross, was a man in a leather waistcoat, staring at the sky. The lights went red and Marie stomped across the road. At the entrance to the train station a busker was playing 'Blowin' in the Wind'. A couple unnervingly similar to her, in age and dress, smiled as they walked past. Marie had thought that a walk through the Cross would be a testing odyssey, but the street was surprisingly bright and short. She slowed down to make it last. There was a 7-Eleven from which spilt travellers garbling in a Nordic language. Cars cruised in both directions, bumper to bumper. She passed a disco with a luridly lit façade, manned by a huge Islander who looked at her blankly. A woman in track pants staggered across the footpath, nearly crashing into Marie. Everywhere was the blare of music, car horns, sirens, spruikers.

'Hey sis!' someone was shouting in the plaza to the left. 'Sista girl!'

Marie turned to see a large black woman in a black t-shirt with *Treaty!* emblazoned across it in red.

Catching her eye, the woman started enthusiastically towards her. 'Got a smoke, sis?'

'Sorry, I don't smoke,' said Marie, hurrying away, handbag clutched tight to her side.

She rounded the corner past a Deco apartment building, brass nameplates gleaming. You would have to be quite wealthy to own something there, thought Marie. So much for the seedy Cross, the people here aren't exactly *poor*. She marched over to the fountain, a floating ball of liquid light. A boy and girl were sitting on its edge and, as Marie passed, the girl turned to throw up in the water. A parmesan smell of vomit arose, reminding her of the shopping trip, and she wondered if it was on her clothes. Rock'n'roll charged out of a bar. Suburban teenagers stood outside, the girls in stilettos nervously smoking and flicking their hair. Aren't they too *young*? But wasn't I their age when I met Ross? Nothing returns, thought Marie, walking on. Nothing twice.

There was a lump of rags in a doorway, slumped forward at an acute angle as though trying to lick his shoe. My god, is he alive? Is he a he? A group of bikies stood around their Harleys, fat oozing between waistcoat and jeans. One with white hair, slurping on a can of Solo, looked like their leader. Outside Stripperama stood a girl in tight jeans, sports bag slung over her shoulder. *Nooo*, she was saying into a mobile. *You're joking*. Marie stopped at a fast-food place and bought a piece of pizza that tasted like melted plastic on cardboard. She ate it walking, realising soon that she had left the Cross, and nothing had happened. She tripped on the kerb. She turned down William Street.

She walked looking over her shoulder for a taxi, but all the vacant ones were streaming up the other side of the hill into the

Cross. She continued down, gnawed by disappointment, pawing with aggression. Why should she have to go home anyway, when the rest of the world was just warming up? She felt like she had been sloughed off and washed away. And isn't it just like you, Marie, to give up and go home? Ahead was the serpentine signage of a tattoo parlour. Marie paused to look through the window. The room was empty. And why shouldn't she be allowed into places like this? she thought, checking over her shoulder with furious resentment. But nobody had looked at her the entire night.

She pushed the door open and walked in. Surrounded by walls of designs, she felt for a minute like she was inside a giant comic book. A tall man with small eyes and long grey-brown hair emerged. A drooping moustache covered his mouth, and stubble the rest of his face. He had a tentative, distracted air. It was him in the photograph on the corkboard behind the counter, straddling a motorbike, two toddlers perched on the chrome body between his thighs, his inked arms stretched around them to the handlebars. He stood in front of her expectantly.

'I want to get a tattoo,' Marie said.

'Righto. Know what you want?'

'I have absolutely no idea!' She hung on to the counter and laughed.

He pushed some portfolios towards her and indicated the walls. 'Plenty of choice.'

She didn't want to put on her glasses. She felt idiotic enough in here as it was. Too old, too fat, definitely too dowdy. There was thrashing guitar music coming from the back room, strangled by a tiny speaker. Marie wanted to be away from the window so nobody could see her. Impatiently, she flicked through the portfolio, chose a red rose, then placed her credit card on the counter.

'Cash only.'

She emptied her wallet with five dollars to spare.

'Neil.' He pointed to himself as he led her through.

'I'm Marie.'

'My sister's called Marie!' His voice was high, with a slight quiver, as though he were trying not to get upset.

On the vinyl couch in the back room, it occurred to Marie for the first time that tattoos hurt, and she began to be afraid. The music crescendoed to a chorus, Neil whistling something unrelated over the top. A sudden desire to laugh hysterically racked Marie. She braced her stomach and looked at the pictures on the walls. A busty girl in denim, a Chinese dragon, a rock band. Body parts livid with fresh designs like offcuts in a forensics laboratory. The tattooist was busying himself with stainless steel dishes and sealed packages. Her heart began to flutter like a moth against the light.

'Where're we gonna put it?' Neil turned to her.

'I don't know,' Marie replied, almost indignant.

'Want people to see it?'

He had placed gold-rimmed glasses on the end of his nose and rolled up his flannelette sleeves. She supposed he saw all sorts in here. A cavalcade of criminals, sluts and rock stars sauntered through her mind. A look of impatience ran across his face. She said, 'Somewhere on my back?'

The door of the parlour burst open and voices filled the shopfront. Neil walked out, said, 'Twenny minutes,' then walked back in. 'Shoulder blade?'

'Alright then.'

She unbuttoned her shirt. There was the cool sting of a swab, then something pressed to her skin. A wave of nerves washed through her, leaving her gelid and sweaty. 'Is it sterile?' she barked.

'You kidding?' He laughed. 'Get sued for farting in public toilets these days.'

Well, that was a detail she didn't need to hear. A whirring began behind her ear.

'So what's the occasion?' Neil asked.

Marie had to think. 'I don't know. My freedom. I'm free for the first time in forty years.'

'To your freedom, then.'

The needles entered her skin.

From the mirror the rose stared slick and shiny as though painted on with oils. It radiated a memory of pain like an ember. In the sunlight, Marie could see every detail. The curl of petals, serrated leaves and thorns, the entire area raised red. It made the surrounding skin look even more tired and damaged.

She had never liked her skin: she lived inside it like a captive. Imported, unsuitable, over-reactive, it kept no secrets. Everything transmitted: spicy meals, tears, anxiety, another long day in the garden. Every ultraviolet hour of her life was written across it, every drink taken. Yet now, finally, here was a mark she had chosen. She had planted her own flag in her own country.

She washed the tattoo, then anointed it with the cream Neil had sold her. A large bloody mary for breakfast to settle her stomach, then a taxi into town to fetch her car from the parking station. She sat inside staring at the repetition of bays in dull concrete. Why did everything have to be the same? Why this preference for neutrality over colour? She reached into the glove box for an indigestion mint and thought about what to do for the rest of the day. She wasn't needed anywhere. When she leant back against the seat, the pleasant, painful reminder of the tattoo lit her flesh. She set off reluctantly in the direction of home, then an arm came down out of the sky and, like a stormchaser, Marie was speeding back to the parlour, trawling the narrow streets behind William Street for a park.

Neil was in a Motorhead t-shirt, writing something into a ledger with a chewed biro. He looked up. 'My first customer of the day!'

She chose an ankleband of jasmine and signed the same piece of paper she vaguely remembered signing the night before.

'I like your style, lady,' Neil said to her in the back room.

Marie was flattered and remotely perturbed. 'Really?'

'Yair, it's like the old days. Punters used to come in 'n' say *I'll have that*. I'd get 'em sleeved up in an hour. Now it's all this consult, consult. They've gotta throw runes or sit in lotus position for three days before they can even decide what they're gonna get! I've gotta get someone to work reception full-time,' he whined with his back to her, preparing needles. 'I can't handle it! I used to smoke marijuana years ago and I think it still hasn't worn off! All this astrology shiatsu bullshit.'

Marie didn't know what to reply. 'No,' she said, placatingly.

She removed her sandal and settled on the couch. It was cool and quiet in the shop. No music played. Sporadic Sunday traffic drifted past. How still these moments where everything changes, hollow yet pregnant, like the eye of a storm.

Neil began to swab her ankle. 'You got a garden?'

'I do, actually. A big one.'

'With roses?'

'No. I tried them but they didn't take.'

'Nah,' he assented. 'Pissy English flowers, aren't they.' He wrapped the transfer around her left ankle and peered at it through his bifocals.

'I have a lot of natives, and a subtropical section along the bottom.'

'That must be a bit of trouble these days, eh,' he said rhetorically.

He switched on the iron, took her foot in his hand, and began to tattoo. How drunk had she been the night before? This wasn't the sensation she had remembered, not this smarting that rang through her leg to her heart like an alarm. Her breakfast bloody mary wasn't sufficient lubrication for the ordeal. Her heart rattled her ribcage like a lunatic prisoner. What am I doing? Why *did* I get a rose? Christ, I can't stand this.

'Fucken politicians,' Neil burst out. 'You know they run their limousines all night while they eat in their swanky restaurants? I saw this thing on TV? All these limos lined up outside this restaurant with the engines running, polluting the fucken atmosphere for, you know, *hours* just so the cars are warm enough to drive the poor pollies home in.'

She had seen the report he was talking about. She had been drunk, shouting at the television. 'Yes,' she gasped, 'I think it's wrong.'

'And we're supposed to feel guilty about going on joy rides?' his reedy voice complained. 'I voted for him the first time around, y'know. Thought he might be the change we needed.'

He let go of her foot and Marie exhaled. 'I did too.'

'They're all the fucken same. It's all downhill.'

Neil looked at her in a comradely fashion, turned her foot, then the pain clawed in deeper. She clenched her eyes then forced them open and was soothed by the dexterity and steadiness of his hand. 'You're bleeding a lot. Y'been drinking?'

Marie said nothing.

'Not a good idea. Turn over?'

Through the ink, more blood welled around Marie's ankle and a hot charge ran through her, an overwhelming sense of herself as flesh and blood, here and now, living and affirmed. To be able to stand and speak and walk away half an hour later felt like a victory. She was flooded with energy.

How could she go home now? On such a sunny day, in an unfamiliar neighbourhood with its buildings crowded together, its gutters of colonial sandstone. The smell of jasmine hit her as she turned the corner. She smiled at an approaching couple, the girl looking back at the ageing woman getting into a pale blue Saab.

The streets came alive as she drove up Palmer past the old church. The terraces with their colourful façades, the businesswoman in her black skirt suit, the bodybuilder straining to bend his muscle-puffed arm to answer his mobile phone. Marie felt like celebrating. She saw a café, parked and went inside.

Did they know? Could they see? 'I'll have a ham and cheese baguette, please,' she said to the waiter as though nothing had happened. 'And a glass of the Lehmann's Cab Sav.' She longed to rest her swaddled ankle on the chair opposite. She ate with appetite and ordered another two glasses of wine in quick succession. Opposite, a well-dressed man was reading the *Herald*. On the front page was the familiar image of a torture victim, naked, bound and blindfolded. The man smiled at her then went back to his reading. So many people out there getting away with murder, so many bodies, so many crimes. And this, now, in her own smug heart, this pounding lust for taboo and severance, this blood seduction. Like coming home after a tryst in Quakers Hat Bay, serving dinner to her family, slick with lies and another man's sperm. This bliss, this murder.

The waiter placed the bill on her table, and she saw a Sacred

Heart tattooed on the inside of his forearm. Thorns encircled the organ, a drop of blood spilt down his wrist, all of it nestled in a bed of flames. So the bells had rung, the bets been laid, and she made her way back into the ring.

Nosing down the alley behind the parlour, sun in her eyes, she made contact with a Jeep. She slowed but couldn't disconnect. She shrieked as metal gouged metal, and in the rear-view mirror saw a man emerge from a building and run shouting towards her. She put her foot to the floor and zoomed around the corner, laughing maniacally. Four blocks away, she found a space where she could park, the wrecked side of her car flush to a wall. Making sure the coast was clear, she walked down to William Street. She wished she could see the man in his damaged Jeep.

When she arrived at the parlour, the tattooist was busy with a client. Marie could see a section of fat hairy back reclining on the couch, then Neil came out and eyed her with bemused wariness. She began to take money out of her wallet. 'I want another one on my right ankle.'

'Whoa.'

Marie looked at him in surprise. 'I feel unbalanced.'

'Don't we all. It's gonna be uncomfortable having both ankles done on the same day.'

She stood her ground with the arrogance of the initiate, and a woman who had the money to buy. 'I'll be fine.'

Through the door, she could see the owner of the back. He had turned, showing a chest blurred with tattoos, the afternoon's work a raw patch on his forearm. Ginger hair surged up his torso to a greying bush around his face. He was grinning at her. Disgusting man.

'You'll have to wait,' Neil said.

'How long?'

'Couple of hours.'

'I'll wait.'

'Give you time to sober up, think about the design you want.' He turned in the doorway on his way back out. 'It's for life, y'know.'

Offended, Marie sat down with some portfolios. Was she that

noticeably drunk? She plonked her handbag on the seat beside her, ate a Rennie then got out her compact. Hard to see herself in this way, in pieces, in the glare, held at arm's length. She didn't look that bad, surely. The glitter in her eyes more mood than alcohol; the usual flushed cheeks, but that could have been sun, or menopause. In any case, there must have been millions of people in the world as drunk as her right now, let alone drunker, she thought defiantly, as she went over to the water cooler and poured herself a cup. So what's the problem? Show me the straight line, officer. I'll walk it.

Night fell on the street outside and, as the alcohol receded, Marie's desire remained white and certain as bone. She chose lilies for her right ankle and settled in for the wait. Minute by minute, the plateau of sobriety extended around her. She began to submit. There was something exhilarating about this exposure; nothing between you and experience, neither barrier nor augmentation.

Every morning a counterpoint of drilling was Marie's breakfast soundtrack. The jackhammer gouging the Hendersons' garden began just before eight a.m. On the other side of the cove a house was being renovated, and each time the jackhammer next door paused, power tools responded across the water in soprano notes.

On Sundays the cove was quiet but Marie had still woken early. She felt shackled, both legs swollen up to the calves as though they had been split open at the knee and lava had been poured in, silting up the ankles. For a while she lay in the throb of her hangover, listening to Mopoke howl at the bottom of the stairs. Eventually she got up and comforted the cat. She showered then dried herself before the mirror, the anklebands glaring up at her. She tiptoed down to the kitchen, across the broken glass of her life. Chastened, she stayed inside for two days, bathing and anointing her wounds.

On the third day she ventured out to meet the man from the nursery. As Jared piled bags outside the laundry, the rich scent of rot filled the air. Beneath his Western Union baseball cap, his weathered face belied the perfect, kinetic sculpture of flesh and cloth that was his body in its faded King Gees. He carried the last bag high against his chest, leaving Marie with nothing but the bottom half of his body to look at: the curve of haunch, the bulge between his thighs. Jared straightened.

'Can I get you anything?'

'I'm right, thanks.'

She spoke to Jared over next door's jackhammer, and Jared said to nobody in particular, 'Ah, the leafy harbourside suburbs.' He had a tattoo of the Southern Cross on his left arm.

Marie couldn't wait to get into the bags of blood and bone to feed her hungry garden. First she had to greet the men from the homewares shop, who delivered the furniture later that afternoon. The lounge suite seemed so big and cold, like icebergs cruising into position. She stood on the edge of the living room, directing them. The lamp that she had smashed and Susan then bought had survived well: they had bent the bottom light back almost to its original shape. Marie kept her old couch facing the view. Looking at the new one, she felt nothing. The drug had left her body.

At the end of the week she began composting and mulching. She was singing to herself outside the laundry when she realised Rupert Henderson's face was at the first-floor window opposite. With its receding chin, narrow jaw and eyes so hooded the lids drooped over the lashes with reptilian lassitude, this face always seemed to be falling, giving Rupert an air of disappointment or disapproval. He was sixty-four and sat on three boards including the biggest insurance company in the country. He had sold his plastic drink-bottle manufacturing business two years ago for an enormous profit, played golf, owned a house in the south of France, and was an American Civil War buff. All of this Marie knew from an article in the *Herald*. From a pole on the top balcony flew an Australian flag. She and Rupert didn't cross paths often, the Henderson house exuding an officious unoccupied air most of the time. Marie waved at the face, which ducked out of sight. Then the window opened.

'Sorry to bother you,' Rupert said down to her. Amidst the portrait of gravity, his mouth was small and clearly defined, like a bottle opener. 'There's a very strong smell coming from your place. I think something might have died.'

'It's just compost and mulch, for the garden. See?'

'It's *very* strong. The smell's gone through our whole house.'

The jackhammer had stopped and a conveyer belt on the far side of the Hendersons' garden was carting disgorged earth and honeycomb sandstone to a skip on the street. Marie could hear this, not see it, since Rupert had built a tall fence immediately on moving in. Four months later, its sharp pine smell was beginning to fade. There was a wife, Celia, but she was out most of the time, busy with charity work. Marie used this as the excuse for her habit of attributing all features of the Henderson house to Rupert.

Across the cove, power tools were starting up again.

'I'm so sorry,' Marie said over the insect whine.

'I just thought I should let you know. It's even infiltrated the air-conditioning.'

'It'll be gone from here in the next day or two.'

'And you have nests in your guttering. We can see them from our balcony.'

'Thanks for letting me know.'

Marie smiled up at her neighbour, whose face from below foreshortened to triumph, but inside she felt furious. Getting this amount of compost and mulch onto the garden in two days would kill her. Bloody Rupert with his swimming pool and flag and mocking little mouth. She missed Pat Hammet and the old house and garden, the sharing of cuttings, the neighbourly updates on the beach and bush. Rupert in his fortress had no idea what was out there, which was the whole point, she bitterly supposed. The environment wasn't a place of participation and exchange for these new neighbours with their fleets of cars and air-conditioned cellars and home theatres; it was a picture safely framed, a display resolutely locked in its box. The jackhammer began again, its vibrations coming through the earth into her ankles, reminding her of the weekend's drunken escapade.

Clouds had come over, grey and close; the harbour lay like syrup below. Marie took an old tomato stake and a jar of water crystals into the top garden. She moved in rows, punching holes into the earth, dropping crystals into them. Rupert thought she was just a stupid housewife, didn't he? Well, ha, little did he know. When she reached the edge of the garden bed she could see down the side path to the bush, filigreed by dead angophoras.

The *Encyclopedia* claimed they were less susceptible to phytophthora: this deadly fungus, which fed off stormwater outlets and the extra nutrients from north shore gardens, was supposed to be slowed by dry weather. But it seemed to Marie that more trees were dying in front of her house than ever before. *I haven't seen any scientific studies but as far I know,* Leon had said in a recent email, *there is no way they can stop the fungus spreading.* Leon attached a link to a petition against internet censorship. Marie signed it and emailed him back: *Don't you think my belt of rhapis would trap those nutrients? That's what it's there for.*

She hadn't heard back. Looking past the bags of compost to the tree skeletons, she thought again of the rainwater tank that could have gone there. She thought of Jared. His tattoo. His bulges. But what was the point in thinking so much about sex, a woman of almost sixty? She drove a stake into the ground.

And was her humus better than cement? she wondered, mixing a vodka spritzer in the kitchen after lunch, sweat dripping down her spine. Was there a scientist in the vicinity who could tell them the pros of clean garden air as weighed against the cons of gluts pouring over garden boundaries like feasts off a Roman table, choking the bush? And hadn't the man who had built this house, before the Kings moved in, torn down a house as magnificent as the Hammets'? Pat had let her know that as soon as they'd arrived. Marie still had the photograph. Burrawong, a stately, mournful Federation, two-and-a-half storeys tall with bay windows; in the middle of the garden, two cabbage tree palms like sentinels. It had been in the same family for three generations. Marie had been crestfallen, felt implicated in its loss. She had fallen in love with its replacement the minute she had entered — the light-filled open plan, the overgrown declivity that spilt into bushland. But in Pat Hammet's living room thirty years ago, looking at Burrawong with its rectitude and tradition, she had felt like her new house: callow, intrusive, unwarrantable.

When Marie had signed the cheque for Jared, she asked him if there was any rain in the long-term forecast.

'Nuh.' He tilted his head back to drink from his bottle of Gatorade, Adam's apple pumping the fluid into his body.

'My garden's really suffering.'

'You think this is bad. You should see the western suburbs.'

He wiped his mouth, thanked her and left.

She slid the invoice into her receipts drawer, then checked her balance online. Slowly but surely, over the last twelve months, it had lowered. With so much of his money tied up in tax liabilities, Ross had manoeuvred his way out of paying a decent allowance. All those things she had taken for granted — lunches with Susan, furniture, the nursery — remained on her credit card like weeping wounds. Then there were the necessities like rates, electricity, visits to the vet, another dehumidification for the rumpus room.

There was no payment due for another week so dealing with the guttering would have to be deferred. Her overdraft would feel that cheque going to the nursery. Through the doorway she could see the lounge suite, lounging away richly and coldly. With a jolt, she remembered her car, gouged all down the side. My god, did I black out? she thought, stunned she hadn't remembered till now. In order to save money, Marie had forsaken insurance this year. She went outside and composted till night fell. Sometimes this place felt like a beast, groaning to be fed and groomed. She resented it.

Coming into the rumpus room through the garden door at dusk, Marie found the television on low. She had forgotten to turn it off again. The six o'clock news was repeating footage of the latest bombing, and Marie could now recognise the victims as easily as neighbours. Broken, bloody bodies staggered past the camera. She stood before the carnage, hot with shame.

Her evening drinks tasted sour: she stopped at five; the following night at four. Jared drove in and out of her dreams in a cloud of exhaust. Fatima the new cleaning lady came and Marie observed her stately grace with envy. Against the window, clusters of bogongs quivered towards the light. She lay awake in the wasteland of bed as the Hendersons' sprinkler system trickled down the path like a bloodletting. A cricket was trapped in her bathroom, its metallic cheep echoing past midnight. Mopoke nosed her way under the sheet and Marie clasped the cat gratefully against her skin.

Clark had said *cunt* in front of his daughter again this morning. The phone had woken him and he had stood blearily over the answering machine, puzzled by the sound of fluey breathing. When it rang again half an hour later, he picked it up. 'Hallo,' said an adenoidal female voice. 'I'm ringing from Chevron at Bondi Junction, and we're offering free hearing tests —'

'You rang me yesterday.' Clark hung up.

He went into the kitchen to make coffee and the phone rang again. Maybe it was his mother. He picked it up. The infected breathing moved into his ear and Clark dropped the handset into the cradle. 'Fucken cunts,' he snapped, turning to see Nell in the doorway holding the neighbour's cat, a fluffy white tom called Kimba with pale blue eyes like the Living Dead. 'Put it down, darling. Daddy's allergic.'

Nell put the cat down on the doorstep where it crouched beneath her stroking hands. 'Pussy, pussy, pussy,' she crooned.

Janice would be at him. She had rung the day after Nell's last visit to tell him grimly that Nell had said *cunt*, and to remind him that Nell was only four years old. Clark retorted that he only got to see his daughter once a fortnight and was therefore unlikely to be the source of the word.

'Dad,' said Nell, as they crawled down William Street in a thick line of cars. 'Can I get a cat?' She lingered on the last letter to emphasise her point.

'Sure. Ask Mum.'

'No,' Nell said patiently. 'We can't have a cat at our place cos of Roger.'

Roger was the yappy terrier who belonged to Chris, Janice's new partner, a barrister. Clark had felt ripped off when the stories of barrister tax evasion finally left the pages of the *Herald* without having mentioned Chris Nickson once.

'I mean at your place. Then I can play with her when I stay.'

'Nellie, darling, your dad's allergic to cats. Remember?'

Nell drummed her feet against the seat. 'I want a catt. I want a *black* catt.'

'Your dad's an infirm old man who gets really sick around cats,' Clark elucidated.

'Oh, you are not.'

Clark looked at her, surprised and flattered. He was constantly amazed by her intelligence and how far ahead of her age she was *conceptually*. He didn't believe in talking down to children. It seemed to be paying off. The State Library was covered in scaffolding, people picking their way along its edge. Clark felt a rush of admiration for his daughter, whose fleshy neck furled beneath her chin when she smiled, whose eyes were becoming more like Janice's — icy, intelligent, chaste and shrewd. He could feel the folds of his stomach sweating against one another like greasy tyres, and straightened his back. The only sort of cat Clark could bear was a dead one, with historical significance, like Trim, Matthew Flinders', whose statue was hidden somewhere in that scaffolding. He launched into a potted history.

Nell asked, 'What did she look like?'

'Trim was a he and he was black and white with a goofy face.'

'Goo-fy?'

'He was the first cat to go around Australia in a boat, Nell!'

Nell looked out the window, and Clark became so involved in what he was saying that before he knew it, like a little paper boat on the whirlpool of life, he was sucked into the harbour tunnel. He hunched over the wheel, silent, bilious, trying not to swear.

Half an hour later he was walking through the light-filled house, calling his mother. He wandered down to the rumpus room with Nell, onto the terrace, and found her outside. 'I'm applying for a PhD,' he told her.

'Oh?' she looked up in surprise. 'And what does that involve?'

'Research and writing for three years.'

'So you will get to write.' Marie was trying to unblock the drain outside the laundry. Her hands struggled in its fetid sleeve.

'*And* get paid for it, if I get a stipend.'

'What are you going to research? Where do you do that?'

'The library, the art gallery, archives, lots of places. It's about interpreting images to construct history. But kind of crimes and misdemeanours, not regular history, more the stuff that gets brushed under the carpet. It's local, of course.' Clark's head began to swarm with ideas too fast to articulate. 'Anyway,' he said, even though this wasn't his real motivation, 'a PhD will help me get a better job.' His real motivation was to write, indefinitely. '*If* I get it, Mum.'

'I think it's a great idea, Clark. I'm proud of you. Look' — Marie held out the bucket to Nell, the mud in it writhing with worms — 'these are what make my garden grow.'

Clark grimaced. Clinging to his thigh, Nell looked from her father to her grandmother, then approached the worms and stared, fascinated. 'Worms,' she said.

'You should have seen the traffic today,' said Clark. '*Un*believable.'

'It's all the tunnels and roadways. They're carving our city into little fortified towns,' Marie said sadly. She packed the mud onto the edge of the herb patch, then led the way into the house.

So here she was after everything, a normal mother doing normal motherly things. That brilliant, fatal conflagration seemed ancient history, the city in ruins, smothered by jungle. She didn't know if she had lost or found herself, here in her kitchen on another sunny day. Some sacrificial urge still burnt inside her. She felt herself revolving on an extreme oval, one moment remote from the fire, the next so close it scorched her. Everything was going to change, and the tattoos felt like protective circles. She poked through the cupboards looking for something to feed them all. Nell passed into the living room, carrying Mopoke, a bag of fur punctured by startled eyes.

'Careful, sweetie.' Clark followed her. 'She might scratch you.'

'She's barely got claws left,' said Marie. 'Put her on her cushion, Nell. She's a very old lady so you have to be gentle.'

'Fucken cunts,' said Nell matter-of-factly, as she staggered over to the cushion to deposit the cat, enormous in her little arms.

'Pardon?' said Marie.

'Nell!' Clark looked at his mother. 'This is Paddington child care, and barristers at home. Can you believe it?'

Mopoke remained in the position she had landed, half standing, half crouching, staring straight ahead. A moth flopped on the floor nearby and she lifted her nose.

'It's the last of the bogongs. Mopoke used to be a great bogong hunter.' Marie looked at the cat sentimentally. 'She used to eat them too. They made a crunching sound.'

Nell stroked the cat carefully into a recline. Mopoke went down, eyes moving from side to side. Clark hovered over them, thinking he must stop saying that big round word *house*, and get used to small, simple *flat*.

'Cunts,' Nell said.

'Pretend you didn't hear her,' Clark whispered.

Marie opened the fridge and laughed into its cold white interior. She wanted to gather up Nell, put her nose into her neck and take in her sweet milky smell. She began to take food out: bread, cheese, ham and bottled dressing, iceberg lettuce in a Tupperware container.

Nell marched in looking very pleased with herself. 'Caniva Coke, Gran?'

'I don't have any,' Marie lied. 'How about water? That's what we're having.'

'I saw Coke in the fridge.' Nell's voice began to rise.

'It's like this all weekend,' said Clark. 'Honestly, I feel like a child abuser when I offer her water.'

'And don't you look smart,' said Marie, getting out the Diet Coke. 'In your new jeans and haircut. What's on the hem?'

'Daisies.' Nell extended a foot proudly. Beneath her fringe peeped a red arc from where she had gashed her head under the magnolia tree last year. Marie remembered the incident more for Clark's hysteria than Nell's.

'They're a birthday present from her stepfather.'

Marie brought the food into the dining room, then plates and cutlery. 'Well,' she said when Clark had sat down, 'I've decided to sell the house.'

He looked at her in shock, then a smile spread over his features.

'That's really good. I mean, it's kind of tragic, but necessary. Isn't it?'

'Pretty much.'

'I got a Game Boy too, Gran.'

'Did you, darling? You lucky girl.'

'And we're going to America for Christmas.'

'Really?' Marie avoided Clark's gaze.

Clark tucked a lettuce leaf into his roll and looked at it glumly. 'I *have* to get fit.' He chewed, eyes roaming the room. In spite of his campaign, the idea of losing the house made him secretly frightened. It would be like cutting off a lifetime's tress of hair, too difficult to maintain, devastating to relinquish. He looked back at his mother. 'It's the end of an era.'

'It sure is.' Marie squeezed her roll shut and brought it to her mouth.

They ate in silence, looking out at the view.

Thirty-two degrees, hot October night. Marie couldn't sleep. Down in the cove a gang of koels began to fight, their outraged caws rising in the darkness. She couldn't use the hose till Wednesday. She lay there mentally listing the tasks. Start researching real-estate agents. Book the guttering man. Prune the kangaroo paws, and everywhere manure, and mulch, mulch, mulch. She was dreading the coming day with its blowtorch sun. But night gave the heat a feeling of luxury.

She went into the bathroom for some water. Mopoke was stretched across the tiles on her stomach, absorbing the cool. Marie drank stroking the cat with her foot. How could you sleep in this heat? Or consider working when the sun came up? How could you do anything but melt and drift?

The heat brought the tattoos up like Braille. The dips and swirls disappeared then rose again, fresh enough to scale slightly, ancient enough that they seemed to have always been there. This language of welts was strangely familiar, as though the needles hadn't so much inserted ink as stripped the veneer from an underlying design.

Her skin spoke in the darkness. Look, this is me. I have arrived.

Marie drove slowly along Military Road. She didn't usually take this route into the city, but she was looking for tattoo parlours. She knew that tattoos, like mobile phones and myna birds, had been proliferating for years already, but she had only just begun to notice them. Like an artist obsessed with a new vision, the synchronicities aligned and she saw her superstition almost daily. The lower-back insignia of the girl in the supermarket, faded adornments on the workmen rendering the Hendersons' swimming pool. She grew discerning, recognising the poor imitations on bad boys in movies. She felt dissatisfied with her timorous, generic markings. A craving had taken root inside her. She couldn't see any parlours on this side of the harbour so she drove across the bridge towards the smog-laden skyline then into the cluttered streets of East Sydney. She passed two parlours in quick succession. Each reached out to place a hook in her eye but she still wasn't ready to stop. She continued up the hill, and at the next sighting began to look for a park.

The tattoo parlour doubled as a body-piercing studio, with a counter of glass display cabinets. There was a wall of designs and a clump of panting rhapis in a wooden stand below them. The man behind the counter was about Leon's age, with a goatee beard into which red fangs were dyed. He was talking to a tiny woman in a pencil skirt and a shirt with the top button done up. Her hair was pulled back in a ponytail and she stood very straight with her handbag perched on the counter before her. She wore black-framed glasses with little diamantés on the arms.

'And I'm thinking, Scary? This?' She placed a fine-boned hand on her chest. 'Switch on the evening news, Bozo.'

'Don't get out much,' the shop assistant mumbled in assent. His earlobes were stretched open by enormous metal tunnels that wobbled stiffly when he nodded. He turned to Marie. 'Can I help you?'

'Just looking, thanks.'

'D'you want to get Indian for dinner?' the doll-like woman said to him.

The designs on the wall were slicker versions of those in William Street. None appealed. Marie found some portfolios on the mantlepiece and began to leaf through them. The further in she went, the more confused and indifferent she became. She had felt some kind of blessing that morning, the image floating, evolving in ether, her body waiting like a dam, but the sense of having been duped now began to seep through her, perhaps even of being the duper. She stole a glance at the old-fashioned maritime designs clustering the woman's arms. Not for her either. The woman's eyes flicked at her, as though she were an insect.

Marie opened the next portfolio. Pages of photorealist portraits. Her heart sank. Maybe she was in the wrong place. Maybe she was being too choosy and what she wanted — amorphous as it was — didn't exist. She opened the last portfolio and three pages in found a tattoo of flames. It rippled off the paper like light. She took the portfolio over to the counter. 'Is this person here today? Can I see him for a tattoo?'

The shop assistant angled his head to look at the photo, and frowned. 'She doesn't work here anymore.'

The woman looked at Marie with sudden interest. 'Has Rhys got her own place?' she said to the shop assistant. 'Good for her.'

'Why's that still in there?' he said under his breath. His fingers slid into the sleeve and plucked the photo out.

'Bloody good choice, if I may say so myself,' the woman said.

'Can you tell me where she works?'

The shop assistant looked at his girlfriend with accusative eyes. She pursed her lips at him. Marie could feel their game somehow favouring her. The assistant wrote on a piece of paper. 'Up the road. And you didn't get the address from anyone in this shop. Okay?'

His girlfriend laughed. 'As if the whole world won't be queuing up soon enough.'

Hot winds from the western plains had settled into the streets of Surry Hills like sauce into a griddle. Marie turned down a laneway. Over back fences vegetation spilt. She passed through the sweet-smelling shadows of jacaranda, their blossoms carpeting the bitumen purple. She turned into a street of plane trees and grand nineteenth-century terraces four storeys tall with flaking façades. A dracaena angled its spiky head over a wrought-iron fence. The frangipani were putting out their first flowers. Now and then Marie touched her hand to a smooth leaf or cold steel to give herself the answer of texture. She stopped at a house with a *For Sale* sign but couldn't see through the window.

She headed vaguely in the direction of the address. She wasn't in a hurry. It had been weeks of nothing but household tasks; now she was off-duty. She knew the area superficially from when Leon lived here but wandering the streets on foot was different from driving to a specific point. She became random as a leaf; she could go anywhere, was open to everything. She passed a girl in checked trousers with straps linking the legs; an elderly couple arm in arm muttering to one another in a foreign language. Between the gentrified houses was an occasional ramshackle terrace, projecting a smell of damp and cockroaches. Marie went into a bakery and bought a quiche, which she devoured on the bench outside. How long had it been since such pure hunger! She checked the address and realised it was across the road.

A bell rang in the far reaches and the door clicked open. Canvases of tattooed ladies danced around her with carnival exuberance. In the next room was a table with a large diary on it, a vase of irises, portfolios and a box of tissues. On the right, a staircase ascended to the floor above. The walls were hung with old photos. There was the tramp of boots then a woman emerged from the back room. She was tall with dark shaggy hair and an angular face into which were sunk large, dark, bloodshot eyes. Her high forehead and full top lip gave her an inquiring, opinionated air. Thick metal hoops hung from her lobes, she was of an indeterminate age, and both her hands were completely tattooed. She appraised Marie with one swift glance, and frank disappointment. She opened the diary on the table and leafed through the pages. She spoke in the tart, ironic drawl of old Sydney. 'Um … d'you have an appointment with Rob?'

Diffident with sobriety, Marie tried not to stare at the grids that extended from the woman's sleeves to the first joint of each finger. 'No. I don't have an appointment with anyone. I wanted to see Rhys.'

The woman shut the diary and looked Marie up and down.

Suspicion was joined by confidence, and mild curiosity. She cocked her head. 'How did you get my address?'

'From a place on Crown Street.'

'Ohhh … Why —' she began, then cut herself off.

She continued to stare at Marie, who squirmed and looked away. 'I saw a photograph of your work there. I thought it was beautiful.'

Rhys sent her a brief smile. 'Just a sec.' She left the room.

On the wall was a photo of *Alice — Inuit Tattooist*, a smiling nonagenarian in a frumpy cardigan with tattoos lining her cheeks and jawbone. Next to this was a photo of a prepubescent girl whose sultry Asian eyes pierced the camera with bold self-possession. A tiny cross marked the end of her nose and the middle of her forehead. She was naked from the waist up, hung with necklaces, her arms tattooed with sleeves of snake scales. Marie could hear the rumble of a male voice, and Rhys's lighter reply. She stepped closer to examine the tattooed girl, when the artist returned and issued her edicts.

'I wasn't supposed to be free right now. Somebody else was due.'

'I'm sorry.'

'I only do customised.'

'That's fine.'

'I got a two-month waiting list.'

Marie was crestfallen. She wanted a tattoo immediately but also felt she had come to the right place and didn't want to go anywhere else. 'I'll wait.'

'Know what you want?'

'Yes. Flames.'

Rhys sat at the table and indicated the chair opposite, and her portfolios. 'Okay, d'you know where? If you want my advice, I think flames go best on the lower torso. The belly is ideal for older women, especially if you've had kids. The texture of stretchmarks, you know.'

'Oh, I've got plenty of them.'

She listened to Rhys's advice while she turned the pages. A Hokusai wave breaking across a calf muscle. A corset delicate as lace down a woman's spine, in black ink only. And all across a large man's back, Australiana bright as a 1930s advertisement. She began to feel excited.

'Alright, my belly. I've had three children,' she added shyly.

'Looks great. I presume you've been tattooed before. You'll have to shave, down to about here, or wax. Think about how big an area you want to cover. You'll notice a lot of space in my designs: bare skin is part of my palette so I tattoo fast, which is good for you. I'll measure you up for the design today.' She plucked a tissue from the box and honked into it. 'Bloody plane trees. I'll pencil you in for the first available and if you want you can go on my cancellation list. I get a cancellation, I text whoever's next on the list. I don't hear back within the hour, I text the next person.'

'I'd love to come in as soon as possible.'

'Yeah, I know.' Rhys smiled. 'You want it, like, *now.*'

She took a deposit, and motioned Marie to the stairs.

Afterwards, what Marie remembered most about the tattoo studio was the photo above the stairs of what appeared to be a cadaver.

Marie walked down the path beside Susan, trowel and pots in hand. She was debating with herself whether to apologise for vomiting in the homewares shop. When Susan had arranged to come and get plants, she hadn't mentioned it, but plenty of things were never mentioned let alone apologised for. Marie decided to wait. Overnight, fifteen centimetres of rain had dumped on the east coast and a thin cloud cover kept the air cool and damp. A couple of lorikeets shrieked as they alighted on the angophora blossoms. Marie noticed a track through its shedding bark, probably made by a possum. The trunk beneath was raw and pink as skin beneath a scab.

Susan kept a hand clamped on her large white hat. 'Wooh! It really does pong.'

'It smells happy; it smells like death.'

'Your garden's really surviving, isn't it.'

'It always perks up after rain. But some things are dying.'

'My last azalea's dead, thanks to these bloody water restrictions.'

'I wouldn't worry about azaleas, Susan. I'll give you some broms.'

'And I hear they're going to toughen them even more.'

'The dams have dropped to forty-five percent.' Marie arrived at the patch of bromeliads and bent down to dig. 'Sometimes I think we're going to run out of water altogether.'

'Not with the desalination plant.'

'I mean in the long term. The whole country.'

Susan stood above her, scanning the garden despondently. 'I'm very unhappy with my gardener. He charges through the nose.'

On her knees beneath this cascade of mild rebuttals, two feet from Susan's gold sandals, from her freshly painted russet toenails, Marie was assailed by a sudden sense of incongruity. *What am I doing with this woman?* She had been friends with Susan since their husbands formed King Jones in the 1970s; even after the cataclysmic split of the advertising agency twenty years later, and worse, they had endured. *We hardly know each other*, she thought as she potted the bromeliads. They walked back up to the house.

'I saw Louise out the window of my car the other day. She looks like she's about to drop,' Marie said.

'It's due in the new year.'

'God, it goes quickly. You're going to be a grandmother!'

'We're getting old, Marie.'

'We're all getting old at the same rate. Nature's democratic by nature.'

Pleased with her platitude, Marie stopped to pick some mint and lemongrass.

'And how's Clark?' Susan asked. 'Has he found another job?'

'He's applied for a PhD.'

'Oh yes. Robert moved home when he did his PhD. He was only twenty-three. Watch out you don't have Clark back on your doorstep, wanting three meals a day.'

'Susan, he's thirty-nine. He's a father.'

'Well, they do say that mature-age students apply themselves better. And Blanche?'

They discussed their children briefly, mechanically, like cuckoos coming out to strike the hour.

'Anyway,' Susan reverted, as they walked up the side path, 'nature doesn't have much to do with ageing anymore. Honestly, Marie, the lengths people go to these days. Sometimes when I'm at the hairdresser's I think I'm the only one in the room who hasn't had something pulled out or put in.'

'You don't need to. You look fabulous and you know it.'

In the shade, Susan's eyes were visible behind her purple UV lenses. She looked at Marie with devious invitation. 'Gina has been getting Botox treatment. Did I tell you?'

'*No.*' Marie's face jutted forward eagerly.

'She swears by it. God help her.'

'Gina always was very careful with her appearance.'

'I don't know. I can understand sometimes why the Muslims hate us. It all seems so self-indulgent.'

'I read in *Good Weekend* that nose jobs are all the rage in Iran.'

'Really?'

'Yes.'

Susan considered this scandalous piece of information. 'Well, there I was thinking they were such downtrodden goody-two-shoes skulking about in their veils,' she said in a cheated tone. 'I wonder if they use Botox as well ... They inject it, you know. Needles! In the *face.*'

'I've heard that Botox is good for migraines,' Marie said smugly. 'Apparently it's one of the most poisonous substances in the world.'

Susan barked with laughter. 'You'd better not say that to Gina.'

'I haven't seen Gina since the divorce, Susan. I've been dropped from her dinner party list.'

'Well, you're not getting out of New Year's at our place, and the Tottis are coming too.'

'I'd love that.'

Susan's witty malicious eyes raked Marie's body approvingly. 'You've lost weight, haven't you? Shall we go in?'

From behind, Susan looked removed and vulnerable. The skin

around her elbows had loosened. Sunday after Sunday on her husband's yacht had sailed deep furrows across her face. Nobody escaped these marks of time, the cracked heels and spotty hands. Nature couldn't be cheated. Rain followed sun as night followed day.

Marie walked into the house affirmed. Common enemies aside, she and Susan had bonded from growth in the same patch, absorbing the same nutrients. As they removed their hats, the air outside began to brighten with cicadas. The clouds parted and a billion tiny legs in the trees around the house grew frenetic with their worship. Within minutes it felt as though it hadn't rained at all; within hours the garden would be completely dry. Was there such a thing as true balance? Nature was also the cane toad plague moving steadily south, the man signing the contract for the pulp mill in Tasmania, the spreading saltpans.

'The new lounge suite!' Susan exclaimed. 'I want to sit in it. Why is it over there? Why isn't it facing the view?'

'I don't know. I like the old one.'

Susan sat stiffly with her hands either side of her thighs, like the man in the shop. 'You have to get rid of it. Put this in front of the view, Marie.'

Marie took the herbs into the kitchen and put on the kettle. She could see Susan move to the old couch, then descend into a recumbent posture, her sandals snaking over the armrest. Her swathed hair hung neatly off the other end. There was something comforting in the sight of feet and hair not biologically related parenthesising the furniture. Marie hadn't had a dinner party since her divorce.

'Oh,' said Susan to the view. 'It's so beautiful here. How can you sell?'

'With great difficulty.'

Susan sat up to face her. She made a pained face.

'I have to, Susan. I can't afford it.'

'Well, you can get something near here, something a bit smaller.'

'The real-estate agents are going to start traipsing through next week.'

'Hugh will handle the sale, won't he?'

'I'm seeing a few others anyway. Just to be sure. God, I'm dreading it.'

A loud groan issued from the couch. 'God. I'm *dying* for a cigarette. I don't know what's wrong with me. I gave up fifteen years ago and all of a sudden I'm getting these *cravings*. I couldn't sleep last night so I watched the late movie. You could hardly see the people for the cigarette smoke.' Susan sat up and looked in outrage towards the kitchen. 'It's a crime to smoke these days. It's a crime to hose your garden.'

'It's all a bit phallic.' Marie sniggered.

'It was a Julie Christie movie. Wasn't she just style incarnate?'

'She's not dead yet.'

'I always wanted to be Julie Christie, cool as a cucumber. The young one, I mean. Have you been watching *Desperate Housewives*?'

'Yes. Out of desperation,' Marie said.

'I think it's funny.'

'But do you think they're really desperate? They're all so perfect.'

'Oh, that's just America. They're all on drugs or plastic surgery. What about the one that was on *Melrose Place*? Do you think she's gay?'

'The one with the long face? Oh yes, she's so *cold.*'

'Oh dear,' Susan was saying as Marie came out of the kitchen. 'Oh my Lord.'

Mopoke was making her way across the floor, back leg dragging. She stopped and miaowed loudly. Marie put down the tray and carried the cat out to her spot beneath the Weber on the deck. 'She's got arthritis,' she explained to Susan, who watched the whole procedure warily.

Susan settled into a recliner. The tide was rising, waves thudding against the sea wall. 'What are those trees?'

'Brushbox.'

'It's a shame they've grown so much. It'll cost you on the sale.' Susan pushed her glasses down her nose and looked over. 'Have you thought about poisoning them?'

'I've thought about poisoning their owners, the Hendersons.' Marie bent to remove her shoes and stretched her feet towards the breeze. 'Their bloody wandering jew is spilling into the bush. I'm constantly pulling it out.'

'You're not allowed to call it that anymore, Marie. And your blackboy is a grass tree, you know. *Xan-thor-rhea,*' she intoned. 'One of the Tottis' neighbours in Clontarf is being prosecuted for poisoning a tree.'

'I read about that. The Norfolk Island pine? Lovely trees! What a creep.'

'He doesn't care. He says the fine is less than what tree removalists charge. There's a logic there, you have to admit … I've asked myself a couple of times if it isn't the Tottis, actually.'

'Really?'

'They know every detail of the story, let me tell you. They even know the type of poison.' Susan picked up an almond biscuit with her thumb and forefinger. 'You're looking very chipper, Marie. Better than the last time I saw you. What have you been doing?'

'I've been getting myself tattooed.' Marie twirled her feet. She had painted her nails too, to extend the celebration. 'I got the first one just after our trip to the homewares shop.'

Susan's face went blank. Marie felt like she had just whipped out a plate of strawberries for dessert, only to find they'd gone off. She had always associated Susan with her new self, the big-spending, freewheeling advertising executive's wife, who had supplanted her old self, the prudish Catholic schoolgirl. She thought that Susan must be joking, that any minute she would laugh.

'Look,' she said. 'You can see the designs properly now the swelling's gone down.'

The corners of Susan's mouth began to turn down, her eyes widening. 'Just like that? You just walked into one of those places and got *tattooed*?'

'That's right.' Marie began to talk excitedly. 'You can't imagine what it's like. You feel so elated afterwards.'

'Don't you feel cheapened? I'd feel cheapened. Marie, you were blind drunk.'

'Well, I felt enriched. And I hadn't had a drink for hours when I got this one.'

'Really.'

'Look at them, Susan. You haven't even looked.'

'No, thank you.' Susan looked in the direction of the Hendersons'. The scrape of trowels drifted over the fence. Marie began to pour the tea. She wanted to crawl away and hide.

'My lime tree is dying,' Susan said. 'Really, I'm at my wits' end.'

'Piss on it,' Marie said sullenly.

Susan swung her head around. 'Why on earth would I want to do that?'

'Nitrate is good for citrus.'

'Who told you that?'

'It's a well-known fact.'

Marie drank her tea too quickly, scalding the roof of her mouth. Every little act, every wish was nature as well, even sitting next to her best friend in a state of alienation was the most natural thing in the world, as natural as disease.

'Marie.' Susan narrowed her eyes. 'Are you sure you're alright?'

'I'm fine!'

The next day Marie sat in the vet's waiting room leafing through magazines. The comfort of animal and the scourge of disinfectant fought in her nostrils. Mopoke hissed through the bars of her hutch at a docile Great Dane sitting between the boating shoes of a middle-aged male opposite. Every so often, Marie's finger rose to a bristle emerging from her chin. She hadn't seen it in the mirror this morning but the message her nerve endings now transmitted to her brain was that it was enormous.

She went over yesterday's scene with Susan. A shard of pain sat in her chest. Her two selves weren't that dissimilar, she reflected now, and neither of them — along with Susan — was in agreeance with this third new self who thought of the Surry Hills tattoo studio with impatience, who anticipated it even more than the appointments with real-estate agents. Susan would have scoffed at the page in *New Idea* now open in Marie's lap —

In	*Out*
Rock music	Dance music
Facial hair (on men)	Tattoos, body piercing
Pilates, yoga	Gym, aerobics
Sunblock, fake tans	Real tans
Hipsters	Shoulder pads
Recycling	Fossil fuels

— but she would have secretly ticked things off the list just as Marie was doing now, because it was always better to be in the *In* column, even when the arbiters were fools. Marie noted with relief and satisfaction that she was only *Out* on one count, and considering how hopeless Susan was at recycling, they were pretty much even. She flicked the pages irritably, compulsively feeling her bristle. Witchy hairs, Blanche called them. To think that Blanche was getting them too. Marie was filled with impatience by all she still had to do.

She calmed her cat as the vet pinched the fold of skin between Mopoke's shoulders and slid a long hypodermic into it.

'This'll do the trick.' He was a small neat man who favoured pink shirts and bowties. He lifted Mopoke up in front of him, saying, 'There you are, Moey!' then kissed her on the top of the head and handed her back to Marie.

'Will she be able to walk properly now?'

'She'll have as much movement as we can give her. I'm going to prescribe some pills for her blood pressure as well. The senility could be caused by that.'

Senility. A fate worse than death. Marie drove home contemplating this, one hand on Mopoke stretched along the passenger seat, head drooping over the edge. Could she herself be going senile? Was that the explanation for these bewildering compulsions? But she had never had high blood pressure, she knew where the toilet was. She felt as lucid as a pane of glass. *Well, we all gained from the stockmarket,* said the announcer on Radio National. *Of course I use the royal We.*

Marie flicked the dial and found a station playing The Animals.

She turned it up and sang along, holding the image of the flames against her belly close and warm like a secret.

Marie always tried to give Fatima a cup of tea when she had finished cleaning, but Fatima always refused. She finished exactly five hours after she began and was always punctual, arriving at exactly nine o'clock in the morning. She was a reluctant conversationalist and of that floating age — late twenties to early forties. At midday she took her packed lunch onto the patio with a glass of water and ate staring into the branches of the scribbly gum that Marie had planted for Clark.

She was gone when Blanche arrived. Marie was just in from the garden, with an armful of birds of paradise. She put them in a vase on the coffee table. 'It looks good in here, doesn't it?'

'Fatima is the *best*.'

'She told me she's a physiotherapist. She must hate cleaning.'

'She loves Australia though. She might be able to qualify here eventually.'

'I don't think she can afford to study. Poor thing. It must be awful.'

Blanche stopped on her way to the kitchen. 'Mum, it's not awful, it's fan*tas*tic! Her kids are in school, she's got a house.'

'She drives all the way here from Macquarie Fields, Blanche. She cleans six days a week. She's been trying to get her husband into Australia for more than two years.'

'Half of Sydney drives two hours a day to work, and works six days, even *seven*. And Fatima's not alone, she's got an aunt here or something.'

'I'm just saying it's hard.'

'Could be harder,' Blanche said, striding into the kitchen.

Blanche was busy in the kitchen, moving the kettle over the burn mark, and the bread basket in front of the corroding grout. She had come straight from work and, in her pointy boots and jacket with asymmetrical seams, looked incongruous undertaking domestic tasks. Her thick brown hair was pulled back in a tortoiseshell clip that sat on the nape of her neck. She looked more like agent than occupier, Marie thought. She tried to imagine Blanche pregnant, and a satisfyingly frumpy and exhausted image surfaced. Not the sort of thing they'd go for in Huston Alwick, oh no.

'How do you like the new furniture?'

'Yeah, it's alright. I think you should get rid of the old couch, but that's just me. Which agent is coming today?'

'The one with all the aftershave. The nice woman is coming as well.'

'Both at once?'

'Yes.' Marie smiled slyly. 'I thought I'd let them at each other. Aftershave is coming with a prospective buyer. It should be quite an interesting mix.'

'Buyers already? Are you that deep into negotiations with him?'

'Blanche, it's an experiment.'

Blanche looked around the living room forlornly. 'It feels weird. Where's Mopoke?'

'I don't know. She's got a sixth sense. She disappeared for hours when the Nice Woman came.'

'I'm not the Nice Woman.'

'Aren't you?'

'Let's have a Campari and soda.'

'It's three o'clock in the afternoon.'

'You always have a Campari after working in the garden.'

'Not before sunset,' Marie lied. 'Anyway' — she motioned to the liquor cabinet — 'I haven't got any, I haven't been restocking.'

'Wow.' Blanche's face creased. 'I can't believe I didn't notice that.'

What she did notice was a fresh bottle of Campari in the pantry, and she was dying for a drink. She rarely drank during the day, but this house or her mother had a parching effect, just as she craved a cat fix when she was here but at home barely thought about them. Blanche didn't know if she needed to be here in order to drink or if she needed to drink in order to be here. Two months ago she would have assumed the pantry bottle was deliberately hidden but now she wasn't so sure. Her mother looked sharpened, knowing, fragile. There was the usual mint waft but without its fumey undertone.

She was definitely sober. Blanche realised that she couldn't imagine Marie in any other environment but this, and that she didn't in fact want her to sell. She wanted the house to be here always. Just in case.

She was dying for a drink. 'You know you've got a bottle of Campari in the pantry.'

'Where?'

'With the lime juice and all that stuff.'

'God. No flies on you.'

'So. One last toast for the house?'

Marie walked into the pantry. 'I suppose I'd better steel myself.'

'You have to act from a position of strength, Mum. You have to name a price. I think you should start at six and a half million.'

'Hugh suggested six.'

Blanche was stunned.

The phone rang and Marie picked it up, said a few words, then returned to her task at the bench. 'That was the Nice Woman cancelling. So there will be just one agent after all.'

'Why not try higher? You can always come down.'

'We'll see.'

In a deft and elegant trio of motions, Marie jabbed the ice pick into the bucket, dislodged cubes and sledged them into two tall glasses. Blanche had always loved watching her mother mix drinks. As a child she had been fascinated by the sleight of hand, the fabulously shaped and coloured bottles like so many potions wielded with shamanistic familiarity. She loved seeing her mother in charge of so potent a ritual, this gateway to adulthood with all its dangers and privileges. Later, when Marie became so undone, the ritual remained as the last moment of governance, the keys turned in the ignition before the crash. But beneath Blanche's desire for her mother to re-occupy this authoritative position were contempt and scepticism. Blanche knew that in suggesting a drink she was throwing down a gauntlet. Could Marie handle it? She couldn't bear the thought of her mother humiliating herself in front of a real-estate agent, especially if she was present. Then again, such a scenario would reinforce her mother's intrinsic inability to take control, giving Blanche an excuse to. And to think that Marie and Hugh had started talking without her knowing.

Marie poked a flamingo swizzle into each drink and handed Blanche hers. 'You can take the Campari home with you. In fact, you can take the whole liquor cabinet.'

'I'll take the Campari, but the liquor cabinet won't go at our place. You've got dirt on your trousers, Mum. From the garden or something.'

'Bloody hell. I only put them on a couple of hours ago.'

A cuckoo crowed across the room, and Marie went to her handbag. She extracted a slim red phone and looked at the screen with satisfaction. 'Good.'

'So you did get a mobile, after all that.'

'Yes, I succumbed. What should I put on?'

'The ochre pants.'

'Which?'

'The linen ones. The shirt and sandals are good. Leave them,' Blanche said encouragingly, watching her mother ascend the stairs.

'What are those things on your ankles?' she asked when Marie came back down.

Marie fetched her drink and took a big mouthful. 'Tattoos.'

'Yeah, right. Are they those wire things? That sit flat against your skin?'

'They're tattoos, Blanche. Let's go onto the deck. It's a lovely day.'

Outside, Blanche looked more closely and was surprised by the delicacy of her mother's feet. In an unusual flourish, her toenails had been painted. It was true that the thick ankles, which were also Blanche's resented inheritance, had never looked finer, but the bracelets that encircled them were unmistakably tattooed on. 'God, Mum, are they real? Where did you get them? Were you drunk or something?'

'At a place on William Street. They were a birthday present to myself. I got one here as well.' Marie patted her shoulder blade.

'*God*. I mean the real-estate agent's coming. With a buyer.'

'Well, I'm afraid I can't take them off.'

'Why don't you put on shoes and socks instead of those sandals?'

'Let's be rational, Blanche. What do my ankles have to do with selling property?'

'There's nothing rational about selling property, Mum.'

'*There's* Mopoke,' said Marie.

Marie picked up the cat and began to drag a brush through her fur. 'We're going to make you beautiful for Aftershave, aren't we?' she crooned. 'Not that he'll notice.' She pressed her cheek against the rumbling purr for brief sanctuary. Aftershave was an unctuous man whose odour lingered in the passages of house and head for hours afterwards. *It's a strong house, it's a wonderful house, and you've just got to believe in it*. Those agents got, what, two percent? Objectively, Marie could imagine Hugh earnt his commissions but the thought of him pocketing tens of thousands of dollars from the sale of her house made her feel ill. The thought of Aftershave doing the same made her feel suicidal. Anger rose in her like a hot geyser, and she drank down a large mouthful of Campari. She wasn't going to let her daughter make her feel bad. She was going through one of the greatest traumas of her life, and as far as she was concerned she had a right to do anything she liked. How stupid to worry about some little squiggles when there was a war going on, people were being tortured, and children were dying of hunger.

Marie knew she should make friends with the real-estate agents: partners in profit was the logical approach. But she couldn't separate her soul from the place. So many years here, so many memories, the shift was so much more than corporeal. And it seemed as well that the more valuable the body, the more evil its undertaker.

'Where is Macquarie Fields anyway?' she asked Blanche out of the blue.

'I don't know,' Blanche said sulkily. 'Why?'

'I just wondered. And what are you working on now, Blanchie?'

God help us, Blanche thought, she must be getting pissed. Never asks about my work otherwise. 'Miele. Domestic appliances with industrial features.'

'Oh yes?'

'It's fun. Loads of animation ... I don't suppose you'd want a washing machine and dryer set would you? Can't get rid of them. Everybody in the office has one.'

Blanche was looking at the cat on Marie's lap with longing. Marie rubbed her hand over Mopoke's face; Mopoke shut her eyes and returned the pressure.

'Is she well?' Blanche asked.

'She's picked up a bit, yes.'

'What time does Aftershave get here?'

Marie checked her phone. 'He's due right now.'

'So. Are you going to give me your mobile number?' Blanche spoke in a constricted voice, and looking into her daughter's eyes Marie realised with shock that she had hurt her.

'Of course I am,' she said light-heartedly, trying to make it all go away.

'It's a funky little phone.'

'Really?' Marie looked pleased. She tilted her glass to her mouth. Go away, she thought. *Go away.*

Appearance was everything. Aftershave alighted from his Prussian blue Audi with a pip of the remote car lock, his violently white shirt screaming down the path at them. He entered the house with topographical ease, as though all its dimensions from the one previous visit had been physically imprinted upon his senses. Marie introduced him to Blanche and he shook her hand with a politician's fervour.

His trousers, Blanche noticed, were Armani. Or, more likely, a copy. She didn't care about copies anymore. Let whatever charlatan who wanted to wear them wear them and be damned by their own crassness. It was true you couldn't necessarily tell these days without looking at the tag (though tags could be faked as well), so in a way it had become a question of conscience. Good. The other problem was with people like Aftershave — legion — whose real suits may as well have been fake for the lack of style with which they wore them. Blanche hated that Australian casualness — the entire country sometimes seemed a gross replica of her little nouveau riche family. She imagined with disapproval Aftershave's suit jacket crumpled on the passenger seat of his car. Sure it was a hot day, but why get an

Armani (even a fake) when you weren't prepared to wear the whole thing. There was nothing intrinsically wrong with the man's looks — he was tall, broad-shouldered and evenly proportioned — but something about his soft, barely whiskered face or floppy blonde fringe belied authority. The cologne was Calvin Klein, pure Oxford Street kitsch, an excess of cinnamon like a grandmother's kitchen. His eyes were evasive, watery. In a minute Blanche took all this in and measured it, seated at the table on the deck in a casual posture, leaning to one side, chin propped on hand. Yes. There were the men who were Armani through to their marrow, and the men who weren't. It was that simple.

'This is my daughter Blanche,' said Marie.

'Oh yes, I could tell straightaway. She looks so much like you.' Aftershave looked from Blanche to Marie. 'Yes, it's in the mouth.'

'The King women are renowned for their mouths,' said Marie.

Blanche sat there smiling.

'So you grew up here?' Aftershave asked her.

'Yes, the family's been here more than thirty years.'

'Well, if everybody was like you, people like me wouldn't have a job. What a fabulous childhood you must have had!'

'Yes.'

Aftershave leant up against the railing with his back to the view. 'Well, we thought we had a buyer, but unfortunately they've gone over to the eastern suburbs.'

'It's early days yet.' Blanche smiled.

'Can I get you anything to drink?' said Marie, finishing hers.

'No, thank you. Christmas is in a month. It is a slightly awkward time.'

'I think it's the perfect time for a house to go on the market,' Marie said. 'People come and look now, then they have their holidays to think about it. I can wait.'

'You're right.' Aftershave nodded. 'You're absolutely *right*.'

'What about that cabbage tree palm? Have you factored that into the price? It's older than the house by decades.'

'We've factored in everything, Mrs King.'

For a while Blanche watched this routine of indulgence, caution and coercion. It was the oldest pantomime in history — the whole world was a marketplace — but again a feeling of unease moved through her. This transaction in the temple of her childhood was absurd, even obscene, and her mother was being predictably hopeless. The cabbage tree palm! Yeah, right. Blanche assumed a warrior attitude. 'I imagine people would be clamouring to buy here.'

'We're doing our best, but I have to be honest. Interest rates may rise any day and we won't get the sort of price we might have twelve months ago.'

'This is harbourside property. This market's never going to fail.'

'Of course it won't *fail*. It's a unique house, a wonderful house!'

'My daughter knows all about the market. Her husband works for Coustas and Stevens.'

'Really?' Aftershave's eyes lit up, then retreated. He stepped away from the rail. 'I brought a camera with me today. I thought I'd take some photographs if that's alright.'

Blanche needed to move before she strangled her mother. 'I have some ideas. I'll show you around.'

'One last piece of advice, if I may?' Aftershave said to Marie. 'You might consider installing surveillance cameras to monitor the front gate. There's absolutely no security here. I came right in. I could have been anyone.'

'But you're just Roger. And we left the gate open for you on purpose.'

'The bottom of the property is also very open. National Park down there, isn't it. Public access? You know how picky buyers in this market can be.'

'Shall we?' Blanche led Aftershave into the living room.

'Photograph the garden,' Marie called from her seat, swirling the ice around her glass, thinking she should take Aftershave through but a lassitude pressed her to the chair: it would be so much easier just to sit here and watch the trees and water.

Like blood flowing into her benumbed body, the Campari inflamed Marie. When they had gone upstairs, she plucked Blanche's drink from its little pool of sweat. The indigestion she expected from her first dose of alcohol hadn't come: energised, she went into the kitchen to mix more drinks. Just as she was beginning her second (third really, counting Blanche's), the little teeth in her belly began to nip. That old chestnut: the indigestion got worse when she drank, but if she drank a certain amount, she ceased feeling it. She ceased feeling anything. That certain amount was about ten more drinks: almost total obliteration.

She had to stop drinking.

Aftershave followed Blanche through the house, scattering pleasantries. He photographed the living room and view from an angle that Blanche hadn't considered but saw at once would be striking. Was it to her that Terry's rant about innovation at today's meeting had been directed? Blanche worried her vision had succumbed to cliché as she followed Aftershave through the rooms now, not the other way around. You could get complacent about the beauty of this place. From your position of comfort all you had to do was lazily lift the frame and something dazzling would be captured. Had Aftershave thought of the bedrooms? Probably not. Blanche waited for him at the bottom of the stairs. 'Come up,' she said, then took off, aware of her arse moving at his eye level.

She took Aftershave into her old bedroom, which had been added during the second renovation, when Blanche was twelve. It was her magical retreat, with its bay window; the realm in which she had come of age, gossiping over TimTams with her girlfriends; throwing up a cocktail of Mateus Rosé and No-Doz after an INXS concert. She remembered the summer her father had given her a Sony Walkman, the wonder of the rich, stereophonic sound spreading from the headphones like flowers from seed. Dripfed aural romance, she fantasised about John Reid, a Shore boy who lived in a big house on Raglan Street and soon materialised in this room in the flesh. They had clumsy, virginal sex, John crying afterwards while Blanche stroked his hair and felt weirdly empty. And all of these memories were twenty or more years old, she reflected, as Aftershave moved around the room looking for an appropriate angle to take a photograph from, crouching beneath the television on its clunky bracket in the corner. She was embarrassed by this: she used to think it was the height of sophistication but now it reminded her of a hospital room. And the view was the least special in the house, she realised with a jolt, just a pathetic inch of Athol Wharf poking across the middle distance. You could see the Hendersons' garden, most of it now the just-finished swimming pool, a pale glinting bowl awaiting megalitres. Blanche wondered if the next twenty years of her life would pass as quickly as the previous, and how many more special things would suddenly appear ordinary, even crass, in the company of a stranger. She felt choked by loss.

'Nope,' said Aftershave, jammed into the corner, the camera hiding his soft blonde face. 'I can't get a decent shot in here.'

'I'll show you the master bedroom,' Blanche conceded, knowing from his tone that he had already decided something. Most likely it was decided the second her mother had spilt the beans about her husband, his rival.

Aftershave would not be so easily manipulated after all. He would not be used as a bargaining chip.

Blanche let him out of the house feeling meek and miserable, then went to join her mother on the deck. 'You shouldn't have told him about Hugh.'

'I know.' Marie stirred her drink with its flamingo and sent Blanche a look of drunken cunning. 'We're not very good at this, are we? I made you another one, darling.'

'I didn't finish the first one.'

Blanche drank in silence. She couldn't wait for Christmas in Aspen. Just her and Hugh, skiing every day, not a family member in sight. The three weeks before departure seemed an age; she longed for a cold white drift to smother this heat and loss and obligation. She sipped the Campari, stronger than the first, and her mouth turned at the bitterness. She stared at the water through the trees while her mother sucked up her red drink like a vampire. And yet she believed Marie's claim of a break from alcohol, leaving no excuse for the revolting tattoos. Just an endemic vulgarity, just like Aftershave. She felt a combination of despair and surrender, on her island in the rising sea. There seemed no middle ground.

Alcohol, her warm night companion. No need for food, everybody gone. Marie drank some Mylanta to settle her stomach then poured a glass of wine and switched on the television. *I want to marry you,* declared the English gentleman in his extravagant collar and high polished boots. *You know your family will never accept me,* the maid said, pressing her face against the ruffles of his manly chest. 'You know your family will never accept me!' Marie chimed to Mopoke, flopped along her thighs. She ran her hands through the fur, a purr rising with the upstroke. She watched television with a sardonic eye, yielding in spite of herself, weeping at the end when the ardent lovers were parted by the Cruel Forces of Society and weeping on through the late news. *Every Australian family has a reason to celebrate,* the Treasurer announced. *The economy is booming.* How like a pig he looked, with his self-satisfied smile. Like a child who had stolen someone's lunch and gotten away with it.

She changed the channel, alighting like a fly on the footage of a face being sliced open. Her stomach twisted. It was *Extreme Makeover.* She watched with schadenfreude and voyeurism, sluicing her solitude with the last of the wine. The bloody scene dissolved into the face of an ordinary woman, dotted lines marking her features. The camera pulled away to show her body while a list was recited: *We're going to give her a brow lift, an upper and lower eyelid lift, a nose job, a crow's feet release, dental surgery, a tummy tuck, a Brazilian butt lift and liposuction.*

An ad for expensive scotch came on, all dark wood and seamed stockings, and Marie went to the liquor cabinet for a glass of Chivas. She switched off the television, scooped up Mopoke and went over to the stereo. In twelve hours she would be at the tattoo studio finalising the flames design and this liquor cabinet and its contents would be no more. She put on the Stones' *12 x 5* and danced across the rug holding the cat.

'Last drinks, Mopoke.' Marie drained her scotch, Mopoke beginning to squirm. She put down the cat and turned up the music. 'And out they go!' She took the Midori into the kitchen, swigged then emptied it into the sink. She went back for the Johnnie Walker. '*Ouch*, Mo, that's about a hundred dollars down the drain,' she proudly informed the cat, who was settling stiffly onto her cushion.

The reek of alcohol filled the kitchen as bottles accumulated by the door. Marie lurched out to the garage with a cartonful, pouring them into the recycling bin with an almighty clatter. What a gorgeous noise, the sound of breaking glass. Wasn't that a song? *I love you, hate you, love you, hate you,* Shirley Bassey howled from the house. The Hendersons' kitchen light flicked on.

She went down the side path in the dark, tripping on a bucket outside the laundry. 'Fuck you, Rupert!' she cackled. The moon slid out from behind clouds, lighting the way into the garden. The heat was everywhere, even in the grass and earth between her toes. She hitched up her nightgown and pissed beneath the lime tree.

She went back into the house as 'Sexual Healing' came on, and turned it up. It was a good song to clean up with, even if a bit close to the bone. She mooched around clearing plates, swelling with virtue when she passed the empty liquor cabinet. Then she remembered the freezer. The bottle of Finlandia. She extracted it, a tray of steaks sliding to the floor. 'Now,' she addressed the bottle, 'I'm gonna have to drink you, oh yes I am.' She chugged it all the way out to the recycling bin. Was that her phone ringing? She went back into the house, no, just the opening bars of 'Le Freak, C'est Chic'. Dancing at a party in Whale Beach after she had weaned Leon. New strappy Charles Jourdan shoes — she had danced all night in them.

She replayed the song and danced with her reflection in the glass doors to the deck. Susan was right, she had lost weight. She did a little striptease, opening the doors to feel the breeze on her skin. She looked trim in her black lingerie, and the sexy anklebands. But she needed those high strappy shoes. She made her way upstairs, a shutter or something banging, then she slumped on the floor before her wardrobe to rummage through the shoes. There, at the back. Oh, so beautiful. Hard to get on, those tiny little holes in tiny little straps. Jesus, hang on to the railing going down the stairs will you, Marie! Her laughter pealed out before her. Finally, through the open plan, she stepped tall and elegant in stilettos and lingerie. *Oooohh, freak out!* She jiggled her hips and flung an arm to the sky, then strode across the room to repeat the move up the other end. She held her breasts, leaning forward to get more cleavage. Bloody shutter banging again. She did a disco swivel for the thrill of the rose tattoo and saw in the doorway two police officers, one banging his fist on her door.

Nausea surged into her stomach. Marie fumbled with the remote. 'What is it? What's wrong?' She held her shirt over her body. It felt like a handkerchief. She looked down at a tickling on her knee and saw blood.

'We've had a noise complaint. Mrs King, is it? Can you turn that down, please?'

'Yes, of course. I'm so sorry.'

They stood there politely until she complied. 'If the music goes back up, we'll have to fine you twenty thousand dollars,' said the older officer.

'It won't, I promise.'

Later, before falling asleep, Marie masturbated with a Rexona bottle. She fluffed up the pillows and lay back working it with sorbolene, imagining the policemen at crotch level. She was hot and desperate and ravaged herself so severely that it hurt to piss for the next two days.

'You're lookin' a bit green around the gills today,' Rhys said cheerily. 'Been out on the razzle?'

Marie felt like dying. A session like last night's was normal a year ago, but now it made her feel as if she'd been run over by a truck. She shaded her eyes from a spear of sunlight. 'Just at home.' Rhys raised an eyebrow. Marie strung a flimsy smile around the mountain of her hangover. 'What do they call it? Home disco?'

'Yairs, well, home everything these days, isn't it? The interior era. Turn around so you can see that in the light.'

Marie stood before the mirror holding the flames over her belly. The design gave her form and strength, her body radiating power from the flames at its core. But above this changing body was the same old face, Marie King, of Sirius Cove. 'Do you think I'm mad?' she blurted.

'Not for getting tattooed.' Rhys was at the corner table, soldering. The blinds beside her were drawn, the blue jet flaring in the dimness. It subsided into a bright painful point, then Rhys stood the soldering gun on its end and pushed her glasses up into a headband. 'I wouldn't tattoo you if I thought you had a screw loose. If you wanna go away and think about it, that's fine. No go-ahead until you're sure about what you're doing. I'll give the spot to the next person on the waiting list.'

'I'm a grandmother.'

'Really?' said Rhys, with remote politeness. In a tone of impatience, her face averted, she added, 'I've tattooed grandmothers. I'm a mother myself, whatever that means.' She pulled a tissue from a box and trumpeted into it. 'Where you from?'

'Mosman.'

'... Right.'

'But I'll be moving out of my house soon.'

'They say that moving house is the second most traumatic thing after death.'

'I'm dreading it.'

From outside on the landing came the slurp of thongs and male voices. 'That's just my partner, Rob.' Rhys sucked her bottom lip and examined her. 'Rightio, Marie. What's it gonna be?'

'I want the tattoo.'

'Tuesday then?'

'Yes.'

Rhys fired up her soldering gun.

'What are you doing?' Marie asked, curious.

'I make my own needles. Some of them anyway. In fact I'll probably be using these to colour you.' Rhys smiled facetiously. 'My instruments of torture.'

She called out in a sing-song voice as Marie reached the top of the stairs, 'Go easy on the home disco, eh? We want you bright 'n' perk-y.'

Marie walked past the warehouse, which contained an art gallery, gym and furniture store, then into the laneway that dog-legged around to Bourke Street. The purple brickwork was covered in graffiti. All around the corner swarmed black and red bats. There was a Warhol-like portrait of a young Elizabeth Taylor and a homage to the Coppertone girl with a dog pulling her knickers off, showing her tan line. How times had changed, Marie thought. Ross had been so jealous of that advertisement: it had won awards and been a people's favourite. Now it wouldn't make it past the censors. At the other end of the wall, slapped on with a big paintbrush, was a fourth-term warning: *IF YOU VOTED LIBERAL I WILL HUNT YOU DOWN AND KILL YOU.*

She walked on past the backs of houses; stopped to look through a fence. She was going to sell with a two-month settlement to give herself longer to look for a new place. Could she live here, with a garden this small, without the smells and sounds of the harbour? What would it be like waking in a street like this, in an area where she knew nobody but Rhys, the tattoo artist, who regarded her with a mixture of curiosity, civility and exasperation. Who kept her in Mosman anyway? The Tottis seemed to have disappeared. She had lost touch with Pat Hammet as well, and the Hendersons may as well have been robots. She didn't doubt it was Rupert who had called the police last night. The Joneses — Susan — that was her last connection.

She walked down Bourke Street beneath the spreading boughs of plane trees, their pods releasing allergens for half a million of the city's inhabitants. She realised how little she knew of the world beyond her territory, how confined she had been. And she felt afraid, and lonely. And excited.

'Did you see Mum's ankles?'

'Why on earth would I be looking at her ankles?'

'She's got tattoos.'

'Hey?'

'Didn't you see them when you were over there?'

'We went to Kurnell today, not Mum's. Hang on a sec.'

Clark put his phone on loudspeaker then dropped it into his lap. Sunday night and he couldn't find a park near his building. He turned the corner and drove slowly along a street of hooded figs, their great gnarled trunks glowing in the headlights. He hated parking here because of the acidic carpet of figs and fig shit dropped by bats at night and lorikeets during the day. It stuck to the car and ate through the duco. The moon had risen while he was in transit and hung above him, warped, pitted, luminescent. The fig trees carved shadows black as pitch. As Clark reversed into a space, his sister's voice piped through. He turned off the engine and picked up the phone. 'Pardon?'

'I said I was there last week meeting a real-estate agent and she showed me these tattoos on her ankles. She said you'd been there. I rang you days ago, you know.'

'I know, I'm sorry. I've been really busy.'

'But you haven't been working.' Blanche was incredulous. 'What have you been doing?'

'Applying for a PhD.'

This wasn't entirely true. The application had been sent weeks ago and Clark had since been applying for jobs half-heartedly. Boredom had set in. And guilt for not working. His house had never been so clean: his CDs were even in alphabetical order. He had done his tax and begun swimming every morning. He missed his daughter constantly, like a yawn craving oxygen; he missed her more than he had six months ago when working full-time and seeing her less. He even missed the sleepless nights and insensate days of the first years of child rearing when fatigue stretched out like a long throbbing pain that you eventually became immune to. He spent most of the day surfing the net aimlessly. How could he explain any of this to his Svengali little sister? People without children just didn't understand the permanent demand of parenthood, any more than people with secure employment understood the vulnerability of the unemployed.

'Surely you mean those henna things,' he said.

'I didn't think of that actually ... But she said she went to a place on William Street. I'm sure they're real.'

His sister in any case could make a drama out of nothing. He closed involuntarily against her emotions like a sea anemone. Getting out of the car, he found Nell's jacket on the floor and walked up to the flat with it held against his face like a poultice.

'Look,' he mitigated, 'William Street is getting so gentrified now it's hard to imagine anything very nefarious going on there. How did it go with the real-estate agent?'

'Hopeless. He didn't stay very long. Mum wasn't very friendly.'

Clark laughed. 'Was she pissed?'

'Not initially … we had a Campari.'

'I can imagine.'

Clark unlocked the door, walked through to his study, switched on his computer, walked back into the living room, switched on the television and muted it. He became bored when speaking on the phone without doing something else at the same time, which irritated anyone he spoke to, especially Blanche, who applied the same fierce concentration to telephone calls that she did to any interaction. This attention to detail was partly a pre-existing character trait and partly a habit from work where so much could hinge on a few words down the wire — the tacit refusal inside affable reassurance, the shadow of a knife about to land in your back. Clark, focusing on the latter, objected to what he considered an overly mercenary attitude to conversation. This was what the corporate world did to you, turned you into a permanent hunter. Except that you didn't actually need the quarry you were bagging, it was all merely for display. The world was literally overrun with these types: everywhere marched the sleekly trained and sharply equipped, in service to greed.

On the other hand, in Blanche's view, Clark's hyperactivity signalled an unwillingness to surrender — to scrutiny, pleasure, relaxation. Anything. And neither of them ever wanted to waste time.

'Why don't you want to talk about this?'

'Listen, I'm totally wiped out and going straight to bed. Can we talk about this tomorrow?'

'I'm going tomorrow.'

'In the morning?'

'We leave at eight o'clock.'

'That's okay.'

'There's nothing else to say,' Blanche said glumly.

'Well, um, have a great Christmas?'

'I have these pains,' Marie said to the doctor. 'Here, mainly.' She placed a hand beneath her navel.

She was lying on the bed, looking out the window at tentacles of wisteria. Dr Cayley's surgery was in a rambling house at the back of Neutral Bay. Marie was shocked by his appearance, stooped and slow, with a thick white beard and eyebrows that burst over the fence of his glasses, up the cliff of forehead. She couldn't remember the last time she had visited. Her memory was of an upright posture, grey hair and trim beard. Dr Cayley had plucked a glass bead from three-year-old Clark's ear, removed Blanche's appendix, and set Leon's broken leg. He had prescribed antibiotics to all the family at one time or another, and put Ross on three diets. With its worn floorboards, ancient camellia bushes and faded wallpaper, his surgery had seemed a place of comfort. But now Marie felt unsure, and an endemic mistrust of doctors reasserted itself.

Dr Cayley bent over her, pressing his fingers into her abdomen while staring at a spot on the wall. 'There?'

'No, not there. I don't know ...'

Maybe she had booked the appointment on false pretences. The pain was so mild today that the impression of the doctor's cold, dry hands was one of discomfort more than anything else.

He continued his examination, suddenly reaching an area that made her cry out. He straightened, satisfied. 'The indigestion tablets aren't working?'

'No.'

'Right. Well, I'm afraid it looks as though you might have ulcers. I'll give you a prescription, but in the meantime you should also go and get some tests done.' He returned to his desk and wrote on a piece of paper. 'I'll give you a referral to Dr Barr.' He paused and looked over his glasses at her. 'Everything going well? Are the children well?'

'Very well. Clark's just been awarded a PhD scholarship.'

'Terrific news! Clark's the youngest, isn't he.'

'The eldest.'

'And I hear you're selling the house.'

His eyebrows twitched, and Marie realised that the mouth hidden in its white bush below was smiling, a polite, even timid, enquiring smile. She had a sudden desire to lie back on the couch, in Dr Cayley's arms. Grief surged into her throat. 'Yes,' she said, her eyes on the pen spinning between his fingers.

'Happy Christmas!' He saw her out.

She handed the receptionist her Medicare card.

'That's ninety dollars, thanks, Mrs King.'

Marie was taken aback. 'You don't bulk bill?'

'Not for three years.' The receptionist smiled.

'I'm sorry, I had no idea.' Marie handed over her Visa card.

'That's good. It shows how long it is since you've been to the doctor.'

Marie drove back to Mosman, her gouged car turning the heads of passing drivers. She searched behind the junction for a park in the shade. The shops were filling with Christmas decorations and the media with stories of spending. Australians had bought fewer motor vehicles this year than the previous — a record year — but sales were still strong relative to other countries. On the passenger seat beside Marie, the *Herald* had a photo of two sisters in Pitt Street Mall, proudly proclaiming the expenditure of their first thousand dollars on Christmas presents. Marie switched off the engine and sat for a while in the air-conditioning. In her rear-view mirror, a woman put down bags from Country Road and Kidstuff and pointed her keys at her Lexus.

Marie walked up to Military Road. It was midday and both sides of the street were sunny. She had forgotten her hat and walked with her head bowed, the sun boiling down between each hair follicle. She was sweating, her socks hot and damp: why hadn't she worn sandals? Automatic coverage of tattoos, she realised, but she felt even more uncomfortable being this hot. It was going to be sandals from now on. From the direction of the oval the thrumming of cicadas came in waves. She walked past the delicatessen and menswear shop, and entered Bonza Brats. A blonde with sloping green eyes and a thin disgruntled mouth was folding clothes on the counter. Her face lit up when Marie entered.

'Hallo! What can I do for you today?'

'I'm looking for a sailor suit. For a four-year-old.'

'What a fabulous idea! I *love* sailor suits. Your timing is perfect.' The shop assistant led Marie to a rack in the corner. 'The retro styles are becoming popular again. These have just come in.' She stood beside Marie, flicking through the clothes. She had glossy golden skin and a fine neck strung with seed pearls. She smelt like the David Jones cosmetics floor. 'I had a sailor suit, you know, and I wore it to death. You can't go wrong.'

'So did I. My mother made it.'

'Oh how *sweet*,' said the shop assistant, gazing into Marie's face. Her elegant, long-nailed hands seemed to see the clothes on their own, rifling to the spot where size 4s hung as she continued to stare searchingly at Marie. Then she shook her head. 'But we don't have the time to do that sort of thing anymore, do we? We don't seem to have time for *anything*.'

The suit was of raw linen with dark blue trimming, dark blue buttons and detailed stitching. Marie turned it, inhaling its fresh, natural smell, imagining Nell inside it. 'Oh, it's beautiful.'

'It's Italian. It's actually modelled on genuine Italian navy wear. It's for your granddaughter, is it? She'll love it.'

'I think it might be too small. She's quite big for her age.'

'We are bigger than Europeans.' The shop assistant nodded. 'And if you buy one a little too big, she'll get more wear out of it.' She pulled out sizes 6 and 8.

Marie was stunned by the price: $500 reduced to $325. But she was late, and she only had one grandchild and she hardly got to see her and she might spend too much time looking elsewhere for a present and time was money, so she found herself walking to the counter and getting out her Mastercard.

'Seven hundred dollars,' the shop assistant said and smiled.

Marie swallowed. 'Oh. I thought it was three hundred and twenty-five.'

'That's just the jacket.' The shop assistant flipped out the waistband and displayed another price tag. 'The dress is more of course. They're both reduced even though they've only just come in. We forgot how hot Australian summers are,' she added. 'It's actually a better garment for autumn. You're getting a real bargain, because it's haute couture quality. It's not mass produced in a sweatshop.'

Marie felt rooted to the spot. She wished she hadn't come in here. She couldn't afford the sailor suit. She made a show of appraising the garment thoughtfully. 'You know, I think I'll go for something a bit simpler. My granddaughter's a bit of a tomboy — she's a really active little kid and I think this might be a bit too formal for her.'

'That's *fine.*'

Marie felt furious. How dare this woman assume she could afford something like that? She sulked over to the rack of t-shirts. There was a selection of colours with an *I* ♥ *DAD* logo for eighty-five dollars. (Were they produced in a sweatshop?) Or, for the same price, t-shirts with ladybirds on them. She chose a green ladybird t-shirt.

'And I hear you're selling.' The shop assistant pulled a sheet of blue tissue paper from beneath the counter and began to wrap the t-shirt in it.

'Word gets around, doesn't it.'

The woman looked at Marie disconcertedly, her fingers pleating the paper. 'You don't recognise me, do you? I'm Penny Brayton-Jones. I went to Queenwood with Blanche. I *loved* your house. It was one of my favourite places to visit when I was a kid. I loved your garden especially.'

'Oh, Penny, I'm so sorry! How are you?'

'Really well.' Penny drew a ribbon around the parcel in a tight cross, held it against the scissors and pulled it to a tight curl, and Marie felt her heart constrict for her home and the raw display of its imminent loss. 'And how's Blanche?'

'She's doing very well.'

'I loved coming to your house,' Penny said again as Marie left. 'You had a pinball machine. I thought you were the coolest people in the world.'

'And how are the children?' Edwina asked ten minutes later, tucking the cape into Marie's collar.

'Very well, thank you.' Marie reached into the rack for a magazine.

'And your granddaughter? Will you all be spending Christmas together?'

'Nell's going to America with her mother.'

'How lovely!' Edwina parted her hair with the thin handle of the brush, revealing a track of grey roots. Practical, bossy and loquacious, with friendly crinkling eyes, Edwina reminded Marie of a home-science teacher. She wore low-cut t-shirts that emphasised her breasts, and high-heeled sandals. She put down the brush and left to welcome a customer. *It is not just the politically active:* Marie read in her magazine. *Just to know someone who might be active could land you in hot water.*

'Hallo, Marie!' the new customer boomed, gripping the arms of the chair adjacent, her own tanned, flaking ones wobbling as she lowered herself to a sitting position.

Marie's heart rose. She spoke to Pat Hammet's reflection. 'I didn't know you came here, Pat.'

'I don't really. Only when my daughter forces me to. No offence Edwina. The problem is me. I couldn't care less.'

Edwina laughed. Pat's hair was still long and her face had become copiously lined but she seemed to be several inches shorter. Colette, Edwina's apprentice, removed something from the crown of Pat's head, and a section of hair gently released. Marie remained bowed to her magazine, lifting her eyes occasionally to this ritual; Pat proud and vulnerable as she came undone, her face diminished in the mass of hair that seemed, in its free state, not to be her own.

'How is Sirius Cove?' Pat asked her.

'She's selling,' said Edwina. 'Aren't you, Marie?'

'You're not,' said Pat.

'Yes, I'm afraid I am.'

'Dear old Sirius. How I miss it.'

'It's too much on your own,' said Edwina. 'Those big houses. Did you know the Braithwaites' went for eight million?'

'Really?' said Marie.

'Oh dear,' said Pat again. 'You're the last one standing, Marie.'

'It sounds like a war. The last who ...'

'Who really loves the place. It *is* a war. Who's your agent?'

'I'm not sure yet. Who did you use?'

'Coustas and Stevens. Absolute sharks. You must come and visit me in my poky little flat near the oval.'

'I keep meaning to ring you about weeding parties in the National Park but I never seem to find the time.'

'I'm not getting out as much. I'm too arthritic.'

'Oh nonsense, Pat,' said Edwina, wrapping Marie's head in plastic.

'I am so.' Pat stared firmly back at her. She turned to Marie. 'Where are you moving to?'

'I don't know. I've been in Surry Hills and Redfern recently. I like it there.'

'Really?' said Edwina.

Pat cocked her head and said robustly, 'I suppose you're young enough to handle it.'

Edwina said to Colette, 'I can take over now.'

Pat went docile while Edwina ran the comb through her hair. Marie turned the page of her magazine to find one of Blanche's advertisements: a tilled field with a row of jocular judges' heads planted like potatoes, in the background a farmer wielding a spade. The sky was bulbous with stormclouds. She didn't know what the ad was for but she loved the image, and felt a surge of pride. 'I'd still visit,' she said to Pat. 'My daughter's in Lavender Bay. Maybe it would take a move across the bridge to get me back to weeding.'

'You know, you can find information about them on the net.'

'Are you online, Pat?' said Edwina, in an impressed, avuncular tone.

'I've been online for years,' Pat snapped.

'I'll look it up,' said Marie.

'I'm addicted to email. I have a MacBook.'

'My son does everything for me on mine. The one good thing

about computers,' said Edwina, 'is that then they're not at all interested in television.'

'What,' said Pat. 'The computers or the sons?'

Edwina emitted a tinkle of laughter. 'I mean as soon as I have a problem, Owen fixes it, and he's only nine! He was writing music on his computer from the age of three. It's amazing. There we go, Pat. I'll just wrap this up so it sets better.'

Pat watched Edwina walk over to someone on the other side of the room who had slivers of silver foil stuck at odd angles all over her head. 'Oh, I'm dreadful,' she moaned. 'She really does mean well. Honestly, Marie. Just give me a good kick, will you?'

They sat there for a while in companionable silence. Edwina could be seen in the mirror, plucking foil from the woman's head like petals from a flower. Marie had been coming to this salon for fifteen years and all of them — Dr Cayley, Edwina, Pat — suddenly felt so deeply rooted in her life that moving seemed impossible. Grief lodged in her throat like a piece of food that wouldn't go down.

'I remember when we first met,' she said to Pat, 'how impressed by you I was. That beautiful old house. I still miss it. You had five children and you worked, I was so impressed.'

'I've become a very ordinary little old lady, Marie, slumped in front of her television every night with tea and biscuits.'

'You never liked television.'

'I made friends with it after Marcus died. I'm addicted to *The Chaser.*'

'Oh yes, they're so funny. Did you see the episode where they came to Mosman?'

'With the plan for the mosque? Yes.'

Edwina clicked back across the parquet. 'Let's check that, shall we, Marie?'

'They can be very naughty sometimes,' said Pat, in a teacherly tone.

'I nearly died,' said Marie. 'It was hysterical.'

'What was this?' said Edwina.

'*The Chaser.* In Mosman. Showing everybody plans to build a mosque.'

'Oh, I was in that.' Through the layer of plastic, Edwina began to massage Marie's scalp.

'Really?' said Pat, bouncing a wink off the mirror to Marie.

'Yes, I had no idea! I was completely taken in!'

'What did you say?' Marie asked.

'That I didn't think a mosque would suit Mosman, of course.'

'You know they're all down at Cliffo beach now,' said Pat.

'Who?'

'The Muslims. In hordes. I was down there recently with Phillip and I couldn't believe my eyes. You see the women in their scarves preparing all the food for the men. Ugh, those big fat men swimming and so on while the women sit out of the way in their heavy black clothes, sweating and serving them. And I thought to myself, What on earth are you doing, you *dopey* women?'

Edwina peeled the plastic off Marie's head. 'I'll miss you, Marie.'

'I haven't gone yet.'

Marie thought Dr Cayley must be wrong but she swallowed her pills obediently along with her Panadol, laxatives, Swisse women's vitamins, and fish and evening primrose oil. Prompted by Penny, she had unearthed the pinball machine in the cellar. Bought decades ago as a folly, it was fought over incessantly, the pings and whirls driving Marie and Ross mad. The children acquired friends who ignored their parents at the door, trooping straight into the house with the glazed-eyed resolve of addicts going to their dealer. The pinball machine was also admired at advertising parties: its glass top, and seclusion in the rumpus room, a magnet for the cocaine coterie. Then seemingly overnight the machine was abandoned and had sat rusting in the cellar ever since. What could you do with such a hulk? And how could she have forgotten its existence? As her house emptied, Marie began to feel the impact of its perimeters as though she were a pinball herself, rattling through the rooms and decades, and all those pills in turn inside her body, seeking targets.

She asked Fatima to come an extra day and help clean out the cupboards. She stood there supervising as the refuse of a rich life spewed forth. Toys, an old tennis racket, broken banana chair, bug catcher, gumboots, school textbooks, two pairs of children's ski boots and twenty years of *National Geographic*. 'Would you like any of these things, Fatima?'

'No thank you.' Fatima smiled.

Marie noticed Fatima had molars missing and thought of the reminder notice for her root-canal therapy. She sat with Mopoke in the rumpus room flicking through the old magazines while Fatima ferried things to the garage. *A man with a scar or a strong, damaged face may often be judged more attractive than one with unmarked features*, wrote an anthropologist in the 1970s. Marie corralled the *National Geographic* magazines into a pile. 'You can leave those.'

More than a purge, the cleaning became a forced investigation. Marie was dismayed by how much of her past was signified by things. How and why did they linger? They irritated her, like something stuck on her shoe. She still hadn't found her mother's embroidery, but an obsolete printer was here.

She was happy to find her university textbooks from Psychology 1, and an old *DSM*. Year after year, she had intended to go back and finish her degree, abandoned with her first pregnancy; year after year she had been too tired and distracted.

The most unbelievable relic was probably the plaster cast from Leon's broken leg, crumbling, grotesque, the yellow insides like an old man's skin. She remembered Leon at fourteen, limping down the path behind Ross, sports bag jerking, face wracked with pain. 'Leon went down in the scrum,' Ross announced, with an undertone of embarrassment.

Marie went out to the patio where Leon was slumped on the couch, leg trembling with Parkinsonian fury. She drove him to Dr Cayley's and, while the leg was being set, rang home from the Red Phone in the corridor. 'It's broken in three places. Why didn't you take him to the doctor?'

'He said he was alright.'

'Of course he did. He's a teenage boy.'

'He won't let me near him.'

'You were watching him play, weren't you?'

'I'm trying to get dinner here for two children, Marie.'

'I can't imagine how hard that must be.'

Ross's sigh billowed through the phone, making her hair stand on end. 'O'Sullivan rang,' he minced. 'Tell Leon he wants to know how he is.'

'Please, Ross.'

'I don't think blokes like that should be allowed to coach football,' his voice rose. 'I'm going to ring the school about this.'

Marie hung up and paced the corridor. She hated her husband for his hatred, and her son for his betrayal. She hated herself for having failed so spectacularly. She took Leon to Pizza Hut on the way home, where he ordered a Supreme with the lot. 'O'Sullivan rang,' she said, watching his face. Leon ate his pizza without looking up. On arriving home, he disappeared into his room for the next four years.

He covered the plaster cast with graffiti of his favourite bands. The names were still legible. Guns N' Roses. Red Hot Chili Peppers. The Doors, The Cure. Marie put the cast back into the carton containing Leon's old magazines, the topmost one showing a Burt Reynolds lookalike with a thick moustache, a strappy leather thing on his bare torso.

'Help me, Mopoke,' she groaned to the cat. She carried the carton to the garage, the gay porn glowing like a fresh wound in her mind. Of course it was her who had saved these things, including that copy of *Colt*. She remembered the hot shame when first coming across it secreted behind Leon's desk after he moved out. It had altered her fantasy life forever, and these shaggy-haired, smooth-skinned men of the 1980s rushed back now like old lovers. She took the *Colt* up to her room with the pile of *National Geographic* and the psychology books.

The flames took two four-hour sessions to complete: the first session the outline and darker reds; the second the oranges, yellows and touch-ups. Marie lay back watching Rhys carve curves into her belly. On the wall was a sign saying *DON'T MOVE KEEP STILL*, next to it metal shelving crammed with books. Sometimes Marie shut her eyes against the pain. There was the tattoo whirr, the tear of paper towels, occasional voices. Below the window a boom box transmitted community radio, crossing every two hours to another language or genre. Marie lay there not wanting translation, letting the emotion of the music wash through her as the needles injected dye into her flesh. She came away from these sessions purged and exhilarated. By the second hour the pain had alchemised and she reclined peacefully, eyes opening every now and then to see Rhys's intense face below.

'Fantastic skin. *Soaking* it up. You were born to be tattooed, Marie.'

Marie grimaced as Rhys wiped the seeping tattoo.

'Breathe.' Rhys switched on the iron again.

Halfway through they had a break. Rhys took out her contact lenses and leant back to receive drops in each eye.

'My middle child has trouble with her contact lenses,' Marie remarked. 'Have you tried the new non-allergenic ones?'

'I've tried everything.' Rhys blinked, hands moving over the benchtop. She pressed a tissue to her eyes then put on glasses. 'Is she your favourite?'

'Pardon?'

'There's always a favourite. Usually the middle child.'

Marie didn't want to answer, but there was nothing peremptory in Rhys's manner and in this room her usual defences seemed unnecessary. 'My youngest is my favourite, but he's gay.'

'But?'

Marie sighed. 'I'm a hypocrite ... I don't like my rose.'

'Sorry?'

'The rose tattoo on my shoulder blade. I don't like it.'

'What brought that on?'

'It's just not me. Do you think I should have it removed?'

'Laser treatment's expensive and I don't really believe in it. But you shouldn't wear something you're uncomfortable with.' Rhys sat on her stool, boots hooked on rungs, shadows under her eyes. Marie realised how tired she must be. Two other jobs already today. She had mentioned a child. 'An alternative is doing something over it.

You'll still see it slightly, like a ghost.'

After her first tattoos Marie had felt like leaping into the air, but these longer sessions made her at once giddy and lucid, as though the leap had been made, the border crossed. Downstairs, while her payment went through, she looked at the photograph of the girl with snake arms.

'I'm glad you like the photos,' said Rhys. 'We didn't want just the usual flash.'

'Who is she?'

'Isn't she beautiful? She's a Kalinga girl from Luzon island in the Philippines. A tattoo like that could take months to complete. A wall of pain.'

'She doesn't look much older than twelve.'

'It was a preparation for womanhood. A woman was considered more desirable if she'd endured that sort of pain. They were headhunters. Rob put her up. He has Filo blood.'

'When was it taken?'

'I don't know. Early twentieth century? Their forests have nearly all gone now. Logged or burnt.'

Rhys indicated the photo over the stairs, which Marie still averted her eyes from. 'I know. He freaks some people out. But he's like our Moses.'

It was a mummified body with the macabre protrusion of skull through parchment flesh, the clavicles and ribs rising like a mountain range in an eroded landscape. In the corner was a close-up of blurred stripes and crosses. 'This is the Iceman they found in the Alps, remember? He had about fifty-eight tiny tattoos. They think they were done to treat some sort of back pain, and probably a stomach disorder. He had whipworm.'

Marie thought of her stomach ulcers. The knife unsheathed inside, the constant shifting around its point. She disliked people who spoke of their ailments. 'Acupuncture,' she said vaguely.

'Well, acupuncture supposedly didn't begin until about three thousand years ago in China. Otzi's Italian and five thousand years old. But most of the tattoos were on meridians and it *looks* medicinal.'

'Did he die of his worms?'

'He had an arrowhead embedded in his chest. He was shot in the back, but I don't know if that killed him. Anyway, I like to tell myself that tattooing heals. I'm a believer.'

The sessions began in the afternoon, the room in sunlight enormous around them, diminishing over the hours to a bright cone from the lamp Rhys positioned over the tattooed area. From ribs to pubis was her canvas, Rhys a quiet worker, gliding on the office chair to decant more ink, returning to Marie's side before Marie even knew she had gone. Then it began again, the searing cut, the graze of paper, the cut, the graze, the whine of the iron.

Marie was trying to visualise stomach ulcers. Did they resemble blisters on the epidermis? Spongy pustules filled with mucus? Or did the aqueous interior give them another structure? She wondered how pliable they were, whether they resided in one spot, suckered to the fleshy lining, or moved through the viscous bile of the abdominal cavity. She lamented her ignorance of the body. She sensed she must begin preparations for the hunt.

Rhys began to score alizarin at the base of the flames. Stung awake, Marie became aware of every perforation, the stark tent of lamplight, the tree outside deepening to silhouette, the mournful keening of Bulgarian women on the radio. And in the moments of acute pain when the interior burning surfaced like a fin through the ocean of tattoo, she was stranded again. She needed distraction.

She read the spines of Rhys's books. *Parrots of Australia. Edo Japan. Bad Boys and Tough Tattoos.* She mentally listed household tasks. The garden was in shape, the rooms cleaned out, she had only the guttering to do. The horizon was clearing and she saw a simple yet radical possibility: she could go back to university and finish her psychology degree. A whole new world could come from that; a smile spread across her features. And it came to her also while lying there that she would engage Hugh to sell the house. All the tortured cogitation associated with this fell away, and the decision made, she withstood the pain easily.

She questioned Rhys about her tattooing. Gradually Rhys

relinquished details. She had dropped out of art school and fallen in love with a young tattoo artist. 'He practised on me, and I stayed with him mainly because I loved being tattooed. Then I got critical of his draughtsmanship; I started thinking I could do better. But I was such a good little girlfriend, it took me another two years to leave him and find my own teacher. I didn't want to threaten him. My boyfriend, that is.'

'We're like that with our men, aren't we. I was like that with my ex-husband.'

'I'm not anymore.'

'Good for you. And what was your first tattoo?'

'A snake.'

'Whereabouts?'

Rhys shrugged, not looking up.

Marie closed her eyes and slipped back down to the half-world of endorphins.

Rhys was all there and yet somehow absent, her only visible tattoos the hypnotic gauntlets, and even these were mostly concealed by gloves. Marie dozed through the final flames, the pain all around her a hot red flood.

Christmas Day was unnervingly quiet. There was nobody here apart from Leon, and he slept in. A sense of impermanence made the house feel to Marie like a holiday rental, the languorous hot weeks stretching ahead filled with the sounds of the beach; her continuing her motherly tasks of cleaning, organising and providing; the inevitable packing up at the end. The inevitable end.

She had a swim in the cove then went into the kitchen to begin preparing food, Leon eventually joining her. Clark arrived late, taking the dishes he had made straight to the table. There was a ham at one end; at the other, the cloth was held down by a breadboard covered in a baguette and a parmigiana. There were green beans with basil, olive oil and garlic; a potato salad with capers and anchovies; a green salad; and spicy chick peas. Lastly, Marie brought out a dish of tuna steaks and turned on the barbecue. There was barely enough room for all the food.

Marie began to sear the tuna.

'Tuna instead of turkey this year?' said Clark.

'I couldn't stand poultry,' Leon said. 'I pass a chicken farm when I go to my nursery on the outskirts of Brisbane. It's this huge tin shed in a paddock, baking in the sun. The bush stinks of death for miles around from the birds that die in there. They just leave them to rot in the cages with the living ones.'

'Are turkeys farmed too? Or are they all organic?'

'I don't know.' Marie served the tuna. 'We used to see chickens slaughtered in Avalon, you know. There was a Chinese market gardener next door who kept fowl. We saw our Christmas turkey slaughtered and plucked nearly every year.'

'That's good. We're so removed from the animals we eat and how they're killed, we don't take responsibility.'

'I didn't take responsibility, Leon. I was a child sneaking a look through the fence.'

'Witnessing is a form of responsibility.'

'My mother hated us seeing it. She smacked us if she caught us. Me and Judy used to hide in the passionfruit vine.'

Clark ate, watching her. 'So you liked seeing them slaughtered?'

'I don't know.' Marie remembered Judy, three years older, digging her fingers into her shoulders to make sure she didn't run away when the hatchet came down. She remembered the spurting, jerking bodies. 'Judy forced me. I cried.'

'The tuna is great by the way,' said Leon.

'Market gardens in Avalon,' said Clark. 'Hard to imagine now, isn't it.'

'We're fishing the seas to death too,' Leon added mournfully.

Clark fussed over his mother, carving the ham, filling her glass. It was a still, hot day, and they ate slowly, hunched over the abundant table, the low liquid hum of the harbour all around them. The sky wore a glary sheath that gagged the cicadas. From the zoo across the water came the indignant cries of peacocks, and from next door those of the Hendersons' grandchildren playing in the pool.

'They use the pool much, Mum?' Leon asked.

'This is the first time I've noticed anyone in it.'

'We should go for a swim after lunch,' said Clark. 'I've started swimming in the mornings.'

Leon moved his chair away from the table, arm muscles tightening. 'Must be beautiful, Bondi in the mornings.'

'Where d'you swim in Brisbane? D'you drive to the ocean?'

'Not much. I miss it. I just keep fit gardening. Cabbage tree needs a haircut, Mum. You got a good tree surgeon?'

'Another thing to add to the list,' Marie groaned.

Clark tried not to look at his brother's muscles and resolved to increase his lap count. When Leon put his hands behind his head you could see the edge of a tattoo around his left bicep. Clark suddenly remembered his conversation with Blanche — how could he have forgotten that Leon had a tattoo? One of those pseudo-primitive things, all sharp curves. He believed Blanche about his mother now, and wanted to see them. He dropped his napkin and took his time picking it up off the floor, but his mother's feet were tucked backwards so her ankles were invisible. He sat up and fixed his eyes on her while Leon talked on about cabbage tree palms. Clark couldn't concentrate on the conversation; he burnt with a need for explanation and positioning. It was as though things had been rearranged in his absence; he felt adrift. Marie looked over and saw him staring at her.

'When's the house going on the market?' he said quickly.

'It's a miracle it's survived this long.' Leon was finishing a sentence. 'Alone and unprotected like that.'

'I'll be talking to Hugh when they get home,' Marie said to Clark.

Leon grinned and raised his eyebrows.

'So you've decided on him definitely?' Clark tried to sound neutral.

'Yes.' Marie gave him a flinty look.

He sensed she wanted him to challenge her but he wouldn't allow himself to be baited. His mother didn't seem to be drinking as much as usual, but he didn't know what she'd had before he arrived.

'God.' Leon patted his stomach. 'Didn't exactly scrimp on the food, did we? Can we wait till later for the pudding?'

'I thought I was cooking less. Why don't you stay the night, Clark? Watch the boats go out in the morning? And at some stage you both have to clean out your rooms and take your televisions and the things I've left for you in the garage.'

'*More* televisions?'

'*Your* televisions.'

'I never watch TV anymore,' said Leon. 'They must be ancient.'

Clark flicked through a quick inventory of what he could do if he stayed here. He could read, go for a swim, watch the test match tomorrow. He could get a look at his mother's tattoos. He ran his tongue along his upper lip and tasted sweat. He was too full to move right now. 'Okay then.'

'Look behind you.' His mother pointed.

On the recliner beneath wrapping paper was a shallow wooden box, the size of a plate, with a glass top. Clark picked it up and gasped. 'This?' Beneath the glass was an enormous butterfly, emerald green with jaffa underwings, almost as wide as his hand. The iridescent body was the size of his ring finger. 'It's beautiful!'

'It's from Leon. I think it's the most beautiful thing I've ever seen.'

Looking closely, Clark could make out the cruel speck of a pin's head in the insect's back. 'You *killed* this? That's not like you, Leon.'

'I found it. It died after laying its eggs.'

'Is it rare? What's it called?'

'I don't think so. It's a Splendid Ghost Moth.'

'How did you preserve her?' Marie asked.

There was a pause. 'I didn't actually. I didn't know how. I guess it'll kind of ... disintegrate.'

'You should put it somewhere special.' Clark held it up to the light.

'That's exactly what I'm going to do. I'm going to get a tattoo of it on my back.'

Clark put down the box. 'Pardon?'

Marie was giving him that same look of challenge as when

announcing that Hugh was to be the agent for the sale.

Leon snorted softly over his plate.

'By the same artist who did my flames.' Marie lifted her shirt to show him a portion of the tattoo.

'Oh no don't,' said Clark in a strangled voice. He reddened and turned away. Blanche had only mentioned ankles. 'Why?'

'Because I want to. Why don't you ask Leon about his?'

Leon remained hunched over his plate, not looking at either of them.

'But Leon's half your age!'

'So what?' Marie said cockily, looking over to Leon, whose eyes were widened in innocence.

What a stupid woman. She was acting like a teenager. She honestly thought it was funny. That sly look she got when lifting her shirt, like a little girl proud of pooing in her pants. The way she tried to draw Leon in, god, the way she *flirted* with him. Maybe he was in on it. The tattoo looked like an open wound. The fact of its permanence appalled Clark. But, hey, it was her body, like he was going to lose sleep over it? Really. An uncomfortable silence descended. Unable to contain his hurt, Clark began to collect the dirty dishes then walked into the house with them.

Marie followed him to the kitchen with more dishes. He stood over the bin scraping plates, barking when she joined him, 'Leave it, Mum, please. I'll clean up.'

'For Christ's sake, Clark. Calm down. It's Christmas Day.'

She heard Mopoke miaowing and found her outside on the patio, looking expectantly at the house. 'Oh my poor darling, locked outside on Christmas Day.' Mopoke walked in a semi-circle to the left then to the right, nudging Marie's legs. 'Come on, Mo, tuna for you!' Marie took her into the kitchen and scooped the scraps onto her plate.

She left Clark sulking over the washing-up and tramped down to the bottom of the garden with the compost. God, he was such a little prig. It only made her want to lift her shirt higher and dance on the table, just to scandalise him. He was like the nuns at school, or her parents. Why was he like this? Hadn't she kept religion away from her children to avoid this very problem? Not for them the lifelong injuries sustained by an upbringing in the torture chamber of the Catholic Church. Not that she hadn't recovered. Still, it felt naughty lifting her shirt like that. It made her laugh now just to think of it. She could see his figure at the window from down here. She had a schoolgirl urge to hurt him even more, then a schoolgirl guilt for her cruelty; then all she was left with was the bitter aftertaste of their disconnection. And Leon who sat there saying nothing. Oh, fuck both of them. Sometimes, when she looked back at her past, all Marie could see was childhood followed by marriage with nothing in between. So starved of adventure, so habituated to authority that she sought it in her sons.

She remembered Christmas in Avalon. She hadn't cried because she didn't want to watch the slaughter, but because she did. She was ashamed of her fascination, the distant thwack of Win's hatchet through bone, the bright red blood splashing onto the ground, the vital sense of ritual and how casual Win was with this momentous responsibility. It wasn't how a little girl was supposed to feel. Animals were being murdered, but their pain to Marie seemed subservient to a bigger force, beyond Win and herself: it was the force of human appetite stretching back through infinity.

Clark didn't want to move until he had digested so Marie and Leon set out on a bushwalk. It was low tide and the sand on the beach was laced with coal run-off. Marie took a bag with her, filling it with weeds as they walked.

'So you actually saw the moth laying her eggs?'

'Yes.'

'Moths and butterflies don't live very long, do they? Long enough to reproduce, and become another animal's dinner.'

'They're more useful as grubs. Splendid Ghost Moths are underground for years. They eat fungus from root systems. I'm always blown away by how beautiful these animals are when they hatch. I mean it's the shortest and least important phase of their life.'

'Why does everything have to be measured in terms of

usefulness? Why can't we just have pleasure and beauty to know how good life is?'

'I'm not saying there's no point to beauty. If there was, it wouldn't exist. It's the Darwinian thing, Mum. Beauty attracts mates.'

'I didn't think *you* would say everything boiled down to procreation.'

There was a crowd milling at the entrance to the zoo. Leon made his way through it, ahead of his mother, and waited for her on the footpath beyond.

'I know you hate my irises,' Marie said. 'But I keep them because they're beautiful.'

'They're weeds. They get into the national parks and take over.'

'I don't let them anywhere near the bush. And there's no point to their beauty. The nectar they give to birds and insects could be given in a much plainer package.'

'We need variety. Nature's the best artist.'

Past the wharf they arrived at the relief of bush. The track curled into a gully then rose up the ridge and entered a tall angophora forest whose canopy was shot with the nerve endings of dead trees.

'I wonder what sort of larvae would eat the fungus from the root systems of angophoras.'

'Poor things.'

'Would fire be a solution? A layer of carbon?'

'Probably help. This sort of bush needs a burn every fifteen years or so I think. But I can't see how they'll ever manage it now with all the houses.'

'Have you seen the mausoleums going up around Taylors Bay? I wouldn't mind if they burnt the lot.'

The harbour unfurled below like rippled silk, cut by the white streak of a boat's wake. They stepped to one side to let a family past. Marie felt reassured by this path worn over millennia with the passage of human feet. How many had walked it in the same state, bellies full, sweating in the afternoon sun. Cold and rain, exposure and famine, seemed impossible today, with the sea all the way to the city speckled by yachts, and one vivid yellow and green ferry.

And on all of those vessels, parties, feasts, enough food and water and diesel for an army.

The path widened to nineteenth-century luxury with sandstone borders and an even gradient above a jetty. All that remained of the dancing pavilion was a foundation wall edging the lawn of the old hotel. A couple of groups were gathering their things and walking up to the car park. Marie and Leon sat on the wall. Across the water, the CBD shimmered in the sun. Marie's weeding bag was full. She looked around for a bin. At the far end of the lawn was one overflowing. She got up and walked towards it. The pile of rubbish was moving. How bizarre. Closer, she saw it was rabbits, scores of them, a twitching blanket of vermin rifling through picnic remains. She turned back with a look of distress. 'Leon!'

Leon started towards her. '*Jesus*. When did it get this bad?'

'I don't know. I should dispose of these at home anyway. I'm exhausted.'

'Give it to me. I'll take care of it. I want to walk a bit more, okay? Maybe have a swim.'

'Thank you.'

How small she looked walking away from him, how frail.

Alone at last. Leon went over to a tap and gulped down warm rusty water, then continued up the road. What he really wanted was to have sex. If he didn't dawdle, in about an hour he could get lucky in the bushes above Obelisk Beach. He could exhaust his stuffed body, cool off in the ocean and finally be rewarded with the eager mouth of a father escaping family Christmas. Afterwards, he could ring home to be picked up. Yep, great idea. Excited, Leon peeled off his t-shirt, tucked it into his shorts, and walked up the path, the bag of weeds dangling off a belt loop.

He had found the moth, which he initially thought was a butterfly, in his room one night a month earlier. It was flapping between his bed and the wall, and from the weight of the sound he guessed it was a creature of substantial size. He lifted his pillow to find the biggest insect he had ever seen.

He had shown it to his housemate, a local, who hadn't recognised it. Leon had been surprised to see a butterfly active at night, but it was barely ten o'clock and this was the tropics and everything up here was still slightly foreign to him. He walked out to the garden holding the insect, large, bright and heavy as fruit on his palm. He tried to put it onto a leaf, but it was raining and it wouldn't leave his hand. It had grown completely still.

He went back inside and looked through every nature book in the house. Sat at the computer googling, insect hand steadily palm up. He couldn't find anything. An hour and a half had passed, and Leon had fallen in love.

Then its body began to pulsate and it turned onto its side and started ejecting eggs from its tail. For almost an hour a stream of white sand fell across Leon's palm while he watched in awe. So fine and copious, there must have been thousands of eggs. He didn't know what to do so went back out to the garden to release them, but everything was waterlogged. The moth had hooked one of her forelegs into his skin so she didn't fall off. He knew now it was a *she*.

When she stopped laying she looked exhausted. Leon thought she would die and felt devastated. He went into the kitchen and made a nest for her with a cereal carton. No sooner inside, she began to lay again, and Leon to panic. He took the carton out to the garden and tipped eggs everywhere. Then the moth went quiet and he took her inside. He noticed she had lost a foreleg and the possibility he had ripped it off made him feel desperate. Three hours had passed and he was worn out. He placed the carton on his bedside table and fell asleep almost immediately.

Deeper along the path now, the bush rose around him like a cathedral. In this interval of leaves and ocean, devoid of people, Leon loved the place more than anywhere in the world. It was the driest he had ever seen it, and this dejected him terribly. He passed an entire gully of brown ferns, the path slippery with sand and fuel. It must have been after five o'clock and it occurred to him that people would be leaving Obelisk. He walked faster, entering Taylors Bay. His mother was right: the new houses were awful, just slabs of cement plonked in the middle of the bush. The thought of another two days in her house made him feel edgy and suffocated. The shock of her plan to tattoo the moth on her back was only just beginning to sink in. He realised he was insulted — more than disconcerted — and also resentful at being implicated in this decision. She was going to take his gift and advertise it to the world, on her body. *My son this* and *my son that*. It took all his energy to resist her and the last thing he could do was rescue Clark with some spurious act of solidarity. He felt sorry for his mother and wanted to do the right thing, but every gesture, like the gift of the Splendid Ghost Moth, seemed to propel her deeper into this clinginess, which only made him want to run. Where to? He had stayed in Brisbane last summer and it depressed him with everyone else in the company of loved ones while he drifted. He could probably find a New Year's Eve party in Sydney, but the longer he stayed here the more likely he was to look up George, and he wouldn't allow himself to do that. A couple of sinewy old ladies in floppy hats passed him with a cheery, 'Happy Christmas!' Then, suddenly, a party of five. *G'day. G'day … Christmas.* The cloud cover broke and the cicadas swelled and, his sanctuary compromised, Leon walked quicker, longing for escape, his favourite porno close-ups sliding through his mind.

He had been woken at two a.m. by the sound of the moth rattling the carton. He knew she would die and he wanted to keep her so he left the lid on and tried to go back to sleep. The moth bashed furiously against her prison walls, keeping him awake. The sight of those eggs pouring from her phallic tail had fascinated and repelled him. Like sperm, but female, it was eggs emerging from an orifice, and a feeling washed over him like that feeling he got from his mother — from so many women — of cloying, soft demand. He lay there in the darkness listening to her die, finally falling asleep at dawn. He identified the moth in a book at the museum two weeks later.

'So,' said Clark to Leon in the rumpus room the next day, 'to what do we owe the honour? Twice in three months after not seeing you for over a year.'

'Mum's frequent flyers.'

'How's the business going?'

'Still struggling. But it's always slow in summer.'

'Is the drought bad up there?'

'Not as bad as here.'

'How's Blanche about the loan?'

Leon slid his eyes over. 'She hasn't sent the debt collectors up, if that's what you mean.'

They were watching the cricket. It was tea break, and a vox pop came on. *My dad got a pig*, said a guy with the stringy blond hair of a sea-sider. *Like a whole* pig, *and cooked like the* whole thing. *I've never seen a whole pig before. Yair, it was great, we just ate like* stacks, *me and my family, and drank heaps-a-beer. We had a great time.*

'To tell you the truth, Clark, I'm a crap businessman. I can't blame it all on the drought.'

'You really spent *all* the money from Dad?'

'We won't go there.'

Clark felt a pang of hunger although they had only eaten an hour ago. He watched the players file back onto the field. He wanted another beer, but the kitchen seemed miles away. He decided to wait till Leon got one. He could hear his mother in the kitchen. 'Did you know Mum's in debt?'

'But how could she be? Dad was loaded when they divorced.'

'He was mean in the settlement. She got the house but not much alimony so she's been burning through credit. That's why the sale's so necessary.'

'*Such* an arsehole,' Leon muttered.

'He rang yesterday when you two were bushwalking.'

'You pick up?'

'Nope. Just let him leave his perfunctory Christmas greeting.'

'He'd be proud of you doing a PhD.'

'No, he wouldn't. He's threatened by anything vaguely intellectual. All that stuff about being a Bankstown boy who didn't even get his HSC and made it big.'

'He hated me gardening too.'

'Let's face it: he wouldn't have been happy with anything except advertising. Or some sort of business venture. Money. Blanche says he's threatened by her though. Because she's a woman.'

'That old chestnut.' Leon sounded unconvinced.

Clark chewed his nails, looking at the TV. 'Hugh!' he said after a while. 'Can you believe it? *Hugh.*'

'Yes.'

The tourists were being bowled out in quick succession, the Australians throwing their hats into the air and slapping each other on the back.

'Jesus,' said Clark. 'They're the only country who can beat us. Come *on.*'

'Why do you want them to beat us? I mean, you wouldn't cheer *England* against us, would you?'

'I'd cheer the Third bloody Reich against the Australian cricket team, mate.'

'Why?'

'Because we need our arses kicked, that's why. We're too complacent. We think we're hot shit but we're just a bunch of fat, rich, beer-swilling pigs.'

The click of Marie's sandals came down the stairs. 'It's Boxing Day,' she said brightly to her sons sprawled on the couch in front of the barking television.

Clark and Leon looked at her without expression.

'And I wanted to take those boxes and things to St Vincent de Paul.'

'It's closed, Mum,' said Leon.

'That doesn't matter. You leave it all in the loading bay.'

'They hate it when you do that,' Clark cautioned.

'Please, Clark. I can't do it on my own.'

Clark touched his chest and looked at his mother then his brother in perplexed outrage.

'Don't worry. I'm putting Leon to work in the garden. He's going to mow the lawns, and help us load up the car.'

Leon sent Clark a smarmy smile.

An hour later, Marie stood by the car as Clark unloaded. She had packed the boxes in a hurry for fear of the backslide of memory or a spurious utilitarianism that would insinuate the things back into her life, so she kept her eyes averted. As the car emptied, she felt her skin peeling away.

'Wow,' said Clark as he came back to the car. 'This is a big gouge. What happened?'

'Oh, I was parked in a narrow street and some idiot sideswiped me.'

'Don't you need to get it fixed so it doesn't rust?'

'When I sell the house.'

Driving along Military Road was a shock for Clark, who always took the back roads. He exclaimed at the boutiques and smart cafés under their pretty awnings.

'I was excited when the first café opened here,' said his mother. 'Cappuccino in Mosman. It was quite an event. Everybody drinks it now.'

'Which one do you go to?'

'That one occasionally when I get my hair cut. But I've gone off coffee. It gives me indigestion.'

'Bonza Brats,' Clark read acidly as they passed the shop. 'God, they're making a mint out of children these days, aren't they?'

And all the way home, the cavity of the boot behind her, the yawning double garage, the walls now free of clutter. Marie alighted mournful, cleansed and dispossessed. She pointed to the couch on the patio, splashed with faded orange and yellow designs. 'We should have taken that.'

'It wouldn't have fit, Mum.'

'Next time then.'

Marie remembered opening the front door one Sunday morning almost twenty years earlier to find Clark passed out in his vomit on the new orange and yellow couch.

'Clark! It's brand new!' She stood over him trembling. 'I was just about to ring the police.'

Clark eased himself into a sitting position. 'Gonna have a shower.'

'No, the laundry.' Marie directed him down the side path and stood in the doorway while he took off his shoes and socks. 'Who brought you home?'

'Louise.'

'Jones? I didn't know you were seeing her.'

'I'm not *seeing* her, Mum. She's just a friend of a friend.' Clark manoeuvred himself behind the ironing board to strip off his t-shirt. 'God,' he muttered to his feet, 'as if I'd be seeing Louise *Jones*.'

'I didn't know you were at the Joneses'.'

'We weren't at the Joneses'. Well, not really.' Clark leant against the wall not looking at his mother, hunching self-consciously around his thin white torso.

Marie found it repugnantly delicate, almost feminine. She decided that once Clark had showered she would make him clean the couch. 'If you want to go out all night and make us sick with worry then you can at least do me the credit of telling the truth about where you were.'

'We went down to the boatshed, Mum. Quakers Hat Bay.' Clark glared at her through puffy red eyes. 'You know the place.'

Marie went back up and cleaned the vomit off the couch. From the kitchen she could hear Leon coming up from the beach. Of course she wouldn't have called the police. Clark wasn't a minor. She had been trembling not just with relief, but also a hangover. She poured two Beroccas, and cooked an enormous breakfast for the boys.

Leon didn't mow the lawns in the end, so two days after he left Marie hired her usual man. She used to do the lawns herself, hefting the mower across the slopes above and below the house. She had taught herself to use it at the age of forty-seven, when Leon moved out of home.

'Why don't we get someone in to do them?' said Ross, who had taken up golf. He was fiddling with the gloves from his new kit. He didn't look at her when he spoke to her, but she was used to that now. In response — she told herself — she had retreated into reserve, and a sort of convivial irony.

'I like doing them. You have your golf, I have my mowing.'

What she liked was the cacophonous lapping meditation, the sense of control, even if just of a little machine. It was good having something to do on the long slow Sundays when Ross was playing golf and her adult children were going about their adult lives. The reward was having a drink on the deck at sunset, with the smell of freshly cut grass as trace of her toil.

But the effort with the mower defeated her now and she looked back with amazement at her strength and zeal. From this distance, she could also see for the first time the flinty reserve and irony as others must have. She realised her solitude had begun before Ross left. She had walked away as well. She had made herself completely impenetrable.

In spite of the drought, the yellowing lawns had struggled up a few inches. From her balcony, Marie watched Scott unclip the catcher and take it down to the compost. Behind her sat two garbage bags full of unwanted clothes. The desolation of space where her husband's suits once hung now extended to her side as well. Corpses of bogong moths lined the edge of the ensuite. Marie shut the door on the chasm of her past.

Standing at the bowser, feeling fluid pulse through the hose in her hand, Marie imagined the tanks beneath directly connected to seams of oil in the earth. Her car was a tick sucking up its weekly supply, injecting its host with poison simultaneously. Inhaling the intoxicating scent of petrol, she imagined the vast seams of black blood running dry, the earth's crust collapsing in on these voids, the entire planet shrivelling like a raisin.

The price of petrol had gone up ten cents in two days so Marie had detoured to a cheaper station in Cremorne. It was hot and windy, the nature strips turning to dust. The traffic thickened like sclerosis. Kilometre by kilometre the air-conditioning filled with a faint perfume of diesel and the bottle of Veuve on the seat beside her sweated away its chill. Marie crawled back to Mosman beneath a pink evening sky, unable to take her eyes off the television in the Mercedes in front. The road extended in a long curve, four-wheel drives glinting to the horizon.

The Joneses lived in a Tuscan villa on Burran Avenue. Marie pulled up and pressed a buzzer in the high pastel wall. She spoke into the grille below the camera. In this moment of arrival, she was acutely aware of her solitude. 'Don't be nervous, Marie,' she muttered to herself as the buzzer clicked. 'Get a hold of yourself.' The gate swung open and she drove down to the forecourt. She was late.

Jonesy answered the door, convivial and paternalistic, and placed a glass of champagne in her hand. She could hear guests on the balcony and the olive bowls were empty. The knots in Jonesy's paisley cravat did not hide his chins. 'First things first, Marie. Come in here.'

He ushered her into the living room at the back of the house, a forest-dark place of antique furniture, rugs, a dimmed chandelier, and paintings crammed across the walls. He stopped before one. 'Look at what my dealer picked up the other day.'

The painting was smaller than Marie expected, not so different to how it looked in reproduction, its smallness accentuated by a wide gilt frame. The swirl of scrub, ochre outback and black slit mask of the bushranger moved through her eyes with the ease of old habits. She couldn't say why she loved the picture so much; it was like birthplace or blood, something undetachable. Yet now, domesticated, its haunting effect receded. The eyes of the policemen all seemed the same, and Ned Kelly less authoritative. It was awkward in conversation with the English hunting scenes either side, the frame the loudest voice of all. She also found herself thinking about the painting in terms of her body and its evolving language. Different people were marked out for different stories: her tattoos would all be organic; her arms would be next. Jonesy loomed over her, breathing. She could see the network of capillaries across his cheeks. 'Well?'

'Is it from the original series?'

'Ross has had his eye on this for years.'

'I love the Ned Kelly paintings. You must be thrilled.'

Jonesy rocked back and forth on the balls of his feet. 'I gazumped Ross for it. He's seething!'

'The frame's very impressive. Did it come with the frame?'

'A bloke in Double Bay did that for me. Four and a half grand. Bewt, isn't it?'

'Lovely.'

Seventeen years earlier, on that first day in Quakers Hat Bay, Jonesy had avowed, 'This has nothing to do with them.'

They were in the boatshed. Marie had come here for a cutting of the bush lemon that grew on the slope behind it. Having only ever seen the boatshed from the water, taking the track from the road was a new adventure. She had stumbled down the gully after Jonesy, enjoying how the lantana tore at her ankles. Jonesy went into the boatshed for secateurs, beckoning her to follow. Nothing visible in there but a glowing window of pearly sky, she almost tripped in the sudden dimness. Then the dark shape of him, his erection pushing against her belly. No need to undress, just him moving over her with rough precision on the old couch. He scratched her breast with his watch when pushing up her bra. She would feel this in bed later that night while Ross slept. And the ache in her buttocks, the lantana scratches. The satisfying physical evidence of living, change and effort.

'Of course not,' Marie had agreed. 'It's just about us.'

They were whispering though the nearest house was over the lip of the hill. It was that dead time of afternoon before children finished school, when workers were comatose with boredom or liquid lunches. In the boatshed, blurred shapes had clarified into a table and chair, sails, a coil of rope. They were side by side on the couch, hands touching, clothes rearranged. Marie added: 'It's been on the cards for a while.'

'Don't forget your cutting.' Jonesy handed her the secateurs as they left the building.

She was surprised when she heard the gushing behind her, as she clipped off a branch of the tree that yielded famously sweet, thin-skinned fruit. It was the sound of him urinating and the hairs on the back of her neck prickled as though she had stumbled on a secret rite, even though they had been fucking only fifteen minutes earlier. She turned to find him looking directly at her. She felt impaled.

'Nitrate.' He winked. 'It's good for it.'

Jonesy rang a week later and another meeting in the boatshed was arranged. In that diesel-and-bait-scented capsule, Marie was distilled to nothing but hunger, nerve endings, an animal nosing at the crack. She left as she arrived, in a state of desperate excitement. It sparked a febrile reconnection with Ross, fuelled as time went on by a fear of loss. Everything that Ross had done was forgiven now she was doing it as well. She became extra attentive, cooked special meals, bought him a silk tie, gave him blow jobs. She was forty-two years old and had never been with another man, and the sense of herself as a skilled, desirable lover was a gift for which she felt the need to thank the entire world. Maybe marriage needed treachery — bushfire cleansing — who could stop all those bodies real or imagined slipping between the sheets with you and your spouse? That sweet violation, to walk through flames and survive. And after every boatshed meeting, Jonesy emptying his bladder beneath the tree, both of them taking its fruit home. Eating a harvest nourished by corpses, Marie thought one night, watching a documentary about trench warfare. She was filled with a reckless joy and power, kicking the house of cards she had so painstakingly built.

Then storms struck, the Pacific driving straight into Middle Harbour, and for two weeks Marie and Jonesy didn't see each other, until Jonesy suggested another meeting place.

He unclipped his gold Rolex and placed it carefully on the bedside table. 'I'm going to have to make a decision about this pastry chef by the end of the week.'

'Doesn't the manager decide things like that?'

From the bed Marie watched him pull clingwrap off desserts. Spit Road hummed below the window. They had come to a motel because the outlet of Quakers Hat Bay had overflowed and Middle Harbour, said Jonesy, stank like a public toilet. The motel room smelt of cleaning fluids and a faint plastic tang that Marie realised was emanating from the new telephones beside the bed. She wasn't hungry. She missed the boatshed, the calm of Middle Harbour, its river feel. She would have rather been down near the water in a cesspit of sewage than up in this neon and cement block. She checked the switch for a dimmer dial, but there was none. Jonesy's foreskin was enormous, like an elephant's nozzle dangling as he brought the desserts over. She thought of it in her mouth, pissy, granular, and revulsion surged through her. And wetness into her cunt.

'You're going to help me decide now,' he instructed.

'Jonesy, darling, we've only got an hour.'

'Well, you never need much warming up, do you? I thought restaurants would be a breeze after advertising. By Christ, I've learnt my lesson.' He settled on the bed beside her, grumbling. 'Everybody wants the same old thing. Innovation is punished.'

Marie ate a spoonful of each dessert in quick succession and told Jonesy that she thought the chef was a marvel and to leave everything at Bel Mer exactly as it was. She didn't want to hear about Jonesy's life, she just wanted a quick orgasm, but the yield of kapok didn't compensate the absence of water slapping pylons, brine and birdsong. She had to fantasise about the boatshed man: knees grazing canvas as she knelt before him, his silky hardness between her thighs.

There they lay in the motel light, a middle-aged man and woman in all their ordinary disgrace. Jonesy was watching her over a spoonful of crème brûlée and she saw a look in his eyes that she hadn't noticed before: a glint of victory, crafty self-satisfaction, and the motive of diversion her conscience had incanted for the three months of their affair shrivelled in the hot truth of her own vengeful heart. The realisation that this was all it was swung into her chest like a hammer. She had sworn she wouldn't so much as mention their names, but she couldn't help it. 'How's Susan?'

'I believe she's playing tennis with Gina today.'

'Really? I should call her. I haven't played in ages.'

'Maybe you should take up another sport for a while.'

In that instant Marie knew that she and Jonesy would never touch each other again. She said, 'Did you leave King Jones because of her and Ross?'

'I can't believe you're asking me this.' Jonesy tossed the desserts into the bin, and began to dress. He shovelled the coins he had left on the dresser into his pocket. 'Ross and I always kept business separate.'

'Bullshit.' Marie laughed. It echoed around the room, a witch's cackle, black and knowing. 'Did you fuck his secretary as well to get back at him?'

Jonesy's head snapped around. 'Well, aren't you the little saint.' He put on his jacket then left.

Now, standing before his new acquisition in his cluttered living room, he pressed her arm for emphasis. Marie had only seen him twice since the divorce, both times in company. Alone with her for the first time in years, he donned the mantle of their meagre sexual history and Marie realised the power of her singleness. She began to feel suffocated by his attention; the need to draw a circle around herself grew inside her like a balloon. She couldn't believe how much Jonesy's touch had once thrilled her. He stood there with the door open to the competitive lair he still shared with Ross, the bets laid casually as napkins on tables, the payment usually a carton of Moët, all that flourish on crotchety parade like an old general. As Ross had been the creative in King Jones, an artistic acquisition was a particular coup for Jonesy. Marie glanced into the lair with contempt, nostalgia and impatience to wrest herself back to the present. But this was the present, and it was still happening. What she really wanted was the future.

'It really is the quintessential Australian story, isn't it. The outlaw, the larrikin. Did you read the book? Susan has a signed first edition of everything he's written. She's in love with him!'

Somebody had come into the room behind them: a tall man with an acute and slightly mischievous gaze. 'And how's our outlaw?'

'You know my great-great-grandfather was transported for art theft?'

'Well, he'd be proud of you.' The man found an aperture as Jonesy turned back to the painting, sending Marie a wink through it. 'Now, I've been sent in here to corral you both.'

Marie caught the wink and followed the man into the hall, hung with etchings of French cathedrals. Susan met them. 'He's been glued to that painting for *weeks*. He'd sleep with it if I let him. You remember David Rosenthal, don't you, Marie?'

'Of course. Hallo!'

'Hallo!'

'Now everyone. *À table*. David, you're on my right.'

Marie remembered David from a party at Sirius Cove, a reticent man talking to the more serious guests. It must have been about ten years ago. He seemed different now. He still had a full head of hair that sprang vigorously off his forehead, but he was looser in manner. Even his face seemed to have acquired mobility: inquisitive, sceptical, on the hunt for a joke. He sat opposite Marie in the large echoey dining room with its parquet floor.

'You bid for it, Dave?' John Totti asked him.

'Nope. He went through Sotheby's.'

Totti drummed the edge of the table with his fingers. 'And what do you think?'

'Can't go wrong with a Nolan.'

'And where have you been, Marie?' Gina was saying.

'Buying petrol.'

'Oh?'

'I went all the way to Cremorne to a cheaper place, which is why I was late. Isn't that stupid?'

'I know the one.' Totti nodded. 'I go there.'

'Actually,' said Gina, 'I meant in general.'

'Marie,' said Susan, 'by the time you've gone to Cremorne for cheaper petrol, you've used up another litre anyway.'

Susan was looking at Gina, waiting for her opinion on the soup. Gina's soufflés could stun a table of ten into silence. Gina carefully worked each mouthful, sucking in her cheeks, watching the conversation with her habitual expression of faint astonishment. Her hair had been cut and a silver streak flared along the left part. Her black top had a sheen through it and an off-centre décolletage. She looked exactly as she always had — luminescent.

'I know,' said Marie. 'It's stupid.'

'They're really taking advantage, aren't they?' said Totti, mainly to the men. 'The price has risen thirty cents in a year.'

'More,' said David.

'In general, I've just been at home,' Marie went on, discreetly checking Gina's face for Botox. She wasn't sure if it was common knowledge she was selling: she didn't want to talk about it. 'I've been fixing things up, having a big clean out.'

'It's such a good thing to do,' said Susan. 'It's very Buddhist, getting rid of things.'

'I can't believe how much stuff I had.'

'Well, you're looking very well,' said Gina. 'You've lost a lot of weight.'

'Thank you.'

'War makes the price of oil go up,' David was saying.

'In devastation is opportunity,' Jonesy rejoined.

'Oh yes, I can see those sheikhs in Dubai, rubbing their bejewelled hands together in glee,' Susan said grimly. 'They've organised everything very nicely.'

'The Americans are controlling the oil, Susan,' said David.

'Du*bai*,' said Totti. 'It's another planet. The things they're doing there.'

'We thought of going,' said Susan.

Marie was stuck on Jonesy's phrase. It sounded familiar, as though lifted from *The Corporation*, which had repeated on SBS last night, or from an article in the weekend papers. Or maybe everything was just doubled by drunkenness. She drank some water as, either side of her, Totti and Jonesy began swapping figures for gold. She tried to ascertain what was in the soup. Something fishy, something spicy, something gelatinous. She said to nobody in particular, 'You know what I was thinking when I was filling up tonight? Maybe, all things considered, we're not paying enough.'

'What things, Marie?' said Jonesy.

Susan had put down her cutlery and was resting her chin on her fingertips, the vertical forearms striped with bracelet marks. 'Come on, Gina, stop torturing me.'

'It's amazing, Susan. I'm still trying to figure it out. It's so subtle.'

'Depletion. We're always complaining about how much things cost. I bought a pair of sneakers two years ago that I thought were expensive but they're still going strong and I garden in them. And considering they were made by child labour and the factory was damaging the environment, and the long-term cost of all that and how long the sneakers have lasted, they were really quite cheap.'

Jonesy barked with laughter. Marie fiddled with her empty wineglass. She was glad to have amused someone but she wasn't really trying to be funny. She always felt stupid in the company of these people, even when it was them who were being stupid. She barged on. 'What I mean is that from my end, as the purchaser, I wasn't paying too much. It's just that the money is going to the wrong place. Does that make sense?' Jonesy had refilled her glass. She gulped some down. 'And considering the water crisis, maybe we should be paying five dollars for a bottle of water.'

'That's what they pay in Dubai!' said Totti.

'If the global economy was properly managed,' said Jonesy, 'nobody would have to pay that much, and everybody would have enough to drink.'

'I'm sick of that word *economy*,' said Marie. 'It rules our life. Every election is run on it. We're not people in a society anymore. We're just numbers in an economy.'

'You've got a point there,' said David.

'I'm sorry,' said Totti, 'I missed the connection between sneakers and water.'

'Running makes you thirsty, Totts.' Jonesy grinned.

'Go to Mario's,' said Gina. 'You'll pay more than five dollars for San Pellegrino, believe me.'

'Mario's is finished.' Totti waved his hand.

'I hate seeing my shower water go down the drain knowing it won't be recycled,' said Marie.

'We don't need to recycle,' said Jonesy. 'Within the next few years there'll be desalination plants servicing every major city in Australia.'

'But Sydney's desalination plant is going to burn enormous amounts of fossil fuels to power itself,' said David. 'And it's going to run whether we need it or not, because of the contract, to the tune of around thirty-three billion taxpayer dollars a year.'

'*No*,' said Marie.

David seemed to be leaning towards her, sending her a subtle signal. 'Oh yes, I'm afraid so.'

'Did you know that nose jobs are popular in Iran?' said Susan to Gina.

Gina widened her eyes.

'I read an article about it in *Good Weekend*.'

'We should all have rainwater tanks,' said Marie, looking at David. He didn't seem to hear. She wanted him to know that she didn't have one because Ross hadn't allowed it, even if that didn't account for the past year.

'The rebates they're offering for those are a joke,' said Totti. 'And how are we expected to suddenly fit such big lumps next to our houses? Nuclear. It's the cleanest power source.'

'But we're too beholden to the green movement to exploit it,' said Totti.

'Well, I know they have a Prada fetish,' Gina said to Susan.

'God, no, that sort of thing is not allowed in Muslim cultures.' Jonesy shook his head at her.

'Middle Eastern women spend a huge amount on cosmetics and fashion,' Gina replied coolly. 'It's an ancient tradition that goes back to the Egyptians. It's part of the decorative tradition you see in their architecture, their rugs.'

'That's right that's right,' David said.

'No,' Jonesy insisted. 'I think you'll find them very restrictive. The women aren't allowed to do *anything*.'

Susan sent Gina an indulgent smile and asked her husband to get another bottle of wine. Jonesy appeared not to have heard her. He was buttering his bread and listening to Totti describe nuclear fission to David. Susan inclined her head to Gina, who was telling her about the similarities between Middle Eastern and Mediterranean cultures. Marie tried to listen to both conversations at once. She wanted more wine. She dipped her bread into the dish of olive oil. It tasted fresh as grass and she revelled in the luxury of all this good food. The desire for wine was maddening, though: wine went with everything, even its own solo self, and not for the first time, Marie regretted the removal of alcohol from her house.

She wouldn't have done it if she hadn't been so drunk. It made her all the more determined to drink her fill tonight.

Susan announced, 'Marie's selling Sirius Cove.'

Everybody looked at her. Marie said, 'So this is my last New Year's Eve in Mosman.'

'Nooo.'

'But you're going to buy locally,' Susan said decisively, then projected her voice the length of the table to her husband. 'Harold, can we have that wine now, please?'

'You'll make a mint selling that property,' said Totti.

Jonesy nodded. 'The market here is very strong even though it's beginning to hurt elsewhere.'

'Harold,' Susan shouted. '*Wine.*'

'Stop shouting at me, darling,' Jonesy shouted back.

'It's this bloody room. The acoustics. We were supposed to do something about it *twenty* years ago.'

'Well, I'm not stopping you!' Jonesy got up.

'All this panic about one drought,' Totti was winding up his polemic, 'when Australia has had them since the beginning of time. Ask my grandparents about water shortages in Sardinia. Honestly, the *panic* in this country when the tiniest thing goes wrong.'

'It's a global problem, John,' said David. 'The Japanese have as many people in Tokyo as we have in this entire country and they recycle their sewage for drinking water and use the waste to irrigate. Why can't we do that?' He leant back as Susan cleared his plate. Again, Marie felt he was inclined towards her, although he was on the other side of the table and not even looking at her. She watched a Hardy Brothers 1999 Merlot pour into her glass from Jonesy's freckled hand.

'I refuse to drink sewage,' said Susan, and left the room.

'I'm going to help you,' said Gina.

'We're never going to agree on this, David. Where are you going to buy, Marie?'

'I don't know. I'm in debt so until the house is sold I don't really know what I can afford.' She took a deep draught of wine.

A hush fell over the table and Marie felt its weight double

beneath the suddenly unanimous masculine and attentive presence. She couldn't lower her voice in time and unintentionally boomed, 'But I've begun to hate Mosman and the belt's tightening so probably not here.' She laughed and addressed her plate, 'I mean I love the bush and harbour ...'

Totti began to fold his napkin. Jonesy watched her from beneath his brow. Marie wished she could remove the words *debt*, *afford* and *hate Mosman* from what she had said, but then she wouldn't have said anything.

Eventually, David broke the silence. 'I'd get a tank if I didn't live in a townhouse.'

'Oh!' Jonesy exclaimed as Susan entered carrying a rack of lamb. 'Look at this! Isn't she marvellous!'

'She's been watching Jamie Oliver.' Gina followed with a dish of flageolets.

'I did ask David to bring someone,' Susan said to Marie later in the kitchen, when she helped clear main course. 'I *think* he's got someone, but he's being a bit coy. God knows I don't want you to think I'm trying to set you up with him or anything like that.'

'He's a very nice man.'

'He's really come out of his shell since his wife died. I know that's a very politically incorrect thing to say, but it happens to be true.'

Marie deposited plates on the sink. She ran water over her hands, cracked with fish emulsion that had settled around the cuticles like brown dye. 'I wouldn't mind being set up. I'm not fussy.'

'Really?' Susan unwrapped a piece of dark chocolate and began to grate it over a pear tart.

'Can I help with anything?'

'No, no.'

Marie sat at the table. 'I'm thinking of going back to uni to finish my psychology degree.'

'Can you, after all this time?'

'I'm going to look into it in the new year, when I've sold the house.'

Susan flapped a hand towards the floor. 'What about them ... are they still there?'

'Of course. Susan, nobody notices them any more than they notice the straps of your shoes.'

'Gina would. She'd notice a speck of dust between your toes.'

The hubbub in the dining room was getting louder.

'That looks fabulous. You really are cooking up a storm tonight.'

Susan continued grating, eyebrows raised, elbows like wings. 'When Robert was a teenager he wanted a tattoo, you know.'

'Really?'

'Yes.'

'And?'

'Jonesy told him he'd be thrown out of the family.'

Marie said nothing.

Susan picked up a lemon. 'A little lemon zest,' she said, then began to grate it, adding: 'He grew out of it of course.'

They could hear David's voice rising. Gina came into the kitchen. Susan sent Marie a fierce hiding look. 'They're arguing about politics now,' said Gina. 'David's on his Arabic bent.'

'It's Jewish guilt, that's what it is,' Susan muttered.

Gina laughed. 'I think he's just a very good businessman, Susan. He's importing some beautiful stuff. *Beautiful*. And he's quite right about Morocco.'

'What about Morocco?' said Marie.

'If you haven't been already then go now. All the Peter Mayles will be down there in a flash and it'll be over.'

Susan pushed back her hair to show long earrings encrusted with stones. 'Did you see these? He brought them back for me.'

'Beautiful,' said Gina.

'Lovely,' said Marie. 'Can I borrow some hand cream, Susan?'

'Of course, in the bathroom. They're prophylactics, traditionally, for the Berber.'

'Will they stop you getting the flu this year?' Gina left a waft of perfume behind her as she walked out of the kitchen.

'She's had a boob job!' Susan hissed to Marie.

'Do you think so?!'

Marie walked after Gina, who had left the bathroom door open.

'Come in, Marie. I'm only doing my lipstick.'

'I'll just get some hand cream.' Marie tried to get a look at Gina's face while rummaging through the drawer but saw only erasure in Gina's sucked-in cheeks, her polished cleavage. She stared at Gina's breasts, then looking up saw Gina staring at her and she quickly looked away, mortified. Her ankles twisted and turned, trying to hide behind each other. She found the cream and focused on it. 'So tell me about Morocco.'

''eelll.' Gina's mouth stretched to receive a coat of lipstick. 'It's hot. It has everything really — desert, mountains, sea. The food is superb. I suppose it's like anywhere — you have to know where to stay.'

Marie wondered why she had begun this conversation. It was another case of can-I-afford-it. Everything seemed to go back to money and money now spelt restriction. And nobody here had the faintest idea what that meant. She simmered with resentment. And here she was trying to perve at fake lips, fake tits. As if that mattered. 'It sounds lovely.' She smiled.

Gina fixed her large eyes on Marie's mirror image. 'You could go on a tour! There are some very good ones these days. Not the dregs you'd think would go on them, but lots of people like us.'

'Really?'

'Yes. Very educational is what I'm told.' Gina lipsticked her mouth with a second, darker colour, then dabbed it with a tissue. 'The guides are Oxford scholars. You know, they speak about a thousand languages.'

'And how are you, Gina? How's the shop going?'

'I love it, but it's exhausting. The clientele are changing. All the new money coming into the area. They're so *rude*.'

'I hate the thought of selling my house to somebody like that.'

'Oh yes, it must be so hard.' Gina capped her lipstick. 'But you don't have much choice, do you? You can't sit there forever picking and choosing. You have to think of yourself and the best outcome in the long term … I think that's a terrific idea, you know. You really should do it. A tour to Morocco, after you've sold your house. What an adventure!'

When Gina left, Marie shut the door for a long, private scratch of her healing tattoo. Back in the dining room the seating had changed, and Gina was now in front of the light and Marie was seated next to David Rosenthal. The Valkyries were storming from the stereo, Totti shouting, 'What on earth are you waiting for? Book your tickets now. Subscribers get a discount. Fifteen hundred dollars, it's so cheap!'

Marie also subscribed to the opera. It was an effort to sit through all those hours of Stürm und Drang, but she felt somehow virtuous afterwards, as though she had fasted, or run a long way. Maybe *The Ring Cycle*, being that much longer, would work like an extended stay at a health farm. Maybe, also, a live version might finally expunge the images of *Apocalypse Now* that charged through her philistine mind each time she heard 'Ride of the Valkyries'. Maybe she couldn't afford it. Maybe she wasn't invited. Maybe she wasn't invited because she couldn't afford it.

'Then it's up to the Barossa for a few days,' Gina added.

'That's the part I'm looking forward to,' said Jonesy.

'The entire *Ring Cycle*?' David groaned. 'I might just join you at the wineries.'

'I agree, David.'

'Oh, come on, Harold. Don't be such a bore. I want to go.' Susan then instructed David to talk to Marie. 'She'll know what to do.'

David told Marie he needed something semi-temporary to cover an ugly fence that he was battling with a neighbour to replace.

'Passionfruit. They grow quickly and live for about six years.'

David looked disappointed. 'I know what I'm like. The fruit will rot while I fill my bowl with peaches from Harris Farm. I was thinking of something more decorative.'

'But they flower. Haven't you ever seen a passionflower? They're extraordinary and they go on virtually all summer.'

She described the flat petals, the stamen reaching up like dancers in their midst, the purple tendrils. She noticed sunspots on the whites of David's eyes and a scrape of bristle on his cheekbone that he had missed shaving. His gaze moved to the flare of her thigh when she crossed her legs, then he frowned slightly to show he was paying her serious attention. Marie talked about the medicinal qualities of passionflowers, for anxiety, some said cancer. A foot poked her beneath the table, and Marie sent David a coquettish look before realising his legs were stretched in the other direction. She could feel Susan's eyes spearing her profile. She remembered her children sitting by the passionfruit vine eating all the fruit in one afternoon. They did the same with the mandarin tree, strewing peels across the grass and returning to the house with their mouths swollen from citric acid. Later from the deck, the glint of peels in moonlight floating over the sea of lawn. It was another time now, and Marie could feel herself coming back to life.

'My son Leon used to call passionflowers "fairy stages". They open out flat, like a podium for the tendrils and stamen.'

'Really?'

'Yes. And they're named after the Passion of Christ.'

David turned down the corners of his mouth. 'I'm not a Christian. I abhor religion.'

'Neither am I, so do I,' Marie hastily reassured him.

'Each to his own,' said Totti.

'Well, Marie,' David said decisively, 'I'm going to take your advice.'

Jonesy pushed back his chair clumsily. 'Let's struggle on through the cellar, shall we?'

David began to clear. 'Come on, Totti, our turn.'

Totti followed, sheepish, baffled.

'I won't have you men messing up my kitchen.' Susan quickly rose. 'Marie?'

'Well, I'm the last man sitting,' Gina said to the abandoned table. 'Are we going into the lounge now?'

'Yes please,' said Susan.

'Fireworks!' Totti exclaimed. 'What's the time?'

'The witching hour approaches!' David did an excited swivel.

'Darling, they're not having fireworks here.' Gina took her husband's arm.

'Well, they bloody well should.'

'It isn't fair, is it?'

'It's an outrage.'

'I know someone who lives in the Toaster. She says that Circular Quay is like a *war* zone at midnight.'

'Oh yes, the ground literally shakes when you're that near.'

'She can't stand it. She spends New Year at Noosa.'

'I don't care! I want fireworks on *this* harbour, right below our house! Now!'

Their laughter faded. Marie whispered to Susan in the kitchen: 'Did you kick me under the table before?'

'It was a prod, not a kick. I didn't want you to speak about cancer. It's what David's wife died of, you know.'

'I'm sorry.'

'No need to apologise.' Susan looked at Marie shrewdly. 'He didn't seem to mind.'

A tendril of Arabic music curled into the room.

'Look at him, will you?' Susan whispered admiringly as they crossed back through the dining room. 'He's not afraid to stand out, is he?'

She smiled at David, perched over the Bang & Olufsen, a flat silver box on a Chinese chest. It was a giant beige cocoon of a room with a triple-seater lounge suite and salmon-coloured rugs. On the mantlepiece was a pair of ormolu vases stuffed with tea roses. Through the French doors drifted miniature voices from parties on Middle Harbour. David turned up the music. Watching him click his fingers and yell to Jonesy, Marie wondered if Susan had slept with David as well. The shrine of marital fidelity seemed so petty now, an inanimate object whose meaning was all externally imposed, and with regulations arbitrary as the marketplace. Leaving the boathouse the final time with Jonesy, Marie had gone ahead and lifted her skirt beneath the bush lemon. He looked at her affronted then walked straight up to the car. It was suddenly clear that the ritual had nothing to do with the tree nor minerals nor even bladder function, but everything to do with territory and gender. Had Jonesy brought others here? His private tree of conquest. The cutting had died in Marie's garden. And why cling so resolutely to that as well? The negatives in her bank statements seemed just marks on paper, her house a mere structure that if lifted away would leave her, this body, intact as ever. She felt so glad in this moment to be alone and released.

'Come on, Susan!' David plucked a scarf off the back of a chair and twirled it over his head. 'It's the Raindance!' He hooked the scarf around her neck and pulled her into the living room. Susan shuffled obediently, rolling her eyes at her husband who sat on the couch drinking Sauternes, stomach protruding.

'You dance like a woman, Dave.' Totti laughed.

'They all dance like this over there. Come on, boys.' He flourished the scarf. 'Get in touch with your feminine side!'

'That's my scarf,' said Gina.

'Well, get up then!' He swished it in her face.

'I can't *move*.'

So David danced over to Marie, and Marie stepped into the next arabesque with him. She danced with glide of silk over her hips, as David pressed her face against his shoulder, the room swirling all around her.

'Marie's certainly kicking up her heels,' Jonesy chuckled to his wife.

'That's putting it mildly, Harold.'

BLOOD

'I REMEMBER YOUR HOUSE,' David said to Marie, one week later in a restaurant in Woollahra. 'There were some beautiful rugs. I can't remember what I was there for. It was summer, a drinks party, but for some reason I see it all as a daytime event.'

'It could have been Boxing Day. We used to have people over for champagne breakfast to watch the Sydney to Hobart.'

'There was one rug with a beautiful dark blue,' David said dreamily, 'like a night sky. Did you know that children go blind making those rugs? The knots are that small.'

David told Marie he had been invited to the party after procuring a desk for Ross, a colonial slab that needed three men to be moved. It was quietly thrilling to think of him moving through her house all those years ago, barely noticed by her, then coming into her life so forcefully at this time. It had to mean something: like a flower pressed between the pages of a book she had had for years but only now decided to open, David seemed to have been waiting for her all along. Destiny. David had furnished most of the Tottis' and the Joneses'. His shop was two blocks away on Queen Street. Marie noticed his posture lilted to one side as though he was partway through a shrug. Or leaning towards her. He was handsome, she thought, scanning the room, a smartly lit space of right angles. She turned back to David in his pink polo shirt. Yes, definitely one of the best-looking men here, of his age. Someone who knew how to enjoy himself. She savoured the thick white napkin on her lap, the white hats of kitchen staff bobbing behind the stainless-steel counter, her cosmopolitan, eastern-suburbs date.

'What do you really think of the Ned Kelly painting?' Marie asked him.

'Honestly? They're terrific paintings, even the third series, which is what Jonesy has although he's loath to admit it.' David steepled his hands. 'But in my humble opinion, he paid too much. He'd be better off collecting emerging artists, but Jonesy has a very conservative eye, bless his soul. He's staunchly old school.'

'They both are. They didn't use to be.'

'Jonesy and I argue all the time. We're on opposite sides of the fence politically. He's a climate-change sceptic, and he votes accordingly. I told him, "If polar bears are rendered extinct by this fiasco, I'm holding you personally responsible."'

'And what did he say?'

'He laughed.'

'I can imagine.'

'He's a good bloke. Warm-hearted, hospitable. Kindness' — David looked Marie in the eye — 'I've come to realise in my old age how important this simple quality is. You've known them a long time, haven't you?'

'Yes, we go way back.'

'Do you want dessert?' David put on his glasses and peered down at the menu.

Marie ordered the citrus crème caramel with chocolate puff pastry. An icy jet of air-conditioning streamed directly against the back of her neck, and she pulled her shawl tighter.

'I met the little grub,' David said. 'Louise brought her over on New Year's Day.'

'What's she like?'

'Wrinkly.' David screwed up his face. 'She looks like Jonesy!'

'Isn't it fabulous being a grandparent? I miss my Nell.'

'Where is she?'

'My son doesn't have a very good custody arrangement.'

'Oh dear. They're a bit hard on us men in that respect. Here. Taste some of my fig soufflé.'

'… Divine.'

'But that's going to change.'

'What?'

'Custody. Everything. When women become equal. Not long now.'

'You think?'

'You should see my Rosie. She's seven and the best in the soccer team. The boys are *terrified* of her. You should see her go! Fastest on the field, hardest kicker, tough as nails. She wants to play for Australia and she's furious that she'll soon be playing with girls only.'

'That's a nice idea,' said Marie. 'Equality.'

As they came out of the restaurant, David said, 'I don't think Susan approves of us going out together. When I asked her for your number she said, "David I wasn't trying to set you up!"'

'She said that to me as well.'

'Are we going to tell her?'

'Tell her what? That you've been consulting me about planting?'

They stood on Queen Street looking at one another shyly.

'I have to get a taxi,' Marie said. 'I'm over the limit. Can I get one here?'

'Of course. But what about your car? The parking inspectors will begin their rounds at nine a.m. sharp. They're ruthless around here, you know, they'll book you for looking in a shop window. Terrible for business; we've actually mounted protests with the council.' David checked the street, clearing his throat. 'You're going to have to come all the way back into town at eight-thirty in the morning to avoid getting booked. You'll have to buy over this side, won't you. You can stay at my place tonight, I have a spare room. I'm five minutes away in Darling Point.'

'Okay then,' said Marie without hesitation. 'Let's walk.'

Over the hill where the shops abated and streetlights were obscured by large old fig trees, the road grew dark. It's my first real date in about forty years, Marie thought. And nothing has changed. We're like teenagers, eager, naughty. She felt a prickle of renewal, the air heavy with low cloud, the scent of deadly nightshade filling the hot darkness. A splodge of moisture landed on her shoulder and she twisted, thinking it was bats in the fig tree but her shoulder was unmarked and David caught her eye, then hand, and held it with warm insistence as they walked down the hill to Edgecliff. She loosened her shawl and when they came out from beneath the figs felt another drop. A faint rumble passed over them. 'I think your Raindance worked, David.'

The rain began to fall more steadily and they hailed a taxi in front of the German embassy. Anxiety about what he would make of her tattoos lurked in Marie's mind, though she wouldn't allow herself to think that anything more than a cup of tea would pass between them, but he reached for her hand again in the taxi and when she looked over he was smiling out the window at the lights of Rushcutters Bay streaming past. He looked so happy. She smiled too. She leant forward as the taxi pulled up, elbowing her way past David to pay the driver.

'I insist. You paid for dinner, I'm getting the cab.'

'No, no!'

'Equality, David,' Marie said firmly.

He chuckled.

She felt him steal looks at her as they walked down the steps to his Darling Point townhouse, and expectation grew so heavy that she couldn't speak, could barely hold her head up, could only wait dry-mouthed while David got out his keys. He kissed her just inside the door and she drank him in. How long was it since the touch of a man — at least two years, because Ross had been sleeping in the spare room by the end. Even then it was a bored, contemptuous, over-familiar husband, not this cocktail of new taste and smell, this never-before-felt, angular body. They passed through a room full of exotic figurines and bark paintings. Polynesian-looking cloths were draped over the couch. There was something optimistic about being in the house of a man open to other cultures.

'These are beautiful.' Marie touched one of the cloths.

'Good for calling cards. A dime a dozen in Tonga. Shall we go to my bedroom?'

He indicated a chair on which she could place her clothes, then went into the ensuite.

She watched him from between the sheets as he went naked and unself-conscious from the wardrobe into the bathroom. He swallowed pills at the sink then climbed in beside her. She pushed against him for the warmth of skin the length of her body, the comforting swell of genitals against her mound. He rested his head on the pillow and she opened her eyes to see him smiling at her. He kissed her neck, her breasts, propped himself on his elbows, his mouth following his hand down.

'Goodness, you shave down there? I find that so erotic,' he whispered. He moved down her body then tensed. 'What's that?'

She couldn't see his face, just the shape of his head between her legs. He moved to let the diffuse street light fall through the window across her belly. His voice came out confused and wounded. 'Is it real?'

'Yes.'

'My god. Can I ask why?'

He came back up to lie beside her. Fighting off a feeling of dread, Marie turned on her side in order to see his face. She remembered the moment of his head between her legs. Her memory could wash a facial expression across that silhouette; it could imagine anything.

'I wanted it. That's all.'

The silence between them expanded, then into it trickled the sounds of the world — a rustling of Moreton Bay figs from New Beach Road, the swish of car tyres. A multitude of impulses charged through Marie. To leave. To slap or to reassure him. Then there was the impulse to howl with frustation.

'I'm sorry, Marie. I have trouble understanding why people do these things to themselves.'

'I love my tattoos.'

'You've got more?'

'Yes, four.'

Marie felt like a blemish on these tasteful furnishings. The mushroom walls, scrolls of Chinese calligraphy, Egyptian cotton sheets. The long wooden body beside her, legs crossed at the ankles. She felt humiliated, and in the slipstream of this humiliation began to grow a brittle defiance.

David's voice came, thin and small. 'Can I see them?'

Marie didn't really want David to see the tattoos now his unease was so evident. She didn't want to be judged or feared, but she had offered him her body and the tattoos were a part of that, so she didn't feel able or even willing to take them away. David stared, reaching out to touch. As he moved, the sheet fell away. He tried to hide his erection.

'Well,' Marie quipped, 'they can't be that bad,' thinking what a nice dick he had, angry with him now, angry with herself for thinking yet another compliment, for noticing this crucial factor and being unable to resist it.

'It's very ... um, beautifully drawn,' he said.

He leant back against the bedhead and she could feel the heat of his skin, the contraction of lungs and trickle of digestive juice along its ten-metre labyrinth to the bowel. The humble, diligent workings of his body, which continued in spite of everything, softened her, even filled her with a kind of awe. They also riled her with their imperviousness. What's in it for me? she thought, feeling robbed. The rustle outside grew louder. 'Rain,' she said.

Then David rolled onto his side and pressed his body to hers, cock twitching against the tender skin of her groin. Desire stabbed her. Viagra, she suddenly thought. Or was it just her? Who cares? She cupped her hand around his balls then bent to take him in her mouth. David groaned, running his fingers down her flanks, 'Such soft skin.'

She wiped herself with spitty fingers and slung a leg over his hips and drew him inside. From above, half shadowed, his face looked sad and wanting, and a feeling of compassion for both of them washed through her. She placed his hands on her breasts, closed her eyes and moved faster. She knew if she leant forward how quickly she could come. The rain was growing louder, an all-enveloping hiss, drowning them out. Marie reached behind to push him in deeper then felt a rush begin. 'Slowly. *Slowly.*'

He kept going for a while with her sated and relaxed, still on him. 'I'm sorry, I couldn't wait ... oh, it's a bit uncomfortable now, David.'

'That's fine, he's fine!' David said, as though his dick was a person. 'He's had a very nice time.'

Later, falling asleep, Marie became aware of frenetic movement. She realised that David was masturbating. He finished quickly and began to snore. She turned on her side and dozed with her back to him. Later again, she woke properly and lay there watching dawn percolate the sky. The Chinese calligraphy began to clarify. From outside, the *cheep-cheep* of a bird. Marie grew more alert with every passing second. It occurred to her that life was nothing but a series of fumbling endeavours, one after another, until you died.

She went for a swim when she got home. Eight a.m., nobody around, birds quiet in the sullen heat. Across the harbour lay the tall buildings of the city, Renzo Piano's acute angle dominant. The reserve was a dry yellow, the sky and sea a dirty grey, and all the yachts in the cove were still. The first bite of water around her ankles made Marie cry out. She stopped to adjust to the temperature, then submerged fully and rose stroking towards the harbour.

Was the studio her opium den? A place of arcane, ambivalent pleasure, the drug administered through modern stainless steel? More prosaically, it had begun to feel like another home, containing another language and family. She loved the domesticity of the old terrace, the mysterious top storey keeping it aloof, the tattooed ladies on the walls of the front room. Often as she paid, she could hear kitchen sounds beyond reception, or encountered friendly traffic, like Rob, Rhys's partner, a short dark man with a black beard of Rabbinical length.

'I wanna get a photo of the flames before we begin today,' Rhys said. 'You okay if Rob takes it? He's got a cracker camera.'

'I'd love one.'

Rhys lifted her chin and yelled behind her. 'Rob!'

Rob appeared, a chain clinking around the hip of his baggy, calf-length shorts. 'G'day Marie!'

'Hi Rob.'

'Gotcha camera, darl? We forgot to photograph the flames — you didn't see them, did you?'

Rob went and fetched a large Nikon. 'Can you stand next to that window, Marie?'

Marie lifted her shirt and lowered her trousers. Rob pressed a button on the camera and the snout pushed towards her and opened its eye. '*Great* job. Looks fantastic!'

The bell rang and two people walked in. Marie recognised the shop assistant and the doll-like woman she had met in the other tattoo parlour. His red-fanged goatee had been shaved off, the metal was gone from his earlobes. It was thirty-eight degrees outside, the hottest January on record, but the girl's shirtsleeves were sharp as blades, her lipstick and hair perfect. 'Christ, it's hot,' she said.

Rob did the introductions. 'Stew, Mel, Marie.'

'What are you getting done today, Stew?' said Rhys.

'The Pud.'

'Last session,' said Rob. 'Touch-ups 'n' stuff.'

'Well, hallo,' Mel said to Marie, examining her flat black shoes and plain t-shirt. Marie felt very Mosman and very sweaty, and cringed from Mel's stare. 'So you *found* it. Good for you.'

'Yes. Thanks for the tip.'

'The boss know you're sleeping with the enemy?' Rhys laughed at Stew. 'Stew's an animator,' she explained to Marie.

'I've left the parlour!' Stew thrust his head forward in delight. 'Got a job at Fox.'

'Gone over to the dark side, eh?' said Rob. 'They make you take your tunnels out?'

'Murdoch or bikies, much of a muchness.' Stew shrugged. 'I can stretch 'em up again.'

'They're like little arseholes when they're shrinking,' Mel remarked, touching the loose rings of flesh that his empty earlobes had become. 'Little ear arseholes. Quite cute really.'

Stew had a tattoo of Felix the Cat on his left forearm and the Roadrunner on his right, delirious with another death. Captain Haddock fumed on a deltoid. Stew himself was like a cartoon character, or a sideshow puppet whose head was on a long stick inserted into the body cavity, bouncing when he laughed as though someone had depressed it. She wished Mel hadn't said that about his earlobes. She kept thinking of things poking through the puckered holes. She tried not to look at them.

'What are you getting done?' Mel asked her.

'A moth, on my back.'

'Oh.' Mel was nonplussed.

Marie felt slightly offended. 'It's colourful, like a butterfly, it's this big. It's called a Splendid Ghost Moth.'

'*Oh.*'

'Mel,' said Rhys, 'Rob's gonna show you the ropes cos I've gotta pick up Travis from school, so I want to get started on Marie. Okay, Rob?'

'Sure.'

'Did you mean the Magic Pudding?' Marie said to Stew.

Stew lifted his shirt.

'Oh,' Marie exclaimed, 'I love the Pud!'

'Isn't it great.' Mel gave his belly a little stroke. 'It is *so* good.'

The Pudding's shading was still fresh, enhancing his livid countenance. He took up a large space, his currant nose Stew's navel, spindly legs disappearing into the lawn of re-growth below. He had a fork stuck in his head that tapered off around Stew's solar plexus. Stew and Rob shot one another a look then, to the surprise of the three women, broke into song:

Eat away, chew away, munch and bolt and guzzle,
Never leave the table till you're full up to the muzzle!

The Pudding's furious face twitched as Stew sang.

'Rightio.' Rhys laughed. 'Tatt looks great. I'm going upstairs.'

'I'm trying to understand,' said Mel, 'this fixation with a pudding. I'm a wog,' she explained to Marie.

'It's not common,' Rob admitted. 'You don't have to be Anglo. I'm not.'

'It's an acquired taste,' said Stew. 'You're a Pud fan too, Marie?'

'I love him, I've still got my original edition. My eldest son played him in a school play. He insisted on the forked version, just like you.'

'Did you make the costume?' Stew said excitedly.

'I couldn't get the fork to stay upright. I couldn't persuade Clark to wear a bowl.'

'Foam. And you use a plastic one and paint it silver.'

'I'll have to remember that. Clark was so cross with me.'

'Clark,' said Mel. 'That's a nice name.'

'After Gable. We loved old movies.'

'Little boys,' said Rob. 'They're so vain. Travis takes like fifteen minutes to fix his Superman cape in the mirror. And that's without the facial expressions.'

Marie guessed Travis to be Rhys and Rob's son.

'How many children do you have, Marie?' Stew asked.

'Three. Clark my eldest is thirty-nine.'

'Same age as Rhys,' said Rob.

'My god, I would have taken her for thirty.'

'She's got that beautiful Slavic skin,' said Mel.

'And, um, do you have any grandchildren?' Stew asked.

'Nell.' Marie smiled. 'Clark's four-year-old.'

'Gosh, you look good for a grandmother,' said Mel.

'You'll have to introduce Nell to Travis,' said Rob. 'Travis would love that.'

They stood there looking at Marie expectantly. Marie felt overwhelmed by their friendliness. 'I'd better go up.'

Clark had been about nine in the play of *The Magic Pudding*. Marie had dressed him in an old pair of Ross's shorts. The huge brown shorts, stuffed with foam, waistband gathered around the boy's chest, created a very pudding-like effect. She remembered her pride when Clark stormed on and roared the Pudding's polemic to the audience, the fork immediately flopping horizontal. The sight of his vulnerable, skinny legs made her ache with tender protection. Ross bellowed with laughter, pinching the bridge of his nose. Marie began to laugh as well, leaning up against Ross, the vibration of their laughter mingling in her bones. 'He's a right little Hitler, isn't he?' Ross said, laughing again.

Clark never lost his enthusiasm for the Magic Pudding. Fifteen years later, in his Honours thesis, he wrote about the character as avatar of colonial greed, prescient of end-stage capitalism. Marie was impressed by the fifteen-thousand-word document. To see her son's twenty-four-year-old mind work with ideas was to watch a bird in flight whose wings till now had been clipped. He didn't express himself like this in the family home — passionate, eccentric, overexcited, mildly pretentious — he assumed instead a surly world-weariness, originally as protection against a father who would have ridiculed such a thesis, but then it became a habitual attitude. With all of them, possibly the whole world, Clark had become bitter and defensive. Marie worried about her role in this, she worried she didn't like him, she struggled to give him her approval. She found him so hard to talk to now. Hopefully the PhD would make him happier. And as she left the room containing three people the same age as her children, she remembered Christmas Day and how much she wanted Clark's approval as well. Paradoxically, the longer Clark lived a non-career-driven life, the more curmudgeonly he became, as though he were anticipating the judgement of the world and pre-empting it by bringing it on himself, on everybody. Marie felt overwhelmed by how easy it was to talk to Stew, Rob and Mel. She felt that if she didn't leave the room immediately she would want to stay there for the rest of her life.

She thought about age as she made her way up the stairs, how it manifested first and foremost on the skin. Then grey hair, arthritis, old injuries waking from the opiate of youth. Desire lessened with age but didn't vanish. Inside your fifty- or sixty-something-year-old body, you continued lusting, your mind oblivious to the flesh crumbling around it.

It was hard to believe Clark was the same age as Rhys. But why was she surprised by Rhys's age when Rhys's poise and wisdom had always held authority with her? Something about Clark's adage that tattoos were for the young. Clark, Blanche and Hugh were so much more earnest than the people here. They had entered a No-Fun zone with adulthood. As their mother, Marie was supposed to be even deeper in this zone. Right up the back, just in front of the remedial chairs, with the retired professors and bingo players.

But age changed throughout the ages, first-time mothers these days old enough to be grandmothers. Men had seniority, regardless of age. Marie's father had been twelve years older than her mother, and that was normal. A mother twelve years older than a father would have been wrong. And back when Clark was playing the Magic Pudding, Marie and Ross were younger than the tattoo folk and her children were now, yet they already had two mortgages, three children and a twelve-year marriage. Somewhere, somebody was not acting their age.

Age changed in other places. In Africa, women her age were still dancing in their hot village streets, like the folk in *Buena Vista Social Club*, shimmying and shaking to their sexy love songs. While in Sydney town, dancing remained the province of the young.

You could take Viagra like David, or have Botox like Gina, get a new liver like Dennis Hopper. You could get new breasts like Nicole Kidman, who looked the same age now as she did ten years ago and probably would ten years hence. *But we cannot buy immortality*, said a doctor in a documentary on cryogenesis that Marie had watched recently. *Our bodies simply aren't designed to last that long.*

She didn't think the tattoos would reverse the ageing process, nor even make it stand still. In some ways they would have the opposite effect. Like tidemarks, they would indicate forever what was happening now.

Marie entered Rhys's room with the frazzled air of a woman who had lugged her baggage all the way up the stairs only to find she didn't need it here. She shut the door on her yapping thoughts and began to undress.

'My faithful tattooed lady.'

'I'm greedy, aren't I.'

'Yep. You're on a mission.'

Rhys lay the transfer across Marie's back, and beneath its gentle adumbration Marie surrendered.

There wasn't much to do in a garden during a January that blazed near forty almost every day. All Marie needed now was to keep it looking good for the buyers. She watered twice a week and on washing days uncoiled the bailing hose from the laundry. She cut grevilleas for the living room. She tried not to go outside in the middle of the day and wore a thicker shirt to protect her healing back.

The guttering man arrived just before lunch. Marie went out to greet him. 'It's going to be boiling up there,' she said.

'I've gotta go to Pymble next. This is the easy job. Harbour breezes, you know.'

She watched him climb onto the roof from the patio. He wore sock guards and his legs were burnt brick red. He touched the gutter and swore, hands flicking away. He moved along in this fashion, clearing the gutter and burning himself in the process. He held up a nest with two eggs in it and called, 'Want me to save these?'

'What birds are they?'

'Probably mynas? Might be a top knot?'

'Destroy them.'

He disappeared over the roofline.

'Were there many?' she said to him afterwards as she wrote out a cheque.

'A couple operational. Couple others abandoned. They don't look after their young very well,' he said disapprovingly. 'Dunno how they're such successful populators. Can I use your tap?'

'Of course. But it'll be hot too.'

He turned it on anyway, then recoiled. Marie went into the kitchen for ice, and cut a chunk of aloe vera. 'For those burns.'

He refused the aloe. 'Best just to leave 'em and toughen up.'

She handed him the cheque. 'And how's business in the guttering world?'

'Really busy. Everybody in Ku-ring-gai's finally clearing their gutters in case of bushfires.'

'Take it.' Marie pressed the aloe on him. 'It's soothing.'

He thanked her then walked up the path to his ute. Marie swept the perimeter of the house of its guttering refuse, scraping up a smashed egg with a handful of leaves. Inside the shell was a half-formed bird; Marie threw leaves over it, annoyed by her distress.

Walking back up to the house, she heard the banksia groaning and thought as she turned how uncanny it sounded, like a creature crying for help, and as she stood there watching, the tree slowly fell. It was a surreal and frightening sight, the old man banksia falling towards the harbour with a groaning woody shriek, dropping dead before her eyes. It was over quickly. Vertical one minute, horizontal the next. She ran inside and rang Leon.

'Must've had something eating its roots.'

'I didn't even notice it was sick.'

'It doesn't necessarily show. Which one was it?'

'The one at the bottom. I planted it when we moved in.' Marie was stricken.

Leon sounded cool as ever. 'That's really sad. I don't know ... Phytophthora? It moves in a line. Could've come up from the bush? Or else the roots've been weakening for a while then collapsed with the rain.'

'We only had two days' worth.'

'That can be enough if it's heavy. Sorry I'm not there to help you dispose of it.'

After she rang off, Marie picked up Mopoke and went out to the deck. Through the angophora, she could see the banksia lying on its side, roots clodded with earth. A red wattlebird alighted onto a flower to drink his fill then threw his head back and clacked loudly at the sky.

The next day Marie went down and cut a dozen mature cones off the tree.

Blanche told him they had broadcast the full execution on cable. Shocked, Clark said nothing though his television had been switched on early in the hope of seeing more news on the matter. He muted it and settled into the phone call with his sister. Watching TV while it was still light outside made him feel like he was sick or on holiday or back in his childhood. Clark had refused to own a television for the first five years out of home, swearing he had already watched enough to last a lifetime. Penny his first girlfriend had one, and after two years living with her he found himself, like any spouse, eating dinner in front of it almost every night. And hating it. When they broke up, he went on a television fast for a year but his life didn't improve. He was too poor to have a holiday and too shattered to attempt seductions. He filed three days a week in the Film Finance Office while finishing his Honours thesis on Australian pop icons of the early twentieth century. He was miserably aware each time he went home and faced his father of how unsuccessful he was.

His financial situation changed with the $300,000 Ross gave him on his twenty-fifth birthday, a sum to buy real estate that all the children would receive. But Clark didn't want to identify as wealthy so he banked most of it and escaped to Europe for three years, where the jobs ended in a nadir of delivering cooking oil in Brighton. He began to write travel articles and, when he moved back to Australia, tried journalism. It was insecure work. He spent more of that real-estate money. Then came the museum job and three months later he met Janice, a publicist for the Sydney Festival. They bought a house together and had Nell. They got free tickets to everything. Clark felt like he had been saved. These were the glory days when things fell into place just as they were supposed to when you were in your thirties. What you never foresaw was how just as easily things could fall apart.

The Sony 23" in his living room had been handed down from Blanche and Hugh when they upgraded to plasma. It was on a stand that Clark could twist around to face the kitchen so he could watch it while he did the washing-up. He missed Janice's Miele appliances and cable TV. He missed their subscription to the Sydney Theatre Company. Although the plays generally bored him he liked to go down to The Wharf dressed in black and stand around drinking by the harbour. He missed the view of the ocean from the Clovelly house. He missed his daughter like a limb. It was galling to see the disappointment on her face when she came to stay. Clark became loud and hearty while Nell soldiered on with polite bravery. It took until Sunday night for them to relax, then he had to unpeel her and stick her back in her mansion. With typical caution, Clark had bought a small two-bedroom flat outright after settling with Janice, who owned most of their house. Now he was kicking himself as with a growing daughter he would have to find something bigger yet the market only got more impenetrable. How could he pay a mortgage on a $25,000 stipend? Blanche and Hugh had been at him for years to invest but Clark remained averse. Consequently he neither made as much money as his sister nor spent as much as his brother. He missed not having to worry about money; he hated this incessant gnawing at the back of his mind. He had liked the idea of marrying a richer woman. He could live the good life without feeling personally responsible; it assuaged his guilt at being born into privilege. Penury was good when you had a safety net but real penury was torture. It was pure humiliation, just as genuine inferiority to a woman was. Clark's uselessness with money began as an amusement in his relationship with Janice — him the Batty Intellectual indulged by her, the Organiser — and ended as one of the main causes of the bickering that chipped their relationship to the bone. He watched TV as he filled the sink and listened to Blanche. Four ads in a row. Better off reading *The Guardian* later to get the full story. Clark still read more than he watched. He rarely bothered with literary fiction, let alone poetry, but read history, biography, crime, the paper every day and a variety of publications online.

'You know they had executions in your old art school at Taylor Square?' he said to Blanche, phone clamped between head and shoulder. '*Huge* public events, those hangings. One guy called Knatchbull got a crowd of ten thousand. Can you imagine?'

'Sounds fantastic.'

'And when they built Darlo Gaol in the 1840s, the convicts from the old place in Lower George Street were moved there on foot. Think of the spectacle, hundreds of crims clanking through the city in chains, everybody coming out to heckle and gawk.'

'Well, thank god we're alive today and not then.'

'But it's still going on. You just saw it on TV.'

'No I didn't. I didn't *watch* it.'

'It's just been removed from us. We don't have to confront anything.'

'I didn't learn anything being confronted by that execution Clark. Except how fucked up the human race is.'

A sunburnt reporter was standing in a paddock of cracked earth. A graph came on showing how low the dams were, then the words *Permanent Drought.* Clark could just make out the reporter saying: *The Murray–Darling river basin, responsible for forty percent of Australia's produce, is dying ...*

'Can we talk about something else?' Blanche said.

'Sure.' Clark muted the television. 'How was your trip to the Evil Empire?'

'Great. We shot lots of people and released ten times our quota of pollution daily, just by talking crap.'

'Did you ski?'

'Well, it was fabulous the first week, lots of powder, then the rest of the time it rained. It was bizarre. We were out when the weather changed and it was like a switch being flicked. After that it was bloody awful to tell you the truth. There's no reason to be there apart from the snow. We just watched DVDs. Have you seen *Ants*? It's amazing.'

'Climate change.'

'It's the latest excuse, isn't it. It floods and it's climate change; there's a drought and it's climate change. Apparently even therapists are doing a roaring trade. Like, *Help me I'm suicidal because of climate change*. Insurance companies too, you know, *Sorry for running up the back of you, I was stressing out about climate change*.'

'Some guy here murdered another guy for using his hose on a non-watering day.'

'No.'

'True. Out in the suburbs. Last week. When did you get back?'

'Four days ago. I didn't hear about that. I'm drowning in emails and I have a toothpaste campaign coming up and I'm still jet-lagged.'

'You should use me as a model. I'm running out of money.'

Was that another Clark joke, or a covert appeal? Blanche wondered. Many a true word spoken in jest. Well, tough luck. No way, José. What you sow you will reap. Clark had refused to wear orthodontic braces as a teenager. The family assumed it was an abjuration of vanity. Blanche disagreed, saying the opposite was the case. She maintained that for a hormone-crazed boy, eighteen months in oral quarantine didn't seem worth a lifetime of straight teeth, but he would regret it later. She, on the other hand, had worn her braces with committed idealism and emerged from her metal chrysalis twice as popular with boys. She could hear the thunking of solids in water beyond Clark's voice.

'I've always thought vampires would make a good toothpaste ad.'

'They're so conservative these days, they'd never agree to vampires,' Blanche said, while a cute little Nosferatu with a white frothy brush held to his cute little fangs materialised before her. 'In terms of hygiene vampires are totally politically incorrect.'

'They never go out of fashion. You could make them quirky, like the Addams Family. *Shit!*'

There was an almighty crash as the salad bowl slipped out of Clark's hands.

'What are you *doing?*'

'Sorry, I just dropped something.' He propped the bowl to drain and pulled out the plug.

'Was Leon here for Christmas?'

'Yep.'

'How was he?'

'Alright. The usual.'

Clark stretched his neck to the left and right, holding out the phone so Blanche's voice tinkled into the air. 'He owes me money.'

'Really?'

'I lent it to him a year ago, interest-free, to keep his business afloat.'

'I don't think the business is doing so well.'

'Climate change,' Blanche said acidly.

'I'm not defending him.'

'And he hasn't even said anything. I mean, wouldn't you even *say* something?'

Clark went into the living room, swivelling the television as he passed it. He regretted his earlier provocations. He realised he assumed an attitude like Leon's — a more polarised view — just to wind his sister up. A fractious exchange was preferable to one of calm affability because Clark felt uncomfortable at anything remotely intimate with his sister. He was also still angry at Marie's decision to use Hugh for the sale of the house, entirely predictable as it was. He began to pace his living room. It was small and the laps quickly multiplied.

'And he's still sending me those bloody online petitions just about every week.'

'Yeah, I just got the Burmese junta.'

'Like it makes the slightest difference. *Anyone* can sign those things, under ten different names and addresses if they want. And he's obviously got enough money to fly down to Sydney twice in three months.'

'Mum's frequent flyers. He didn't stay long.'

'Of course. And did you see her tattoos?'

'Ye-ep ... You know she's got one on her stomach now.'

'Hey?'

'On her stomach, flames or something. And she's getting one on her back of a moth.' To appal Blanche, because it would make him feel less appalled, he added, 'Like, you know, *big.*'

'... *Jesus.* Are you serious?'

'I know, I know.' Clark walked up and down, up and down.

'What is *wrong* with her?'

'She's freaking about the sale.'

'Do you think that's why she's on this bender?'

'It's not really a bender, not in the normal sense. She wasn't that pissed on Christmas Day. She said she saved the liquor cabinet for you, but when you didn't take it she took it to Sotheby's, and she's packed all our stuff. Every time I go over there I come home with another carton.'

'I didn't want the liquor cabinet. It was ugly. I took a carton last time I was there.'

'You'll never believe what ended up in my last one. Speaking of teeth. Your plate.'

'God, really? I haven't gone through mine yet.' Blanche began to sound mournful. 'I must admit I'm beginning to feel a bit wrenched by this sale. It's our loss too, you know.'

'And your husband's gain.'

'For Christ's sake, Clark. He hasn't even given her a valuation yet!'

'It's in the bag, though.'

The telephone ticked with silence. Blanche's tone changed. 'So who's your preferred agent? Go on, you've had three months to choose.'

'I don't know. They all give me the creeps.'

'Why?' Blanche said in a voice shiny with curiosity and challenge.

'The Sydney property market is grossly inflated. It's awash with easy money, and money corrupts.'

Blanche snorted. 'Yeah, we should all be buying our groceries with gumnuts.'

'I'm not talking about daily necessities, I'm talking about profits for the elite few.'

'Like *you*, Clark. And there'll be more when our parents die!'

'Mum's only fifty-nine and she's heavily in debt!'

'Hey, I've got a great idea! Why don't you do it?'

'I'm not a real-estate agent.'

'Yeah, but in your opinion a real-estate agent doesn't do anything but take money so why don't you step in and sell the house? Mum likes you better than Hugh — I'm sure she'd be *thrilled*.'

'I don't want to,' Clark protested, 'I don't know how!'

'You're all so fucking superior, aren't you? Hugh's bloody good at what he does, you know, and I'm sick of you all giving him such a hard time!' Blanche slammed down the phone.

Shattered, Clark sank into the armchair opposite the television. After a while he realised it was dark outside and that he was watching a toothpaste advertisement with the rapt focus of a child. It was set in an office, everybody smiling and bending close to one another as they passed files around, the final shot lift doors closing on the corporate lovers kissing. All those ferociously perfect white teeth, all that sterile osculation. He knew Blanche would have done a better job than this; he rued upsetting her. He had discovered her plate nestled in the pewter cup of his fifth-form debating trophy. He had washed it, drenched it in Listerine then stood facing the bathroom mirror trying to ease it into his mouth, but it was an uncomfortable trespass, the plate refusing to fit over his teeth. He had walked back into the living room holding it gently between his lips like a cat with a bird, and standing over the box containing his childhood, he was overwhelmed by the physical intimacy that leapt across decades through plastic and metal. He experienced a sudden sensation of disembodiment, an almost vertiginous feeling of mortality. The real reason Clark had refused to wear braces was a phobia of any kind of interference with his body. He seemed to have been born with it and learnt to disguise it so successfully that not even his family perceived it. He hid pristine behind his façade of shabbiness. He drew about him the worn and comforting veil of flaws.

The pain was always there. Marie grew accustomed to it and, like a boxer, instead of stepping away stepped right into it. She visited Rhys twice more for the moth, leaving a fortnight's healing time, coasting down from euphoria to land in the pit of fear again. The fear became an energy. She no longer closed herself to it, letting it sing freely along her veins until it was a need that could only be sated by the affirmative puncture of inky needles.

On Rhys's couch, her mind wandered. Hugh had visited yesterday and deemed the house ready to be advertised. Mopoke was deteriorating again. Marie's bowels were hardening as well, from all the stress, she presumed. David had been silent since their date. She could have rung him. She wouldn't need to go through Susan; she had found him in the phone book. She had stood in the kitchen with it open on the table, flicking through the pages then following her finger down the column to *Rosenthal, D, Darling Pt.* She wondered why she was seeking out the number of someone who was so clearly uncomfortable with her. But then, she replied to herself, he had come around. He was fascinated, really. Is that what you want? she parried back. To fascinate someone, like a specimen? The memory of him masturbating next to her filled her with revulsion. But maybe it was she who had failed as sexual partner. Her sessions with Rhys were longer this year, the pain alleviated by Rhys's patter. Through all the disruption in her life now, tattoo plans acted as anchors. She took to the pursuit with decisive zeal as though it was all long overdue. The initial dream, the floating image, then the corporeal manifestation.

She didn't like the journey to the studio. She missed her old Deco Sydney with its trams and ramshackle buildings: this twenty-first-century city of tollways alienated her. Refusing to register for an E-tag, she found it hard to get around. She caught the ferry into town sometimes and for those ten minutes crossing the harbour, she was in paradise. The CBD was in its summer limbo of tourists and workers in equal numbers. At Circular Quay there was a fifteen-minute wait for the train followed by a fifteen-minute walk to the studio in its no-man's-land between Central and Redfern. On the day of the last moth session, Marie decided to get the bus instead and read the paper while waiting. No rain had fallen on the catchment area and the dam was lowering to thirty-five percent. One hundred thousand hectares of native woodland were being cleared each year in NSW alone. Protesters who had burnt the flag at a demonstration were called *unAustralian*. The Catholic and Anglican Archbishops of Sydney were meeting with politicians to emphasise their opposition to abortion and gay marriage. She read that Hugh Jackman had clashed with paparazzi on a recent visit to Sydney, and that CEO payouts had risen an average 13.5 percent as compared to 4.2 percent for full-time workers. The bus didn't arrive and Marie moved on to the world news. The US vice-president estimated the war may last for decades, the rising demand for biofuels was causing a world food shortage, and a US music lover claiming to suffer *iPod ear* was suing Apple Computer. By the time Marie arrived at the studio an hour later, her indigestion was raging.

As the iron buzzed across her shoulder blade, she clamped her teeth together and breathed. When the wave subsided, she began to speak. 'I've been cultivating a caterpillar on my irises. It's amazing. It's green and orange and has furry crests on its back. I'm not sure what it turns into.'

'Maybe it's a moth. You know what moths are called in French? *Papillons de nuit* — night butterflies. I've been thinking they're the great unsung mystical creature — all the mysticism of the butterfly, along with the *night*.'

'I read that butterflies for the Greeks represent the soul.'

'Yeah, for a lot of people. Some Native Americans. The ancient Slavs.'

'Mel said you were Slavic.'

'Did she?' Rhys said evasively. Her feet appeared in Marie's sightline. They were in thongs, a bluebird on the left, a scarab beetle on the right, black chipped nail polish on the first toe of each. A wad of paper towel landed in the bin near them. Rhys said: 'I've started a garden.'

'Out the back?'

'Yep. Before Christmas Travis and me found some plants on the street and put them in, then I planted some herbs. We got a hose to bail the washing machine and everything took off. I've just eaten my first chilli. It's so fulfilling. I love it.'

'I'll bring you some seedlings.'

'I want to grow banksia. I used to make up stories about the banksia men when I was a kid. How big is your garden?'

'Probably as big as this block. I've been blessed.'

'You've been there a long time so things you've planted'd be quite mature by now, eh?'

'Yes. The oldest is a scribbly gum I planted for Clark.'

'No wonder it's hard for you to leave.'

Rhys hadn't drawn the moth exactly as it was; it had been transformed. Marie tracked the design in her mind's eye, feeling the right wing fill in. Here, through Rhys's majestic hybrid, the red rose would ghost, like a plant disappearing, a site reclaimed by the bush. Marie often fantasised this demise for her house. Like the Burley Griffin house in Clifton Gardens, abandoned by its owner, dilapidated beyond repair, the bush creeping back over it. Marie thought of her old man banksia, carted off two days earlier, for a fee of four figures.

'In early Christian writings,' Rhys said, 'moths represented temptations of the flesh.'

'I'm not surprised. Christians are obsessed with sex. Is gardening a temptation of the flesh, do you think? The feel of earth in your hands ... The Garden of Eden ...'

'I don't know. Much as I'm in love with my new garden, I'd still prioritise a fuck.'

Marie was initially shocked by this candour. Then she walked straight through the new doorway. 'So would I. But my garden will be there the next day.'

'I mean a good one, with someone you love. That you get to cuddle after.'

'I had a date with someone recently.'

'Did you have a good time?'

'Well, things were fine until he saw my flame tattoo. He got a real fright.'

'Oh dear.'

'But he took a Viagra.'

'Ri-i-i-ght.'

'And I took advantage.'

Rhys smiled. 'Did you have some too, did you?'

'Oh no. He didn't offer me any. I mean I'm just assuming he took Viagra. For a man in his sixties to perform like that, you know.'

'Careful, you're moving. Maybe he was just really turned on. They act disapproving, but it turns them on and they can't admit it.'

'He hasn't rung me back though.'

'Bastard.'

'*Ouch.*'

'You wanted hard core, Marie, all this colour on the spine.' Rhys's tone turned droll. 'Maybe he just ran out of Viagra.'

'It's alright. I still have my compost.'

Rhys snorted. 'You wanna watch it if you ever have Viagra, Marie. Or have you?'

'Oh no,' Marie said primly. 'I've heard it's bad for the heart.'

'The *clit*, you mean.'

'Oh.'

'Maybe it's just me. Gawd, I dunno, the clitoris is not designed for a big blue pill. It's ex*cruciating*. It just goes on and on and *on*. I couldn't walk for about two days. Honestly.'

Marie laughed. 'How did we get onto Viagra?'

'The moth. Sex. Your date.'

'Does the tattoo work like a charm? Like a hunting talisman?

You know, tattooing the temptation on me will bring it into my life? Or is it more like a branding? The mark of the harlot.'

'*Harlot*? You crack me up. I don't know, Marie.'

'I hope it's a charm.'

'Oh, all my tattoos are charms, lady.'

'Maybe they're the same thing anyway.'

There were footsteps on the stairs, lighter and quicker than Marie had heard here before.

'My son's just home from child care.' Rhys put down the iron and went to the door. 'I'll take him upstairs. Won't be a sec.'

'Travis? Bring him in. I'd love to meet him.'

'Yeah? He's a good boy. Knows the drill around tattooing.'

Marie arched her back like a cat, enjoying the heat across her shoulder blades. She became aware of a presence behind her, heard a whisper, 'It's a butterfly!' She lifted her head to see a moon-faced boy standing close. He was wearing a t-shirt that said: *Snakey did it!*

'It's nearly finished, Trav,' Rhys said. 'It's called a Splendid Ghost Moth.'

Rhys introduced Marie to Travis. Travis huddled against her thighs.

'She's like that priest lady,' he said as Rhys ushered him out.

As she returned, the sound of a television came loud through the ceiling. She went back upstairs then the room above went quiet.

Through the final licks, the noise rose again.

'He's *so* naughty. He knows I'm working and can't keep coming up there.'

'Isn't he allowed to watch it?'

'He's rationed.'

'What about Rob?'

'Rob's got a client at five. He's a pushover anyway and it's not really his job.'

'You're very conscientious. The television was always on in our house. No doubt my children are all permanently damaged as a result.'

'I wasn't allowed to watch TV when I was a kid. Only on weekends.'

'Oh? You had a strict upbringing?'

'Catholic on my mother's side. But it was my father who was thingy about TV, and he wasn't religious.'

'Catholic!' said Marie gleefully. 'I was brought up a very strict Catholic.'

'I'm not surprised.'

'I'm well and truly lapsed,' Marie reassured her. 'My husband was atheist. Our children went to Anglican schools, much to the horror of my parents.'

'I don't believe in that lapsing stuff. You never stop being a Catholic, you know.'

'Oh yes, you do, if you don't practise, you're not worthy, you can't get the blessings without the effort. You can't take holy communion.'

'Listen to you. *You're not worthy.* I don't think you can ever get rid of it, to tell you the truth.'

Marie had an image of herself in her first-communion dress. The church in Avalon. Stained-glass windows. A sense of the ocean swirling three streets away, but she was trapped inside this stuffy church, sitting ramrod straight next to her mother, trying to concentrate on the droning priest, battling a sense of dread.

'That's a depressing thought,' she said.

'My Catholic half knows it's Catholic, believe me.'

'How?'

'Well, half of me is very moralistic. I'm half superstitious too, and Catholic moralism is tied to superstition I think. Half of me mistrusts pleasure. Half of me is mildly, um, half homophobic.'

That was quite a lot to digest. Lots of different facts, in different areas, like the little touch-ups that Rhys was doing on her back. Rhys delivered the final fact with an undertone of shame. Such a familiar feeling, Marie realised, along with fear.

After a while she asked, 'Do you see much of your parents?'

'Nup.'

'They're not in Sydney?'

'My father racked off about twenty years ago, haven't seen him since. My mother's still in our childhood home in Earlwood. That's where I grew up. John Howard's suburb. Although in his day it wasn't woggy.'

'Do you get on with your mother?'

'No,' Rhys said with finality. 'Where should I take these antennae to?'

She pulled out the mirror and reflected Marie's back into the full-length one on the wall. The wings fanned out like spinnakers, the translucent green of tropical water; the ridges of the moth's body mimicked her vertebrae. Marie turned her neck the other way, and Rhys tilted the mirror. From behind, she looked transcendent. With her fingertip, Rhys drew lines. 'Here? Or here?'

Marie lay back down, overcome. 'Into my hairline.'

After Rhys had finished, she said, 'It's the best one so far.'

'Ooh yeah.'

'Who's "that priest lady"?'

'There were two Anglican priests I tattooed. I think Travis was saying that because you're around the same age.'

'What did they get?'

'The white rose of Jesus or something. That design wasn't mine. The other one had a crucifix on each arm, high up. I loved those, I based them on designs that Christian pilgrims to the shrine of Loreto used to get hundreds of years ago. Interesting women. Very religious.'

'I admire those female priests so much. They're well ahead of us on that count.'

'See what I mean?' Rhys laughed. 'You're *such* a Catholic.'

She snapped off a length of Glad Wrap and taped it over the tattoo.

'What other older women do you tattoo?'

'A biker's wife. I don't know. I don't notice the age, I notice the designs.'

'The designs are all yours.'

'*Now* they are, they didn't use to be. God, Marie, you wouldn't believe all the people with their little Celtic thingies or they want Sanskrit or Chinese for *love* or *healing*? The place I used to work had heaps of walk-ins like that, most places do. They bring you these characters and you say, *Um, I don't think it means love* and they're like *Yeh it does, yeh it does!* So you tattoo all this stuff that probably means *fuck off, whitey* or *shoe shop* or whatever, thinking, It's your funeral, baby.' Rhys took Marie's blue shirt off its hook and held it open. 'Nice,' she said. 'Silk, is it?'

'It's very old. It's my favourite shirt.'

'I've done about five different Kanji for *healing*,' Rhys went on. 'No wonder the world's so sick.'

Marie put on her shirt. 'I've decided on a passionfruit vine next. Down my arms.'

'That'll be very visible.'

'Yes. I've decided I'm coming out.'

'You want to stay on my cancellation list, I presume? You've used up all your appointments.'

'Yes, always.'

At dusk Marie took the cones from the old man banksia and placed them on the Weber. She filled a bucket with water, mixed herself a lime bitters and soda, and stood by the barbecue, tongs in hand, blowing on the cones till little flames licked their edges. Slowly the follicles opened in the heat. Next she soaked the charred cones in the bucket of water and left them to dry, then she shook the seeds from the follicles, prising out the recalcitrant ones with a twig. Mopoke followed her as she worked, settling onto the flagging to watch her pot the seeds. 'The old man will give birth to lots of little babies,' she said to the cat as she rubbed the seeds between her fingers to remove their papery wings. 'Yes, Mopoke! He will!'

The soft, greasy charcoal from the banksia cones stayed around her cuticles for days.

In the first year of the war, Blanche had made her mark. Within a week of the Opera House sails being protest painted with *NO WAR*, she had an ad up for Dulux outdoor paving paint. It went to press and television, the latter a fifteen-second newsclip. She used an article in the *Herald* as well as Channel Nine's hyperbolic report about activist vandalism and the amount taxpayers would fork out to have the Opera House cleaned. Old-school simplicity married to new-school irony. *Next time use Dulux outdoor paving paint*, said the copy. *Impossible to remove.*

Cheeky. The advertisement had won awards all over the world. It was what really got Blanche noticed. Even her father had been on the phone raving. Terry had worried that Sydney Opera House would object, but instead they were glad for the free publicity. And Terry had worried that Dulux would find it too notorious, but like almost half of Sydney the company's marketing manager had been to the anti-war rally in Hyde Park, and nobody could object to an ad that appealed across the board. When approached by people raising money for the activists' court costs, Blanche had politely declined, saying she was firmly non-partisan in her views.

Forever now the curving white sails of the Sydney Opera House daubed with the words *NO WAR* in red would be associated with Dulux, and Blanche. Everybody in Huston Alwick was queuing to work with her when she was appointed a creative director. Blanche chose Lim, more for his sex appeal and exoticism than his copywriting talents. She chose Kate for similar reasons, and because she still had a photograph on her desk of the painted sails. Kate was black and spoke in a tough Manchester accent and wore Gaultier jackets over tight ripped jeans and cowboy boots, and Lim was half Vietnamese half Swedish with a broad Australian accent. All in all a formidably cool team.

Blanche sat up straight with her arms stretched either side in oblique curves so she resembled a bell. Three p.m., another lunch break at the desk eating chocolate and yoghurt, her back was killing her. She had one leg longer than the other and her sacrum rotated, her shoulders tilted from scoliosis, and her right breast bone stuck out more than her left. Nothing could be done about this, nor about the rib that continually popped out as a consequence. Blanche was condemned for life to the chiropractor, Nurofen and heat packs. She undid the top buttons of her shirt and glanced at her sternum. Crooked as ever. She stretched into her bell pose, looking out the window at her patch of harbour. She envied Terry's office for its view of the Opera House. Still, her view wasn't bad. It was like meditation: at this time of day if she sat still and watched the same spot for long enough, she would see the windows of the eastern suburbs gradually absorb the afternoon sun till they glowed so brightly she had to squint.

Blanche had left her door open and Lim moved so quietly that he was standing beside her desk before she even noticed him. 'Willy Wonka's here.'

Blanche redid her lipstick, gathered her papers and walked down the corridor with Lim. He was twenty-nine years old and six foot two, his high school full-back physique already softening. His thick black fringe hid lazy intelligent eyes. There was a flirtation in their rapport with a sexy undertone of threat. Lim was like a large sleek animal who swam alongside her as a buttress, equally capable, Blanche knew, of flipping and crushing her any time. This made her power over him that much more exciting. He was a strong ally in meetings: men loved his laconic heftiness, women his softness.

Kate was still at her desk, on facebook. 'Hiya.' She looked up vaguely.

'Meeting.'

'God, yeah, sorry.'

'Let's hope he likes it,' Lim said as they approached the door. 'This guy is so humourless. He honestly thinks his company's recipe comes from a Nobel Prize laboratory or something.'

'Lim. Narva's a good product. And he'll love it.'

William was at the window, discussing the cricket with Terry. He was a surprisingly dowdy man, considering his job, all checked shirt and mismatched blazer and tousled curls.

'William.' Blanche moved forward, hand extended. 'We're in *love* with your chocolate. We've completely demolished everything you sent us. I feel like I've discovered El Dorado,' she said, addressing this to Terry. 'Narva's been going since 1806 and I'd never heard of it!'

'It was confined to the East until recently.'

'I'd *love* to go to Slovenia. I think it sounds fascinating.'

William smiled. 'Narva's from Estonia.'

'Come and sit down, William,' said Terry.

'We're really excited about working with a chocolate company,' said Lim. 'I read that cocoa beans can't be cultivated on cleared land, so you need to conserve a particular type of rainforest ecosystem around the plants for them to thrive.'

'Really?' William knitted his brows. 'That's interesting.'

'Anybody for coffee?' said Kate. Blanche pushed the tray of petits fours towards William, and after he refused took an éclair.

'So, William.' She held eye contact. 'Chocolate. Gourmet chocolate like yours is essentially feminine. It's elegant, special, we savour it. It's associated with luxury.'

'Women crave it at that time of the month.' Kate nodded at Blanche.

Blanche gritted her teeth. Terry sat back, foot propped on knee, smile playing at the corners of his mouth. He was cultivating a hybrid of Beckham and Branson with his cropped beard.

William looked from one to the other. 'We don't want to alienate any portion of the market. We don't want people to think this is just another piece of fluffy confectionery. This is the highest-quality chocolate. It's better than most foods you buy in health-food stores. It's actually *good* for you.'

'Exactly,' said Blanche. 'And that's how we've framed it. Remember how attractive to *men* a feminine product can be, William.'

'I switched to James Boag because of those seamed stockings,' Lim chipped in. 'Truly. How are those ads? And they're *still* going.'

'We're using the concept of feminine in a broad contemporary sense.' Blanche spread some papers out on the table. It was a good excuse to push the petits fours, which were wiggling their little arses at her, out of reach. 'What Kate means is that chocolate — *quality* chocolate like Narva — is full of magnesium. Muscle relaxant, heart tonic, such a crucial mineral. Some scientific studies recommend a piece a day, as you would know, William. The reason we crave it is that we *need* it, *scientifically*.'

William watched her, nodding. 'That's right, that's right.'

'It's an aphrodisiac for the same reason,' said Lim.

'I honestly get a little rush when I eat it,' said Kate.

'Kate? We've gone for an urban feel,' said Blanche. 'To do with the demographic in the areas where most of the billboards are. Also because we think there's potential for the Asian market.'

Kate hit PowerPoint and her first image came up, a man and woman in sepia tones, the man feeding the woman a piece of Narva, and Blanche forgave her everything because it was so well designed. 'These are just roughs,' said Kate.

'It's timeless,' Blanche enthused. 'Everybody loves the '20s. Fun, excitement. Class.'

The next slide came up with the cocoa percentage, the company stamp and Blanche's copy. *The love drug.*

William looked over, tickled but unsure. 'I was really keen on trying a new angle here. And using the quality of our ingredients to our advantage. Chocolate always has such a *soft* image.'

Blanche pursed her lips. She crossed her legs and felt her rib pop out. 'William, science is *boring*. Until you show the effect it has on our actual bodies, the things around us. The things we touch and see and *feel*. Narva *is* a love drug, quite literally. But we don't need to go into the details. Nobody has the time to read them. People are sceptical. They're stressed from a long day at work. They have enough energy to be seduced by this beautiful couple then maybe to take in the amount of cocoa and how long you've been making the chocolate. They just want to relax. They want the comfort and luxury of Narva. They'll see a report somewhere else that tells them about the merits of pure cocoa. They'll make an automatic association.'

'But then anyone making chocolate with a high cocoa content can say the same thing. Anyone can make that claim.'

Blanche leant forward. 'But they're not. Only *you* are.'

William turned back to look at the image. Behind Blanche's shoulder blade, a bullet wound began to throb. She could have thrown her arms around William when he turned back and said, 'I like it.'

She ushered everyone out of the room, then discreetly helped herself to a profiterole.

'You,' said Lim, on their way back down the corridor, 'are having a Negroni on me after work.'

'I can't, Lim. Hugh and me promised each other we'd have dinner together. Great work by the way, Kate.'

Kate grinned. 'There's a new barmaid at the Shanghai who makes Negronis to die for.'

'I won't keep you from your husband. Just one drink. Because. You. Are. A genius.'

'Okay then. I have to run some errands so I'll drive up. Six o'clock.'

Lim had their drinks waiting when she arrived. 'Cheers, dears.'

'Where's Kate?'

'She said she'd come later. She's still working.'

'You're kidding. I didn't see her at her desk. She's always stuffing around.'

'I know. That's why she works late. I'm going to see Cirque du Soleil tonight.' He pronounced it in perfect French, oblivious to how sexy he sounded.

'You speak French fluently, don't you?' Blanche looked at him in awe.

'My grandmother was French.'

'Are they good? The Cirque?'

'They're amazing, yeah. Amazing make-up and costumes.'

'God, I can't believe I've never been to see them.' Blanche groaned. 'I never get out anymore, Lim. I'm turning into an old woman.'

Lim made a sad face and Blanche pouted back at him.

'They're on for the next fortnight. Treat yourself.' Lim moved forward so Blanche could smell his breath. 'Let's go do a line.'

She leant against the wall watching the back of Lim's head as he chopped up the coke on the toilet seat.

'I wish they hadn't renovated,' he said. 'The other toilets were so much better, they had those big shelves behind the cistern. *So* uncivilised, making us do it like this.'

'God. I've actually got cravings for Narva. Can you believe it?'

Lim straightened and gave her a straw. 'This'll cure that.'

Blanche snorted slowly, messing up the line, using each nostril.

'I'm really bad at snorting coke.' A little white cloud floated out of one nostril as she spoke.

Lim said nothing, hoovering his line in a nanosecond.

One by one, the teeth along Blanche's upper left jaw went numb.

'It's good stuff, that chocolate,' Lim said, pinching his nostrils.

'I'm excited about it, you know. I mean, we are *launching* it. I so hope it takes off. I want cinema! How about what you said about the rainforest ecosystems and all that, isn't that amazing?'

'Yeh, yeh, and I'm sure it's true.'

'I mean like the chocolate market world over has increased by something like five hundred percent in the last twenty years alone, and most products these days, if you said that, you'd be straightaway hit with a whole bunch of awful facts about commercial exploitation to make you feel guilty about the impact of increased crops on the environment or something, like what soy's doing to the Amazon. D'you know anything about that?'

'Yeh, yeh, yeh.' Lim was nodding. 'What? Oh yeah, they're clearing it.'

'But I mean it's so nice to know that for once it's actually *okay*, you know?'

'Yeah.'

'And how about coca?' Blanche's eyes gleamed deviously.

Lim frowned. 'I always get mixed up between them. Then there's guarana ...'

'But aren't they all related? Like how does cocaine grow? Isn't it a bean?'

Lim was standing very straight with his back to the wall. 'I don't know. I'm the last in the food chain in that one.'

Blanche felt so excited she wanted to gnash her teeth. 'Why hasn't the cocaine market ever taken off in Australia? It's so bloody expensive like there's a stranglehold on supply, I've never figured it out.'

Somebody came into the toilets. Lim rolled his eyes and whispered with stagy seduction, '*The love drug.*'

'I better go home and fuck my husband now,' Blanche said airily over her shoulder as she walked back into the bar and swooped onto their table just in time to save their Negronis from a zealous waiter. Lim tittered.

They drank and watched the bar fill slowly with suits.

'What are you doing this weekend?' Blanche asked, realising one second later that he had already told her.

'Apart from the circus, just having a quiet one. Maybe the beach. My girl's just bought a flat in Bronte.'

Something lanced into Blanche's chest. She rummaged through her handbag, thinking of the phrase *stabbed by jealousy*. She tried to retreat from her body, shaken by the vehemence of its feelings. 'I didn't know you had a girl,' she said, trying to be flippant.

'There's a lot you don't know about me, Blanche,' Lim replied with heavy innuendo.

'Really? Do tell.' Rummage, rummage.

'I can't. Then you'd know it.'

A bitter glob fell down the back of Blanche's throat and she sucked up the last of her drink. Her rib twanged angrily. Her car keys were in her hand even though she didn't want to leave. 'Sometimes I can't understand why Terry comes to every meeting when he hardly says anything.'

'He wants to watch over his minions.'

'Hal-looo.'

'I mean, that's *his* line of thinking.'

'He still doesn't trust me. Even though he promoted me for my signature risk-taking.'

'Fuck 'im. We'll give the old farts a run for their money.'

Blanche only had four blocks of the Pacific Highway to drive, but on a Friday evening it could take half an hour, longer than walking. She pulled out of the underground car park and drove up the hill and when the lights went green, like a little metal tooth her black BMW slid into the chain of cars heading north. Thirty-six degrees out there, ten less in here. She plugged in her iPod and scanned to Radiohead. The cocaine was ebbing now and her backache moving to the fore. She noticed how premenstrual she was, her legs needed waxing. She felt dirty.

Half an hour later, she was sliding the gear into Park, pushing the remote, and watching the garage door rise before her. She pulled back into Drive too soon, nearly skinning the hood of the car. Hugh was in the shower when she came into the house. She dropped her keys into the bowl on the mantlepiece and went into the kitchen. It was hot and stuffy, the windows shut all day against a promised storm that never came. Blanche opened the freezer and rested her forearms inside its gelid shock, then withdrew a carton of cookies'n'cream ice-cream. She took it into the living room, switched on the television and ate watching the news.

Hugh crossed the hall wrapped in a towel, then returned to the doorway in shorts and singlet, drying his hair. 'André's wife moved out this afternoon,' he said over the top of the television.

'Really?'

'Yup. The removalist van was packing the last things when I got home. Adios!' Hugh spoke with a note of triumph: both of them had sided with André because his wife had screamed louder.

'Fantastic. We might sleep tonight.'

Hugh draped his towel over the back of a chair and sat down. 'I saw this place today that might be perfect. I want to take you to have a look at it tomorrow morning. It's got a view.'

'You've got the day off?' Blanche said excitedly.

'No. Before my inspections.'

'I wanted to sleep in tomorrow and maybe go to a gallery, Hugh. You promised me you'd get a free Saturday. I was having drinks tonight and I came home for you.'

'I'm sorry, pooky. It's just crazy at the moment. I sold that Deco place in Kirribilli in one week, didn't even advertise it.'

'You really want to go ahead with this now? With the downturn and everything?'

'Downturns are good. They bring back the investors.'

'I don't think I can handle another mortgage right now, Hugh.'

'Why not? The more you have the easier it gets. And we'll get money from the Sirius sale in a few months.'

'Are you sticking to six million by the way? Isn't it more like six and a half?'

'Better to be conservative, then when you get more you're over the moon.'

'Will you take the usual commission?'

'I think it'd be wrong if I didn't do things by the book.'

'The book might say we should give mates rates.'

'We?' Hugh arched an eyebrow.

'Get out of town, Hugh.'

Hugh kissed her on the forehead then got a bottle of white wine from the fridge. 'Ultimo's a safe bet.'

Blanche stared at the television, spooning ice-cream into her mouth direct from the carton. A line of tanks rolled towards a crowd, Molotov cocktails shooting through the night.

'Blanche, can you at least look at me?'

'Hughie, I'm really tired, okay? I'm pre-menstrual and it's been a big week.'

Hugh poured her a glass of wine and muted the television. 'What are you doing, pooky? It's half empty. Have you eaten all that? I thought you were trying to lose weight.'

Blanche sighed and stretched along the couch, lifting her legs onto Hugh's lap. Hugh looked worn and jowly. There were camels on his boxers, all heading in the same direction — nowhere — around and around his hips. He looked so unsexy that she felt sad. 'You can talk with your middle-aged spread.' She poked her toes into his armpit.

He jammed it over her foot. It was hot and moist and comforting, like a mouth. 'I know. We both have to go to the gym.'

Miffed, Blanche turned up the television. A kookaburra laughed in the bedroom and when Hugh walked out to answer it, Blanche began to eat the ice-cream again. Why did they play such shithouse ads in prime time? What an embarrassment. No wonder Australia was the laughing-stock of the world. Her mind became keen and predatory, slicing through each twenty-second slot with the clinical precision of a surgeon removing tumours.

'Hey, Stav,' Hugh spoke into his phone, watching her from the doorway. 'Yeh, yeh I'm working on her.' Blanche raised her eyebrows over the spoon moving towards her mouth. The ice-cream felt fantastic slipping down her throat. The quicker she ate it, the deeper it retained its chill, cooling her from the inside. She scraped the bottom of the carton, thinking how wonderful it would be to get fat and really go to seed. Attached to Hugh's arm, she would wrap red lamé around her corpulence, tie a ribbon around her fat waist and go as a giant Christmas bauble to the next realty Christmas party.

Hugh shut his phone and came over, slinging her legs back up.

'Ow, ow,' she protested.

'Did you have a bad day?' He massaged her calves.

'No, my back's out. When are you going to Mum's?'

'A week or so. When the ads are ready. Did you finish the copy?'

'Yeah, I emailed it straight back to you.'

'I was out of the office all arvo. Stav wants to come tomorrow morning too. He's got the keys to the place next door. We can look at them both then have brunch at the Fish Markets.'

'Do we have to have brunch with Stav? He's so *boring*.'

'Dimitri's going to retire soon, and Stav will take over the agency.'

They stared at a mob of shoppers charging through the doors for the Australia Day sales as though fleeing a tsunami. Security guards waved their arms with the alert ineptitude of schoolboys playing cops'n'robbers. Blanche hadn't told Hugh about her mother's tattoos; she hadn't known how. She had thought it would all blow over, but if what Clark had said was true, they were only spreading. The ice-cream was glued to the pit of her stomach, a warm, sticky pool. She gulped down wine to dissolve it.

'Shall we order Thai?' Hugh said. 'Or the new wood-fired pizza?'

'I need to tell you something. I had a weird conversation with Clark when we got back.'

'Oh yeah?'

'About Mum.'

'Is she okay?'

'She's started getting tattoos.'

'Hey?'

'She's had all these tattoos done, I don't know why.' Blanche ran her hands through her hair then rested them across her face and looked shyly through the paling of fingers at Hugh. 'Clark sounded pretty upset.'

'I didn't see anything when I was there last week.' Hugh frowned. 'I thought she looked really good.'

'Well, they're there, even if you can't see them.'

'Why didn't you tell me?'

'I don't know. I thought it was stupid.'

'Tattoos? Your mother?' Hugh started to laugh. 'Are you serious?'

'It's true. And she's getting more.'

'She's such a fruitcake, your mum.'

'Really?' Blanche's eyes swung onto Hugh's face, beaming challenge and enquiry.

'Well, she's supposed to be selling her house, not getting tattoos! And doesn't she want to be a psychologist now or something?'

Blanche drank more wine. Hugh kept laughing, shaking his head. 'It's not funny,' she said.

'Well, I think it is. What else is it? Tattoos!'

'Stop laughing, Hugh!' Blanche lifted her legs off his lap. 'It's not fucken funny. Okay?'

'I'm finish, Mrs King,' Fatima called from the hall.

'Come into the kitchen,' Marie called back, from where she was reading an old *National Geographic* while she waited for Hugh to arrive.

Fatima came in, rolling down her shirtsleeves and buttoning the cuffs.

'Would you like a cup of tea?'

'No, thank you, Mrs King.'

'Oh, go on. Sit down and have a cup of tea with me.' Marie got out a cup and set it on the table. 'You've been working nonstop for hours. Have a break.'

Fatima perched on a chair. 'Thank you.'

'I've been reading about tattoos in your country,' Marie said brightly, pouring tea.

'What?'

'Tattoos. Drawings on the skin with ink.'

Fatima looked at her in puzzlement.

'How they're mostly done by the women. And to ward off sickness. Here.' She touched the corners of her eyes. 'And here.' She touched her forehead. 'Look.' Marie showed Fatima the *National Geographic*.

'Ah.' Fatima glanced at it politely. 'Duck.'

'Duck?'

'*Daqq.*' Fatima pointed to the word in the headline. 'It's old, not many anymore.'

'That's sad. Is that because of Sharia law?'

Fatima was inscrutable. 'I'm from city. We don't see much in city. Only the people do *daqq* who are prim ...'

'Primitive?'

'Yes.' She wrinkled her nose. 'I don't like.'

'Yoo-hoo!' Hugh's footsteps came down the path.

Fatima cleared her throat. 'Mrs King, your cheque is no good.'

'Pardon?'

Hugh walked in.

'My bank say your cheque is no good.'

'Hi, Fatima!'

A blush scalded Marie's face. 'I must have used my old chequebook. How stupid of me. I'm so sorry, Fatima.'

Fatima ignored her and smiled at Hugh. Superior little cow, thought Marie. She was only trying to be friendly. Days like this she wished she hadn't given up drinking.

'Did the cheque bounce?' said Hugh.

'Don't worry.' Marie reached for her handbag. There was five hundred dollars in her wallet, and the next session with Rhys had to be paid for. Tattoos had the highest priority, up there with food. 'How much do I owe you?' she said, trying to hide the cash.

'Two hundred thirty. The bank charge me ten dollars for cheque.'

Hugh had his chequebook out and was writing in it already. Marie reminded herself he would soon be making the equivalent of some people's annual wage from the sale of her house. As Hugh tore the cheque out and handed it to Fatima, she said, 'You'll keep note of everything, won't you, Hugh.'

'Not a problem.'

'I go.' Fatima pocketed the cheque. 'Bye-bye, Mrs King.'

Hugh was holding a boutique arrangement of natives, lilies and orchids. The sort they sold up at the Junction for around seventy dollars. He handed it to Marie, then stood back and examined her. 'How *are* you?'

'I'm good. Aren't you kind.'

'Ready for the big sale?'

'Yes.'

'Because it is a big one.' Hugh looked at her with emotion. 'You're being very brave.'

He opened his briefcase and took out a sheaf of laminates and papers in plastic folders. 'This is going onto our website. This is the listing. And this is the main one.' He shuffled through the advertisements, isolating the glossiest. 'We're going to run this in "House of the Week" in *Domain*.'

'Right.'

'It's a real coup. It's a jungle out there, Marie. I mean, "House of the Week" is as good as it gets.'

'It looks great. Did Blanche write the copy?'

'Joint effort.'

Exceptional Family Home Offers the Ultimate Lifestyle

- *Designed with the style-conscious family in mind*
- *Brilliant multi-use living and entertaining areas maximise the enjoyment of this unique harbour-side position and harbour views*
- *Vast open-plan living and dining area flows with full-width east-facing deck*
- *Rumpus room with potential to create games room and cellar, opening through French doors onto terraced gardens. Room for a swimming pool*
- *Gourmet kitchen interacts with patio; sep. butler's pantry*

- *Grand master ensuite with panoramic views of exclusive Sirius Cove*
- *Walking distance to the ferry, and waterfront reserve*

It was strange seeing her house described as a package for someone she hadn't met. She was humiliated by Hugh writing out that cheque even if she could persuade herself that in a roundabout way it was still her money. She shuffled through the advertisements, aware of Hugh looking at her with the same piercing interrogation as when he had first walked in.

'You've done well, Hugh. I like how you've presented it.'

'Such a lovely house. Such lovely light. And so *cool*.' Hugh took off his jacket. His underarms were wet. 'Stinking out there!'

'It's cold here in winter, actually. South-east facing can be a problem.'

'But it's summer we're selling it in, isn't it?' Hugh wandered around, looking at things. 'I'm sad actually. I want to do the right thing by it … Are you sure you don't want to paint the kitchen? Buyers are conservative, you know.'

'They can paint it. They'll paint it anyway.'

'Listen. We're thinking of changing tack. We think that the way to get the best possible figure is throw all the buyers together into an auction situation. It's not worth anyone's while to make a mistake so we're advising a more conservative approach.'

That word again. Marie shifted around the pains in her stomach that had begun to move like snakes to their music. 'I read that clearance rates are around only forty percent at the moment.'

'Not here. The only places in Australia that aren't feeling the pinch from interest rate rises are the lower north shore and eastern suburbs of Sydney. It's depressing, really.'

'Why don't we set a figure, and see if we can get it? I want to know who's coming here after me, I want to be sure they'll look after it. And if we can't find anyone within a month then we'll go to auction.'

Hugh didn't look totally convinced, but he ceded.

'They'll kill the cabbage tree palm, won't they.'

'God, no. They're not allowed. A client of mine in the eastern suburbs bought a row of houses in Bondi. Backpacker hostels, absolute flea pits. He built apartments and a mature Norfolk Island pine was interfering with his plans and he had to go through an unbelievable amount of money and red tape to move it. It ended up costing him around fifty thousand dollars. And your buyers won't be making money from apartments on this site to compensate.'

'You mean it's a liability?'

'There are ways around it. Look, I know how hard this is for you, Marie. I have to tell you all of this so you know exactly where you stand.'

Marie could see what must have been a patch of piss gleaming on the floor of the living room. She hadn't seen Mopoke all day. She and Hugh must have stepped right over it. She fetched a rag and bucket then went to clean it.

Hugh followed and stood over her talking. 'You'll still be alright. You'll still have easily enough to buy yourself a bewt little place.'

'I know.'

Hugh fell silent. Marie became aware of his mass behind her and realised he could see the tattoo on the back of her neck. When she stood, he turned away, embarrassed. She threw the pissy rag into the bin.

'Look, ah, I've got to go. I'm picking up Blanche. Call or email if there are any changes you'd like made to the ads. Anything you're not comfortable with, any questions.' He regarded her with the same piercing interrogation as when he had first walked in. 'Anything at all, Marie. Okay?'

'Thank you, Hugh.' Out on the patio, she gave him a pot of germinating banksia.

When he had gone, she went in search of Mopoke and found her asleep under the bed. She hauled her out and cleaned her rheumy eyes. She walked around holding her, cooing, 'Where have you been pussy cat? Were you hiding from the real-estate agent? It was only Hugh. You know Hugh.'

Mopoke felt so light. Her teeth could no longer handle biscuits: her breath had a trace of rot. Beneath the thick fur, her muscles were giving way to bone. She began to purr against Marie's chin. 'Come and get some fresh air, Moey.' She carried her down to the bottom fence and deposited her on the ground. Mopoke stood there with her legs splayed. Marie wondered if she had dermatitis now, the goo from her eyes seemed to be increasing. 'Come on, puss,' she pronounced it *pus*, walking ahead and calling in her gooey cat voice, 'Pus-pus, here, pus! You can make it!'

Mopoke didn't move.

Marie picked her up and carried her back. She found it hard to look up at the house these days. It seemed to be reproaching her. And the garden, trees and birds, the very air in the rooms. There was something colossal in the mood surrounding her; she felt guilty for abandoning her custodianship. There was a breeze coming off the harbour and Rupert's flag was flying straight and proud. 'Well,' she muttered as she entered the house. 'I'm leaving.' She threw a shirt over her shoulders then went up to the Junction for groceries.

It wasn't just the Hendersons, the metastasis of flags was everywhere even though Australia Day was almost two weeks ago. There was a woman outside the pharmacy in an Australian flag shirt and cap with an Australian flag backpack. There were Australian flag scarves on mannequins in clothes shops. The Lebanese corner shop had planted a large one outside the door. Cars had miniature flags flying from their windows like limousines. It made the suburb looked like Pennsylvania on Fourth of July, decked out in its red, white and blue. And all the cars were shiny, all the houses big, and all the shops were crammed with luxury goods for the well-fed blondes of Mosman.

Clark was late to the seminar, the only seat free in the front row next to a woman with chestnut hair. When she turned and smiled at him, he glimpsed a jutting cheekbone and a fine web of laugh lines. The lecturer droned on and Clark found himself wanting to move closer to the warmth of this woman on a hot afternoon on the third floor of the university. 'What did he say?' He inclined his head to her. The woman shrugged, turning a pen in her long fingers, looking straight ahead. Clark watched the fingers, fascinated as they released the pen then stretched themselves in the crook of the woman's arm. Never a good idea sitting in the front row: when his eyes moved back to the rostrum, he found the lecturer staring straight at him. He looked at the floor and tried to concentrate. He couldn't understand a single word. Soon, he was looking at the woman's hands again. Suddenly her ring finger clicked backwards, startling him, her face impervious as the top joint of her finger snapped like a tiny mechanical toy. She was double-jointed, in the same place as him! It seemed one of the most momentous discoveries of his life. Eyes on the bore addressing the room, Clark stretched then snapped his own finger back. She snapped hers. He snapped his again.

Then she was walking to the front of the room, her height unravelling like a beautiful secret. My god, she wasn't a student, she was a member of staff. Clark squirmed. He realised he was in the wrong seminar. She was talking about law. He stayed, mesmerised.

He approached her afterwards to apologise, and she laughed. They stood there awkwardly as the room emptied around them. 'Anyway,' Clark said, 'you don't have to worry about me misbehaving. I won't be in any of your seminars.'

She was tall and broad across the shoulders and wore no make-up. Her bone structure was almost Aztec — strong lips and cheekbones, fine prominent nose. She shifted her bag up her arm and looked at Clark shrewdly with eyes that could have been green or brown. 'I'm sure I could stop you misbehaving if I had to. What are you doing?'

'A PhD. Cultural Studies. I can't believe you've got a double-jointed finger!'

'It's a good party trick, isn't it.'

'We should form a circus act and tour the country.'

They walked down the corridor to the lifts, not speaking. Clark was aware of her keeping pace with him; those shoulders seemed to carry her entire body in its passage of tensile, swinging grace. As they drew up to the lifts, he finally allowed himself to look at her and found she was smiling. He wanted to tell her that he was seeing his daughter this weekend for the first time in six weeks and he was jumping out of his skin with joy. He wanted to tell her everything. 'What are you doing now? Want to go for a drink?'

'I can't, sorry.'

'I'm Clark, by the way.'

'I'm Sylvia.'

He googled her when he got home. Typing in *Sylvia* and *Law* and the university, he found she was an associate professor, had published several articles on law reform, and that her surname was Martinez. Ah, Spanish. In an instant she was starring in a blockbuster movie as an Aztec princess — no, she wasn't enough of a bimbo. A shaman then. He did an image google and found a photograph of her at a book launch, in a group of five academics, and another thumbnail that when enlarged became too pixellated to see her properly. She looked ordinary in these photos, but now he had her surname as well he googled *Sylvia Martinez* and found four entries on MySpace and seven on facebook. Sylvia Martinez, twenty-three, California. Sylvia Martinez, thirty-six, physiotherapist, Wyoming. A teenage Goth in Brisbane. None was her. They didn't even look like her. But as the hours rolled on and Clark wandered further into the Westfield of the web, he began to wonder what, in fact, she *did* look like. He only had one encounter to remember and he had rubbed it raw. Was her skin pale or tanned? How big were her eyes? And what were her breasts like? He waded through forty-six entries on Sylvia Martinez, finding an occasional bureaucratic detail that vanished on contact with his memory, like snow. All of this Clark did on the living room couch in front of a documentary about the war in Sudan, his takeaway cooling beside him. There were so many Sylvia Martinezes in the world that his epiphany began to drown beneath the banality of all those lives: a little billet-doux buried in junk mail.

Feeling like he had eaten too much greasy food, Clark took his laptop back into his study and plugged it in. It sounded like a plane trying to take off. It would be just his luck for his computer to die on him now. He shut it down and went back into the living room and ate his congealed pad thai. An hour later he realised the television program had changed. He switched it off and went into his study to try to do some work. He opened a book and stared at the paintings by convict artists. These had always been his favourite works from the early colonial period. Now, looking at the naïve portrayal of blacks around campfires, the stiff English redcoats, he wondered why. He wondered if it was a part of him that craved mollification that loved these bright colours and childish lines. How naïve could you claim to be, after years of incarceration and journeying across the world? And he wished he hadn't restricted himself to the north shore: he wanted to talk about the Aboriginal carvings behind Ben Buckler of a man being attacked by a shark, surely the ur-image. He realised he was saying all of this out loud, to Sylvia. He went to bed and lay awake thinking of her, the ocean humming in the distance, or was it the wind in the she-oaks outside his window, an endless breathing eventually lulling him to sleep.

On Saturday morning, with Nell here, he was in the kitchen early making breakfast, thinking about Sylvia Martinez. When he went into his study with a glass of juice, he found Nell still in bed, the neighbour's white cat crouched on her chest. Nell's eyes were closed and she was running her hands down Kimba's flanks, smiling. He was purring sonorously, his claws working the covers near Nell's neck. Clark knelt next to the little fold-out bed and the cat jumped off. Nell whined and Clark placated her. 'Have some orange juice, Nellie.'

The cat returned when they sat down to breakfast and Clark let Nell take it on her lap. It sat in that same Sphinx pose, bum poking towards him. He peeled Nell's egg and mashed it on the toast. Nell watched him, kicking her chair softly, stroking the white cat. Clark placed her breakfast before her. 'Look how much your hair's grown.'

'Yep. I'm gonna grow it long.'

'How long?'

'Down to my knees. Down to my *feet*.'

'How was America?'

'Good.'

'What was your favourite thing?'

'We ate hotdogs.' Nell chewed with a dreamy look. She ferried a little piece of toast and egg down to the cat's mouth.

'Don't feed him, darling.'

'He's hungry.'

'His owner will feed him.'

Nell pursed her lips and tilted from side to side, then lowered her body over the cat and made purring noises.

'Was it cold? In America?'

'Yep. Nope.'

He reached over and tucked her hair behind her ear. It was so thick and lustrous. Her mouth was a crystallised strawberry, her skin a peach. She looked so gorgeous he wanted to pick her up and squeeze every atom of air out of her body, and suck her chubby little arms. He almost had to grit his teeth against this ravenous love but, when Nell got up and went to the toilet, he saw how much more weight she had put on and repugnance shivered through him, followed by guilt. He wanted to love her unconditionally: to be the opposite to his cold, critical father. Nell toddled back in and climbed onto her chair.

'You know Auntie Blanche was in America too?'

'Yeah, but they went skiing, but we went to California where it was hot and we stayed with Chris's friends at the beach and then we went to the desert and and and I rode a donkey!'

'Wow, a donkey! Did you swim?'

'Yep.'

'Want to go for a swim today?'

'Yep.'

'We can snorkel. Bondi's completely flat and we can look at the fishies and seahorses next to the rocks. Did Mum pack your new snorkel?'

Nell shrugged. Clark went into his study and looked through her bags but found only a change of clothes. He pulled a pair of swimmers off her shelf, gathered up towels, sunblock, hats, water. Nell was watching him from the door. 'Daddy, can we take Kimba?'

'No.'

'Why?'

'Because his owner won't like it.'

'But he's hot. He wants to go to the beach.'

'Nellie, cats hate beaches.'

'I saw a lady in America with a cat on the beach. We can put him in a bag.'

Clark walked back into the living room and Kimba ran out the front door. 'See? He heard "beach" and he ran away!'

'Nooo. He ran away from you,' Nell said with quiet conviction.

'Are you going to put on Gran's Christmas present?'

'No.'

'Come on, darling, it looks great on you. It's a ladybird! They bring you luck.'

'*No.*'

'Okay, okay.' Clark squeezed sunblock onto his fingers and Nell tilted her face, her blue eyes looking into his as he lathered. Outside, he took her hand. Again, he had the urge to squeeze her, to literally take her flesh into his mouth and consume her. She trotted by his side along the street. The she-oaks gave way to paperbarks.

'Have you got my snorkel, Dad?'

'No, Mum forgot to pack it. We can swim and you can use mine.'

There was a pause, then Nell said firmly, 'No.'

'Why not?'

'I don't want to. I only want to use *mine.*'

Clark didn't know what to say to this. They walked along in silence.

'I don't want to go to the beach, Daddy.'

They stopped and waited to cross the road. When the cars had gone, Clark stepped off the kerb but Nell wouldn't move. She yanked back her hand and stood there glaring at him.

'Come on, Nellie. You said you wanted a swim.'

'I don't wanna use your snorkel!'

'Why not? It's a great snorkel and it'll fit you.' Clark knew it wouldn't but figured he could bluff something else by the time they got down there.

'*No.*' Nell began to cry.

A car drove past tooting and Clark stepped back onto the kerb.

The snorkel problem alerted him to the fact that Nell might no longer fit the swimmers he had brought down for her today, which were almost a year old. He was dreading another scene. A car stopped at the *Give Way* sign next to them and the woman in the passenger seat stared out her window. Clark felt ashamed of the fat, blubbering child by his side. He wanted to slap her. Then came the guilty aftertaste.

'I don't want to.' Nell stamped her foot.

'Nellie, you're *such* a good swimmer. You're like a fish!'

'I don't care. I wanna wear my new snorkel!'

Around the corner, the cicadas grew louder. They marched up Clark's ear canals and swelled inside his skull. He felt utterly defeated. The southern sky showed a pall of purple-brown moving up to Sydney from bushfires in the National Park. 'Okay, darling, we'll buy you another snorkel, okay?'

Nell considered this a moment. 'Can I have a ice-cream too?'

'Yes. After we swim, we'll get an ice-cream.'

'And chips, I want chips.'

'We'll see.'

From the distance came the high white noise of humans and motor vehicles stretched by the ocean. Clark crouched to pick Nell up. He lifted her in front of him, feeling strength flow down his arms and across his chest. He pressed his face against her belly and growled, and she laughed, then he put her onto his shoulders. He enjoyed the weight, his morning swim muscles bracing it. And everything he did, everything he said, all of Nell's behaviour as well, was for the imaginary audience of Sylvia. He felt a sensation rise at the back of his nose and realised his whole body had been carrying tension since Kimba's arrival that morning. The sneeze rushed out of him with gale force as they crossed the road. Nell laughed, placing her hands on his cheeks. Then a section of ocean appeared, and they reached Campbell Parade and the beach stretched before them, a vivid kilometre of pale yellow sand teeming with people. Clark sneezed and sneezed, his arms either side of his head balancing his daughter on his shoulders.

Marie thought her ideal house would have three rooms, a small garden and a water tank. Bedroom, spare room/office and a room for Nell. The garden would be completely drought-proof. The swamp gum, still not planted, would be the first into the ground. In the office, she would study for her psychology degree. It was like paradise. And what about solar panels, wouldn't that be great? But whereabouts would this house be? A three-bedroom house could cost three million dollars in Mosman or a million in Dulwich Hill. In Surry Hills it varied between. Looking at the ads for houses in *Domain*, she felt a combination of fear and excitement but quickly grew bored. In spite of her need, the thought of looking seriously at properties nauseated her. She wished she could close her eyes and wake up on the other side of the whole process, the conversion to her new life complete.

She escaped into town with a gardening book and some *National Geographic* issues to give to Rhys, as well as a pot of banksia seeds.

Mel was working in the studio that day. 'Hallo,' she called as Marie walked in.

'Hallo,' Marie replied.

The paintings of tattooed ladies in the front room had gone. In their place hung embroideries of Chinese dragons. It was only two weeks since her last visit, but Marie noticed that Rhys's hair had grown, spilling below her collar at the back. She had a new tattoo inside her left forearm, a small ouroboros that she got for Travis's birthday.

'Such a gorgeous boy. He looks so much like Rob.'

'You think?' Rhys laughed. 'Rob says that too. Wishful thinking. The moth heal well?'

Marie unbuttoned her shirt and let it fall from her shoulders. She could hear the rumble of Rob's voice in the room next door, a female counterpoint, then a buzzing iron.

'Lov-erly,' Rhys drawled at her back.

'I brought you some presents. You should see some shoots from this in the next week or so. Keep the soil moist.'

'Oh, thank you!' Rhys's face broke into a surprised grin, but there was something else in her expression that retreated and hid, something sad. She placed the pot on the windowsill then sat on her stool, looking at Marie. 'I haven't done a design for the vines, just some flowers. I could do them freehand, but I also wanted to talk to you more about them. Have you had lunch?'

'No.'

'I need to eat.' Rhys took a shirt off the back of the door. 'Let's go and discuss the tattoo over lunch. There's a good Thai down the road.'

Marie knew the place by sight. She could orient herself in the area now. She knew the jacaranda branch that she saw from Rhys's couch grew from a tree across the alley where she sometimes got a fluke free park. Further down was the electrical wholesaler, graffiti of little men running beneath umbrellas down its brick wall. She bought pastries sometimes from the sourdough bakery, and water from the corner shop, and often parked further up in front of the housing commissions. She knew the difference between the Sunday calm and midweek rumble of Crown Street a block away. The jacaranda was completely green now, not lilac as when she had first visited.

'What happened to your tattooed ladies?' she asked Rhys as they walked out onto the street.

'Hmm, that's a bit of a sore point. The artist took them back.'

'I loved those tattooed ladies. Why?'

Beneath the beating sun they put on hats and sunglasses. Rhys had a surprisingly heavy tread. She walked in strides, skirt clinging to her thighs, and talked looking straight ahead, making it difficult to read the expression on her face. 'I had an affair with the artist and the paintings were here on a sort of long-term loan so when things didn't work out they had to go.'

'Oh.'

'Anyway, Rob got to hang his Chinese silks. He gave me a good dressing-down of course.'

Marie felt bad for Rob. 'Well,' she said generously, 'you've obviously got a very strong relationship.'

'We're good mates.'

'I was never really mates with my husband. We were lovers —

for me teenage sweethearts. Then partners running a family, then we were enemies. We never talked about the infidelity. That's probably part of the reason it kept happening.'

'I like that word *lovers*. It's real. About the heart, and the body. Funny how we say *partner* these days, as though *girlfriend* is too frivolous and *lover* too emotional. Or carnal. *Partner* has only been around a decade or so. It's kinda clinical, like even love has been economically rationalised.'

'But it's perfect for you and Rob, isn't it? Working together. Living together.'

'But we're not *lovers*.' Rhys laughed, horrified. They were entering a restaurant called Thai Me Up. Rhys sat at a window table. 'We're *business* partners. Rob's like my brother. Always trying to set me up with someone. Natasha was his idea. Natasha's the artist.'

'Oh.' Marie smiled politely and looked down at her menu. She felt somehow cheated. It had never occurred to her that it was a lesbian who had been injecting ink into almost every spare inch of her body these past three months. It was exciting in a retrospective way, like a feat of bravery accomplished because you had no choice but to go ahead and survive. It was also mortifying. She couldn't look Rhys in the eye. She raked through all their past encounters for signs she had missed. She was overwhelmed by all she would have to rearrange. She worried she had become too intimate. She felt briefly angry, remembering Rhys laugh at her remark that Travis looked like Rob. And to think she had confided in her about David. Oh yes, she had been made a complete fool of.

But there was still the question of paternity — and there were such things as bisexuals — maybe she wasn't so stupid after all. She glanced at Rhys, who was sitting with her usual straight-backed posture, the menu lifted between her hands. Her skin in places was blotchy from the heat.

'Forgot my bloody glasses,' she muttered, as though aware of Marie's eyes on her. Her shirtsleeves were falling away and her hands had become objects of discussion at the adjacent table.

Marie felt a surge of defensive solidarity: she wanted to tell the whispering businessmen to mind their own business. Yes, she *liked*

Rhys. A *lot*. She seemed so well adjusted. She was kind and sensible. Still, this feeling of revulsion at the thought of lesbians. Angry, ugly, overweight women, dressed like construction workers. Man haters. There they sat in judgement on her, anyone really. Leon didn't have any lesbian friends, let alone Clark or Blanche or, of course, Susan. In fact, when Marie thought about it, she had never met a lesbian in her life, apart from Blanche's surly, thickset PE teacher about whom the rumours had been rife. She wondered about Travis. She wondered about turkey-basters and IVF. What did they do? *Syringe* it in? It seemed a repulsive, if necessary, procedure. Like putting ointment onto a sore. Rhys signalled to the waitress who came over with a notepad, greeting Rhys in melodic Thai.

'I'll have the pumpkin snow peas, please. With beef. Marie?'

'Paw-paw salad, thank you.'

The waitress, around fifty, was petite, muscular and heavily made up. She wore a tight t-shirt with the logo *It Ain't Botox, Baby*. 'You wan' drinks?'

'No, thanks.'

'So you're a lesbian!' Marie said when the waitress had gone, feeling the word clunk onto the table. 'I don't have any lesbian friends.'

Rhys smiled, a little shy. 'Gawd, Marie, I don't know what I am. I think some of the capital L lesbians would have me burnt at the stake.'

Marie thought about this for a moment. If the pyre were in Mosman, she might be on the stake adjacent.

Rhys added cryptically, 'Sorry, that was my Catholic half speaking.'

Marie laughed, but the revulsion remained and she began to hate herself just as much. She didn't want to be in the same camp as people like her ex-husband or the Mosman pyre-builders. She channelled this self-hatred into a glare at the businessmen staring at Rhys. She took solace in the fact that Rhys liked her. After all, she reasoned, if she were a crass, ignorant bigot, Rhys wouldn't have anything to do with her. 'I think it's great all the ways women can have children these days,' she said. 'You have a lot more control.

IVF, for instance, has come a long way.'

'I guess so, but I'm hopeless at control. That's why I fell pregnant with Travis. One silly night with a friend.'

Their meals arrived and they began to eat.

'... So you're bisexual?'

'No. I prefer women. I'm queer.'

Marie still didn't understand. Paradoxically, she understood that Rhys also had no definites, but that was the point. She felt marooned, as though she had turned the page of a book only to find a section missing. She forced the food down, her stomach clenched with embarrassment. 'I'm sorry.'

'What for?'

'All my prying. It's none of my business who you sleep with,' she said vehemently.

'It's okay.'

A woman carrying a huge backpack passed the window. If Marie craned her neck, she could see her car in the distance, parked behind a red Jeep. Across the road, workmen in helmets were waist deep in a manhole. The lawns of the park in front of the housing commissions were completely brown, the colour of earth. An old Aboriginal man sat on a bench, taking white bread from a plastic bag, tearing it up and scattering it to the pigeons.

'So, the vines. What did you have in mind?'

'Down my arms.'

'Like to your wrists?'

'Yes.'

'How big?'

'Quite fine, but with passionflowers here and there.'

'That's quite a visible tattoo, Marie.'

'Yes, I know.'

Rhys leant over her plate, chewing thoughtfully.

'I love those gauntlet tattoos,' Marie said to her.

'Thank you.'

'Who did them?'

'My first teacher. After my apprenticeship had ended.'

'I covet them actually.'

Rhys put her fork down. 'I'm not gonna tattoo your hands, Marie. I think tattooing hands is illegal, though that could be urban myth.'

'How can it be illegal?'

'Some English law dating back to when people were considered the property of the Crown. On their death their head and hands might be delivered to the king, so they couldn't damage the goods.'

'So how did you get yours done?'

'Oh, the king'll have my head and hands chucked into a ditch, *big* time,' Rhys said obliquely. 'Seriously though, I cop a bit for these. I wouldn't wish it on you.'

'Why did you get them?'

'Because while the English king is chucking me into a ditch, a Dayak goddess will be admitting me to heaven.'

'I didn't know the Dayaks had a heaven.'

'Kind of. They had to encounter all sorts of obstacles and cross the River of Death to reach it. Only the souls of the tattooed could cross because tattoos provided light for them in the afterlife. The men would have their headhunting tattoos, and the women their gauntlets which described their talents like weaving or whatever.'

'You see why I want them? I'll need somewhere to go when St Peter refuses me.'

'Oh, you don't need gauntlets.' Rhys laughed. 'The goddess'll love you as you are. You'll be fucken *blazing*. Anyway, bugger the law, that's not what stops me. It's just too full-on, all the judgement. You can choose to show the ones you have so far. They're on non-public skin. With tattooed hands you don't have a choice unless you're wearing gloves, which happens once a year in Sydney. I get searched every time I go through customs, like squeezing out my toothpaste searched. You can't rent a house. You can't get a job.'

'I don't need a job.'

A look of scorn flashed across Rhys's face, then she said evenly, 'Fair enough.'

Marie wondered for the first time what she would do with this psychology degree. She couldn't imagine a workplace. She pushed the issue out of her mind. 'Do you regret the gauntlets?'

'I've grown into them. But I got them just before I fell pregnant and I did for a while, like taking Travis to child care was hard in the beginning. I was totally gung-ho and I had no idea what being a mother meant in the eyes of the world.'

'It means purity. It means service.'

'It means Nice. But there is a power in motherhood. It's just proscribed. You operate within those parameters, and you can access it. You can even reinvent it a bit.'

'My son-in-law, the real-estate agent, saw my moth tattoo. His face.'

'You're the mother. You've got the power.'

'I don't have the power,' Marie said in surprise. 'I never did.'

'Of course you do. You're the *mother*.'

'They ran rings around me. Still do.'

'I can imagine. Just having one.'

A pigeon with a deformed foot was hobbling on the footpath, pecking at crumbs. The deformed foot was like a clump of melted plastic, Marie thought, watching it pitilessly.

'You gotta take the power,' Rhys said with quiet insistence.

Marie looked at her.

'When does the house go on the market?'

'This weekend.'

'Scary.'

'I'm ready.'

'Okay. Let's start today.' Rhys formed a beak with her thumb and first two fingers and drew an undulating line to her forearm. When she finished she put her hands behind her head. Marie was again startled by the new ouroboros. A tattoo that size would take barely an hour. It seemed incredible how quickly and permanently things could change.

Susan stayed on the street tooting the horn of her new car, a fawn Peugeot convertible with leather seats and a GPS. Marie brought up a plastic bag containing the last pot of banksias, and Susan popped the boot. Then she noticed it. 'My god. The sign!'

The *For Sale* sign was around two metres tall and featured a photograph of the view taken from the living room. Beyond the sign was the real thing, rich with subtle movement.

'It's enormous, isn't it?' said Marie, building a nest for the pot in the boot of Susan's car. She slid into the passenger seat inhaling the cocktail of diesel, leather and brine.

'There's a little house in Awaba Street that's come onto the market, you know. I saved the ad for you. It's in the glove box.'

'I'm not staying in Mosman, Susan.'

'Why not? What's wrong with us?'

'I can't afford it.'

'Well, I think you can. You just need to be more positive. Aren't you even going to look at the ad?'

'I don't like it here anymore.'

Susan didn't reply. They drove up to Avenue Road. 'At the top of the hill,' said the GPS in an English accent, 'turn left.'

Susan obeyed, turning beneath a small sandstone bluff. The street was split, the corner guarded by wooden railings before the drop. Back from the road, buried beneath a cloud of crimson bougainvillea, stood an old Spanish mission house. Further along, an ancient Alexander palm towered over the suburb. After thirty years here, Marie still greeted her favourite things like a child rereading a fairy tale. These rare sites, whose decades hadn't been erased, soothed her.

'Does that thing tell you where to go even when you know the way already?' she said irritably when the GPS issued another direction.

'I can't switch it off.'

They drove on in silence, then Marie said, 'So how are you, Susan? Is everything alright?'

'I've had a shit of a week.'

'What's going on?'

'The painters are still here so Fatima can't hang the washing and every time I go outside *reeling* with paint fumes I'm nearly beheaded by a ladder. You should see them, sauntering around saying *fuck this fuck that*, knocking off at two every day. I took the Pajero to the mechanic because it was using up so much petrol and

he said I need a new carburettor then lo and behold the battery
dies as soon as I get it back. So there I am waiting for the NRMA all
morning, dodging painters and of course the car isn't running more
efficiently so that's another thousand dollars down the drain.'

Marie wondered if Susan had any idea what it was like to have
your cheques bounce. The car glided quiet as a boat through the
verdant curves of Neutral Bay. 'Well, this is a lovely car. I feel like a
million dollars in this car. It's intoxicating.'

'It runs on biofuels. Or it's supposed to. That's why we got it.
And two months later we find out we're responsible for food riots
in Bangladesh or wherever. Fabulous, isn't it.' Susan's mouth settled
into a grim line.

'We should have caught the ferry. Walked up to the gallery
through the gardens.'

'I don't have the time. I'm doing my shopping on the way
home.'

'How's Jonesy?' Marie tried to sound enthusiastic.

'He's in Singapore. Honestly, sometimes I feel like I could
murder someone.'

'I know exactly what you mean. Sometimes I think life is one
long act of self-control.'

'Self-control!' Susan barked.

After a while she said, 'You didn't come to *La Bohème*.'

'I'm sorry, I got the dates mixed up.' But Marie in fact hadn't
renewed her subscription. She had arrived home fifteen minutes
before the opera began, fresh from a session with Rhys, thinking
of the Joneses in seats E15 and E16. She had picked a lettuce and
watered the garden as the harbour sank into dusk. She had made
herself a salad with tuna and boiled eggs and eaten it with a book
lent her by Rhys, the opera loud on the living room stereo to drown
out the yapping of the Hendersons' new shih-tzus, Ming and Tang.
She had luxuriated in this time alone with her house, knowing she
would be up early to arrange things with Fatima for the Saturday
inspections. She left the house for these, finding evidence of
strangers when she returned: a crumpled tissue on the bathroom
floor, on the couch a long red hair. Worst of all, cigarette butts

in the garden. She had learnt paranoia after the first week, and in spite of Hugh's vigilance acquired the habit of locking everything she could and placing paper over the contents of the most private drawers. 'How was it?' she asked Susan.

'Absolutely exquisite.'

They were driving to the art gallery to see the blockbuster Renaissance exhibition. It was surprisingly cosy with the roof open, the acutely angled windscreen and windows proving excellent buffers. An even cool emanated from the seats and floor. Susan drove with both hands gripping the wheel, bracelets clattering. Every so often she glanced over at Marie. Marie's shirtsleeves were covering her half-completed vines. She liked her body now, with all its changes and secrets and stories. She no longer had the sense of hiding when she dressed. The daily ritual of alteration and censorship had given way to enjoyable enhancement and the judicious coverage of parts of herself that might need protection.

'Bridge, left lane,' said the GPS. 'Tunnel right.'

'Well,' said Susan. 'David rang me for your number.'

'Yes. We went out to dinner.'

'And?'

Marie was disconcerted by how much David's silence still hurt. 'It was ages ago, Susan.'

'And what happened? Did you go home with him?'

'Yes.'

Susan waited for more, but Marie had no desire to confess. The car swept onto the Cahill Expressway, Susan shaking her head. 'So *David* saw your tattoos?'

Marie's throat went hard and dry. She said nothing.

'Doesn't it hurt?'

'Nothing hurts as much as giving birth, Susan. Believe me.'

'But we don't seek that pain. We have no choice about that.'

'If you want the baby, you go through the pain. If you want the tattoo, ditto.'

'Rubbish,' Susan snapped. 'I had epidurals.'

'I didn't. And my relationship to pain was altered forever.'

'I'm sure your children would love to hear you compare them to tattoos.'

Laughter flew from Marie's mouth.

Susan took the corner hard at the end of the expressway, pitching Marie against the door. She kept glancing over. 'Are you covered in them now, are you? How many are there?'

'I'm not going to undress for you here, Susan.'

'I don't want you to undress for me at all, thanks.'

'Jesus Christ, when did we become such prudes?'

'I'm not a prude! This isn't about sex!'

'I didn't say it was!'

'I-don't-like-tattoos!' Susan's hand struck the wheel with each word. 'You can never get rid of them, and people change.'

'Exactly.'

'They last forever, Marie.'

'Not as long as oil paintings.'

'How can you compare them with *art*?' Susan scoffed.

'Just shut up about it will you!'

'I'm just stating my opinion! Why do you take it so personally?'

'Because it *is* personal! That's the whole point! The tattoos are *me*.'

'Oh no, they're not. I've known you for thirty years, Marie. You can't just change overnight.'

'You just said that people change!'

'All your talk about water tanks and sweatshops, is that what this is all about? You never cared about that sort of thing before. Getting tattoos isn't going to change *that*.'

Marie was going to say, *Better late than never*, when a ream of burps emerged from her mouth, harsh and bitter like sulphuric gas, and she began to laugh again. First at her body's anarchy, then at the world she was a part of, the stupid, narrow world that promised you freedom then punished you for taking it. Helplessly, she laughed and burped as they shouted their way into the Domain.

'I can't believe you're so upset over a silly tattoo!'

'No, Susan, *you* are. And if it's so silly, why is it so reprehensible?'

'I'm *worried* about you, Marie.'

'I don't need your fucking pity!'

'I can't talk about this anymore! I want to go and look at the art!'

The people waiting on the art gallery steps watched them arrive, Susan smiling in a queenly fashion as she slowed down and turned triumphantly into the one free parking space. Out of the air-conditioning, the heat wrapped around Marie like a blanket. She began to sweat. Susan was looking up and down the street, one hand on the parking meter as though steadying herself against a wind. With a long red fingernail she poked the bay number into the keypad. 'Fabulous. There's an hour still paid for. That should do us.'

Marie took off without a word, straight into the gallery bistro where she downed a scotch in two gulps.

She moved alone through the crowded rooms, leaning closer to the paintings for the spill of seeds from cut fruit, the luxurious sweep of fabric, the blood spurting scarlet from Holofernes's neck as Judith plunged her sword in. The exhibition was packed, Marie often forced to stand behind people and crane her neck to see the pictures; yet even from here she could make out the detail of lizard's scales disappearing into darkness, the grimy toenails of Caravaggio's boy. All that rich, creamy white skin: how real was it in the end? Not a mark on the prostitute modelling as Magdalene, yet while Caravaggio was casting from the streets, the local vagabonds were scorching insignia into their flesh with gunpowder. What would his brush have made of their Angel Raphaels and Virgin Marys? Did he delete them for the Church's continuing favour? As she turned the corner into the last room, Marie caught sight of Susan. Susan looked away. Marie left the gallery.

These beautiful flaws. The tiny black mazes, ruined homes of parasites, that scarred the ironbark pews in St Mary's, a reassuring complication greeting Marie's fingertips as she sat down in the hallowed cool. The continuous fundamental meal of nature gave her sustenance. Strange how she was only ten minutes' walk from Susan in the gallery. Susan would never think of coming in here. Sanctuary, Marie thought. She knew their fight wasn't about the petty detail. It was a deeper schism, and she didn't know how to heal it. She looked down the nave at the altar, holy water drying on her forehead, and tried to empty her mind.

She was struck by the automatic gesture of dipping her fingers into the font and anointing herself on entering. The grandeur and solemnity of the cathedral was so tempting, and her own importance as a member of this ancient, godly club. Visitors whispered up the back. Praying people dotted the pews, others walked up the aisles to light candles. She noticed that half the people were Asian. A new congregation, but hardly a new church.

She remembered mass in her childhood. Sunday mornings were awaited with dread, a blot on the fresh page of the weekend. She remembered the drone of the priest and her desire to avoid sitting next to her father, her fear of punishment and wrongdoing. Her mother sitting forward, forehead pinched, a crease forming between closed eyes. Maybe this was when she was recovering from her hysterectomy. Marie knew nothing of her mother's problems at the time, only that her family was smaller than nearly every other in the parish, giving her a feeling of social diminishment. She couldn't remember when she learnt about her mother's hysterectomy. You didn't speak about these things. Sickness, the body, gynaecology especially. Her mother had died of something unrelated, her requiem the last mass Marie had been to. She loved the swing of censer over coffin, the frankincense and muttered prayers. It seemed a magical arcane rite, like the anointment with holy water. After years' absence, the responsorial psalms had risen to Marie's lips naturally as breath. But the truth was that in her childhood holy water held no appeal: the insufferable boredom of regular worship robbed it of all meaning, let alone exoticism. *Blessed are those who fear the Lord ...*

All the blood shed by Christian swords, the afterlife clogged with the souls of burnt infidels. Muslims, Jews, witches, homosexuals, apostates, heretics, wayward women. How many sins would she have to confess to Archbishop Pell or his acolytes in the confession box that she passed now on her way to light a candle? Bless me, Father, for I used birth control and I wish that every woman in the world could do the same. Bless me, Father, for I was unfaithful to my husband and I don't regret it; I regret only not having fucked more men. Bless me, Father, for on top of the fornication there was my drinking, but though I regret the pain it caused I don't regret the fun.

Bless me, Father, for I don't believe we go to hell for sinning nor to heaven for being good. I don't believe the meek shall inherit the earth. Bless me, Father, for I don't even believe in your bearded God.

But somebody, please, bless me.

Marie lit a candle for each child and a fourth for her grandchild. A fifth for a new owner to take care of Sirius Cove. A sixth for the bush and ocean around it. She hesitated then lit a seventh candle for Rhys. The eighth was for her new life.

She remembered the Sacred Heart on the waiter's forearm that fated day months ago like a call to arms. There was another Sacred Heart from a story of Leon's about George's family. During her hours on the toilet, this story returned to her. George's sister Anna, an artist, had been shunned by their mother for hanging a painting of the Sacred Heart in her toilet. George, previously, had been beaten up by his father for being gay.

Were the Anglicans any better? Marie wondered as she left the cathedral, hat pulled low on her head. Thinking about religion always put her in a rage. The Anglicans were *worse*, she decided; they were so pallid, at least the Catholics had style to their hideousness. Better art design, higher drama. The only thing the Anglicans had going for them was the ordination of women, and the Sydney diocese had banned that. Marie thought sourly of the Pope's funeral, all the old men bishops in their Byzantine finery sucking on the teat of the patriarchal god.

She crossed the wind tunnel of Whitlam Square and moved into the warren of Surry Hills laneways. She considered stopping at a pub toilet but her insides remained cemented. Self-disgust shadowed her. She fought it off. Why, she pursued her interrogation, was shit profane? The benign vegetable ooze of babies' seemed exempt; even Clark had been proud of changing Nell's nappy. Then later to the toilet, accompanied, encouraged. Then the ascension to privacy. The subtext of shame. So a child learns.

She wished sometimes she had a god, for protection, wishes and confessions. But what god would bless her on the toilet and listen to this prayer for a purge? After bran, prune juice and pills, what solution was there but one of the spirit? Every morning Mopoke sat in the bathroom staring at Marie as she strained. Sometimes she squatted in her tray beside her, looking up sympathetically, tail dragging in the litter. Marie would hold the tail aloft but Mopoke was constipated as well. She remembered the cat in her elegant youth, digging holes, perching over them with faraway concentration. Then the inspection and neat occlusion.

Marie walked in the sliver of shade next to the fences. She couldn't wait to get to the studio, to be hit by the adrenalin of tattoo.

Oh Lord, deliver me from this evil. Oh God, relieve me.

A fortnight after their first meeting, Clark and Sylvia were drinking beer in his car overlooking Blackwattle Bay, continuing a conversation begun at the pub before closing. They talked about everything — the university and funding, the law, the water crisis, Palestine, the federal and state governments, a fond reminiscence of Norman Gunston, and how jogging on cement fucked your joints. Had Sylvia sought him out? Had she been thinking of him too? Looking up from his notes as he walked through the foyer, Clark had found her standing right in front of him. 'Let's have that drink now,' she'd suggested. The hour at the pub had passed in seconds so they bought takeaways and drove down to the light-strewn bay. It was a marvel to Clark to hear his stories tumble into the ears of a woman he barely knew.

He spoke about his mother's change. 'I'm worried about her. She was drinking too much for a long time and really messy after my father left. She's anxious about the sale of the house. Sometimes I worry she's completely lost it.'

'My father had an anchor tattooed on his forearm. He was in the navy.'

'We should introduce them.'

'I don't think he's *quite* in your mother's league, Clark.'

Clark couldn't help but be disappointed. 'What's he like? Spanish?'

'Was. I loved him. He was Maltese. A short-arse, like a foot shorter than my mother. He was a bit hopeless but a lovely man.'

Sylvia told him that her parents had been jazz musicians in Brisbane. Her father had died when Sylvia was twenty-seven and her mother had eaten herself into a ball of depression on the Gold Coast. Sylvia had fled to Sydney twenty years ago when Queensland was a police state.

'Do you ever go back there? Visit your mother?'

'I hate it there, but I'm beginning to hate it here as well.'

'Why?'

'I feel more and more controlled. Pressured by rising prices. Everything feels so corporate. Even universities are corporations these days. I went to see a band the other night and as we went in the girl on the door said, *I understand you're eighteen years of age*, very stiffly as though reading from a rule book, and I'm like, *Actually I'm more than twice that, I'm forty-one.*'

Clark registered her age with more alarm than he did the draconian door policy. It was at least five years more than he expected. The other side of forty, though less than a year to go for him, seemed an aeon away. It was the country where his mother lived. And the equation of older woman and younger man didn't sit easily. Clark registered also Sylvia's anger and eloquence, with admiration and a little fear. He registered her ethnicity. Her surname. Married name? She could be divorced. He realised with a start that he had given away his googling, because she had never told him her surname. But she didn't appear to have noticed anything untoward; she was still talking.

'I walked into the venue feeling flattered at first. Then I thought, Fuck this, she's young enough to be my daughter and she's only said that because she's done some dumb course or been told by the manager that she is legally obliged to say that stupid line to every punter. It's insulting! They're teaching courses like this at our university, and I work in the profession that's strangling us with this onslaught.'

'I know what you mean.'

Sylvia looked out at the passage of a boat across the water, her face blue in the moonlight. 'I feel guilty about my mother. We're always hard on our mothers, aren't we? It's like a Greek tragedy, we can't help ourselves, it's like the natural instinct is to want to kill them. In order to live. It's different for men though.'

'How do you mean?'

'You're sentimental about mothers. You can afford to be.'

Clark thought about how perfect this paradigm was for Leon and Blanche. Leon took his mother's love for granted. Blanche was the opposite: she often seemed to hate their mother. He considered how much of Blanche and Marie's vexed relationship wasn't due to the mysterious vagaries of female relations that he had always held at arm's length with something he considered to be respect, but to a banal treachery caused by the narrow confines of their similarities. And in that flash of insight, he didn't see his mother as the usual victim. He saw only the awful intractability of the whole dynamic. This ushered in an empathy for Blanche, which worked on him like a balm.

He had been avoiding his mother this year. He hadn't taken Nell to see her. Something had broken when Marie began getting tattooed. He also harboured an obscure resentment towards her for letting the house go, even though he supported the decision. Often lately, the house surfaced behind Clark's eyelids clear and animate as a person. He could almost see truculence in its façade at the mention it had received in Jonathan Chancellor's *Title Deeds* as adman Ross King's old residence. The house had really been their mother's. Ross had been the renovator, tearing into it and re-dressing it like an overzealous parent continually changing his child's clothes, while Marie maintained the daily care. And where was Ross in all this? Blanche would know. She hadn't wanted to join her brothers in cutting off Ross after he left: she had always worn her independence on her sleeve and her father's favour on her heart. Clark supposed it was fitting for Ross to remain silent about the sale because he had wanted it all along: somewhere, somehow he would be celebrating. It was probably better he stay away.

Clark's protective shield around his mother hardened; he regretted their discord. Her life in that house was almost as long as his in entirety. Everything he had first learnt about the world, his primary sensations and obstacle courses were in that house and to lose it was to lose the very foundations of his life.

'Mother Madonna, you know,' Sylvia was saying.

'Isn't that more of a wog thing?'

He knew he was taking liberties by using this word. He wanted the intimacy it might provide. Sylvia gave a little smile. 'Yeah, but not only.' She placed her stubbie in the cavity near the gear stick and wiped her hand on her thigh.

'Look at your hands. They must be as long as mine.'

Clark held up his right hand and Sylvia placed her palm against his. They looked at one another over their fingertips then his hand was on her face and he was leaning over, kissing her. She moved closer, sighed into his mouth. He had a lurching sensation in the pit of his stomach, as though something were cracking open.

Sylvia stroked his cheek. 'Let's get out and sit on the grass.'

Clark took a towel from the back seat and spread it across the ground. They lay beneath the sky holding hands, listening to the lap of water. There was a faint track of stars, and dominating the skyline the peaks of the Anzac Bridge, humming in the distance. Then they were kissing again, he was unbuttoning her shirt, her hand moving to his belt, his on her breast. Then a rake of headlights over their bodies. They froze, listening to the ignition cut.

Clark's erection died and he was relieved. Sylvia locked her arms around his torso and squeezed him so hard that a bark escaped and echoed around the bay like a shot. He squeezed her back harder and she yelped. They lay there laughing inside the dying echoes. Holding this willowy body, he thought of the mother that had birthed it, bloated with despair on the Gold Coast. And what of his own mother, what now had he come from? How our bodies change. His static life had kickstarted, he had the feeling of being on the verge. He held Sylvia's hand against the sky, touching the ring on her finger. 'Your wedding ring, huh?' he said facetiously.

People wore rings on any finger these days, Clark told himself.

He still wore his because he liked it as a piece of jewellery and it fitted on no other finger but the fourth. The transferral to his right hand had been his indication of divorce but men, it occurred to him now in a panic, sometimes wore their wedding rings on their right hand. Didn't they?

'Yes,' she said.

'What, are you married?'

'Of course. Aren't you?'

'No. Not anymore.'

Of course he knew she was married, he had known all along. Martinez was her husband's name; he had realised that as soon as he started googling her. But he hadn't wanted to believe it, he had told himself that, like Janice and Blanche and so many women their age, Sylvia used her maiden name at work. But even that scenario could have meant there was another name, another person ...

Sylvia turned on her back and settled her head against his chest.

'Oh, it's such a beautiful night.'

Blanche loved the TV shoots. The big trucks with their cargo of men and gear, a macho arena through which she prowled with feline toughness in her pointy little boots. Morrison the director was a Swinburne graduate who, straight out of film school, had made a feature about a crim that went on to win two AFIs. Blanche loved his gritty aesthetic and was surprised at their first meeting to find a pale, clerkish boy with an apologetic posture. Morrison wore white shirts every day that looked as clean at six p.m. as they had at eight a.m. He hardly spoke to anyone, whether out of shyness or arrogance Blanche wasn't sure. She didn't want to interfere in his work. She went on set once, to ask for more long shots. The rest of the time she sat in the green room with Kate and Lim, watching the shoot on a monitor.

'How much chocolate d'you reckon they've eaten by now?'

'The girl's spitting it out,' said Kate.

'No.'

'Truly.'

'He should be shooting her in profile,' said Lim.

'Is there any chocolate up here?' said Blanche. 'I'm hanging out.'

'We've finished it.'

Lim looked puffy in the face today, hungover maybe. Blanche realised that she didn't desire him anymore, and she felt abandoned. Her BlackBerry beeped. *How is my precious pooky? A buyer came through Sirius today but still no definite offers. What time are you coming home? x*

Not too much longer hopefully, Blanche texted Hugh. Out the window, the fading claw marks of cirrus stretched across the eastern sky. She could hear the women from the production company gossiping below, Rachel the art department coordinator and one of the set designers, a horse-faced woman with lank white hair. They had gone outside to suck on their cancer sticks. Rachel had a low, sexy voice full of innuendo, with a touch of sibilance: the sort of voice that drag queens emulated.

'... the most indulgent display of spending. I've got about forty-seven thousand dollars in petty cash up there you know.'

'The budget's the same as *Bondi Boys*.'

'Oh, more. Because you have to take into account ...'

'... nuh. Going straight to video.'

I'll let you know when we're finished. Blanche put her phone back into her bag.

'I worked on an American ad for sleeping pills in November,' said Rachel. 'We went all the way to Perth to film one shot of moths flying in a window. Can you believe it?'

Blanche sometimes wished she smoked. She wanted to go outside now, to get away from the monitor. She knew that ad. It was for Pfizer. Slated to play North America, Australia, the UK and Germany: cinema, internet, print, television. Not exactly small fry. They just didn't get it. Blanche wanted to land like a cat among the pigeons and be taken into Rachel's husky, knowing confidence, but if you didn't smoke you looked suss hanging around outside, all lurkish intent and dangling hands. You looked like you were running away from a problem or desperate for friendship or something.

Morrison was doing another take of the man putting chocolate into the woman's mouth. She was peeling her lips back, her whole face contorting. Make-up came in and dabbed her face. The man rose to stretch then stood there nodding at Morrison's directions. He had thick eyelashes and a short dark beard, and Blanche couldn't take her eyes off him. Oh yes, the ritual of smoking with its imperative and relief was immensely appealing at times like this.

'God, this country's fucked. *No* money for film. I'm *so* over it.'

Blanche shut the window and left the room. She walked down the corridor to the toilet, where she sat for a long time leaning forward, chest on thighs, contemplating how scuffed her boots had become from the scungy set. She should get some cowboy boots: Kate's looked good scuffed, they looked good any way. Blanche reapplied her lipstick, left the toilets and dropped coins into the chip machine for Twisties. She was reading the fat, flavourings and colourings she was about to consume when Rachel appeared. 'Hi Blanche!'

'Hi Rachel!'

'He-ey, it's gonna be great.'

'Yeah, they're a great team.'

'No, really.' Rachel nodded. 'Good on you. It's so classy.'

'Thanks. You too. Want a Twistie?'

'Okay! Oh no, actually, I *totally* pigged out at lunch.'

'You sure?'

'Absolutely.' Rachel continued on her way to the toilet, turning at the door. 'Hey, great job, yeah?'

'Thanks, you too.'

Blanche went down to the set eating her Twisties. Amazing how fantastic these little twisted yellow things full of crap tasted. She'd been eating them since she had teeth. Who was it who discovered that if you put the empty packets into the oven, they shrank to perfect miniatures? It provided endless fun after school. Did packets these days react to heat in the same way? Her wheels began to spin. Why hadn't anyone made a good Twisties ad? Little idiosyncratic battler of a cheesy snack thing that kept on keeping on. More to the point, why didn't she have the Twisties contract? Maybe they thought they didn't need to spend money on advertising ... Never say never. She should get Twisties for her circus lust. She could kill it.

There was activity around the catering van and the crew looked as though they were packing up. Blanche remembered the organic carrot cake they'd been served for afternoon tea, and went and saved the last piece from the bin. She gobbled some down then sidled up to Morrison and suggested the woman be sitting upright instead of lying in the man's lap. Could they slot it into Monday's shoot? Morrison blinked thoughtfully. Blanche offered him a Twistie. He seemed about to say something when his mobile went off.

The man in the ad was on Blanche's mind. That eagle tattooed across his chest, which she saw as he stood in the corner changing, aware of the eyes of every woman in the room on him. Pecs like half rockmelons, a ring in one nipple. She caught his eye and he glanced away coldly, and it suddenly occurred to her that he was gay. It was a tragedy that she would never get to have sex with the man with the chest tattoo. She walked up to the green room for her bag, throwing the Twisties and cake into the bin. She had nothing to complain about; she had a loving husband, was steering another successful campaign, but she felt unaccountably troubled and dissatisfied.

She drove home with a knot in her stomach. It swelled into a painful psychic node beneath Hugh's attentive hands as they made exhausted perfunctory love that night for the first time in months. Blanche shut her eyes and imagined the trapeze artist's chest pressing against her breasts, as she tilted her hips to receive him, Hugh, him. She dozed fitfully till dawn and woke to the smell of coffee: Hugh padding into the bedroom with a tray and the papers.

The traffic into town was slow and the galleries had opened by the time they arrived in Danks Street. The first one was showing Tait Green, an art school colleague of Blanche's.

Hugh, as usual, was discussing Sirius Cove. 'I got the photos I took of the garden printed, which Marie loved. Even though they didn't get used for the ad, they'll be a good record. She just wants people to appreciate it, you know.' He turned to Blanche meaningfully.

'Yeah, I know.'

'Two buyers now. I'm putting my money on the lawyer couple.

They're second-generation Mosman: her grandparents live in Kardinia Road. They've got two kids, eight and ten years old, who play in the bush. They love the house. I don't think they'll pull it down, just a bit of reno. But the price isn't ideal.'

'Will you go to auction?'

'I think so.' Hugh moved along to the next artwork, a pair of trainers made from Blu-Tack, mounted on a plinth, enclosed in a glass cabinet. 'I paid Fatima for her.'

'Hey?'

'Her cheque bounced, and I was there. Don't worry, pooky, we'll just put it against the sale.'

'Oh, I'm not worried. Just don't tell Clark. Okay?'

'Course not. She must be getting them done quickly. She's got one on her back. It goes right up her neck into her hair.'

'I don't want to know, Hugh.' Blanche spoke in a low voice.

Behind the white desk in the white corner, the white gallery assistant was doing something on her mobile phone.

Hugh stared at the Blu-Tack trainers. 'Amazing. Adidas. They're *perfect*.'

'Seven and a half grand. Jesus. What's the point?'

'He's having a joke, isn't he? Putting them in a glass cabinet like that? Isn't he saying that it's us who put our trainers and brand names on a pedestal?'

'Half the time I think that irony's just a veneer.'

'What for?'

'Nothing. It's a veneer for nothing.'

They moved to the end of the room where paintings covered the wall. Hugh continued talking quietly. 'You know Pasadena? Just up the road from Marie? Not as well situated, but it's got a home theatre, Gaggenau, five bathrooms, pool, six-car garage with wash bay. Air-conditioned wine cellar. I mean she's got pretty stiff competition is the thing. Stav's handling that property, and he reckons it'll go for seven to eight.'

'So the market *is* going down.'

Hugh crimped his mouth.

'Come on, Hughie.'

'Well, yeah, compared to the beginning of summer. But not compared to three years ago.'

Blanche nodded sadly. 'The market's going down.'

Hugh said in a loud whisper, mildly outraged, 'You know Stav gets racist remarks sometimes? He's like second-generation Australian. I think it's outrageous. I mean, we're all supposed to be equal in this country. It makes me feel really ashamed.'

'We *are* egalitarian. You should see Kate and Lim, they're positively revered. There are stupid people everywhere, that's all. It's just ignorance.' Blanche moved alongside the air-brushed canvases of gridiron players, close enough to take in every detail. 'I *hate* this stuff. It's all surface, surface, surface.'

'It depends what you want. Technically, he's amazing.'

'So are computers.'

'Come on, pooky.'

'Tait used to paint blue circles at college. That's all he painted for three years solid. Blue circles. I'm not kidding.'

'I should tell Stav about these,' Hugh said to the gridiron players.

'Why? I didn't know Stav was interested in art.'

'He's not. He's just looking for stuff for his pub. He's decking it out as a New York bar.'

Blanche placated herself with the apprehension of no more than three blue dots on the walls around the room, on this, the last day of the exhibition. (She wondered when blue dots had replaced red as sale markers; whether they were using them in Woollahra now as well, or just here in Waterloo. She wondered if it was an ironic comment on the blue genesis of Tait Green.) She couldn't believe that Tait, head nerd at COFA, was holding his seventh solo show in Sydney alone. She couldn't digest the three-page CV, the words *Shanghai*, *Berlin*, and *grant* and *award* like drops of acid in her eyes. She steered Hugh towards the exit.

Outside the air was dense with coming rain. Dark cloud hung on the horizon. They walked past a row of terraces with pretty gardens.

'God, it's changed around here,' said Blanche. 'It's so nice now.'

'I still wouldn't buy in Redfern.'

'Why not?'

'You've still got all the housing commissions down the road.'

'But housing commissions give that authentic inner-city feel. People like that.'

'Too many break-ins. If you don't have a lock-up garage, woe betide your car.'

'I heard that most of the Aborigines have been moved to the western suburbs.'

'They're still down near the station. You see them when you drive past. I know a bloke whose wife had her bag stolen at the lights there from the passenger seat of her car. They just opened the door and took the bag. Completely brazen! Terrified her. And you never know when there's going to be another riot.'

They headed down to the new bistro in Danks Street. Along the footpath, its umbrellas gleamed like mushrooms beneath the purple sky. At the end table were a man and woman in black. With her high slanted fringe, the woman was definitely a curator. Definitely Beth, Blanche soon saw. She stopped to say hello.

'Blanche!' Beth grinned up through her sunglasses. 'Long time no see!'

They introduced their husbands. James — Beth's — smiled and folded the travel section and placed it on the seat beside him. He wore his watch loose like a bracelet, and black thongs and long black shorts. The blonde hair on his forearms seemed to have been conditioned and combed. Blanche tried to remember whether or not Beth had been with him the last time she had seen her. Their hands were linked beneath the table in a gesture of sexual propriety; they emanated contentment.

The Hillsong church on the next block was spewing its Diesel and Tsubi congregation out to the footpath while a line of Toyotas and four-wheel drives emerged from its underground carpark like a series of metal turds. On the wall of the grey edifice in huge lettering were the words *JESUS Saves Us*.

'Have you just been up to Tait's show?' Beth smiled at Blanche.

'Yeah, it was really good.'

'Isn't it?'

'Absolutely loved it,' Hugh said.

'He works so hard,' said Beth.

'Yeah,' said Blanche. 'I was telling Hugh about the blue circles.'

'Discipline.' Beth nodded. 'He's totally zen. Did you know he doesn't even drink tea anymore? No alcohol, smoking, drugs or coffee, yoga every day. *And* he meditates.'

'Amazing.'

'Apparently they love his work in China. The art market is going *off* in China. Are you still with Huston Alwick?'

'Creative director!' Hugh placed a hand on Blanche's back.

James smiled up at them from beneath his visored hand.

'Wow! Blanche is advertising royalty,' Beth explained to him. 'Her father is Ross King.'

'Oh right.' James examined her keenly.

'I *so* loved that No War ad. *Everyone* was talking about it.'

'Was that yours?' said James excitedly. 'That was excellent.'

'And are you making any art?'

'All the time.' Blanche laughed, adding, 'You mean my own work?'

'Yeah.'

'God, no, I haven't got the time.'

'I know the feeling. Blanche was a great drawer at college,' Beth told James and Hugh. 'You *were*. Drawing's making a comeback, you know.'

'How about you? How's it going at the MCA?'

'Oh, you know. Bureaucracy. Dead wood. Permanent funding crisis. There's one curator who's an absolute *dream* to work with. But I hate my boss.' Beth grinned.

'I know the feeling.'

'There are some good things coming up. I should get your email.'

The Hillsongers were heading towards them. Blanche shifted her bag down her arm and began to work the zipper to extract one of her cards. A waiter brought out two plates of eggs Benedict. Glistening folds of smoked salmon scattered with dill slooped across the white china beneath Hollandaise sauce. The waiter placed the meals before Beth and James then pulled a giant pepper grinder out from where it was wedged in his armpit. Blanche's stomach growled.

'I ordered a skinny cap as well,' Beth told the waiter.

'Yes, ma'am, it's coming.'

'Look, why don't you join us? Quick, so the Christians don't sit here ...'

Blanche laughed, and she and Hugh sat down.

'No offence,' said Beth. 'I mean nobody here's a Christian, are they? I mean there's nothing *wrong* with being a Christian. *Aaarghh ...*'

'I believe in God,' said Hugh.

'Hu-ugh. He doesn't go to church or anything,' Blanche explained.

James nodded. 'I go to midnight mass at Christmas. The singing's beautiful.'

Beth waved her hands. 'Each to their own. I'm totally fine with it. I mean we just bought a house in the block behind them so I'm hardly allergic.'

'Really?' said Hugh.

Blanche examined her menu although all she wanted was exactly what Beth and James were having. She considered the buttermilk pancakes with blueberries and ricotta but they would be too fattening. Maybe if she got hash browns with her eggs it would seem different to Beth and James's. But then it would be too much food. Hugh could help her eat it, but she didn't want him getting fat any more than herself. Beth was one of those skinny women who could eat what she liked, judging by the way her eggs were disappearing into her size-10 figure. At college Beth had seemed frivolous. She had had a lot of boyfriends and missed a lot of classes and was always hungover. She failed sculpture, which she had done with Blanche, who had topped the class. Beth's real talent lay with theory: she wrote her thesis on Arte Povera and went to every art opening in Sydney and every conference overseas as a postgrad. And now she was an assistant curator at the Museum of Contemporary Art. Just goes to show, thought Blanche, better to be a pisshead networking slut than a hardworking talent. Then again, Tait had been a conscientious nerd. Well, obviously you couldn't get by just being *normal*. Blanche wondered what they earnt at the MCA. The heads of the major theatre and dance companies were on six figures these days: the top museum administrators must be on par. Again, Blanche rued her decision not to stick with art, but she had to admit that advertising had given her greater independence and greater security at an earlier age. She could still smell the sour cockroach kitchen of the Chippendale house she had lived in at nineteen while at art college, then fled to return home a year later. Nobody who wanted anything to do with art, it seemed at that time, would rise above that. But Beth and Tait had.

Anyway, who said that advertising wasn't art? The same people who claimed to ignore the divide between high and low art, who lauded ironic commentary on popular culture, and kept 'art' books of Australiana — most of which was old advertising designs — on their coffee tables. Blanche knew in her heart that she was a better artist than Tait Green and had said more with her Dulux ad than he had with a dozen pairs of Blu-Tack Adidas. Oh, how she loved being creative. Because while she sat here looking at the menu, maintaining a conversation and reminiscing about Beth and art college, deep in the mud of her exhausted mind the seed of an idea was cracking open. Diet Coke. *Better than sex.* A rumpled bed, sleepy hornbag of a bloke, the sheets tented by a bottle. She shut out the voice that told her how unsatisfying her sex life with Hugh was. She let the idea alone, watching it out of the corner of her eye, careful not to frighten it away.

She looked up the street and liked what she saw. A large furniture store across the road, another bistro and a landscape gardening place with huge agaves in pots along the footpath. Amazing how nice it was here in the heart of Redfern, Sydney's biggest slum just ten years ago. Only a handful of the Christians had stopped in the bistro, and they were so well-dressed that pretty soon you forgot they were Christians. A truck rolled into the drive of the whitegoods warehouse ten metres away and opened its back doors to accept a load of fridges. Blanche imagined moving into this neighbourhood and it didn't feel like such a bad idea. Even Marie had mentioned looking here. Not that she'd want to live in the same suburb as her mother.

'So this is your local!' Hugh said.

'We love it,' said James. 'We were in Woollahra before, and it just got too much.'

'Twelve dollars for a jar of cream at Jones the Grocer,' said Beth. 'We called it Jones the Grosser, as in, you know, with two s's. *And* the biggest carbon footprint in the whole of Australia, after Mosman.'

'Fascinating,' said Hugh. 'Blanche and I were just talking about how much it's changed around here. Can I ask how much you paid?'

'Hugh's in the business,' Blanche said peremptorily.

'Oh *right*,' said James. 'Well, Redfern is going *off*.'

'You too?'

'I'm an architect.'

'We'll have to show you our house. James did everything. We've got solar panels, a tank. Skylights.'

'An absolute wreck when we bought it.'

'Really?' said Blanche. 'How do you find room for a tank in a terrace?'

'We built a deck out the back and put in a native garden. The tank is a bladder and fits under the deck. I don't know how anyone lives with themselves these days who *doesn't* have one. We *love* it. We're going to die there.'

Hugh's leg was jiggling up and down. He looked from Beth to James and back again. 'Can I ask how much you paid?' he said again.

'One point seven five. It's three storeys.'

'Whoa.'

'But eighty K on renos.'

'Still.'

'Last exchanged for two thousand pounds in 1963,' Beth said proudly.

Blanche and Hugh made noises of amazement.

Hugh went inside to order and Blanche listened to Beth and James describe their new house. They asked her about hers. She told them about the heritage sandstone cottage in Lavender Bay they had bought five years ago after marrying and as she spoke she regretted how rarely she and Hugh had people over. Yet they loved their house and had bought a seven-thousand-dollar teak dining room table and kitted out their kitchen with the express purpose of having dinner parties. But there was never enough time. Blanche wanted to change this. She wanted her and Hugh to be like they were today every Saturday, out together enjoying the world, in the company of friends.

Hugh came back out. The stormclouds were receding. Far off in the distance thunder rumbled and overhead the sun pushed through cloud, turning the light a purple green. Blanche felt as though she were sitting inside a giant bruise: painful, tender, healing.

It was raining in Mexico for the fourteenth day in a row and millions of people were being evacuated. Towns were flooded to the rooflines, humans and animals alike were drowning, more rain was predicted. But all across the eastern states of Australia, skies remained blue, and in Sydney the temperature continued to rise.

Marie spent Saturday going through her finances. Six months earlier she had stopped her health insurance, saving about two thousand dollars a year. Stopping her car insurance had lost her thousands, as the gouge had begun to rust. She was late with her rates and water bills. She still hadn't paid the tree surgeon and her credit cards were almost at their limit. A letter arrived with the Visa bill: *Dear Mrs King,* **Enjoy 2.99% p.a. for 6 months on a single purchase over $500.** *Why not treat yourself to something you'd really like with an ANZ Great Rate?* None of the buyers had made an offer on the house and Hugh had counselled an auction. She refused to be worried by these lowered expectations, the price still enormous in her eyes. Each night on the news she watched the stockmarket fall. She held shares in half the major companies with red downward arrows beside their names and supposed it boded badly but she still couldn't feel real danger. She was like a drunken teenager driving down a dark country road.

Yet to be without money was a frightening thing. Money

brought a sort of peace. It was the access it gave you, the broadened world, to walk into any place and know that whatever you wanted was just a signature away. To leave big tips and luxuriate in your benevolence. Even back from explicit display, money was a cushion. It didn't matter if the washing machine broke: a new one was just a phone call away. Marie knew she was sliding. Her spending had reduced over the past year and the boundaries of necessity kept shrinking. The orchids could do without food and she could do without fancy restaurants. She knew where she had gone wrong. She could have seen it coming with the mandate for reduction in Ross's settlement. She was also aware, subliminally if nothing else, that there remained an impulse in her to spend because she didn't quite believe this asset was truly her entitlement; her treasure was also her albatross and the impulse to destroy was all bound up with the impulse to preserve. The sadness of losing it contained also relief. Therein seemed to lie the possibility of feeling.

And then what would happen? Becoming dependent on her children horrified her and would in any case be impossible with her sons. Leon didn't care about money, which was part of the problem, the way he had so carelessly spent so much. Clark was prudish to the point of parsimony. It was Blanche alone who was comfortable with money, as skilled at making it as she was at spending it. There was no question: Marie would have to get a job.

Adapt or perish was the headline in Saturday's paper. The article stated that if Australia didn't implement a carbon-trading scheme within the next two years, the cost would be the loss of the Great Barrier Reef, the demise of the Murray–Darling, up to 9500 heatwave deaths per year, GDP collapse, inland migration to escape rising sea levels and severe storms, Pacific atoll refugees and political instability in neighbouring countries. Marie still hadn't grasped exactly what a carbon-trading scheme was. She read every word of the article, depressed and confused.

She turned to *Domain*. The feature was about swimming pools. *I know that Bondi Beach is only a stone's throw away, but a swimming pool adds that element of privacy and luxury that's very important to people in this market*, said a real-estate agent, next to a photo of a pool by the ocean. The shot made the pool look as though it were bleeding straight into the Pacific. Clark never mentioned people like this: he had nothing but praise for Bondi. The prices for semis were around two million. What would it be like living near her eldest son? She might get to see Nell more often. Nell might even stay for a weekend. Marie went back to the feature article where a couple were interviewed who had renovated their Surry Hills terrace to include a swimming pool, but not moved in when the wife fell pregnant as they feared the pool would be dangerous for their child. The house was priced at two and a half million. Hardly her sort of place with all that glass and metal. The ad for her house was reduced to a quarter page this week. She thought immediately of the lawyer couple, whom Hugh had advised her to meet on their second visit. The woman so pale you could see the veins on her forearms. The bluff man in his high-waisted chinos and ironed polo shirt was the talker but clearly, also, obedient to his wife. The grumpy boy and girl. Marie took comfort in the family's froideur, interpreting it as respect, and realised she had mentally passed the house to them already. She threw the paper into the recycling bin.

When the sun began to recede, she put on a load of washing and went into the garden. The coconut ice grevilleas were clustered with honey-eaters. The callistemon looked as though it had thrips. It was too hot to turn the compost. Just unravelling the bailing hose took all her effort. Ming and Tang snarled along the fence each time she went into the laundry. 'Shut up, you little shits,' Marie muttered. She went inside for an iced cordial and in the afternoon switched on the tennis.

Fifty minutes into the third set when they were back on deuce, David rang. Taken aback, Marie began to pace around the living room with the phone. A luxury liner was steaming towards the Quay, its windows lit up like opals. As the sun sank, the harbour caught fire. Drawn by the strange light, Marie walked onto the deck. Her mind, on hearing David's voice, went immediately to Susan. Had he heard about their fight? He sounded friendly in a tentative way. He said he had been overseas. He didn't seem to offer this an excuse for his silence, and his lack of guile eased Marie. It was the twenty-first century after all, so her own silence might have had explanation due as well. She thought back to the beginning of the year and it seemed an age away, the weeks since filled with irrevocable changes, but David spoke as though they had only seen each other recently and nothing untoward had happened. He said he had been catching up on his journal reading since returning to Sydney.

'And I thought about you,' he said warmly.

'Oh?' Marie was flattered, but she wasn't going to succumb. She checked her reflection in the glass doors: pretty good, but she could do with a hair cut. Christ, her hands looked terrible, though. Wrinkly old-lady hands.

'I'm a subscription junkie and a closet anthropologist. Everything worth reading on the subject comes through my letterbox. Did you know that Joseph Banks had himself tattooed? Isn't that extraordinary?'

Marie didn't know that, and felt a bit miffed that he had beaten her to the information. She said, 'Another specimen for his collection?'

'I knew he *wrote* about them, but not that he had one done on himself. He said he couldn't understand how the Tahitians put themselves through such an ordeal. I wonder why he finally succumbed.'

'Maybe it was something for himself.' Marie sat in a recliner and stretched out her legs. They needed waxing. God, Marie, stop it will you. She left the light off and listened to David talk about Banks. Metallic orange drained from the body of water before her, the outlines of trees sank into gloom. The beauty of this view still astonished her and she wished for someone to share it with. Every night, the opera of sunset, like bathing in champagne.

'He had a Maori head, with a moko on it. He brought it back to England with him.'

'God, David.'

'He didn't mean any harm! *They* sold it to him. Banks was a man of insatiable curiosity. He taught us *so much*. Isn't it astonishing when you read about these things? Can you imagine being in a ship with a cargo full of plants and animals the likes of which you've never seen, that may as well have come from Mars? The *Sirius*, Marie!'

Marie thought of the human head carried to the other side of the world, mounted in a cabinet and stared at like an object. *It. A head.* She thought of the person who had smiled and scowled and kissed and wept through that tattooed face. The crowds at those colonial exhibitions were immense, with queues for miles; the most popular exhibits living natives, in dioramas. Reading about this made Marie feel dirty, as though she were in the audience too. She was as pleased by the arrival of the information about Banks's tattoo from David as she was disturbed. She had been gorging on Rhys's books and stories for months, with nobody to share what fascinated her. But David was talking so much it was hard to get a word in.

The cove was almost black now, the harbour to the right still glowing with the last sun. Marie had often imagined the *Sirius* being careened on this side of the harbour to keep the sailors away from the vice of Sydney Cove, the most bored and reckless sneaking across for women and rum. A hundred years later, doctors and lawyers and merchant bankers settled here to keep their children from the same. In the Kings' case it had worked, though Marie now felt far less self-congratulatory. What was vice anyway? Whoring and drinking didn't look nearly as bad to her now as they used to. She had been cooped up alone in this house for months getting it ready: relief came in the city, getting tattooed. But crossing the water at night held other prospects and here was a man she'd slept with on the phone, a possible accomplice. She was desperate to get out and have fun. She really wanted to let her hair down. She wished she hadn't conjured up those sailors scrubbing the deck: they made her think about the Aborigines dying of smallpox so prolifically that they couldn't be buried, their bodies snagging in the rocks below. She tried to imagine the bush without fungus, or lantana, alive with snakes, to flush this horrible thought from her mind. It didn't work.

'The *Sirius* never made it back to England, did she? It was a flagship, wasn't it?'

'Yes, yes, I know,' David said with brisk good humour. 'Poetic licence.'

Marie went back into the house and poured herself a Diet Coke with ice and lemon.

'Then it became fashionable among the European aristocracy,' David went on. 'Prince Edward had himself tattooed before he became king, and sent his sons to the same Japanese master. Apparently *all* the European aristocracy visited this man, in Yokohama.'

'Hori Chiyo!' Marie interjected. David was like a guest who offered to help at a dinner party and ended up taking over the whole menu. Yes, this was *her* territory; she elbowed him out of the way. 'I have a book here about all that. He used ivory sticks and coloured inks. He tattooed half the European navy. When they banned tattooing in Japan a rich American set him up in business in New York.'

They began to talk over the top of each other, David relaying the story of Count Tolstoy, a relative of the writer, pulling his shirt off at dinner parties when he'd had a bit to drink, and showing all the tattoos he'd acquired in North America and the Pacific.

'And Lady Randolph Churchill. Churchill's mother.'

'Is that so?'

'She had a snake tattooed around her wrist. She hid it beneath her watch.'

'And what about you?' David said cheerily.

The fine lines on Marie's arms were healing. 'I've been getting mine done too.'

'*Really?*'

Marie trailed off. She remembered David's Darling Point townhouse, the studs of halogen lights in the ceiling, the Sepik River carving of a man-creature grasping a phallus that flowed in a continuous curve from groin to mouth. The plane of David's chest, his back to her in the dawn.

'Well, I won't be looking at Sirius Cove much longer. The auction's in two weeks.'

'You're going to auction? That's quite an event. How do you feel?'

'I feel like I'm in a trance. I'm looking forward to it in a way.'

'You're being very brave.'

'As much as I love it here the place has become a burden.'

'You're going to need some distractions. Why don't you let me take you to dinner?'

Marie was determined to be rational about this. So what if he wanted something from her. Didn't everybody want something from somebody? In return, she could get something from him, couldn't she? A change of scenery from her couch and the television. The sex wasn't exactly great, but that could have just been first-night awkwardness. David was making an effort: once he got to know her better, he would understand. She didn't want to come across as acquiescent, let alone desperate. She said she was too busy this week but next week was a possibility. David suggested Level 41.

All through dusk the temperature remained steady at thirty-nine. Night brought no relief. Marie made pasta for dinner. Mopoke came into the kitchen and ate her entire meal at Marie's feet then rubbed her thank-you against Marie's calves. Then she moved slowly across the living room out to the deck where she sat like a statue with her back to the house and her face to the harbour.

The tennis moved into the fourth hour. Livid marks grew beneath Safin's eyes. There were tantrums on the court, a racket smashed, umpires yelled at. Between sets, the players sat on the sidelines staring into space with wild-eyed exhaustion, their thighs wobbling between the hands of physiotherapists while the commentator recited a litany of injuries and surgical procedures. Marie wondered if those big floppy shorts didn't make playing in a heatwave more difficult. You couldn't see anything in them. Replays of 1970s matches were pornographic by today's standards. She missed them.

That night in bed she heard a mopoke calling across the cove. She lifted her head off the pillow to hear better. The cat trod lightly up the bedclothes and settled into the crook of her belly, flicking her tail up to rest against Marie's chin. A second bird on this side of the cove began to answer the first, and Marie went to sleep like that, the softness of the cat's tail against her jawline, listening to the vibration of birdsong over water: *mo-poke, mo-poke, mo-poke.*

'He must've been doing his research,' Rhys said to her the next day. 'You must've made quite an impression on him. You and the aristocrats,' she added facetiously. She was shaving Marie's chest, extending the vine.

'I think most of my ancestors were farmers,' Marie replied with fortitude.

'Anyway, aristocrats were seen as totally removed. They may as well have been savages for the eccentric realm they occupied.'

'Such an alien concept, isn't it? Aristocracy?'

'We've got an upper class in this country, we just can't admit it. We're one of the richest nations on earth and still all pretending to be Aussie battlers,' Rhys said.

'We still have a bit of the frontier mentality. Maybe that's why we love four-wheel drives, because we still think we live in the bush.'

'Yeah, battling the elements, struggling for our patch or something. And still trying to plant the flag with this real-estate obsession.' Rhys was speaking in that acerbic tone that Marie had once feared but now recognised as rough, honest humour. 'As long as you work hard, anything goes. Like the dude at Macquarie Bank who makes seventy thousand a day but works eighteen hours, so he like *earns* it.'

'Seventy thousand a *day*?'

'Ya ... Anyway, so says me. I'm a workaholic too.'

Marie had noticed the increase of traffic in the studio. A man Clark's age with a narrow moustache, coming down the stairs when she arrived today. A woman the time before. Mel always at the counter. 'Why don't you cut back? Wasn't that the idea of Mel?'

'The demand is too strong.'

'You're incredibly popular, aren't you.'

'Tattooing per se is getting popular. And I love my work.

I mean, I'm a full-time artist earning my keep. How cool is that? I'm living a life of luxury.' Rhys pushed a button on the boom box and ambient music filtered forth. 'Anyway, so much for aristocrats. They stopped getting tattooed as soon as poor people got into it so it's a working-class art, really. Appropriated by the middle class.'

'Well, here I am, Rhys. Conducting a full-scale takeover.'

'Oh, you conquered long ago, Marie.'

Marie wasn't sure if this was a good thing. If she hadn't changed, as Susan attested, then Mosman had taken over tattooing. If she had, then it was the other way around. Maybe, more realistically, it was a murky place in between.

There was the slap of latex gloves being pulled on. Marie's ears carried this sound to her brain, which translated it into a message to her body: sweat glands release, heart rate increase, saliva cease. 'Lachlan Murdoch has a tattoo.'

'Yairs, our Lachie, on display at the tennis last night. Lachie hates the elites, mind you.'

'You watched it? I never would have picked you for a tennis fan.'

'I'm not really. I just love the spectacle of big sports competitions. I'm agog at what they do to their bodies. I mean, they think we're hard core — what about *them*?'

'It's exciting, isn't it. The way they push themselves to the limit.'

'Watching the AFL is pretty much the only time I feel in tune with my fellow countrymen. I'm even learning the rules.' Rhys grinned.

'I'm more shallow than that. I barrack for looks or personality. It is gladiatorial, after all.'

Marie noticed her usual position on the couch now put her closer to the sun. The light moving across the floor would soon reach her yet the notion of changing seasons and imminent cold was completely at odds with this heat. The indigenous people said that Sydney had six seasons but now it felt like neither six nor four, but one: summer. Rhys began to tattoo.

After a while Marie said, 'Why do you think the men wear such enormous shorts these days? They don't look very practical.'

'That's John Howard's fault. That's when it started. Prudery.'

'But the women's outfits just get skimpier.'

'G-strings make good television.'

'I could never wear g-strings. To my husband's despair.'

'No way. *Crack attack*. Chicks do get to wear better clothes in general though. That's one good thing about being a woman. Can you turn this way a bit?'

Marie obliged, wincing.

'Hurting?'

'It's more my indigestion.'

'I'll make you a mint tea when we have a break.'

Marie gazed at the wall as Rhys moved over the painful, bony part of her chest. Rhys tattooed with her head tilted, close to the working hand, her other hand holding the skin around the area taut. She was wearing glasses today, and a rare sleeveless shirt. Sweat brimmed in the divot of her neck. Behind her, tacked to the wall next to the *KEEP STILL* sign, was a flyer advertising something called *FAST*. The letters were in slanted script zooming over a naked man on a trapeze. He had a cute little cartoon face and from his genitals cartoon fluids spurted. An array of names that sounded like circus performers spilt beneath, and *Nonstop Shows!* Marie wondered about these tantalising flyers and the world they contained. How you could be living right next to something and never see inside it. The cellular structure of society, like a hive, cheek by jowl the wealthy lawyer, the tattoo artist, the housing-commission Aborigine.

'The thing that gets me about this egalitarian thing,' said Rhys, 'is how much it's about sameness. Like we're all earning the same wage and living the same life in the same place in the same skin. Bollocks to that.'

Bollocks, thought Marie. One of Mel's words. The constant seepage between hive cells. And how far away — unreachable — some were from others.

The third hour was upon them and Marie was detaching. Through the windows on warm currents of air came the drilling of cicadas. It was Sunday and the whole suburb was quiet, the singing from the Greek Orthodox mass up the road mingling with Cleveland Street traffic. Travis was with his father. Every time Marie thought of Travis, she thought of Nell. She missed her granddaughter with a visceral ache. She knew Rhys worked on Sundays for the extra money. Marie, on the other hand, saved money as parking in all the surrounding streets was free. Often she had to factor a parking ticket into the cost of a tattoo but on Sundays she drifted into a quieter peace. From Rhys's boom box came washes of sound and strange voices muttering, a slow undulation pulsing beneath. Watching her blood rise from the lines on her chest, Marie considered the almost identical lifeblood of plants and animals. She'd read that a molecule of chlorophyll contained thirty-six atoms of hydrogen, oxygen, nitrogen and carbon arrayed around an atom of magnesium; while a molecule of haemoglobin contained exactly the same except that at the centre was an atom of iron.

She considered herself now, the white skin everywhere broken and coloured. Awareness of difference had come to her, and its corollary, awareness of judgement. She took measures in public because of this, and with the right dress code could maintain her previous position. And that was the thing as well: to recognise what she had taken for granted: a *position*. To recognise its ebb.

At dusk she emerged from the cocoon of Rhys's room. Downstairs was alive with voices. Rob came out to reception. 'Just printing flyers.'

Rhys passed one to Marie. It was for *FAST*. 'It's a night that Stew and some poofs run. It's a boys' striptease.'

'Girls this time too,' said Rob.

'It's fun. You should come, Marie.' Rhys's eyes twinkled with mischief, equal parts invitation and challenge. 'They've found a warehouse, which is like a *miracle*.'

Poofs. The word sounded suddenly cute and fluffy. It had a spring in its step. Marie said uncertainly, 'It sounds like fun.'

'What'd you get, Marie?' Rob asked.

'We extended the vine across my chest and put some passionflowers on it.'

'Oohh, bewdiful.'

Stew came and stood on the other side of Rhys. 'You're gonna need somewhere to show those off.'

Marie tucked the flyer into her bag and left the studio with images of bronzed musclemen striding around a stage in hard hats, waggling their bulging g-strings over her face at a chintzy table in a chintzy bar. A not-altogether-unpleasant fantasy except she didn't want to be like one of those screeching desperadoes on hens' nights. Let alone a post-menopausal tragic. Then again, she couldn't imagine Rhys inside such a chintzy bar either, though Rhys was clearly going to *FAST*.

On the streets of Surry Hills, Marie could never predict who she might see. Tradesmen outside the electrical supplier. The smart lady who tended the vintage shop on Crown Street. Youths in jeans outside the acting school. She didn't cover herself up here and it was a second liberation, after tattooing sessions, to walk these streets with the air on her bare skin. Nobody looked twice. *You're gonna need somewhere to show those off* ... it was the first time anyone apart from the tattooists had responded to her work in celebratory terms.

She had to walk all the way to Marlborough Street today. She passed two skinny men in eccentric clothing, wheeling around a warehouse on their bicycles. 'Hallo!' They waved to her. 'Hallo!' She waved back. Further down the alley an old man was retching into the gutter. There was a couple on the corner, the man chopping the air, saying, 'She has absolutely *no* idea.'

She crossed the road. Walking ahead was a woman in a singlet with silver-grey hair. Closer, Marie saw flowers beneath the white cotton. She hastened her steps, saw a waratah on one shoulder, crimson rich. Beautiful, prolific tattoos floated down the woman's right arm. She was in good shape, and middle-aged by the look of that silver-grey hair. Marie was excited, gaining on her fast.

She came abreast and looked over eagerly and when the woman turned to her, Marie saw a tear tattooed on her cheek. She saw a worn, damaged face, the eyes like closed shutters, wary and hostile. They ran down Marie's arms, then lit up. Marie hurried onwards.

The woman called out in a cigarette voice, 'Nice tatts!'

Marie turned and said politely, 'You too.'

Nice tatts.

'Oh,' said Edwina, as she tucked the cape into Marie's collar.

It wasn't a surprised vowel, more affirmative, as though she was just checking up on something. At the sink adjacent, Colette and her client turned to look. Marie leant her head back into the crevice of the basin and shut her eyes as Edwina's fingers rummaged across her scalp.

Edwina seated Marie in front of the long gilt mirror then went to greet a customer. Marie picked up a copy of *Vogue* and opened it at an article on the history of the bikini. Colette wheeled her customer over and installed her next to Marie. When Marie raised her eyes she found Colette again staring at her nape. She caught her eye and smiled. Colette quickly looked away. Her customer, a dark-haired woman that Marie didn't know, leant towards the mirror to inspect her face from a variety of angles while Colette waited, comb in hand. Marie lowered her eyes again and read the same paragraph over and over. Edwina returned and swiftly and silently cut Marie's hair. Then she mixed up Marie's hair dye.

After a while, Marie said, 'And how are you, Edwina? How's business?'

'Oh, you know, ticking along. Can't complain.'

'And your children?'

'They're very well. Exhausting me as usual.'

'That's children for you.'

Edwina was wearing a peach-coloured v-necked t-shirt. A fine gold chain hung down her tanned chest, with a pendant that disappeared into her cleavage. Marie tried not to dwell on this pendant: she tried to look Edwina in the eye. Edwina raised her eyebrows and smiled with bright, professional solicitude as she poked the dye brush into Marie's roots. Marie looked back at *Vogue*, which was quoting from a 1951 edition: *Our readers dislike the bikini, which has transformed the coastlines into the backstage of music halls and which does not embellish women ...* She read on in the sticky silence.

Ten minutes later Edwina said, 'There we are, Marie. I'll just leave that to set.'

'Thank you.'

Edwina clacked across the room to where a blonde woman with freshly washed hair awaited her. The reception desk, a white oblong table on an oblique angle near the door, was dominated by a large vase of lilies whose scent was tangible even here, beneath her skullcap of hair dye. Marie inhaled gratefully. Outside, sunlight seared the paving.

'It's going to be forty-three degrees tomorrow,' said the blonde as Edwina began to cut her hair.

'Oh, I don't believe it. They always get it wrong.'

'I wouldn't be surprised — it's almost that now.'

'I wake up every day *dreading* the heat, you know.'

'I can't quite believe it, to be honest with you. I mean things *melt* when it's that hot, don't they?'

'I was in the desert once, and it was forty-nine. You can't move. You can't do anything.'

'I think it should be a public holiday,' another customer pitched in.

'You're absolutely right!'

'Edwina, get on the phone to the PM, will you?'

Gales of laughter.

Marie watched them in the mirror, smiling and trying to catch their eyes.

'Why *me*?'

'You're upspoken!'

'I'm not going to do your dirty work for you, Jane!'

'Isn't it *outspoken*?'

'I'm not *dirty*.'

More laughter.

Marie left the salon and walked down Military Road in the direction of the deli. Everybody was moving slowly, seeking the shade. She passed a blonde in tennis clothes, wheeling a pram. Two Queenwood girls came out of Country Road, each holding a mobile phone to her ear. The uniform had changed since Blanche's school days. Hats were compulsory again, for health reasons, not propriety. The girls wore theirs jammed beneath their elbows, and Marie could see the border of foundation around their jaws, the clotted eyelashes, the expertly applied tints in their hair.

They waved at a Mosman High boy in a Jimi Hendrix t-shirt and an eyebrow piercing that looked infected. A middle-aged man in Tommy Hilfiger was walking up behind him. 'Dylan! Hurry up. Your mother's expecting you at home right now.'

The deli was a cavern of relief, its wooden shelves stacked with beautifully labelled jars. Marie filled her basket with olive oil, mustard, marinated fetta, parmesan, a vat of Nice Cream and a litre of organic apple juice. She took her purchases to the counter and handed over her Visa card. 'Is there any wholemeal bread?'

'No, sorry. There's no wheat flour left in Australia because of the drought. Try spelt. The spelt's excellent.'

Marie added a spelt loaf to her shopping.

'Thirty-eight dollars and fifty-five cents, thanks.' The cashier ran Marie's card through the machine, plucked out the docket then bit her lip. 'I'm sorry. It's been refused.'

'But I just used it at the hairdresser's!'

The girl's head tilted with embarrassment. 'Sorry. Maybe you just reached the limit now.'

The limit on that card was fifty thousand dollars. Marie was aware of someone behind her. She reached into her wallet for her Amex and passed it over, ears burning. The girl ran the card through. Her mouth pulled to one side. 'I'm sorry ...'

'That *too*?' Marie's voice sounded harsh in the dim, quiet shop. 'The card gremlin's really got me today, hasn't he? There must be a mistake. Can't you ring them?'

'It's Saturday. There's nothing I can do. You could ring customer service?'

Marie glanced around and saw that the woman behind her was Gina.

'Well, hallo! How are you?'

'Hallo, Marie.' Gina smiled at her and the cashier in turn.

She gave Marie, in a reluctant manner as though fighting a

compulsion, the quick once-over that Marie associated with men, desire, younger days. But there was nothing erotic in this scrutiny. Marie's heart began to accelerate. She opened her wallet for the third time. Inside was a twenty-dollar note. 'I'm so sorry,' she said to the cashier, 'I'll have to go and sort this out with the bank. On a hot day like today! I'll be back.'

Gina's slim, tanned form moved aside. Marie stopped on her way out. 'We must catch up, Gina. I'll be gone soon.'

'Oh yes, the sale! Yes, we must.'

Marie crossed the road and made her way towards the car park. Well, she thought, better to be coiffed than fed. She didn't want to go to the bank in case she couldn't get cash out as well, nor to the supermarket to spend her fifty dollars. She had enough food for a few days. She wanted to run away and disappear. She thought thirstily of the cove. She had parked her car at the end of the car park beneath a peppercorn, but the sun had swung around and was now sheering through her windscreen. She passed a woman shutting the door of a red Toyota with fragile determination, carrying an old-fashioned basket. Pat Hammet. She fell upon her with relief. 'Pat!'

Pat looked up from beneath her old sunhat. 'Hallo, Marie. This is unexpected.'

Marie wasn't sure what this meant. 'You won't believe,' she said breathlessly, 'my credit cards just got knocked back. Both of them, in the deli!'

Pat peered at her. Something flickered across her face. Embarrassment, perhaps pity. She put down her basket and opened her wallet. She had an elderly tremble in her hands, noded with arthritis. She drew out a one-hundred-dollar note.

Marie was stricken. 'No, Pat. Please. It's just a mistake. In this weather!'

'It's alright. I understand.'

'Thank you, really. It's just a terrible inconvenience.'

Pat tilted her head to one side. 'Now what's this I hear about you and tattoos?'

'Pardon?'

'I thought you'd moved out of Mosman. You even mentioned Redfern or something. And then I heard that you were covered in tattoos!' She checked Marie with the frank appraisal of a schoolmistress checking a pupil's uniform. It seemed to Marie, as a woman drew up in a silver Mercedes, that Pat was speaking extremely loudly. Booming. Like a deaf woman.

'The auction is Saturday week but I'm getting a two-month settlement so you'll still see me,' Marie said. 'You should come over before the house goes.'

'Who are the agents?'

'Hugh, my son-in-law. Coustas and Stevens.'

'Right.' Pat raised her eyebrows. 'And are you interviewing your buyers?'

'God, no. I escape when they come. You met all of yours, didn't you.'

'Oh yes. Gave them a thorough grilling. Fat lot of good that did me. That Celia was born in Mosman, you know.' Pat put on a mincing voice: 'She told me, *Oh, it's a lovely house, we won't change a thing, we love the bush.* I can't bear to go back there, Marie. I can't even look at what they've done.'

Marie decided not to tell Pat about the swimming pool.

'But you,' Pat prompted.

'I'm fine about it, Pat. I've let go.'

'I couldn't believe my ears. Tattooed! Then I thought, Well, Marie's an original woman. But she's not *stupid.*' Pat stood back and let this compliment sink in. The Mercedes woman smiled as she walked past with her lime green polyurethane eco shopping bags. Marie felt as though she were falling off a cliff. She could see every detail of the rock face, feel every flicker of wind. The humming of cicadas morphed into a relentless pulse.

'My car's going to be a furnace. I have to go.'

Eyes like claws. Marie walked to the end of the car park and unlocked her car. The seat branded her thighs. In the rear-view mirror she saw her hairdo had collapsed in the heat. On arrival home she stripped off her clothes, put on a costume, slung a towel over her shoulder and went down to the cove. It was high tide with jade depths for a good ten metres. Marie breast-stroked out with her head above the water, cheeks burning. She swam over the mysterious low-lying kelp into cooler water. Then she lifted her arms and dove under for the full relief on face and scalp. Her foot spasmed with cramp and she realised the tension that had gripped her for the past two hours was still in her body; but even in this state, raging and alone, her entire being surged with love for this place. She floated for a long time facing the sky, every cell in her body singing to the water and trees.

She walked back to her house uncovered. In the Hendersons' kitchen window, Rupert's glowering face appeared. She stripped and showered. It was a new person in the mirrors of her ensuite. Someone vibrant, expressive and particular. Someone radiating humour and life. She walked around her bedroom naked, exulting in her shouting, shrinking, wrinkling body. Fuck you, she thought. Fuck. You.

Ten kilometres inland, fifteen minutes' drive from Bondi, the mercury rose. Clark could feel his arms burning as he drove and he took his right hand off the wheel away from the sun. The sunspots he'd had burnt off his forehead last year were itching again. It wasn't a day to be out in, especially not in a car with dodgy air-conditioning. The streets shimmered and were eerily empty as though a bomb had been dropped. It was inhuman. But he had arranged to meet Sylvia and, having Nell all weekend, this was the only time he would get to see his lover. And Nell had been miserable in the heat this morning: an air-conditioned building would be better than the beach where they would only roast more. Yesterday the sand had actually burnt his feet.

'Is Gran coming?'

'No, she can't.'

'Why not?'

'She's sick.'

'What's wrong with her?'

'Nothing serious. She's just got a cold. We can ring her when we get home if you like.' He added, 'We're going to meet a friend of mine instead.'

'Who?'

'She's called Sylvia.'

Nell made a face and hunched her head into her shoulders. 'Daddy, I'm *hot*.'

'I know, Nellie. It's *for-ty-five-de-grees* out there, and we're going as fast as we can to a big air-conditioned building where you'll see dinosaurs and snakes.'

Nell made a whimpering sound.

'You're being *such* a good girl. We're nearly there.'

He found a park in Liverpool Street, locked the car and took his daughter's hand. They walked around the corner past the old police headquarters, hugging the thin strip of shade, Nell jerking his arm. He was excited about introducing his lover to his child: a circle was being joined.

In the deep cool mouth of the museum foyer, they stood looking up at a huge suspended skeleton. The arrangement had been to meet Sylvia here or, if she hadn't arrived, in the reptile gallery. But in she came, right on time, and walked over to where Clark stood with Nell beneath the vast mobile of bones. Sylvia's face was livid, her shirt clung to her back and her hair hung limp. She had told Clark the last time they met that she had been a state swimmer and he now thought of water every time he thought of her body, her long limbs streaming past in a wake. He shivered with the sensation of his sweat cooling, turning his shirt cold and wet against his back.

'You believe this weather?' Sylvia said.

'Pretty freaky.'

Clark introduced Sylvia to his daughter. Nell looked her up and down, then pointed to the skeleton and announced, 'I've got dinosaurs.'

'Have you?'

'Yep. Tyrannosaurus.'

'This is a whale skeleton,' said Sylvia, bending over. 'So you might see one of these alive one day. Can you imagine?'

Nell stared at Sylvia sceptically, in case there was a joke in the air. She looked at the skeleton, then at Sylvia again and twitched her mouth as though resisting a smile. Clark took this as a good sign.

They moved off through the rooms. The place seemed more vibrant than Clark had remembered. After several years working down the road, he found the Australian Museum had crumpled into a corner of his mind like a relative in her dotage whose sour, faded clothes belied her rich past. He was an irrevocable humanist and had always preferred the smaller sociological museums to this edifice of nature. But today it was as though he had caught the old woman by surprise and all her secret cabinets were open, her treasures revealed.

He followed Nell and Sylvia down the ramp. He was surprised by the position of the mole on Sylvia's clavicle, which only his fingers had previously seen. He had thought it was lower, near the armpit. Nell had taken Sylvia's hand and was peppering her with questions, each of which Sylvia answered with perfect lozenges of information.

She glanced back at Clark. 'I used to want to be a marine biologist, you know.'

'Really? And why didn't you?'

'I was crap at science. It was a romantic idea, really. By the end of high school I realised my desire was more about the ocean and swimming and collecting things on the beach than serious scientific study.' She made a little face. 'David Attenborough was my pin-up boy.'

Nell said, 'I wanna go and look at the snakes.'

'That's exactly where we're going, darling.'

'I'm not scared of snakes.'

'What about you?' Sylvia asked him.

'I know you're not … What?'

'What did you want to do? Did you always want to be a historian?'

'I'm not a real historian. More an amateur riding on the coat-tails of Cultural Studies. First I wanted to be a film-maker, until I was at uni and realised how much film depended on money. I think in retrospect it was just about looking. Watching. That's why I've chosen this image-based concept for my thesis. I'm from the television generation.' He grinned. 'I'm a natural perv.'

Sylvia touched his nose with the tip of her finger. His heart pounded. 'You're sunburnt,' she said.

Nell laughed and prodded Sylvia. 'We went to the beach yesterday.'

'We went boogie-boarding, didn't we, Nell?'

Nell launched into a garbled description of their day at the beach, and Sylvia listened attentively. This was their first proper daylight meeting, and Clark was trying to look at all of her without either her or Nell noticing. Sylvia was up till now a series of angles, like a cubist painting. The prism of cheekbone beside him at the seminar, pale blue forehead in the car by Blackwattle Bay. The shallow yet well-defined cleavage he had burrowed into that night and again a week later, in his car at the end of Victoria Street, the first time they fucked.

Nell stopped before one of the cabinets. Clark pressed a button and the light hit Nell's and Sylvia's faces. Inside the cabinet were stick insects, indistinguishable from the sticks on which they were posed. Sylvia pointed them out to Nell, sent Clark a look, and he saw it again, the fragile moue, an entreaty of some sort, or a gift. A tender, flushed expression, like the inside of a shell. He saw also that her eyes were green, and scarred with amber flecks like shrapnel.

They followed Nell, turning on the cabinet lights as they went, talking quietly.

'Franco's flight gets in about nine.'

'Well, we're going to have an early pizza back in Bondi. Why don't you come?'

'No, no. She's going home tonight, isn't she?'

'Swim this heat off. A dusk swim. Beautiful.'

'You guys need to have your last evening together.'

'Look at her,' Clark whispered. 'She *loves* you. *Come.* Please.'

Sylvia regarded him solemnly, saying nothing.

They were passing through the children's activity room. Clark was hoping his daughter would find something to hold her attention for a while so he could sit down with Sylvia and just be. But Nell was in a typically purposeful, garrulous mood, aware of her role as leader of the day's expedition. She fell onto a framed

butterfly and clutched at the glass. 'Oh, darling, darling, *darling.*'
It was a magnificent, bright purple specimen, large as Nell's hand,
and Clark found himself thinking how well it lent itself to design,
how decorative and two-dimensional a creature it was, perfect for
a tattoo for example, unlike, say, a tiger or a horse. He thought all
of this naturally, without panic or the smallest note of resentment
towards his mother, just a matter-of-fact aesthetic appraisal that
washed calmly through him. He followed Nell out of the room.

Sylvia was right behind him. Her hand brushed his arse. 'Okay. I
will.' Then, as though released from a bond, she wandered around
the next room on her own.

In the snake gallery, the exhibits looked old and neglected. The
dowager retreating into her frowsy shawl. An Asian man in brown
clothes peered into the taipan cabinet. His wife sat on one of the
benches reading a sheaf of information through glasses with pale
pink frames.

'DNA,' Clark whispered to Sylvia.

'What?'

'I look at these old stuffed snakes, and wonder, if they go extinct,
how on earth they could bring one back to life by taking DNA from
those mouldy old scales. That's what they're claiming they'll try
and do with the thylacine.'

'Apparently our ancestry going back millennia can be read in
our DNA. And the length of one person's DNA goes to the moon
and back something like eight times.'

'What, the DNA they find in a drop of saliva?'

'I don't know actually …'

'My brother told me that Australia has the fastest rate of species
extinction in the world.'

'Gold medals to us.'

'Which snake can kill you, Dad?' Nell asked.

'One taipan contains enough poison to kill a thousand men.
That's what it says here.'

Clark felt as though he were in an ancient tomb, dazzling,
decrepit, sombre as time. All this death but it didn't touch him.
Outside, the sun was killing half the city's plants; the rivers were

drying up; the whole world was dying. His beloved childhood house was about to be sold, but Clark was unfazed. The taipan could have burst from its cabinet and sunk its fangs into the Asian tourist, and Clark would have remained calm, all-powerful.

Sylvia went to find the toilet and Nell marched out of the gallery through a different door. They found themselves at Kids' Island, a fenced-in playground jammed with luridly coloured apparatus, toys and dress-ups. Every single parent and child that had come to the museum had ended up in here. The noise was deafening, an unbroken communal screech, like feeding lorikeets. Clark unlatched the gate and entered with Nell. He stood against the wall near a woman in a dark green dress with fatty shoulders. She was saying enthusiastically, 'Yes, yes, it's a very safe environment, it's very cut off,' to somebody that Clark couldn't see. And he watched Nell playing on the slippery dip, happy in the cacophony like a man in a cloud of confetti.

Nell shot out of the slippery dip's mouth and tramped over. 'Where's Sylvia?'

'I don't know. Do you want me to go and find her?'

'Yeh.'

He turned to the dark green dress. 'Would you mind watching my daughter for a minute? My partner seems to have gone missing.'

She looked at him suspiciously. 'I'll only be here another ten minutes.'

'That's fine. Thanks.'

Nell dived into the tunnel below the slippery dip. A boy was waving a seagull glove around. 'I'm gonna peck you!' he declared.

Nell found a snake and rammed it on her hand. She poked it in the boy's face. 'Well, I'm gonna shoot you with venom! In the *eye.*'

Clark left the playground, latching the gate behind him. *My partner.* He contemplated the possibility that he wouldn't see Sylvia again and began to panic. He hadn't seen her for about fifteen minutes. How could she have got lost? The toilets were right here. But maybe she went into different ones. And maybe she had gone, freaked out. He was more and more conscious of how illicit her time with him was. He wandered around in circles in front of the toilets then the door opened and Sylvia was standing before him, smiling. They stood in the alcove talking quietly.

'Where's Nell?'

'Playing. Where were you?'

'Here.'

'I got really worried. Nell was asking after you.'

'How sweet.'

Clark glanced around, stepped forward and put his arms around her. 'She sent me to find you,' he whispered into Sylvia's hair, inhaling her smell. Her eyelashes flicked against his forehead like little insects. She took his head in her hands and began to kiss him. He was like a teenager with her, instantly hard. 'Is there anyone in there?' He nodded to the toilet door.

'No.'

Sylvia led him in. Clark recalled a gay party he had gone to years earlier with Leon. The first time he had taken ecstasy and the only time he had gone out with his brother. He had never experienced anything like it. The toilets were a hive of activity, a whole world unto themselves. Prowling predatory men outside the men's, stink of piss, treacherously wet floors, out-of-it people. How afraid he had been, and fascinated. He had fled the men's then followed a couple of guys with a reassuringly non-sexual air into the women's. Every cubicle had two or more people in it; another party was going on in here, as unremittingly salacious as the men's, yet light-hearted. He waited for ages then was finally in a cubicle, surrounded by sounds of snorting, giggling, groaning, shuffling. The toilet was blocked but he didn't care because adjacent he could hear two women having sex. He lifted the seat and unzipped but was so distracted by the sound of them that he couldn't piss.

Sylvia took him up the end to the disabled cubicle and the moment they had latched the door, somebody entered.

'Phew!' Clark whispered.

Sylvia grabbed his belt and pulled him over to the wall, whispering insinuatingly, 'What about your daughter?'

'She's fine.'

'Are you *sure?*'

He pressed up against her. Serenely he watched a clip of the dark green dress taking his daughter by the hand and leading her outside to where a male accomplice awaited. *Take her.* The next clip showed Sylvia kissing a woman, their breasts pressed together. There was the sound of a toilet flushing, running water. He sucked the laughter out of Sylvia's tongue. He imagined her DNA coursing down his digestive tract and a million little Sylvias hatching in his gullet. He undid their zippers and pushed between her thighs and she slid her hands down the back of his jeans, clutching his arse, kissing him deeply.

Forty-six degrees. Each day hotter than the one before, the heat moving stealthily into every corner of the house. Going into the pantry, days after the cool change, and finding pockets of hot air trapped like bad memories on the top shelf. No refuge, no respite. Marie lived in the rumpus room with the television. She watched the evening news. *I love God,* said the newly elected Christian independent, *and I love my family.* The dams had dropped to thirty percent. Skeletons of livestock littered dry watercourses. In her muggy upstairs room, Marie stretched out naked, her body melting against every surface it touched.

Half her herb garden died in the heatwave. On the hottest day, the lavender bushes were scorched. She hadn't gone outside till six-thirty and was covered knees to head, still her calves burnt. Even standing on the deck in the shade the very hair on her arms had seemed to singe. What visitation was this, so close to the auction? None of the buyers showed much interest in the garden but this blitzed expanse would surely shear thousands off the price. Like a storm, the event approached her with its own momentum.

She spent the late hours of the day pruning, then washed off the dust with a swim. The lawns of the reserve crunched beneath her feet like toast. The news said the heatwave death toll was three, all elderly people in the outer suburbs. But the death toll of plants must have been in the millions.

David was wearing a navy jacket and the same mild, spicy cologne. He had a tan and his hair was clippered so short that his bald patch was imperceptible. He looked younger and more masculine. 'What a lovely balmy Sydney night,' he said as they walked into the building. 'And you look ravishing.'

'Thank you.' Marie got into the lift with the heat of his eyes upon her. They rode up to Level 41.

The restaurant wasn't how she remembered it. Surprisingly, it resembled a boardroom. Plain, functional, almost austere. A young woman in black was sitting on one of the couches, drinking a mini-bottle of Moët through a straw. But the room was irrelevant. What mattered was the panorama of night harbour wrapped around the steel and glass cylinder like a black scarf shot with diamonds. They walked to a window table and Marie handed her shawl to the waiter with a thin moustache. David ordered champagne and antipasto. It arrived almost immediately.

'I'd like to propose a toast for the sale.' David lifted his glass. 'Everything ready for the big day?'

'Yes. My son-in-law is handling it. They're auctioning on site, and I'll be on a bushwalk.'

'In the lap of the gods, hey? You aren't in the least bit curious?'

'Morbidly. That's why I'm keeping away.'

'And where are you going to buy?'

'I've decided to cross the bridge. I'm not sure where to exactly.'

'Good idea. The eastern suburbs is just about the only place that's going to survive this downturn.'

'You don't think things will get better?'

'Oh, sure. It's only a matter of time.'

He was pretending not to look at her breasts. She sat with her shoulders back, looking straight at him, enjoying his tortured avidity. The champagne had immediately penetrated the walls of her stomach and was fizzing along her arteries straight to her head. She ate some prosciutto and rockmelon. The waiter reappeared, elegant in his charcoal jacket with his vintage moustache and bottle opener angled rakishly into the wide pocket of his apron. His attentive hovering was directed towards Marie, even as he stood beside David.

'I think I'll have the spatchcock. Marie?'

'I'll have the skate.'

'Excellent choice, madam.'

'And a bottle of the Wirra Wirra.' David slid his glasses to the end of his nose and looked up. 'It is the 2004, isn't it?'

'Yes, sir.'

'Good.'

'I think things will only get worse,' Marie said, when the waiter had gone. 'We're running out of oil. The war has sucked the American economy dry. We're addicted to fossil fuels. The evidence of climate change is irrefutable and we're not doing much about it.'

'Well, the Chinese dragon is certainly going to torch us. And when it comes to the environment, they make us look like *saints*.'

'And we're mortgaged and indebted to the eyeballs. Just like the Americans.'

'I'm not. I think it's irresponsible.' David rested on his elbows and contemplated Marie over his fingertips. 'Did you know that the Dutch economy is one of the strongest in the world because of individual savings? The stingy Dutch! Saviours of the national economy.'

'Well, *I'm* indebted to my eyeballs.' It occurred to Marie that it might be her turn to pay tonight, which would set her up for another public shaming. Then again, it was David who had invited her. 'But I'll be bailed out on Saturday.'

'Be careful.' David wagged his finger.

'What about your business? How will you survive?'

'I really don't care. I'm not a materialistic person, Marie. I have my little flat and a house down the coast. I don't own many shares. I have my *objets d'art*, but I'm not fanatically attached to them as such. They all pass through my hands at one stage or another. I'm a highly adaptable, frugal person. I might even retire to New Zealand. Buy a little farm. You didn't know I was a good bushman, did you?'

'No.'

'I'll have to show you some time.'

'What about twenty years from now? What do you think our grandchildren will have to contend with?'

'I'm not worried about my Rosie. She's a genius. She's going to save the world.'

They leant back for the arrival of their perfectly manicured meals. The waiter filled their wineglasses then settled the bottle into its bucket with a snug, wet crunching. A boat strung with lights in the shape of a dragon glided beneath the harbour bridge. David was watching her with a cheeky, slightly lascivious grin. 'So,' he said, 'Lady Randolph Churchill. *Show me.*'

Feeling slightly uncomfortable, Marie unbuttoned her cuff, revealing the dark green end of a vine on her wrist. Further back, on her forearm, bloomed a passionflower.

David reared away and glanced around the room. 'How far up does it go?'

'All the way.'

'Show me later, show me later,' he said, waving his hand. He lowered his voice and pincered his wrist. 'I thought it was just a small thing here ...'

Hopelessness began to fill Marie like cement. She set her face and picked up her glass. 'Tell me about your overseas trip, David. Where did you go?'

'I wasn't overseas. I was in the desert.'

'In this heat?'

'Yes. Mad dogs and Englishmen and overworked dealers. It couldn't be helped.' David ate with his head down, not looking at her, carefully placing a portion of each vegetable onto the meat on his fork before placing the combination into his mouth.

'Whereabouts?'

'Balgo. Off the Tanami Track. An obscure place that hardly anyone's heard of.' He put down his cutlery. Again that look of dread and excitement crossed his features. 'All the way to the top?'

'Yes. Was it a buying trip?'

'I don't call them *buying trips* per se. There's more to it than that.' His eyes roamed the room, bright, conspiratorial, then came back to rest on Marie's breasts. 'And here? It is, isn't it. My god.'

Marie wanted to do up all her buttons. 'It must be beautiful out there,' she said in a clipped voice.

David looked at her cagily. 'Actually, it's a mess. Alcoholism, petrol sniffing, domestic violence. The communities are completely dysfunctional. It may as well be overseas. It is another world. A third world.'

He was trying to impress her with his brush with misery. She was supposed to act girlish and naïve while he dealt with life's harsh realities. Next thing she knew, she'd be keeping his dinner warm. At least he could still take her out and not have her make a scene. Marie sawed at her skate, hating her politeness as much as his rudeness. Deep in her blood, deeper than tattoos, the program to obey. She tried to scoop up the celeriac purée but most of it drooled through the prongs of her fork. Her posture was gradually closing in on itself, shoulders drawing towards one another protectively. At the table adjacent was a woman with pale pink lips outlined in maroon, giving her mouth a pushed-forward look. Her legs were angled in this direction, through the split in her skirt. David's eyes flicked over, took them in, flicked back onto Marie's breasts, then her face. A new expression was growing on his, like a weed sprung after a day's rain. He continued in a tone that was something between pleading and threat, 'There is nothing beautiful about women walking around with black eyes and children stoned out of their minds at midday, and raped babies.'

'No, there isn't.'

'Did you know that petrol sniffing now costs our health and justice systems almost eighty million dollars a year?'

A hot prickle ran over Marie's skin. Shame bloomed deep inside her. She looked around at this five-star corporate diner, remembering it was a client of Ross's who had brought them here in thanks for a successful campaign. They had sat in a large private room. Glaxo Wellcome, someone like that. A monumental Western Desert diptych stretched across the wall. There was a table of half-a-dozen or so men, two or three women. She would usually end up talking about gardening at these lunches, if she talked at all. The private room was still there, the door to it opened by a passing waiter, showing it to be empty tonight. At the table behind, another couple had just been seated. Marie noticed that almost every table in the restaurant was for two — everywhere were sleek couples in suits and pearls; at night it was clearly a place for romancing. A fog of disappointment had descended over her and David's table. She couldn't tell if she disgusted or attracted him. He was acting as if she did both. I'm going to get through this dinner, she thought with resolve. I'm going to eat and drink my fill, and hold my own. She remembered the curve of his arm when they danced at the Joneses'. The piercing eyes and amused mouth — mischievous, yes. And opportunistic. Predatory even. And she had wanted to be taken by him. So this was what it felt like. David flicked at his sleeve. There was something of the wounded child in his expression as well; she fought off the instinct to comfort. 'I meant the *place*, David. The art. I thought you would have been looking at art.'

'I bought some prints. When they're not drunk, some of them are very fine printmakers.' He lifted the wineglass to his pursed lips.

'Well, that's saying something. I was a bit of a drunk not so long ago but I couldn't print to save my life, drunk or sober.'

David sank his head between his shoulders and glared out from the trenches at her. 'I did Anthropology at university, you know, Marie. And I've travelled to almost every country on this planet, not to mention Aboriginal communities around Australia, and I refuse to buy this romance about indigenous cultures.'

'I'm not selling romance, David. I'm not even giving it away.'

A couple walked past, the man and David exchanging brief nods.

'That was the head of the Commonwealth Bank,' David said when the man was out of earshot. 'God, if only he knew!' He smiled owlishly at Marie. 'You are a feisty one, aren't you?'

'Am I?'

'Oh, don't get me wrong. I *like* it!'

The waiter glided in to pour the last of the wine. Again, he gave Marie that look. It was more than respect — it was warmer, filial but comradely. Marie wished she was eating dinner in the kitchen tonight. David's eyes were like wet tissues on her breasts. She hunched tighter, pressed her face to the view. Below her, like the languid leg of a woman, the long dark shape of Bradleys Head stretched across the shining water. If she leant out further she could see a cluster of lights around the foreshore of her house and garden. How small and irrelevant it seemed from up here.

'You wouldn't know that half the city had burnt, would you? Looking at it from up here.'

'I had to go to Windsor today. You should have seen it. A lunar landscape, completely bleached.'

'I feel like we're living on the edge of an apocalypse.'

David laughed as though she were being silly. 'The councils have already started replanting. How was your fish?'

'Delicious. Aren't most of the market gardens that supply Sydney out at Windsor?'

'Oh yes, food prices will be going up. No doubt about it.' David pushed away his half-finished meal. He sat back with his napkin still tucked into his collar, creating a warped dickie.

The waiter came to clear. 'Dessert, madam?'

'I'll have a look at the menu.'

'Sir?'

'No, thank you.'

'None for me either, then.'

'Go ahead, Marie, go ahead!'

When the waiter had left, David lowered his voice and said, 'So, all over your arms now, are they? And where else did you say?'

Marie cringed and kept her eyes on the menu. 'It's hard to explain.'

'I saw a bloke once who'd had himself tattooed all over, even his face. They were all blurred, ooh it was dreadful. He might as well have been *black*.'

Marie rose. 'I won't have dessert, thank you. I'm going to the bathroom.'

She was blooming, a dark flower, hot with colour. She walked past the diners feeling strange and raw and defiant, and into the palatial bathroom of granite and marble. The entire wall was a panorama of the Finger Wharf and South Head. She pressed her face to the glass. She could make out the swoop of New South

Head Road, the restaurants of Rose Bay, large white houses and square apartment blocks. The whole headland sparkling and gay as a party. All that gravy. All that stew.

She washed her hands and touched up her lipstick. David was signing a credit card docket when she returned. She collected her shawl and waited for him by the lifts. He stepped in after her, pressed the button and stood against the mirrored wall. The lift began its plunge.

Then David's finger was running along her collar, his voice was in her ear, 'Oh, I can't wait to get you home and get a better look at you.'

Marie spun and slapped him across the face. David stood back with vacant eyes, hand on his cheek. The lift bumped to the ground and Marie walked out through the foyer. Behind her, David began to laugh. It came to her then that their waiter had been the man with the moustache she had seen at Rhys and Rob's studio. She kept walking, the sound of David's laughter ringing in her ears.

For three days before the auction, storms lashed Sydney. Seven-metre waves from cyclones up north pounded the coastline. Even Mosman beaches were heaving, the sand at Sirius Cove thrown up across the reserve, and people surfing in the harbour. Marie loved it. She thought she should stay near the water in her move, close as possible to this wild weather.

Clark and Nell arrived at the house at eight o'clock. Marie was in the kitchen taking a pot of coffee off the stove. Fatima was already here, cleaning the upstairs bathroom. From the patio where he came out with his mother to drink coffee, Clark admired Fatima's gleaming hair and full high breasts as she flung open the window above the kitchen. She sent them a brief wave then continued along the sill with her cloth. The sleeves of her starched pale pink shirt were turned up over pale pink rubber gloves. A gold chain slooped out of her cleavage and glinted in the sun.

'She's so elegant,' said Clark, aware he was looking at Fatima for the first time without imagining fucking her. Sylvia had obliterated every other woman, even the most tenuous fantasy, from his mind.

'Isn't she,' said Marie. 'She brings her own gloves you know. It's all part of the look.'

They went into the house. All the rooms gleamed, and when Blanche and Hugh arrived and Leon rang at the same time, Clark felt cheerful. It was the fact of family assembly as though there were a celebration, the momentousness of the occasion giving him a feeling of tragic importance. It was his mother and daughter playing together for the first time since before Christmas, and everything being okay. It was also his tryst with Sylvia the night before, the giddiness of love, himself as a giver and receiver of pleasure: occupying his body more fully than at any other time. He went out to the deck to gaze at the harbour glittering in the morning sun, and his eyes prickled with tears.

'Big hug, Mum,' said Leon on the phone to his mother. 'You must be nervous. What time is the auction?'

'Eleven. I won't be here. Clark, Nell and I are going to walk to Clifton Gardens.'

'That's a fair way.'

'Not as far as Obelisk.'

Leon laughed, embarrassed. 'The heatwave get the garden?'

'It's completely scorched.'

'Bummer.'

'They wouldn't notice it anyway.' Marie was enjoying the cavalier person she had woken as today. She had barely slept and felt sharp and reckless, cut off somehow, unattached to anyone or anything. Blanche came out of the kitchen.

'Where's Mopoke?' she mouthed.

'Just a minute, Leon. Upstairs I think. I'll put you on to Blanche.'

But she did not feel immune to the soft, warm cat in the patch of sun on her bedroom floor. She picked up Mopoke and put her on a jumper on a chair then dragged the chair into a sunny corner, knelt and buried her face in the cat's fur, not wanting to go downstairs. Somebody entered the bedroom. She could feel them standing behind her. It was Nell. 'Come here, darling.'

Nell walked over and fitted herself into the crook of Marie's arm. She stroked the cat with both hands. 'What about Mopoke? Will she stay here?'

'No, she'll come with me.' But Mopoke might not survive the move. Marie was shocked by this possibility, and that she hadn't even thought of it till now.

'I miss the house,' Leon said to Blanche. 'I've been dreaming about it.'

'Really? What?'

'Weird stuff. Like I was coming out of my bedroom — here that is — and I kind of fell through the door of my housemate's bedroom, down into this whole other house which turned out to be ours. It was supposed to be auction day but it was total chaos. There was a party in the rumpus room. There were cupcakes with like, um, tattoo designs on them. Butterflies … It was all kind of '80s, like an advertising party. I was trying to plant a callistemon in the living room, kind of into the Persian carpet and Dad went off at me.' Leon laughed quietly. 'Mum was bonking Jonesy …'

'Ri-i-i-ght.'

'That was a bit weird.'

'What was I doing?'

'I don't know. I can't remember.'

'I got your email petition. About Africa.'

'Oh yeah.'

'Pretty full-on thing to get on a Friday afternoon after a long week and today to look forward to, Leon.'

'Well, it is full-on. They're raping babies because they think it'll immunise them from AIDS. It's a very real problem.'

Blanche didn't think it was the time to ask him about her loan, nor could she wipe it from her mind. 'What difference do you think my signature can make?'

'So we just sit back and do nothing?'

Blanche looked at Hugh on the couch with the Saturday papers. He emanated solid calm. He sat with his elbows on his knees, scanning the main section with a frown. He was wearing the golden mallet tiepin Blanche had given him when he got his auctioneer's licence. He flicked his left arm forward to glance at his watch, then continued reading. She could see Clark on the deck smoking a cigarette. When did Clark start smoking again? She thought he was on a fitness campaign; he had been looking much healthier lately. She felt a bit sorry for him in that tiny flat, back at uni, living on a pittance. It seemed such a thin life. His thesis made no sense to her: she thought of Beth and her impenetrable writing on Arte Povera. Postgrad scholarships to Blanche seemed like three years' subsistence wages to wallow in solipsism. Entire art degrees were done in theory alone now. What was that line about people who talked the most about sex being the ones who had it the least? She listened to Leon with half an ear. Why had her brothers turned out like this? So untogether in so many ways. They'd been given everything. Hugh, on the other hand, had grown up in the Shire. Meat and three veg, public school, father sold lawnmowers. Hugh's family gave her things like pharmacy moisturiser for Christmas, which moved Blanche for the gesture; her brothers gave her nothing. Yet Blanche could hate going to Hugh's family gatherings for the same reason she loved them: the easy-going camaraderie that masked a profound indifference about each other and the world in general. The only thing they didn't seem indifferent about was the fact that Hugh and she still had no children. She longed for that indifference: anything but this constant striving, and constant dissatisfaction.

'I know what you were doing now.' Leon was jubilant.

'What?'

'You were in the garden. You'd given birth to a cat.'

'Great, Leon.'

'It was actually quite gorgeous. You were in a white dress. It was really kind of … tender. Y'know?'

'You hate cats! And I've never worn a white dress in my life.'

'It's a *dream*, Blanche.'

'Do you want to speak to Clark? I'll hand you to Clark.'

'Didn't you wear a white wedding dress?'

Blanche walked out to the deck and handed the phone to Clark. 'It's Leon.'

Back inside, Hugh ruffled the paper and read out loud to

Blanche: *'Mosman in a recent poll topped the list of Australia's best-paid areas with an average wage of $93,656 for both full- and part-time workers, more than double the New South Wales average of $41,407. When non-wage income was added it was $99,609.'*

'Very exact figures,' Blanche remarked. 'But they can't have calculated properly if the non-wage earnings are only around the six-thousand-dollar mark. Even we earn loads more than that. Although they'd be expert tax evaders around here, wouldn't they.'

'That's cynical.'

'How else d'you think the woman from James Hardie avoided paying the asbestos victims?'

Blanche was hurting. Discussing the opening bid on the way here with Hugh, the reality had hit. Nobody could afford these prices anymore except the unbelievably rich. She was locked out. She would be forty in a few years, she was successful and hard-working, yet she still couldn't afford to live in the area she had grown up in. Her parents had bought this house when they were so young: it was so much easier for their generation. She seethed with resentment.

'It was the company, not her. You sound like your brothers, pooky. We'll be fine today is all I'm saying. Totally fine.'

At nine-thirty Stavros arrived, and Hugh cleared up the newspapers then went into the kitchen to confer with his colleague. Marie had locked her wardrobe and placed scarves over the contents of her drawers. Fatima was crossing the open plan as Marie reached the bottom of the stairs. Fatima smiled and went into the kitchen to get her cheque from Hugh. Stavros was spreading the registration papers across the table.

'You put out the sandwich board?' Hugh asked him.

'Yep. And a couple of signs up the street.'

'We have to watch the guy next door. He's touchy. We can't put anything outside his property.'

'The tall bloke?'

'Got a couple of little dogs.'

Stav, short and neat with slicked-back hair, was glancing in every direction, his eyes alive with excitement. 'He's loving it! He's at his gate asking me a million questions. He'll probably come.'

Marie came into the kitchen. 'In that case it's about time we left.' She shook Stav's hand and went into the laundry for an old water bottle and filled it with water from the filter.

Blanche followed her. 'The house looks great, Mum. You've done a great job.'

'How do you think we'll go?'

'Good. Hugh has seven registered. He's optimistic.'

Marie became aware of the smell of her own perfume in the enclosed space. She had also put on lipstick and dangly earrings, all for a mere bushwalk. It was her on sale here today as well, no matter how far away she was, but she wanted to leave the house before anyone arrived. Blanche was the perfect overseer in her crystal necklace. 'You look nice. That's a nice necklace.'

'Thanks. How long do you think you'll be out for?'

'As long as it takes. We want to walk all the way to the Navy café.'

'And Mo? Where is she?'

'Upstairs on the chair in my bedroom. Will you look after her?'

'I'll make sure she's not disturbed, don't worry.'

'Pat Hammet told me a story about this house when we moved in. Burrawong, I mean, the house that was here before. It was built in 1927, a few months after the Crash. It took two years. The owner was an architect and his wife was an interior designer and he'd built entire suburbs of Melbourne.'

'They were developers?'

'Burrawong was built as a luxury house for them and their daughter. And all through the '30s when the Great Depression was on, Pat said the family was off on cruises, touring around Europe, giving parties when they were home.'

'Were they here long? Why did they sell?' Blanche asked.

'I don't think they sold till after the war. Because, I think, they wanted to go back to Melbourne.'

Blanche looked at her mother, unsure why she was telling this story. She seemed weary, aloof, calm and guarded. Her hair had arranged itself in a lucky sweep around to one side. It was a sort of beauty, Blanche realised. A soiled, private beauty as though she had woken from a long night of illicit love-making. She suddenly saw her mother's future as an open space and fervently wished for a beneficent population to fill it. 'It's exciting, Mum. It's your new life!'

'They survived the Crash,' Marie said, oblivious. 'Unlike my grandfather. Do you think it's because they were property developers? I don't think I'll survive.'

'You'll be fine.' Blanche glanced down the passage at the men in the kitchen. 'You'll have enough to pay your debts, buy a decent place and even make investments. It's not the '20s, Mum. We're not going to have another crash. Australia's got one of the strongest economies in the world.'

There was a knock at the front door.

'Mum,' said Blanche, 'I need a definite decision. Do we go below the reserve?'

'Yes.'

'Are you *sure*? No limit?'

'No. Sell. Sell no matter what. I'm taking my mobile. Ring me when it's over. Where's Clark?'

'In the garden with Nell. I think they're waiting for you.' Blanche held up her hands with fingers crossed. 'Fingers crossed, Mum.'

They hugged, then Marie walked down the side path and through the garden, onto the bushtrack with Clark and Nell.

The first people through the door were a couple in their forties. A tall athletic man, probably Lebanese, and his suntanned wife with a leathery neck and chunky gold earrings. The woman registered and the man picked up the floor plans. They spoke to Hugh and Stav on the deck then went down to the garden.

Twenty minutes later, Blanche was at Hugh's elbow. 'Nobody's coming.'

'Be patient, pooky.'

She went down to the garden but the couple had disappeared. She went into the rumpus room, heard the flush of a toilet, the woman's voice in the laundry. She went back upstairs. It was ten-fifteen and the house was still empty. She went onto the patio, buzzed the garage door up, and saw her mother's car was deeply gouged all down one side. Jesus. Drunk driving? Hadn't she cut back? But the gouge was rusty ... God, another expense. Hugh would be writing out cheques for months with this long settlement. Blanche stayed in the garage inhaling the rough, rich, comforting smells of oil and petrol till she was calm. When she went back into the house another couple had arrived. They looked like the Mosman lawyers, the woman ghostly pale in a crisp shirt and ironed jeans. 'They're the ones,' Hugh said out of the corner of his mouth. Then Rupert and Celia Henderson were in the kitchen, consulting the floor plans, wandering across to poke their heads into the study. There was a Chinese man in black trousers who nobody seemed to know. A loud woman in a floppy white hat with a tall young man who looked like her son: she was registered. Stav flitted around chatting to everybody. Blanche watched the Hendersons. She followed them up the stairs, at a discreet distance, into the master bedroom. 'Can I show you around?'

'Thank you!' Rupert turned. 'Blanche, isn't it?'

'Yes.'

'Isn't this a lovely room!' Celia said. She was standing right next to Mopoke, asleep on her chair. Blanche moved over to stand beside her. Mopoke lifted her head.

'Not much of a bird-catcher these days, are we now.' Rupert pursed his bottle-opener mouth then indicated the door to the balcony. 'May we?'

'Of course!'

She had never seen her mother's bedroom like this. Packed away, fakely domestic, like a serviced apartment or luxury hotel room. Not so much as a drop of water on the bathroom sink, the washers folded in diagonals, crisp new hand towel. Her own bedroom was a white void. Blanche waited for the Hendersons with her hand lightly touching the back of Mopoke's neck. Just as they came back into the bedroom, the cat began to purr. She saw the Hendersons to the head of the stairs then went into the hall toilet. She slid a finger into her cunt then inspected it. Not so much as a hint of discolouration, and yet she felt just about ready to burst with PMT.

As she rose, a cool slick broke out on her forehead and she turned quickly to heave into the bowl.

'Auction Toilet,' Hugh had said cheerily in the car that morning. 'Watch out for that.'

'What's Auction Toilet?'

'People get nervous and take a dump. Or even throw up sometimes. On-site auctions *smell*.'

Hugh looked pleased. She watched him out of the corner of her eye as she drove and he went through the papers in his lap, marking things with his Lamy, alert as a hunter, the energy sparkling from him infectious, intimidating.

All morning he had been unusually unaware of her and that was attractive too, having to strive to get his attention. Hugh was in control, he was the dominant figure today, and it was she who was weak-kneed with the stress of it all, stinking out the toilet. She could hear Hugh's voice raised in greeting and instruction to the people in the house. 'Folks, have you all registered? Registration papers in the kitchen, don't leave it too late, folks.'

A woman passed Blanche on the stairs. 'Is there a toilet up here, do you know?'

Blanche held out her hand. 'I'm Blanche King. The toilet's down the hall on the left.'

'Oh, you must have grown up here! Oh, it must be hard for you.'

'My mother will be happier elsewhere.'

'It's a lovely house. *Lovely*.'

About fifteen people were milling around the open plan. Hugh and Stav had taken up position against the living room wall, the harbour on their right, the kitchen on their left. The faint smell of sweat hung in the air. Blanche looked at her watch. It was eleven o'clock. Her stomach expanded and contracted like a bellows. She arranged herself between agents and bidders. Outside was complete stasis, a dense white light as though the sky had been covered with greaseproof paper. Hugh spoke up.

'Ladies and gentlemen, it's eleven o'clock and we're going to begin the auction of this beautiful house on this warm not quite sunny day. Four bedrooms upstairs, the master bedroom directly above with ensuite and a balcony overlooking one of the most exclusive parts of Sydney harbour. *Look* at this view folks. Words can't describe. There's a rumpus room downstairs that you can keep or improve upon. Room for a cellar, games room, gymnasium, anything you want. Oak-panelled study, marble bathrooms and Persian carpets, the latter *not* included in the price, I'm afraid.' Hugh waited for a response then continued. 'For the home decorator there's plenty of potential for extensions.'

Hugh orated with both arms on the move, his accent imperceptibly broadening to Strine as he rapped out the legal conditions of the auction then returned to his spiel about the house. He glanced at the papers in his hands occasionally, and Blanche felt herself hypnotised by his hubris. She wished he came to bed like this. Her hands were sticky with sweat; she wanted a glass of water. Looking around the room she saw that everybody else was mesmerised by Hugh as well. His sentences ran faster, the words joining and flattening like fettuccine, noded by the occasional joke.

'Speaking of warm, what better place to be during a heatwave than on the harbour feeling the breeze come off the water. Look at this deck, folks, perfect as is or improved by your own designs. What better thing to do of a summer afternoon than while away your hours and mind your own business with a champagne or beer? Look down on the garden: a work of art, or your new swimming pool and watch your kids play. Is there a better place to bring up children than here surrounded by trees and water? Sniff the air! You're in the country! Is there a better place to entertain, relax, put your feet up after a hard day's work because *you-know-you-deserve-it-folks*. They say this is the most beautiful city in the world and I agree, and I'll wager you this is the most beautiful location in the most beautiful city. I'm gonna start us off at five and a half million today, ladies and gentlemen, then you're taking over.'

What? thought Blanche. They've gone down five hundred? Nobody else seemed surprised. People smiled coyly, as though pulled on stage by an entertainer. Rupert's eyes were gleaming, riveted to Hugh.

'There's an eerie silence in this room.' Hugh raised his eyebrows theatrically.

Stav cleared his throat. A sulphur-crested cockatoo squawked from a tree on the border of the bush and one of the women laughed gratefully.

'That's right, he's protesting because I didn't mention the birds. How could I not mention the wildlife! I've been visiting this house for years and there are days you can't *speak* for the noise of the lorikeets. Come on, folks, whaddaya say? I'm in your hands. Once in a lifetime, ladies and gentlemen, this property hasn't been on the market in nearly thirty years. With all due respect none of you look like you can wait another thirty.'

Blanche saw Stav's hand extend and Hugh said, 'Five five ten, good as gold away we go.' She did not see who had bid. A silence fell again that was filled with more of Hugh's good-natured goading then the lawyer put up his hand. The bid rose again, it was someone behind the corner in the dining room, the Chinese man, Blanche realised as she edged a little closer to Hugh. The bidding climbed slowly to five million six hundred thousand then stopped. 'There's that eerie silence again ...' Hugh stood with his arms raised either side. 'Can we move on, folks?'

The fridge shuddered to a halt and on top of the hill someone's lawnmower burst into action. The tinkling sounds of the harbour mocked the tension that stretched across the living room like elastic. The silence deepened and in its far reaches Blanche could hear Ming and Tang howling in the heart of the Hendersons' house. She looked at Rupert, whose eyebrows had come together in an acute angle as he stared at the Chinese man, then back at Hugh. Blanche remembered the Hendersons had paid a pittance for the Hammets', Pat not caring enough to get a better price. She remembered Hugh coming home from his first auction wild with excitement, a bottle of Moët Brut, two dozen roses, talking about the bids leaping one hundred thousand dollars at a time, seven to eight million in less than a minute. The twenty-first century had started with a bang and not ten years on was beginning to whimper. This awful, still, glaring light; heavy heat, even the harbour seemed baked to a crust. Blanche ran her tongue around her acidic mouth.

The bidding began again — the Lebanese, the lawyer, the Chinese man. With both arms, Hugh plucked the numbers from the air like a conductor. Blanche watched him, edging all the while towards the kitchen. There was an acceleration, the increments decreasing simultaneously, and Blanche's heart began to gallop. Then it stopped altogether. Hugh stood with a finger raised. 'Five six hundred and seventy, folks, where do we go from here, I've got five six seventy from the gentleman in the corner.' Hugh addressed himself mainly to the lawyers, but they ignored him, whispering heatedly. He looked across at Blanche, then one by one at every person in the room. His accent was now completely flat, like a race caller's, and even when he looked directly at her Blanche didn't feel he was seeing her, only the job, and this callousness made her hate him, while admiration and sexual pull flowed harder through her. 'Five six seventy, ladies and gentlemen. I'm in your hands, whaddaya say?' Hugh waited. 'Going once.' Blanche slipped into the kitchen.

Hugh came in as she was pouring a glass of water. They conferred in urgent whispers. 'Grinding halt. What do we do?'

Blanche opened her phone, called, waited then snapped it shut. 'She must be out of range.'

'Shit.'

'Sell.'

'Five six *seventy*?'

'Yes.'

'You wanted five eight at least, didn't you?'

'Um, *I* actually thought we were starting at six. Remember?'

'We couldn't, pooky.'

'Okay, if we're not going to get the price we want today, then when will we?'

Hugh pinched the bridge of his nose. 'I've never done this.'

'There's a first time for everything.'

'My instinct is to pass it in.'

The narrow space between them seemed an abyss. Blanche felt frozen. 'I can't believe we're selling to that Chinese guy,' she muttered.

'They've got money, those Chinese.'

'I just mean it'd be nice to sell to someone who knows the area and appreciates it.'

'I don't know what's happened to that lawyer couple.' Hugh sounded wounded.

Blanche listened to the silence of a house full of twenty people.

'Stuff it. Mum said sell. So we sell.'

Hugh put his hands on her shoulders. 'Your call. You want me to sell, I sell.'

'Sell.'

Hugh walked back into the living room followed by Blanche. He smiled and raised his hand. 'The property is on the market, folks. Any price below reserve will be accepted.'

Blanche saw Celia cock her eyebrow at her husband. Rupert frowned and stared at Hugh. The male lawyer put his hand up. Hugh sprang to life.

'Five six seventy-five, five six eighty-five, five seven folks, five million seven hundred thousand dollars.' He grabbed the bids. The lawyers put their heads together, the woman shaking hers. Hugh watched them. 'Five seven, ladies and gentlemen. Where do we go from here?' Hugh sought out the Chinese man. The Chinese man shook his head. The female lawyer began to weep quietly. 'I've got five million seven hundred thousand dollars from the gentleman in the corner … Place your bids now, folks … Going once … going twice …'

Hugh waited. The kitchen clock ticked. The air grew tense. There was a clearing of throats, people glanced around. The woman who had passed Blanche on the stairs fell into a coughing fit. Hugh brought his fist into his palm. 'Gone!'

The lawyer began to weep freely then walked out of the room. Her husband, red-faced, glanced around then followed Hugh into the kitchen to sign papers. Rupert and Celia clapped. The Lebanese couple lingered, the woman sitting on the lounge, blinking tears from her eyes.

Blanche moved mechanically to the door to see people out. 'Interesting,' Rupert said blandly to her as they passed. 'Very interesting.'

'I do hope your mother is happy with the outcome,' Celia said, smiling. 'Give her our regards.'

The male lawyer was shaking Hugh's hand vigorously when the female came in to find Blanche.

'I just wanted to say thank you,' she said, wiping her eyes. For a second, Blanche thought she was going to hug her. The woman looked around the room. 'I can't believe it — it's *ours.*'

After they had left, the house fell eerily silent. Like it, Blanche felt drained and hollow. She went outside and through the bushes saw Stav on the street folding up the signs. She went down the side path and found Hugh on the lawn, beneath the angophora. He turned at her approach, his face clenched. 'It feels so unreal,' she said.

Hugh shook his head. Then he managed a choked 'Sorry.'

'It's not your fault, Hughie. Maybe it's this.' She indicated the scorched garden. 'At least it was the Mosmanians. I feel much better knowing the house will be taken care of.' She was waiting for an embrace or kiss. He had taken off his jacket and was damp around his armpits. He frowned and toed the grass. It was rare to see him this angry. She was touched that he had loved the house that much. She drew a little closer to him. 'I've never seen you auctioning. You're quite the showman. I was impressed.' She gave him a nudge. 'Your accent goes totally Aussie.'

'Puts 'em at their ease.' Hugh shrugged. 'You don't want to come across as a ponce.'

A breeze had come up and the trees were moving restlessly. A motorboat idled in the cove. Hugh hung his head. 'I can't believe it I can't believe it. Five million seven hundred thousand dollars when we were talking about six and a half only a few months ago. I can't fucking believe it.'

'It's o*kay*, Hugh,' said Blanche, although she didn't think it was.

'It was bad enough coming down from six five, but *this*?'

'And how come I didn't hear about the five-five starter, by the way?'

'I didn't want to stress you out.'

'There's a bottle of Moët in the fridge, but I don't feel like drinking it.'

Hugh kicked the grass. 'I'm overdue with payments on Ultimo.'

Blanche opened her mouth in shock. 'You *bought* that place?'

'Yes.'

'Why?'

Hugh said nothing.

'Why didn't you tell me? I didn't even like it! *Why?*'

'Because it was a good investment!'

'But why didn't you tell me?'

'I paid for it with my own money.'

'You wouldn't have had enough.'

'I got a loan. I'm allowed to make my own investments once in a while, Blanche!' he whined. 'I just wanted to put a big slab down and stop stressing about mortgages for a while. And I wanted to take a holiday, a proper one. You know we owe thirty thousand dollars on Visa?'

'Just sell it, Hugh,' Blanche snapped. 'I'm sure you'll make a mozza.'

'Fuck.' He kicked the grass again. '*Fuck.*'

Blanche walked back to the house then up to her mother's bedroom. She picked Mopoke off the chair, took her onto the balcony and rang her mother's mobile again. This time Marie answered.

'Mum.'

'Yes. How did you go?'

'Sold.'

'Good.'

The abrasion of wind came through the phone.

'Are you having a nice walk?'

'It's lovely.'

Mopoke squirmed. Blanche put her down and felt her sacrum click out of place. Immediately, it began to thrum with pain. 'We didn't get that much, Mum.'

'That's alright. The best price of the day was what we agreed.'

The three of them had been walking for over an hour and, through the trees, Marie could see the old Defence Force buildings clustered whitely along the headland. Since Taylors Bay, where Nell had had a tantrum, Clark had carried his daughter on his shoulders and his face was now shot through with pain. A branch had come off the angophora next to Marie. Red sap oozed from the wound. The bark rumpled around the knob like skin, the sap dried into amber. Only another ten minutes then she could sit down. Have a cool drink. Nell clamoured to get off her father's shoulders and, like a cat sensing grief, grabbed Marie's thighs. Marie passed the phone to Clark. She leant back against the tree, placed her hand over her eyes and wept.

The blinds in Terry's office were half drawn and it took a few seconds for Blanche's eyes to adjust. She sat on the white, undulating couch. She wanted to lie down. She had thrown up after breakfast and felt queasy ever since. She wondered if it was due to her chiro treatment the day before: her bowels and entire digestive system felt squashed. In spite of her empty stomach, she felt disgustingly bloated. Her thighs rubbed together when she walked. Unable to think of anything she wanted to eat, she had worked through lunch, then gone into the meeting and pitched for Diet Coke on an empty stomach. Terry was looking out the slit of window at the Opera House, foot propped on his knee, Puma sports bag on the floor beside his desk. It was two o'clock and he appeared to have spent lunch at the gym again. He said to Blanche, 'Why?'

She watched his jiggling foot, shod in a winklepicker, the end of which he stroked compulsively with his fingers. 'I thought it was a good idea, Terry. And so did my team.'

'I don't check up on creative, you know. That's your job.'

'It was my idea. I'll take the rap.'

'I could see that, actually. Lim wouldn't have put forward something like that.'

Blanche let this remark sink in.

'It's hip and sexy. And Coke could do with some sexing up.'

'Really? I wouldn't buy something because of a guy with an erection.'

'Terry, it's a *metaphor.* And I buy products with sexy women on them all the time!'

'Like what?'

Blanche's mind went blank. Terry smiled and jiggled his foot some more.

Blanche thought about how the one holding the purse strings was always the real boss, and how tired she was of fighting. She thought about Neil French saying, *Women inevitably wimp out and go suckle something.* If that's the attitude you had to have to be a celebrity exec, then god help her. Terry was definitely the one who'd pulled the Dulux ad off YouTube, just when it was going into the top ten. He was jealous. Blanche remembered her dad's claim that Jonesy was a failed artist.

'Look, Coke ads are always so juvenile. Why do we have to be afraid of risk? Risk is sexy. You were saying only a few months ago that you wanted us to be more edgy. Remember the underwater Levi's?'

'A masterpiece. A *cinematic* masterpiece. The market for Coke is mainly juvenile.'

'Not for Diet Coke.'

'Blanche ...' Terry looked bemused.

'What?'

He raised his arms. 'It was *ludicrous.*'

'So is wearing jeans underwater. Ludicrousness is the spice of advertising!'

'I mean it was ludicrous to take that pitch into Asher — you know what he's like.'

She realised that second that Terry was wearing the same Tsubi jeans she had seen on a Hillsonger a fortnight ago in Redfern. Ha! She clamped her grin. She wanted to grab Terry's winklepicker and snap it off. Maybe he was gay. Photographed in the *Telegraph* with an *Australian Idol* finalist. Yeah, right. He had never so much as glanced at Blanche's body. Not a single joke let alone flirtation had ever passed between them. Maybe he did fuck women but hated them. Wouldn't be the first. He only liked her when she made the agency a bomb, or won a prize. He sighed, and right over here, three metres away on his new couch, Blanche could smell his rank breath. Her nausea stirred. How outrageous for him to come in here with such bad breath and not think he should do anything about it.

'Coke, Blanche. *Coke.*'

'Fantastic couch,' she said, with total sincerity.

'Marc Newson. Nineteen eighty-six. Their marketing team is on the verge of advising them to go elsewhere so you'll have to come up with something else fast.'

Blanche nodded without looking up, absent-mindedly as though in response to her own deep thoughts, because while the part of her sitting here was hating Terry diligently and passionately, thinking the couch must have cost tens of thousands of dollars and Terry would have had the agency pay for it, another part of her was trapped in a fantasy of straddling Terry in his chair, pulling out his cock, the fuck moving to this couch, aggressive and desperate. A hideous, frantic fantasy all in one split second sprayed across her mind. She felt herself blush and was glad for the half-closed blinds. She couldn't speak. Terry smiled at her, eyebrows raised, hands behind his head. 'What's that ad for manchester, with the guy in the bed? Bold for its time.'

'I can't remember.' Blanche rose to leave.

Although she could remember the ad, and that it was around twenty years old. But her idea was a completely different angle.

God. How could she have thought those disgusting thoughts about Terry? Where did they come from? Like birdshit dropping out of the sky into her eye. She was ashamed and angry as she went down the corridor. Was it something to do with neuroscience? Neuroscience was everywhere now, have to do something with that ... But, Jesus, get out of my head, *please.* Blanche stopped to get herself a cup of water from the cooler. Yeah, okay, so the chocolate ad had been sexy too, maybe she could let sex go for a little while. Still, it was a great idea. It would have been noticed. She dropped her cup into the bin and went down to Lim and Kate's office to deliver the news.

'It was too radical for this industry,' Lim hissed.

'That is such a shit,' said Kate to her computer, looking up guiltily as the swish of a full suit landed. Blanche had trashed solitaire and every other game on Kate's computer twice, and Kate just reloaded them. She could have had the nous to mute it. 'Better than googling porn,' Kate quipped.

'Okay.' Blanche hung on to the doorframe. 'I'm going to Mac up the Revlon.'

'I'll do it,' said Kate.

'No, it's fine.'

Blanche went back into her office and shut the door. They had to think up a new pitch. She had to go through the media schedules for Narva. There was a meeting with Roche in two days. They had to think up a new Diet Coke pitch, and fast. Blanche had had a dozen sheets of top-quality art paper and three boxes of charcoal delivered, all on the office-supplies account. She had a craving to draw, with charcoal soft as kohl, to feel it working into the grain of her skin while her fingers worked it into the paper. But when would she find the time? She lay on the floor, pulled her Thai silk pillow beneath her head and dropped Refresh into her eyes.

So her childhood home had been sold and a wall had risen around Sirius Cove. She had been relieved that her mother and Clark hadn't attended the auction because the loss had felt so personal. Let alone the ignominy of the price. She couldn't have borne it with them there; somehow the punters hadn't interfered with that intensely private ritual of letting go and grieving: like an audience they had wrapped a warm anonymous blanket around it. It was strange to think of her mother still there, sleeping, eating, probably even still gardening in this house that now felt like a corpse. It was a death yet here Blanche was, at work as usual. When she should have been marching down the main street in a funeral cortège, the world witness to her grief. She unzipped her skirt to free her legs and one by one brought her knees to her chest. It was cold in the air-conditioning, which made her back ache more. She realised she was crying when Kate knocked. She hoicked down her skirt and scrambled to her feet. 'Come in!'

She was standing, hands on knees, as Kate came in.

'Ya righ'?'

Blanche couldn't get used to Kate's vernacular for *How are you?*

It always felt like an interrogation and put her on edge. 'I stood up too quickly,' she panted. 'Headspin.'

Kate stood politely by the door. When the thrumming in her head had subsided, Blanche went and sat at her desk. 'My back's out.'

'D'you have a good osteo? I've a fan*tastic* osteo, I'll give you her number. I've also been getting loads of acupuncture lately and it's totally changed my life.'

'I've got a chiro.'

'Don't you find chiro a bit *violent?*'

'I need a bit of violence,' Blanche said with a touch of the ham. 'I'm tough.'

Kate smiled. She stood awkwardly in the middle of the room, a bag of cashews in her hand. She had taken to wearing long white socks beneath her cowboy boots, short kilts and sleeveless shirts done up high. A quirky old-fashioned rock'n'roll look. Her legs were disgustingly athletic and smooth, and covered in goose bumps. Look at that amazing black skin. No sunburn, no cancer, so healthy-looking. Blanche wished she had skin like that.

'I just wanted to apologise for before,' Kate said. 'It was out of line.'

'It's okay. Sit down.'

Kate sat on the edge of the couch with her feet together, her huge liquid eyes on Blanche. 'I just trashed solitaire. Promise. I'm really sorry, hey. I'm itching to do some work, honestly. I'd really love to do the Revlon. If you're busy or stressed, whatever I can do to take a load off.'

Blanche looked at the pillow she had left in the middle of the floor. She felt like she'd exited the toilet with her skirt stuck in her knickers and been haplessly walking around like that ever since. She hated ceding. Delegating work was a form of ceding. Having her vulnerabilities on display like this was ceding. 'Okay,' she said, ceding. A shiver ran through her body. 'It's cold in here, isn't it.'

'You alrigh'?' Kate said again. 'You look really pale.'

'I'm just stressed.'

'D'you eat lunch? You can't skip lunch.'

'I ate some yoghurt,' Blanche lied. 'And fruit. I had a big breakfast. I just feel so leth*argic*.'

'I'd offer you a cashew but I'm not sure they'd be good for you.'

'That's fine, I don't feel like one anyway.' Blanche had received more Narva that morning, but didn't want to get the block out in front of Kate because then she would have to give her a piece, and she wanted to keep it all for herself.

'What blood type are you?' said Kate.

'I have absolutely no idea.'

'Cos you know it's important to eat according to your blood type?'

'Really? Why?'

'It's all about antigens and how your body absorbs food. Different blood types have different antigen markers, and they react badly with certain foods. And stomach acidity and digestive enzymes vary too, according to types, so we all absorb food differently. Like, you know how sometimes you eat what you think is a really good balanced meal and you end up all bloated for no reason?'

Blanche didn't know what antigens were but right now felt as bloated as a puffer fish. The cashews smelt incredibly strong and strangely repulsive. She tried to pay attention to Kate's rapid-fire speech. 'Well ... yeah, I guess so.'

'Exactly!' Kate sat forward, her speech accelerating. 'So if you absorb and digest food more efficiently you're bound to lose weight and function better. It goes back like tens of thousands of years, to BC, to how our ancestors ate. So blood type O came first, then A.'

'Oh, okay. So you'd be O because you're black?'

Kate's eyes narrowed. 'We *all* came from Africa, remember?'

'Right.' Blanche squirmed. 'I really didn't mean ...'

'It's fine. B came last, when we started nomadic societies and started to move around, so B gets to eat most things. I'm AB, the most recent and rarest type. It only emerged about a thousand years ago.' Kate smiled about herself as though she were the latest, most efficient product; the meanest machine. She ate more cashews. Blanche was overwhelmed by their odour. She had never even known that nuts had a smell until now. Kate said, 'Are you vego?'

'No.'

'You shouldn't be vego if you're O.'

'Well … I don't eat *that* much meat, I don't think.'

Blanche reflected on her diet. A double-shot latte when she got up, made at home. A second from Machiavelli's on her way into work, with a croissant or muffin or Portuguese tart. A third coffee with lunch but never after three. She had stopped smoking when she was twenty-nine and taken ecstasy a few times in her twenties, but not for years, not since Hugh, who hated drugs. She didn't count her occasional lines of cocaine. 'I stopped smoking when I was twenty-nine,' she said.

Kate nodded. 'That's good, that's really good.'

For lunch Blanche usually had a Caesar salad or focaccia or roll-up. Not much meat there. Dinner was usually Thai takeaway or sausages, steak or pasta. Her favourite foods were red duck curry, fish cakes and wood-fired pizza with goat's cheese, rocket and kangaroo. 'I think I probably eat more poultry and fish than red meat.'

'Everybody thinks that's better, but in fact if you're type A you should be practically vego and avoid dairy. D'you eat much dairy?'

Blanche felt suddenly despondent again, remembering chocolate, corn chips, cheese on toast, a million and one random snacks. What relation did Pringles and Twisties have with the food of BC hunter-gatherers? she wondered. She was hopeless at keeping track of this sort of thing, never wrote down her periods, for instance. She had to admit that she didn't really know what she ate, when it boiled down to it. She felt completely out of touch with her body, trapped inside it like a snail in a shell.

'How old are you? If you don't mind my asking.'

'Thirty-seven.' Blanche pulled a face.

'God, you look great for thirty-seven. You only look about thirty-three. Anyway, all the nicotine would be totally flushed out of your system by now.'

'Yeah, my lungs feel fine.'

'You should do a blood test, honestly. I've changed my diet and

I feel incredible. I've lost weight and I've got like *so much* energy. Type AB is quite rare but good cos it allows me to eat a variety. The hardest thing was cutting out chips and hamburgers — I was a closet McDonald's binger, you know. It's about exercise too, as in the type suitable for your blood type.' Kate looked shrewdly at Blanche. 'You strike me as an O, you know.'

'Really?'

'Yeah. Dunno why I think that. But I bet you are. Most of England is O. Maybe that's why I can tell.'

'Oh.'

'You shouldn't be eating yoghurt for lunch. High protein, low carbs is what you need. And you should be doing aerobics and running.'

Blanche groaned. 'My poor gym membership!'

'There's loads of research on it, just google and you'll find a million articles. It's fascinating.'

'Okay. Thanks, Kate.'

'Should I do the Revlon, then?' Kate stood up.

'Yeah. That'd be great.'

'I'll have it done by five.'

'Great!'

For the rest of the afternoon, Blanche slowly made her way through a block of Narva with almond slivers as she googled blood types and diet. The nausea did not abate, nor, weirdly, the smell of cashews. Chocolate was the only thing she could hold down. She was surprised to find how much information there was that backed up Kate's theories, sceptics notwithstanding. She googled female executives and creative directors and found five depressing articles that all alluded directly or indirectly to sexism in the advertising industry and the glass ceiling. Then she realised she had read two of the articles already. She checked her email and side-surfed onto YouTube and got envious, inspired, angered and bored by a variety of ads, then ended up on the MySpace page of a fabulously rich and successful American executive, thirty-six years old, a big deal at Apple, with enormous lips, tits and muscles, sunbed suntanned, a tiger tattoo on her upper arm, kissing her boyfriend, a chumpy guy in a baseball cap. *So* LA. Then she went onto the facebook login page and was considering joining, for about the tenth time, when Kate was back in her office with the Revlon print. Blanche looked over with glazed eyes. It was flawless. 'That's great, Kate! But maybe … yeah, um, maybe you could move the print down a little?'

'Okay. Where to?'

'Here?'

'There?'

'Yeah. And maybe, try a different font? Not so kind of schoolbookish, y'know?'

Kate flipped the print around and examined it. 'Yeah, yeah, I see what you mean.'

'Thanks, Kate. You're a godsend.'

Less than a week after the auction, Marie drove to Rhys's studio although it wasn't the studio she was going to tonight but Rhys's house. She had fretted over her wardrobe for nearly two hours, finally settling on a sleeveless black dress with a shawl. She rang the bell and heels tapped over the floorboards then the door was opened by a woman with long black hair and big arrogant lips, painted dark red. 'Hi, I'm Natasha.'

Marie followed Natasha's short leather boots and fishnet stockings up the stairs past the tattooing rooms to the top floor. Natasha was big, majestic, with a swinging gait and large sultry eyes that slid back watchfully to Marie behind her. On the landing they passed a room, Marie seeing through the crack of the door toys, small shoes and clothes in disarray, then they went into the front room. The walls were crowded with bookshelves and pictures. There was a television, a computer and an old-fashioned stereo with a turntable. Frankincense drifted from a cone in a dish. The wide balcony was fenced by wrought iron and covered at one end to create a sort of sunroom.

Rhys called out from her bedroom, 'Babe, can you get Marie a drink?'

'G'n'T?'

'Lovely, thanks.'

There was a kitchenette at one end of the balcony. Natasha went to the bar fridge and mixed a drink for Marie. It was eight o'clock and daylight had faded. Marie sat on the edge of the couch, shawl draped around her shoulders. Natasha brought the drink out. She was tightly laced into a corset, birds in silhouette flying across her broad milky chest. Lines of diamantés forked from her eyes across her cheekbone. She looked like a character in a movie, something between concubine and cyborg. She lit a cigarette then walked away to smoke it by the window. She intimidated Marie with her size, diffidence and imperious beauty. She leant on the windowsill, exhaling harshly as though in a hurry. In the street light, Marie saw her face was completely unlined and she realised how young Natasha was, how much of the haughtiness was bluff and naïveté, a shield for nerves.

'So,' said Natasha, 'I've seen photos of your tatts, Marie. It feels quite an honour to finally see them in the flesh. So to speak.'

'Thank you.'

'Especially the moth. What's your next piece going to be?'

'We have a bit more to finish on the vines. Then I'm thinking of an angophora.'

'A what?'

'The most beautiful tree in Sydney.'

By the time Rhys limped in with one boot half laced, Marie and Natasha were huddled beneath the light pulling back their clothing to show one another Rhys's artwork. Rhys put on a record and sat on the couch watching them while she thumbed a text message into her mobile. A beep returned immediately. 'Poor little Trav. He so wanted to come. He cried when Paul took him. I felt so bad.'

'Why not bring him?' Natasha blew a plume of smoke up to the ceiling. 'I'd help you look after him, you know that.'

'Because he's five?'

'Five now?' said Marie.

'He's just started school,' Rhys said proudly.

'Us Russians would have everyone there,' said Natasha, pouting. 'The kids'd crash at the back of the room when they'd had enough and the party would go all night.'

Again the haughty tone, a sort of pitching of herself against Rhys, who stiffened to meet the impact. All the while the two gazed at each other with a frank, dark lust.

'He's going to a birthday tomorrow. Can't have my kid turning up to his friends' parties trashed. Eight, I reckon. In the holidays.' Rhys pulled out a compact and began to apply make-up between sips of her drink.

Something had been completed by penetrating the top of the house. Every bit of furniture in the tattooing room one floor down, every crack in the wall and every book spine, was known to Marie. Downstairs had also become familiar, but always this floor above, with its TV chatter and footsteps or long silences, had remained impenetrable and so had grown in Marie's mind to something large and exclusive. The whole house, due to these hidden realms, had become a castle. Now it was just a collection of rooms in which people lived and worked: an ordinary house.

'Does Rob live here too?'

'Sort of. He has a room in the middle floor at the end, next to his studio. Rob doesn't live anywhere, really. He lives out of a bag. And his beaten-up Mitsubishi.'

'I admire that. Being unattached like that.'

'Oh, Rob's not unattached.' Natasha laughed. 'More like polygamous.'

'You should go house hunting with Rob, Marie. Rob loves looking at real estate.'

'Really?'

'He's totally obsessed,' said Natasha. 'He's on *Domain* like every day.'

'Pot calling the kettle black.' Rhys smiled into her compact.

'I'm just a real-estate pornographer,' Natasha replied cryptically. 'It's just a fantasy.'

'Rob owns this building,' Rhys explained to Marie. 'He owns like eight houses.'

'My god. Who would have thought?'

Marie was cravenly disappointed. Once again real estate enclosed her like a prison. More likely it had never gone away, but she had idealised the tattooists as free of this national obsession with land ownership. Now it seemed like everybody was locked inside, pacing around, measuring space, keys clutched tightly in hand.

Rhys went on, with both resentment and admiration: 'Rob's like the local eccentric. He's the goon in the corner of every party but he's a raging capitalist at the same time and nobody knows it. He's incredibly good at it. He's got shares as well. His studio is full of all the best equipment and pigments, he eats nothing but organic, he's up to his eyeballs in real estate but he only owns one pair of shoes and rides a bicycle everywhere he can.'

'Doesn't pay any tax,' Natasha chipped in. 'It's all negative geared.'

'You know,' said Rhys, 'I've got a bit of a problem with one person owning that much, but Rob is so good to me and Travis, I wouldn't be in business without him. I couldn't live here either. Mainly, I couldn't tattoo independently, and that's phenomenal.'

'These guys,' Natasha said proudly to Marie, 'are the last ones standing. They're the only non-bikie tattoo establishment in the whole of the inner city.'

'But we don't talk about that.' Rhys snapped shut her compact and stood up. She was wearing a corset as well, and made up, in high heels, she looked like a queen.

'Look at you two,' said Marie. 'I feel so underdressed.'

'You look gorgeous,' said Rhys.

'You look fabulous.'

'I haven't worn a corset for forty years. In fact I don't think I've ever worn one.'

'They're comfortable if they're well made.'

'You've got an hourglass figure — you're perfect for corsetry,' added Natasha.

'Yeah, she is, isn't she.'

'There is the red one, babe. You never wear that anymore.'

Rhys disappeared then returned with a red satin corset. She loosened the laces and held it up to Marie.

'Not with this dress.'

'Totally with that dress. Come on.'

Marie stood.

'Turn around,' Rhys instructed.

She fitted the corset and Marie did up the front clasps. Hand on hip, Natasha swept the two of them with an approving gaze. Rhys began to tighten the laces while Natasha stood in front, holding Marie's hands. 'Lean into it.' Marie leant and gripped Natasha's hands as the corset embraced her tighter, pushing her breasts up. There was a point at which it felt comforting like a poultice, then it touched a pain. 'No, looser.'

'Like that?'

'Bit more … Yes.'

Rhys and Natasha walked around her, cooing in admiration. Marie ran her hands down her firm curved sides. She felt regal, sexy, contained and powerful.

Natasha said, 'My lipstick. Here.'

Marie applied it over her lighter one. Natasha and Rhys raised their glasses to her, Natasha saying a word with a buzzing sound, Rhys replying.

'What are you saying?' said Marie.

Natasha said it again, slowly, 'Naz-drov-ee-ay. *Nazdrovye.* Russian for *cheers.*'

'Slav.' Rhys pronounced the word slightly differently. 'We're having a corset party. Isn't it gorgeous? *Nazdrovye*, Marie.'

The men on stage were dressed in black, with little red shorts and pillbox hats. They had blackened eyes and pale faces and were capering in a line to a sarcastic pop song. All the stage was red, with old-fashioned curtains looped either side and bolts draped to the floor. The crowd welled and carried Marie towards the far wall on which hung a banner saying *FAST*. She saw the stage again briefly, the men dancing naked, then they were gone.

She found herself next to a piano that had been shoved against the wall. Girls sat on top swinging their boots, one with cones on her head through which her hair had been pulled making giant ears or something medieval. Sitting in the middle, feet on the stool, was a barrel-chested Asian in white beret and sunglasses, chomping on a cigar. Marie was hot and vaguely frightened. She couldn't see the exit or Rhys and Natasha.

The curtains were closed and a man in devil's horns and leather trousers stalked onto the proscenium to introduce the next act. Sweat poured off his white face as he shouted into the microphone. The crowd began to heckle him good-naturedly. The Asian on the piano above Marie jutted his head forward and screamed, 'Show us yer cock!' in a girl's voice, then jabbed the cigar back into her mouth with a triumphant leer. Marie tried to move away but there was nowhere to go. People pressed against her. The devil disappeared and music began to blast through the speakers. One of the girls on the piano jumped off to dance. Marie strained to see Rhys through the bodies.

She saw a skinny man in thongs and an Osama bin Laden t-shirt dancing with a fat girl in black. She saw a man so black that all she could see were the whites of his eyes and teeth beneath a tweed cap. There were girls in lurid hotpants with lurid hair, and a creature all in green, impossibly tall, with a green face and head-dress. The music was harsh and doom-laden and joyful all at once, a cascade of drums over low swinging chords and a belligerent male voice that seemed to be giving orders yet there didn't seem to be any rules here in the normal social sense, and Marie began to relax. Nobody knew or cared who she was. The other thing was this: everywhere she looked she saw tattoos. Lacing down the back of the cone-headed girl's forearms, an anchor on the Asian girl's arm. A middle-aged woman with a panther headed up her skirt. She also wore a red singlet on which was spelt out in diamantés: *I bang for Jesus*. Marie removed her shawl.

When the curtains parted again and she stood on tiptoes, the loud masculine Asian prodded her. 'There's room up here, mate.' Marie tried to ignore her but she was holding out her hand, so she clambered up.

From here she saw the columns were wrapped in red all the way to the end of the room where a bar had been set up. That must be where Rhys had gone to buy drinks. Slung down the walls at intervals were banners with designs of victorious bodies in Russian

Constructivist style — in detail Marie saw they were actually lewd and facetious. And the banners and costumes and riotous music all made her feel like she was in some dive cabaret of the Weimar Republic.

In front of the stage, people began to sit on the floor and what had seemed a raucous, forbidding crowd now took on an air of obedient expectancy, like children at a recital. A boy came on dressed for the beach, sucking a lollipop. He looked so young; a slender, conceited, young god, and Marie caught a whiff of adolescent Leon at Balmoral, walking across the sand to buy ice-cream, speedos askew showing tan line, all eyes upon him. She thought of Tadzio as the boy lolled on his towel, oiling his chest and legs, while a man with a pot belly and grey beard — Aschenbach — sauntered on wheeling a hotdog stand.

He began pulling out hotdogs, rivers of mustard and tomato sauce coursing down his singlet. He was squirting sauce into a bun, reaching beneath his apron as Tadzio peeled off his shorts and crawled towards him. Then Aschenbach pulled out his penis and began to masturbate it in the saucy bun. It seemed like the real thing. Was he *really*? Marie strained for a closer look. He jammed the whole meal into Tadzio's mouth and the crowd roared. The Asian girl drummed her heels on the stool. Marie was thunderstruck. Heat rose up to her face then erupted in a cheer. The applause faded around her lone voice and Marie realised that Rhys was below, signalling with cups of beer.

The curtains closed and the devil reappeared in a pink baby-doll and suspenders and stockings. 'Wasn't that great? Give it up everyone!'

Marie followed Rhys, who cut a severe, elegant figure, greeting people as she went. In her wake, beer slopping onto her wrists, Marie received inquisitive looks, the occasional smile. Closer to the stage she recognised the devil's tattoos. It was Rob.

'Show us watcha got, Robbo!' somebody yelled.

'Aw SHUD-DUP. Youse're all a buncha desperadoes!'

'Here,' said Rhys, lifting a bag off a chair for Marie.

From the back: *'Get it off!'*

Marie took in the room from this new angle. At the advertising parties all those years ago, the masks had remained nice all night; even by the end when plastered with alcohol, the uniform was still magazine slick. Sometimes there was cocaine and just about everybody including her had indulged in an illicit grope, but like most of the wives, most of the time, Marie had stayed nice. You got used to the disgraces, the script didn't vary much. But here it was the other way around. On stage and off, the masks were interiors erupting through propriety, disgrace was celebrated and, inside this vulgar intestinal display, Marie felt like a pod in a jungle, about to burst open in the heat.

When she looked back at the stage, Rob had his baby-doll around his ankles and was running through the previous acts, squinting at a piece of paper in his hand. Marie gawked at his long, left-leaning penis in its thatch of black hair. She gawked at the crowd. She saw a man in jeans with a white beard, extensively tattooed, an obese man in a t-shirt that said *Butter Bin*, and a priest in a cassock with grotesque, protruding black teeth and a hefting posture as though he were carrying something. Her eyes returned to the tattooed man. She pushed out her breasts and looked in his direction, feeling her tattoos glow. Eventually, his eyes drifted over. He glanced at her sourly.

Maybe he hadn't seen her. Marie moved to an angle that enabled her to watch Rob and still see the tattooed man out of the corner of her eye. A pain jabbed her stomach; she tried to ignore it.

'Put it away, willya, mate!' somebody yelled at the devil.

Rob pulled up his dress irritably and introduced the next act.

Tom Cruise from *Magnolia* roared through the speakers and a woman with red glitter lips, in stuffed y-fronts, strode on stage and began to mime him. *Respect the cock!* She thrust her pelvis forward. *And TAME the cunt.*

The woman with the panther tattoo sat beside Marie. She was wearing a badge that said *Tammy, Christian Youth Worker*. 'How are ya, luv?' she said in a Kiwi twang. 'Havin' a good time?'

'Yes.' Marie leant back as Rhys moved across her to kiss Tammy on the cheek.

'How are ya, babe? I hear you left the AIDS Council.'

'I'm at the Cancer Council now.'

'Out of the frying pan into the fire.'

'I love it there. I'm doing education.'

Tom had stripped off her t-shirt and y-fronts to glittery stars-and-stripes underwear and was speaking through what looked like a giant vagina around her head, breasts swinging. Tammy passed Marie a joint. Marie took the smoke into her lungs and held it, staring at the tattooed man, who had, she noticed now, fine long legs. She exhaled woozily, announcing, 'I'm a legs woman.'

'Oh yair?' Tammy drawled. Rhys cocked an eye at her.

'It's unusual in women, isn't it. It's usually the other way around. But I like legs.'

They followed Marie's gaze.

'Oh,' said Rhys. 'Gavin.'

'Not a good idea.' Tammy winced.

'Misogynist prick.'

Marie swallowed a mouthful of warm beer. She could feel a pulse fluttering in the corner of her left eye. She squeezed it but the pulse wouldn't stop. Tammy was on her left side. She ducked her head so Tammy wouldn't goggle at her hideous gigantic uncontrollable tic.

'Remember I drove for him when he was sick?' said Tammy. 'You forgive 'em for being pricks when they're that sick. But I don't put up with it now.'

'Nor should you.'

'He's gay, Marie.'

'That's alright. My son's gay.'

Rhys and Tammy laughed.

'Oh dear,' said Marie.

'I got your Eckies,' Tammy said to Rhys.

'What are they like? I can't afford to be too fucked tomorrow.'

'Just have a half. They're good.'

'Ta. Marie?'

'Thank you.'

Rhys broke the pills in half and shared them around. Marie

swallowed hers then remembered she had never had the drug before. She felt scared and at the same time determined to ride her fear, like a teenager. She stared at the stage. Tom now seemed to be a he again, swaggering about saying: *Hi y'all, yeah it's great to be down under; we're just out back countin' money.* The joint returned and Marie puffed on it greedily then Tammy disappeared. Rhys nudged her. 'I'm going to the toilet. You gonna be alright here?' Marie nodded, her mouth dry.

She watched the last performance on her own, a military man with a stockinged face, shaking to heavy metal. Behind him jerked two drag queens in masks with gaping teeth, bloodshot eyes and little blonde wigs, and as the music crescendoed the man stripped off his uniform to reveal a veined and muscled body, his penis a pointy dagger. Marie sat holding her wrists, feeling her pulse quicken. The drag queens twitched like skeletons and the music screeched like breaking machinery and the man stripped again, to bone, his face a skull, and danced maniacally. Marie had to look away. Through a gap in the crowd, the priest appeared full-length. Now she saw that what he had been holding was a metre-high doll dressed as a boy. Its arms were wrapped around his legs, its face buried in his crotch. Aghast, Marie looked back at the stage. The military man was thrusting his penis into a globe atlas, over and over, until it deflated. Sweat ran down Marie's spine.

This fluttering in her stomach must be the drug unfolding. It made her nervous and excited. She got up and wobbled along the wall till she found the toilets. Inside, her bowels opened and she left the cubicle refreshed. She regained her seat feeling weird and therefore right at home with these people.

Rob emerged from the crowd and sat beside her. He was back in his leathers and a western shirt, his make-up splotchy with sweat. He was evidently pleased to see her. 'How's it goin'?'

'Good!' Marie's tongue felt like a slab of wood. She could see the priest shuffling with his hands on the boy doll's head, holding it against his crotch with a lecherous sneer. Another man picked up the doll's feet, wrapped them around his hips and began to thrust. The doll flopped helplessly between them while people looked on, laughing or grimacing. The scene terrified Marie.

'Great crowd,' said Rob.

'You've trimmed your beard,' Marie managed. 'It suits you.'

'Thanks.' He offered her a drink from a blue metallic bottle. Marie wanted to wipe the nozzle but thought it might be rude. Besides, she was parched. Her eyes felt so dry they seemed to be dangling on sticks in the air. She took a long swig. It tasted divine. Clarity was immediate. 'You've put fresh mint into it or something.'

'Yeah. I freeze water with mint in it to take out. Stays cold all night. No plastic bottle waste. You like Stew's show?'

'Which one was that?'

'Just now. He was the main guy.'

'Oh.'

It was hard to find all these grotesqueries funny. The reality behind them stayed with her. It was like looking at a person whose skin had been flayed: no matter how beautiful or benign they were, you were still looking at viscera, the movement of blood and shit, the bare bones. Reality. At the same time a delicious inner warmth was moving down her back, through her limbs. She wanted to throw her arms around Rob.

'How'd the auction go?' he asked.

'Well, I sold.'

'Wow. After thirty years, was it? That's big.'

'Yes. But it just happens, like it's just another day.'

'Like death. The sun still rises. The birds still sing.'

Marie had another sip of Rob's water. The party boomed on. 'It was last weekend but it feels like a thousand years ago. It feels like I've been amputated.'

'Where you gonna move to?'

'I don't know. Rhys said you'd be the man to ask for help with that.'

'Did she?'

Natasha appeared, a marble statue robed in black. 'Going to the bar. Place your bets.'

'Drinks on me.' Marie gave Natasha a twenty-dollar note. Her hand shook slightly.

'Are you sure?'

'Yes. Please. Water for me.'

Natasha turned, and the crowd parted.

'Do you really own lots of properties?' Marie said to Rob.

'Yeah.' Rob laughed, slightly embarrassed. 'I got into it when I was really young. I was crap at school and this Economics teacher told me about the stockmarket, and's like, *Here, I'll show you a few things.* I had five hundred dollars saved from my weekend job and I invested that and it doubled then I invested it again, it doubled again. I couldn't believe it. It was the '80s.'

'What about the houses?'

'I bought my first one at nineteen. Got the deposit from the stockmarket investments.'

'Precocious.'

'It's a game. It goes both ways. I lost twenty thousand on gold the other day y'know. Don't put your money into the stockmarket, Marie. Not now.'

The music was growing louder with thumping bass and muttered incantations and sirens whirling like blades. Tadzio was dancing nearby in a pork-pie hat with a bird on a spring bouncing on top. His boyfriend without the beard and gut didn't look at all like Aschenbach. *Are you a freak?* said a female vocal. *Are you a freak?* Mel came and sat on Marie's right with a friend. They huddled over an electronic oblong in Mel's hand, her fingers fluttering across the screen. 'It's on YouTube,' she said to her friend.

'Where do you want to live?' Rob asked Marie.

'I want to stay by the water. But it's expensive.'

'Sydney's ridiculous.'

'Einstein the talking parrot!' Mel's friend shouted. 'Dontcha love yer iPhone?'

'Broc-coli,' Mel croaked back in an American parrot accent.

'You play your cards right,' said Rob, 'you can get a place to live *and* a rental property, and support yourself while you study.'

'I've done my sums. I'll probably have to get a job.'

Rob said in a low voice: 'You be our receptionist when Mel leaves.'

'What a great idea. Why do you stay in Sydney, Rob?'

'For work. And Rhys has to stay near Travis's father. What about you?'

'I've never lived anywhere else. I wouldn't know where to go.'

'Like we did consider Newcastle, but I'm not sure if they'd let us work there either.'

'Who's they?'

'Just business.' Rob shrugged. He leant forward and looked into the crowd, his shoulder blades like wings through the fabric of his shirt. The girls on Marie's other side stared at the iPhone, pressed it to their ears. There was something irresistible in the music: it seemed to ripple beneath Marie's feet. The pain in her stomach was gone. Somebody stopped to talk to Rob. Marie unpeeled her thighs from the plastic chair and stood up.

'Look at you,' said Mel in parrot. 'You're all *wet!*'

Both girls pitched forward, screaming with laughter.

Marie moved into the throng of dancers. She passed a group of men and women stripped to the waist, slick with sweat, smiling through heavy-lidded eyes. The Asian was shouting over the music to someone, '... *mined the fuck out of it.*' She saw Tammy with Butter Bin. She headed towards them and they made her welcome. There was a pause in the music and the crowd stilled, and looking around Marie felt a rush of love. She wormed on through, *excuse me, excuse me*, hands touching her shoulders, her back, people smiling as they gently manoeuvred her on her way.

The music began to build. *Come on ... come on ... come on ... come on ...* She passed the strange green creature who was fanning itself and looking around regally. On sighting Marie, it bowed and smiled. A piano melody spilt forth like a trickle of gems, and Marie found she was stuck. Then a cool cylinder was placed in her hand, followed by a pile of coins, and she saw Rhys and Natasha. Arms encircled her from behind: Stew. 'You scared me with your performance!' '*Good.*' Marie drank from her bottle and felt the fluid course through her body, reviving every cell. A horn sounded across the dance floor, plaintive, urgent, then came an outbreak of violent percussion and Marie slipped down to the bassline. There were bells and whistles and a woman fiercely whispering, *Take me upwards*, and Marie wrapped herself deeper into the bright coat of music, feeling the heat of the people around her, melting into their atmosphere. Somebody was smiling and touching her arms, *Beautiful, beautiful*, and her body became a ribbon threading through their mass, a pillar of salt dissolving into the pool of them, and she had no past, she had no future, just these dancing feet, this breath, this skin. *Take me upwards.*

Rhys's doctor worked in a terrace off south King Street dominated by a gnarled old hibiscus covered in red flowers. The air in the corridor was bitter with Chinese herbs. The worn floral carpet and fireplace in the waiting room reminded Marie of old aunts in Tasmania. She took *New Idea* from the rack and read an interview with a rock star in which he apologised to the journalist that he was late because he had been turning off all the powerpoints in his hotel room. His band was headlining at a green-powered concert. A photo showed him seated in front of the rig in lotus position.

The doctor nodded at the bottle of ulcer pills that Marie had brought in. 'How long've you been taking these?'

'Just over two months.'

'And no relief?'

'Yes. Sort of. But I'm not sure if it isn't because I've stopped drinking. Then the pain comes back. I don't know.'

'Okay. Hop up here and I'll examine you.'

She was a small woman with thick glasses and front teeth that stuck out judgementally. 'Who's your GP?' Her hands roamed over Marie's abdomen, pressing here and there. 'Why haven't you gone to see him?'

'I wanted a second opinion and Rhys recommended you.'

'Ah, I see. This is Rhys's work?'

'Yes.'

'Fair enough.' The doctor grinned and her teeth became joyful, childlike. Marie was positive she was a lesbian.

She began to whimper when the doctor's fingers found a painful spot. She dressed again and sat through a ream of questions, extended her arm for a blood test, took the sheaf of referrals. Leaves skittered down the side path. The doctor looked at her gravely. 'You need to see Dr French as soon as possible.'

'Do I need to worry?'

'It's never worth worrying.'

'What do you think is wrong with me?'

'I really can't say. Make those appointments as soon as you get home.'

The strangest memories came to Marie that afternoon in her garden. Charmaine Solomon's recipe for hibiscus flower curry that she had marked years ago but never got around to cooking. The high surf of wind through the bush at dawn: this with a mournful pang, as though she had left the place forever and wasn't in fact right next to the same bush now, but on a windless day. Beneath a pink, streaky sky, eating oysters with Ross on Palm Beach the evening he had asked her to marry him. Standing in line at the bank, heavily pregnant with Blanche, holding her bladder so tightly her teeth hurt. And furthest but somehow clearest, lying in the bath as a child, counting the frieze of tiled penguins along the wall, suddenly realising that she was Marie, touching her skin in awe, realising it was what contained her in this world.

All the memories were equidistant, and she was alone on another planet.

It took three days for her to produce a stool sample. In her recalcitrant belly a layer of hot rock burnt away her appetite and stilled her bowels. Her next appointment with Rhys approached and still she couldn't shit. She dutifully marked properties in Wednesday's paper, but felt too bad to go on inspections with Rob. By now she had become obsessed with her bowels, this Lutheran curse, the devil's work, each day she hoped for the blessing of evacuation. Impossible to concentrate on anything else as her belly shrivelled around its mysterious agony. Oh, for that most private of ecstasies, a big easy shit. To eat, drink, shit and sleep, all those daily pleasures she had taken for granted. Until it finally emerged in a long, painful release. Marie was elated.

The next day she arrived at the studio smiling. There was a

small crowd at the counter being managed by Mel. Marie went straight up the stairs.

'My cousin had a twisted bowel thing,' said Rhys.

'How does that manifest?'

'She got rushed to hospital. She nearly died. It was scar tissue from a fucked IUD in the '80s.'

'My god. I had an IUD.' Marie thought of her mother. Hysterectomy. Oh no.

'I didn't mean to freak you out. I mean it's really good you're getting checked out.'

'My IUD. Wouldn't that be just typical. To be punished for having contraception.'

'Bless you, Marie.'

'I'm sick of these tests. I was supposed to go house hunting with Rob on Wednesday.'

'That'll keep.'

'I've left it all so late.'

'Look. My cousin was fine. She had surgery and it was all sorted.'

Rhys bent over Marie's arm and the sunlight shone on the dull roots of her hair. Marie was dismayed by grey hair on Rhys, her ageless shaman. 'I hate getting old,' she snapped.

She wondered about the final barrier of dermis against which the ink drilled to a rest, the eternal stain filtering its picture through millions of renewing cells. She considered herself from the inside: tongues of fire, wings of a moth, the flower-studded vines weaving them together. And all the spaces of bare skin between like chinks of sky. She had read an account of a woman who had been fully tattooed in a matter of weeks, her husband working as fast as possible to make money from his wife in the sideshow. One hundred years later, Marie was possessed by a similar sense of urgency for different reasons. She was afraid of what the pain inside could mean. Rhys worked until dark to finish the passionflowers, one just inside her left forearm, on her upper right, the third on her chest, the vine curling and winding between. The flowers were maroon, purple and orange, with the clarity of botanical drawings.

Marie left the studio feeling closer to completion.

The days went by in a barrage of tests.

Sludge of barium, white hospital walls, IV'd tranquilliser. They X-rayed her oesophagus, her stomach in two parts. A gastroscope was inserted down her throat, the tube worming deep into her gullet. They told her to fast, to strip and put on a gown. They laid her on a table then slid her into a tunnel, nothing at all in that total enclosure but machine sounds and pounding fear. They opened her veins and took her blood, repeatedly. Ultrasounds, endoscopies, the swift sadistic punch of biopsy needles. They anaesthetised her and cut incisions in her belly through which they inserted a microscopic camera. Bewildered, Marie surrendered her body to each invasion. It was a battleground and she a mere spectator. Coming to after the laparoscopy with the murmur of doctors' voices overhead, men she would have dined with not three years ago as the wife of Ross King. Gingerly they lifted her gown to examine her dressings, their eyes like cockroaches scuttling over the fresco of tattoos.

Clark threw himself into the ocean and swam along the rip to the sandbank. He dragged his thighs through the water then stopped to watch the waves. It was early morning and the sky was still pink. Behind him, office workers were huffing across the sand with their personal trainers. Sleek bodies in new sports clothes with heart-rate monitors jogged along Queen Elizabeth Drive. To his right, surfers perched among the waves like gulls. He always thought of them as birds, bobbing on the water, then the sudden take-off. Soon they would become black crows, when the sea turned cold and wetsuits were donned and his favourite season in Bondi began.

His mother was having another biopsy this morning. She had looked so good the day of the auction, who would have thought. He remembered the flames, how the skin rose stridently with colour, and how the compact nature of her body had surprised him. Clark had never desired a woman over forty until Sylvia, but Sylvia looked younger and was in the same generation as him, so she didn't count. The fact that Clark was at university with adults young enough to be his children was impossible to ignore. There were millions of people this age all over the world now. It seemed like only yesterday that he had noticed his first white pubic hair: this morning he had discovered a whole clump. Over forty was old — he would soon be old; his lover was already — all that awaited him was more white pubes, more younger people, more possibility of his own terminal illness. His mother's age, on the other hand, used to be reassuring: he had always taken comfort from the fact that her body moved in another orbit, purged by maternity of any endemic sensuality. Yet that day he had seen a woman in her, defiant and strong. The older he got, the closer in age to him she seemed.

A wave approached and Clark began to swim but missed the peak and churned along unsatisfyingly for a few metres. By the time he regained the sandbank, the sun was another millimetre higher, shearing straight across the Pacific into his eyes. A wave came and he pushed off hard, charging to shore in a mane of foam.

In Icebergs sauna he soaked up the gossip. Somebody had died in the surf on the weekend. A South African woman mistakenly swimming at the south end had received a head injury from a board and was dead by the time they pulled her to shore. Clark didn't believe them at first, but the quiet precision of the discussion convinced him. He didn't know who the men talking were, only that they were in the sauna every time he came here. His age, brown and fit, they sprawled across the wooden benches with the comfort of natives. They would be here in forty years' time, replenishing the ranks of the old lizards who swam and sunbaked at the pool all year round. Clark increasingly emulated them. After living in Bondi for a year, he wanted the same committed future, to settle and grow this place in his bones. A pale slouched man entered as he left, greeting everybody eagerly. Something about him unnerved Clark. Blasting himself in the showers, it came to Clark that the man was his döppelganger and a longstanding fear of not being cool enough to hang with the big boys surfaced. God, he was a child today. He walked home haunted by the dead woman and the fact that her story had not been publicised. How stupid to assume information of any calamity was available with the flick of a switch or for a few coins at the newsagent's.

So many deaths you didn't read about. So many murders. Clark wasn't looking forward to today's research. He had ransacked every early colonial painting he could find, but his mind remained closed. Each day it became clearer that he didn't feel confident with the material till photography, as though he needed the imagery to be as close to real life as possible.

His thesis was at its best in the early mornings, in that liminal space between sleeping and waking when it filled his head as a glorious tome. But when Clark came to the library he drifted. Words rose up like battalions and filled the horizon, bearing down upon him. He ended up back at his table by the window with the old comforts of Max Dupain or inner-city crime-scene photos. Nineteen-fifties Avalon, reminding him of his mother. The brothel on Palmer Street. The Tradesman's Arms — now East Village where he was going to meet Sylvia at six o'clock — back in the days when crims and hookers drank there. The photo of Sylvia in his phone. And once he began to think about Sylvia, he couldn't stop. He ended up thinking about her all day long.

He got to East Village early, ordered a schooner and sat at the window looking onto Palmer Street. He knew there was something wrong by the tone of Sylvia's text messages this week. He also knew that she loved him, which made him feel invulnerable. If they loved each other, anything was possible. He hoped that something was wrong in her marriage. He pictured her troubled face, kissing her tears, his little flat her succour, and a feeling of contentment flooded his body.

'Hallo, stranger.' Sylvia sat down beside him, schooner in hand. She pulled her stool closer so their thighs touched. He could smell her hair.

'I didn't see you come in.'

'I snuck up on you.'

'How are you?'

'Wiped out. This always happens to me at the beginning of first semester. I can't believe the workload, though it hasn't changed. What about you? How was the library?'

'Great! I spent the whole day thinking about you.'

Their hands coiled around one another like mating snakes as they drank their beer, smirking stupidly, watching Darlinghurst roll from day to night.

'Franco's beginning to suspect something.'

'Really? How do you know?'

'Text messages at midnight.'

'Don't you have your phone on silent?'

'I forgot. I switched it on when we came out of the movies and two came through straightaway.'

'Sorry,' said Clark, not feeling it in the slightest. What he really wanted was to shout his love for her at the top of his voice and send a thousand text messages at once. *Ping ping ping ping!*

'We have to put the brakes on.'

Clark nodded soberly. 'My head understands, my heart howls, but' — he stared at her — 'my dick didn't hear that at all.'

'That just went straight to my cunt,' she said matter-of-factly, staring back at him.

'What?' he said, just to hear her say it again.

'You saying "my dick".'

His excitement grew at the feeling of all the people in the room behind them, the idea of themselves as spectacle, their hidden engorged genitals. 'Maybe we should lock them in the toilets together and let them sort it out. We can wait for them here. Give 'em a lift home.'

'Bugger that. They can walk.'

'Home together.'

'You know that's not possible, Clark.'

'It is at my place.'

'Okay then. I get to sleep earlier without my cunt anyway.'

'I don't.'

Sylvia laughed into her beer then put it down. '*Clark.* I'm serious. We have to put the brakes on. I can hardly work. I'm really stressed.'

Clark looked at his lap, prickling with insecurity. 'I hate having to talk about this in public.'

'I don't trust myself when I'm in private with you.'

'Are you dumping me?'

'I'm in love with you. But I'm also married.'

The pub was filling with suits. The music was getting louder. Two men came and sat beside Clark.

'Right,' Sylvia said determinedly. 'Let's talk about work. Tell me about your thesis. The photos.'

'Not just photos. It's visual representation. Images.' Clark felt irritated: he had told her this more than once. 'But it might have to change.' The scent of male cologne was invading his nostrils. It was the man next to him, spreading his elbows, laughing loudly. Clark longed to smell Sylvia's hair again.

'You mean you might have to imagine without visual prompts?'

'My imagination's working overtime at the moment, believe me.'

'Cla-ark.'

'Okay, okay. The problem is that my relationship with the early paintings is changing. I'm feeling mistrustful towards them. You know that I'm eschewing the notion of authenticity, cos it's all about conjecture, myth making, the politics of representation. But I keep favouring photography and the twentieth century. It's like a drug, drawing me back.'

'Why do you think that is?'

'Crime-scene photography isn't trying to tell a story. The ego of the image maker let alone cultural presumptions are absent so I can have a more unmediated relationship with the image. I don't have to interrogate the motivations of an artist. The photos are like prose, George Orwell's pane of glass.'

Sylvia nodded, watching him, and he remembered their first drink together, how avidly she had listened to him and how consciously he had used his brain to seduce her. Janice had hated intellectual conversation. Sylvia loved it. Her husband was some kind of businessman. Probably never picked up a book in his life. An intellectually starved relationship. Clark decided that second that he wouldn't let her go. He would use anything and everything in his power to keep her. He heard the man next to him say: ... *fucked a guy in one of those apartments ...*

Sylvia said, 'But there's always a motivation behind an image, even if it's prosaic. And there's no such thing as no cultural presumptions.'

'Yee-aahh, maybe.'

'And wouldn't it be more interesting for you to write about things that are slippery rather than straightforward? Isn't a thesis supposed to change as it goes along, like a discovery?'

'It's not just that. I've probably seen more crime-scene photos of this street alone than all of the north shore put together. The available material just doesn't correlate to what I wanted to write about.'

The man next to Clark was guffawing loudly. Clark wanted to punch him. He remembered the painting of Governor Phillip speared in Manly Cove and felt excited. The heavens opened. Today's decision that pre-photographic images were impenetrable was a cop-out.

'What *did* you want to write about?'

'Crime and misdemeanour on the north shore, as far back as possible.' Payback, he thought.

'What constitutes crime?'

Clark's mouth opened and shut. He took a swig of beer then turned to marvel at Sylvia. 'I actually don't know.'

Sylvia put her arm around him. 'I think it's a fantastic idea. The more ambiguity the better.'

'Anyway, you'd be the expert on crime, wouldn't you?' Fate, he thought. Exactly the woman I should have fallen in love with at this time!

'In some areas but not others. The law is totally specialised.'

Feeling her body this close, knowing it would be sleeping with another tonight, Clark fell silent and miserable. He looked at the church on the corner and remembered graffiti that had been scrawled beneath its *Jesus is Coming* billboard the first time he had come to Darlinghurst. *Wear a raincoat.* It had been there for years. Or had it? Maybe he just read it somewhere and superimposed it onto his memory. But he did remember coming here for coffee back then, how grungy it was. Nearly all the cafés run by working-class

Italians. In the park diagonally opposite he had seen a heap of bands at an anti-nuclear concert, including The Go-Betweens and Laughing Clowns. Opposite it again, on the site of the old pie factory, was the white edifice of Republic, where the loud fag next to him had *fucked some guy*. It was so easy for them. All the whinging and declaiming, but it was so fucking easy.

'Is your place like that?' He pointed to Republic.

'God, no. It's 1920s. Art Deco.'

It was also easy to imagine the flat that Sylvia shared with her husband, somewhere at the back of Potts Point where a few blocks had been saved from the developers. There would be moulded ceilings, floorboards, plants on the balcony. White walls, white crockery. Ikea. Clark didn't want to know the address. He didn't want to wake up howling beneath her conjugal window. He followed the passage of a man with a briefcase past the pub to the next block where he unlocked the door of a renovated terrace. Another fag, no doubt.

'Mr Lawyer or Computer Whatever has just gone home to one of Tilly Devine's old brothels. If only he knew. I think of her whenever I drink in here, screeching at her girls. All the sly-grog crims drank in here. You wouldn't know it now. It's so nice and clean.'

'Now there's an interesting chapter that I could certainly help you with: prostitution as crime, or not. Some of these houses are still brothels.' Sylvia pointed to a terrace. 'I worked my way through uni in that one for two years. It was called Sweethearts.' She gave the name a flirtatious spur. 'Then I moved to A Touch of Class. We all called it Touch Your Arse.' She laughed. 'And Sweethearts of course, became, Cheaptarts.'

Clark sat shocked and silent beside her. A button had been pressed, a wall gone up; beyond it Sylvia was on her back, spreading her legs for the masses. The image filled him with lust and anger. A hot gritty wind rushed into the pub as a group entered the Palmer Street door.

Sylvia was rubbing his thigh. 'Come on, Clark, I thought you'd be fine with it. You talk about your Tillys with such affection.'

'I am fine! I am!'

'Can I get us another beer?'

'That'd be great.'

When Clark spoke of his own past, he wasn't calm like Sylvia. He flashed over certain periods with an unresolved mixture of shame and accusation. He came away from their trysts intoxicated by all he'd learnt and all that remained to be disclosed, but suddenly the fact that she'd lived forty years without him filled him with despair. He would remain excluded from her past forever. He thought with bitterness how hard it was for them to find a time and place to make love, while all those others had just walked in off the street and had her.

Once he had gone to a strip show in the Cross. On a drunken spree with schoolmates after the last HSC exam, he had followed a flashy spruiker off Darlinghurst Road. He remembered the stairs, the smell of cheap cleaning product, the pink-lit stage and scrawny girls, one of them older than the rest. She was the one he fixated on, her sagging breasts strangely arousing. Desire and disgust tangoed aggressively along his arteries. Then an elbow in his ribs and the boy next to him was yelling at the stripper, 'Hey, Mum, Clark hasn't done his homework.' Clark joined in and they were thrown out for heckling. The stripper would have been younger than he was now. Sylvia returned with two beers. Clark drank his deeply, cringing at his snide, superior adolescent self.

Sylvia took his hand. 'Talk to me.'

'I'm worried about my mother.'

'I thought you said the house sold. Won't she get her fresh start now?'

'It's not that. She's been having tests. Something's wrong.'

'You worry too much, sweetheart.'

'Yeah, I know.'

'Cheaptart.' She nuzzled him.

They said goodbye in their usual spot by the building site, hugging against the cyclone fence.

'What are you doing to me?' Sylvia pressed her face into his neck. 'I want you so much.'

Clark's eyes stung. '*I need you.*'

They called each other sweetheart all the time after that. Or, occasionally, cheaptart. They texted each other every day. *What are you up to sweetheart? x. Sitting in the uni café quietly dying at the thought of my supervisor … & yr hands down my pants. xo. Are you digging in those archives sweetheart? Wish you were digging in me. x. Sweetheart, I miss u. xo. Cheaptart where r u, haven't heard from u in HRS. R u ok? xox. Terrible news sweetheart. My mother has cancer. Call me. xoxo*

WATER

MARIE CARRIED HER SHOPPING down the path and left it by the front door. Six p.m. Already dusk. In one day, it seemed, the sun had swung further away from the earth. Cockatoos were making a racket down in the reserve. She uncoiled the hose and began to water the bed where Iceland poppies were waiting to sprout. The pointlessness of it mocked her. Why had she planted these seeds when she knew the house was going to be sold? Why had she clung to the idea of the garden outliving her? But now her stupidity might pay off, in a way she had never imagined. Like rounding the corner of an unknown road and suddenly seeing cliffs drop before you. Sometimes you were going too fast to stop. And here she was, watering the garden anyway. Stupid, stupid, stupid.

Inside the house, she lit a candle on the coffee table. She picked up the phone to ring Clark but, feeling mute and disinclined to duty, put it back into its cradle. *Six months*, it was ridiculous. Two more months here, then where? And the oncologist delivering the news like a morning paper. It seemed too shoddy a story to pass on to anyone. Marie sat in the living room listening to the sounds of the house, sensing the bodies and food and conversation that had passed through it. She felt flattened and transparent, a woman of dusty air projected onto the couch.

Her mother had lived for decades after her hysterectomy, eventually dying of a heart attack. Two years later, her father had died in his sleep of a brain aneurysm. Marie wondered now about her mother's final hour, whether or not she knew she was dying. A moment of terror as she realised the pain in her chest was fatal, then the eternal dark. Unless in fact she had wanted to die. She had her God. Not for her, the eternal dark.

Marie didn't want to talk to anyone for fear they would blame her. She hadn't looked after herself, she had drunk too much and eaten badly, she had held sadness and anger in her stomach all these years until they turned against her. She hadn't gone to the doctor early enough, she had ignored her symptoms. She only had herself to blame.

Nothing had changed, people were still the same. Every sickness was a curse, every dying a punishment. And every death a murder, or suicide.

The garden at night was a cool, deep space filled with the sounds of crickets and one late willy-wagtail. Marie stepped across the lawn, lifted her nightie and squatted beneath the lemon tree. The moon slid from its veil, flooding her to the marrow, and everything around her lit up like a stage. She could see the crinkled furls of hibiscus, and high up in the angophora the lit cigarettes of a possum's eyes. And so it might happen as she had originally wanted. The garden might outlive her.

Leon didn't know what to pack because he didn't know how long he would be gone. His housemate's girlfriend agreed to sublet his room for a while, so Leon pushed his clothes up one end of the wardrobe, ran the vacuum cleaner over the floor, and boxed some items out of the way. He didn't know where his mother was with everything; she sounded exactly the same on the phone. They had talked about the garden, him automatically suggesting that he bring some cuttings, her automatically agreeing. He would realise the folly of this by the time he was collecting them but continued for the sake of palliation. His mother had the same voice, the same advice. *Drive safely, Leon.* He had driven just over the limit all the way down the Gold Coast then the sky closed in and the fender in front approached as bushfires near Grafton engulfed them. He wound up his window and slowed to a crawl. The acrid smell of burning stole through every opening in the vehicle. He reached back to touch the damp newspaper around the cuttings and found it rapidly drying. And what would happen when the two-month settlement period was over? Where would his mother go? The crack across his right boot dug into Leon's foot as he worked the pedals. And how the fuck would he make money down in Sydney? Well, the house had been sold, and he would be helping his mother. So she could buy him a new pair of boots. Those Timbalands he'd had his eye on …

Blanche was sick too. 'Vomiting a lot,' she'd said on the phone. 'I don't know if it's a bug or some twisted psychosomatic empathy thing.' When Leon asked her how work was going, she told him she had lost a big account, her voice uncharacteristically strained with tears, enabling Leon to become even cooler, as though his feelings were drained into the dam of his sister's grief. He let her run the conversation, dabbing it with the occasional murmur, like a lion absently patting a cub.

What he felt deep down was a mulish resistance, everything charged by high alert. He was dreading the thought of his mother incapacitated. A cold alone could provoke impatience in Leon; the reverence and inertia of serious illness would be intolerable. He felt immensely irritated at having to leave Brisbane just when the business had got to its feet and the work season begun.

And yet he chose this. More than anything he felt relief at being taken from the humdrum of normal life into a drama where he would play a main part. His mother had told him not to rush down and Leon had interpreted this as a plea for company. After her phone call, he paced around the house lifting things and replacing them, forgetting his movements like a goldfish after one lap. He smelt burning food for half an hour before realising it was his own dinner. He could have stayed in Brisbane a few more weeks, finished the job he was doing and waited for the bushfires to burn out, but instead he had left five days after the news. For an hour around Kempsey he was trapped behind a semi-trailer, the parched forest coughing dust against his windscreen, a bloody sunset seeping into the land. He drove into the night, wide awake with excitement.

Yet here she was as though nothing had happened, in the garden in her old sunhat and gardening shirt when Leon arrived early the next morning. He walked down the side path and found her mixing up Seasol by the tap. He was astonished by how wiry and energetic she seemed. Her body felt so firm when she embraced him.

'The garden looks fabulous.'

'It was at its worst on auction day, actually. It's recovering now.' She held Leon at arm's length and examined him. 'Look at this beard. You smell of bushfire.'

'I need to have a shower.' He reached for the bucket. 'Can I do that for you?'

'No, no. I know where I'm up to.' She looked at him again. 'I *like* that beard.'

Leon wandered around while she worked. 'You don't really need to be doing this, do you?'

'Not officially. But my babies are hungry, so as long as I'm here, I may as well feed them.' She pointed out changes. 'I put a lilly pilly in place of the banksia. What do you think?'

'It seems happy.'

Looking up at the house, pain bore down upon him, and Leon rued not having been here for the sale. It had taken his mother's illness to wake him up. He had sworn after his two trips to Sydney at the end of last year that he wouldn't come back except in the case of emergency; he hadn't regarded the loss of the house as an emergency, and he couldn't believe that now. It made him glad to be here. The house stood above facing the morning sun, oblivious to the churn of his emotions. Marie saw his expression. 'Yes, it's so sad.'

'I'm sorry I wasn't here now.'

'You didn't need to be. Clark and I weren't.'

'I mean here in general. In Sydney. I might not have seen any of this again.'

Marie stopped by the door just before they went inside, and looked down at the harbour. 'It's so beautiful, isn't it. You must miss it. I'm sure going to.'

When she removed her hat and long sleeves, Leon noticed deep grooves in her forehead and alongside her mouth, the glitter of fatigue in her eyes. He was astounded by the brilliance of the vines coursing down her arms, and how comfortably she wore them. He couldn't help staring.

'Oh, look. You haven't seen the moth.' She reached over her

shoulder and pulled back the cloth of her t-shirt. The moth hung
before him, hypnotic, disturbing, cousin to his gift that was now
displayed over the door to the kitchen. Even partly obscured by
clothes, it seemed big as a kite, the wing shimmering silkily. He
wanted to touch the luxurious green, every line careful as a
Rousseau brushstroke, but he couldn't think of anything to say.
His initial joy at seeing his mother so light-hearted and capable was
giving way to disconcertment.

'I'm reverting, Leon. I've decided my mother was right: if you
can't say anything nice, then don't say anything at all.'

'They're, um, the colours are amazing.'

'I thought you'd appreciate the moth for obvious reasons.'

'Yeah.' Clearly he had been privileged by this viewing. It sat
heavily in his lap like an over-extravagant present, mocking the
sympathy he'd been accumulating since news of her illness. She
didn't seem to need him except as an audience. 'I'm sorry, Mum.
I'm a bit overwhelmed, that's all. I brought you a bottle of wine.
Do you want a drink?'

'It's eight o'clock in the morning, Leon!'

'I've been driving all night and I'm arse around with the time.'

Leon felt queasy. He hadn't eaten. He went out to the ute to
fetch his bags, took them upstairs and had a shower. His mother
was lying on the couch when he came back down, asleep it seemed.
He went into the kitchen to make coffee and toast, and by the time
he brought them out to the deck, Marie had roused and was sitting
at the table, brushing the cat on her lap.

'So what are the doctors saying? When do you start
chemotherapy?'

'They don't know if I'll have it yet.'

'Why not? Don't they need to act fast?'

'The decision will be mine. I'm going in next week. One good
thing about doddery old Mopoke, she's very easy to brush now.'
Mopoke stretched her head out and the sound of her purr rumbled
over to Leon. Marie flipped her around like a cushion and began
to brush her stomach. Mopoke squirmed feebly. 'She's on so many
pills now, poor thing. More than her mother.'

'What are you on?'

'Painkillers, laxatives, anti-nausea tablets.'

'You have lost weight.'

'I've been hearing that for months. It used to be a compliment.'

'Are you in much pain?'

'It comes and goes. It's like bad indigestion. More irritating than anything.'

Leon waited for more but his mother just cooed and brushed the senile cat. 'Clark said something about six months.'

'Don't worry, Leon, I'm going to beat this. Your mum is tough as old boots, you know.' She swung her attention to his tattoo. 'When did you get this?'

'When I got to Brisbane. We talked about it. It's nothing.'

He thought of the sauna and its parade of bodies, the guys who were desperate for you to see their tatts. How pointless it all seemed now. Or was it just her, barging in, shrivelling Leon's fantasy land? He regretted his dumb tattoo. Did his mother think they occupied the same territory?

'You should be careful about getting too much sun on this, Leon. Who did it?'

'I can't remember.'

'It's a Dayak design.'

'It's just a tribal tattoo, Mum.'

'You could have got a Celtic armband. You're half Celtic.'

She dropped his arm and left his hand in hers. Her clammy hand, like an amphibious animal. He hated her and hated himself for rushing down here. Of course she could beat the cancer; there were new treatments all the time, most people survived it these days, didn't they? Did Clark have any idea what he was talking about when he said six months? Leon stared out over the dry listless garden. 'I've never seen Sydney like this,' he said wretchedly.

'You'd be celebrating your mother's side,' Marie mused. 'I don't think your father has any Celtic ancestry.'

And why was his room the only one with a bed left in it? He would have preferred to stay in Clark's attic. Lying on his back, a feeling of holiday boredom engulfed Leon. He went to the window and, looking out at the harbour, the eternal blue sky and moving tree tops, he experienced a moment of disorientation, forgetting what time of day and even what month it was. It came to him that it was the end of March, but with the heat it could have been January, October even, the hot one of last year. Time seemed to be standing still. All the while the disappearing seconds sapped him. He could barely motivate himself to go to the toilet. He moved finally, throwing his dirty clothes into a corner then unpacking. Placing underwear in his old sock drawer, his fingers touched glass. It was an old Vegemite jar, full of dust. He rolled it between his palms in surprise. It was a childhood time capsule, once containing the decoy tails of skinks caught by Mopoke that Leon had collected as little trophies of saved lives. He had considered it years later when packing to leave home, the tails by then brittle as burnt matchsticks. Now the jar's contents were completely desiccated. He put it on the windowsill, letting light through it, wondering if his mother had deliberately saved it. His presence here didn't make the slightest difference: he couldn't save her.

Susan rang when Marie was getting ready to go to the vet. 'I'm sorry, Marie. I'm so sorry. First the sale of the house. Now this!'

'That's alright,' Marie replied curtly. 'It isn't your fault.' She wondered how Susan knew. The Mosman gossip mill gleely churning away, no doubt. She should have charged entry fees.

'Do you have a good oncologist?'

'Yes.'

'Because I was going to recommend Dr Rossmann who looked after Delia Braithwaite.'

'Delia died. And Rossmann is at the Royal North Shore.'

'Of course. Where are you?'

'The RPA.'

'What on earth are you doing at the RPA?'

'That's where the referred specialist was. The North Shore's no better.'

'You're not wrong there. Women miscarrying in toilets and so on. And are you eating?'

'Yes.'

'Sleeping?'

'Yes.'

'Are they going to operate?'

'No.'

'When do you start chemotherapy?'

'I don't know.'

'Is there anything I can do?'

'No.'

Mostly she was lying. The oncologist, Dr Wroblewski, was stiff and impenetrable. Eating was as difficult as sleeping. Chemotherapy as soon as possible was highly likely, and Susan could have done plenty. But it was true they weren't going to operate. The cancer was too advanced. It clung like an epiphyte to the wall of her stomach, millimetres from her spleen and liver. It was buried in the very pit of her, yet she still could not accept it.

She had woken in a rage.

'I knew there was something wrong with you.' Susan began to cry. 'I *knew* it.'

Marie held the phone away from her ear. She had fantasised about this moment often enough. By the sickbed of her dreams, perfidious friends and family would be sorry. All conversation would cut to the chase; there would be no bullshit. The worst offenders would be turned away at the door. Desperate for entry, they would recognise their villainy and beg for her forgiveness. The fantasies would end there, with her all-powerful in her throne-bed, deciding their fate.

'When can I come and see you?'

'Any time.'

'Are your children with you? Louise said Leon was coming down.'

'He arrived yesterday. Do you want a word?'

Leon had just walked into the kitchen, his face creased with sleep, and without waiting for an answer from Susan, Marie handed the phone to him. He looked at her enquiringly. 'It's Susan,' Marie whispered with a sadistic smile. She put the steaming phone into his hand then went to find her handbag.

What she hadn't factored into her fantasies was the burden of allaying the distress of others, let alone facing her own. There was no door: everybody had free passage, just like the tumour. And she wasn't in bed, let alone on a throne. She was stuck in the corridor in the middle of the madding crowd. Illness clouded as it enlightened; old arguments remained unresolved. She was sick of answering questions that were unclear even to herself, and ashamed of her dysfunctional body.

She needed to push them all away, she could only swallow the facts in private. This bitter pill, like a tapeworm writhing in her mouth, going down. She couldn't bear their fear on top of her own, hatching an army in her interior, ready for its rampant feasting.

She drove up to the Junction in a glorious roar of rage and burnt rubber, Mopoke on the passenger seat, chin and paws hanging over the edge. I'm not helpless, I'm taking my cat to the vet. You think I'm sick? Look at *her*. I'm the nurse, not the patient. Don't even think about changing lanes, you bastard. I've got right of way, I've got cancer!

She marched into the waiting room with Mopoke, realising at that moment that she had come out with her arms bare. She scoured the seats for someone daring to gawk at her. *What would you know?* she would say with a glare. *Have you got cancer?* But there was only a young man with a muzzled pit bull. One move on my cat, Marie thought, and you're *dead*. The man glanced up, smiled vaguely, then returned to his yachting magazine. Marie strode into the surgery ready for battle with her diminutive vet, but he took one look at her arms and lit up. 'What beautiful work! Who did those?'

'Rhys,' Marie snapped.

'Rhys! I tried to get an appointment with her, but she was booked out.' The vet rolled up his shirtsleeve and showed Marie the head of a tiger that was slinking around his elbow. 'I got this done by Huey. Do you know him?'

'No,' said Marie, taken aback. 'It's lovely.'

Mopoke crouched on the table between them. The vet secured his sleeve, put his hands on the cat and cooed. 'And how are we today, Moey?'

'She's having trouble pooing again.'

'That's because her hips are getting so frail. The arthritis.'

Mopoke let out a long miaow. 'It's alright, sweetie.' Marie stroked her.

The vet picked up the cat, kissed her on the forehead, and took her into the room adjacent to give her an enema. Marie stood behind the closed door, and at the sound of Mopoke howling, tears burst out of her face.

Blanche caught a cab into town to drive Marie home from hospital in Marie's car. Marie had parked on Missenden Road and, by the time her consultation was finished, a fine had been slipped under the windscreen wiper. She looked pale and unsteady as she shut her door. Blanche steered into the traffic. 'This was the last test, wasn't it?'

'For the time being.'

'God, it's endless. Are you in pain?'

'They gave me pethidine.' Marie closed her eyes behind her sunglasses. She was happy that Blanche was taking her home but also wished she was alone, so she could fart freely. The longer she held her wind, the more the cramps increased.

Broadway was a concrete valley divided by a stagnant metal river. Blanche wondered if her mother was asleep or merely absent. She inched down the hill.

Marie had her eyes open now and was looking out the window. 'I'm sorry you have to do this awful drive, Blanche.'

'It's fine. But I don't understand why you aren't at the North Shore.'

'The Pacific Highway would be just as bad, wouldn't it?'

'Probably. And it's a bit of an abattoir, that hospital by all accounts. The traffic's bad because everybody's avoiding the cross-city tunnel.'

'So they should.'

'I use it. It's quicker. Work pays.'

'All these bloody tunnels and roadways. They carve up the city into little fortified towns then they make us pay for it. It's a form of segregation.' Saying so much made her bilious; Marie tried to settle her stomach.

'There's no public transport, and we need to get around. In all the surveys, people prefer cars. You can't turn back the clock, Mum. Sydney's a car city.'

'Well, I'm sick of it. I'm going to move over this way, so I won't have to drive so much.'

Another pointless conversation about the future. Unlike her brothers, Blanche didn't believe her mother would survive long enough to set up another house, but she played along. 'We'll find somewhere for you to rent while you recuperate. Hugh's pretty confident he can stretch the settlement to three months. The owners don't want to move in straightaway.'

The *owners*, thought Marie. 'They're going to renovate, aren't they,' she said flatly.

Blanche said nothing.

By the time they reached Elizabeth Street, Marie could hold on no longer. A damp gust escaped and she sat there mortified. 'Sorry.'

'It's okay.' Blanche wound down the window and switched the air-conditioning to full. She gulped some air then told her mother, in an attempt at solidarity, 'My chiro does this thoracic adjustment where he lifts me up from under the shoulders with a towel against my back, and yesterday, instead of cracking me, this big fart came out.' She laughed to help the story along. Marie responded feebly. She could feel her mother's effort and pain. She could still smell her. She tried not to gag.

On entering the house, Blanche immediately went to find Mopoke. She was shocked by the crotchety wobble and poking hip bones. She plunged her nose into the fur. 'She smells like old lady.'

'I'll take it that's a compliment.' Marie opened her handbag and stared in vaguely. She sat at the kitchen table then stood with a strange expression on her face and left the room. A thrumming began in her ears as she entered the bathroom then she was sliding down the wall. She slumped on the floor, head roaring, tiles icy beneath her sweating palms, then she crawled over to the toilet and hung over the bowl, every organ in her body heaving. There was nothing but bile. She gargled and splashed her face, then sat on the toilet till she had regained her balance.

'You look like your name,' she said to her daughter back in the living room.

'Christ, we're a pair, aren't we. I just threw up in the laundry.'

Marie took off her shoes and lay on the couch. 'Have you had a pregnancy test?'

Blanche looked incredulous. She couldn't even remember the last time she'd had sex with Hugh, besides which, they used condoms. He slid into her mind as he had been that morning, pouch-eyed, saggy-hipped, slurping juice from the carton. She pushed him away. 'I think I've got a bug. You've run out of lime cordial.'

'Leon will be home with the shopping soon. I used to throw up constantly for the first three months, and with you I had something called hyperemesis. They put me in hospital for five days.' She lay there stroking the cat, enjoying the breeze and the return of hunger. 'Blanche, darling, what we both need is mint and lemongrass tea. And toast with Vegemite.'

'Okay.'

Blanche walked down the stairs and through the rumpus room into the garden. The mint was scorched but the lemongrass was thick and high, sprouting seeds in the middle. She clasped some roots and yanked. One came free, the other sliced her palm. She began to cry. She cursed Terry and everyone at work. She picked some scorched mint, unable to stop crying. She felt like an idiot. She went into the laundry and ran water over the cut and rinsed her eyes, then went back upstairs.

'You've been crying, haven't you?'

'I lost the Coke account.'

'Oh, darling, I'm sorry.'

'Terry's furious.' Blanche began to cry again.

Marie watched her with pity.

Blanche walked rapidly to the bathroom but once inside found she couldn't vomit. She didn't know why she was crying. Because of the lost account, because of the lost house and the pathos of picking herbs there? Because her mother might be dying, because she might be pregnant. Because along with the dread that this possibility brought was a flash of soft baby's skin, the wondrous lightness of a newborn. She hadn't cried for years: this tear-streaked fragile woman of the last few weeks was a stranger to her. She was poise, cool, and smarts personified. She braced herself over the sink, wanting to purge all of it.

Four hours later, Blanche rang her mother with the test results. 'I can't believe it. You knew, didn't you.'

'I'm not sure I knew anything much this afternoon, Blanche.'

'Are you feeling better? Have you eaten?'

'Much better. We've just had pumpkin soup.'

Blanche could hear the television in the background, tuned to Channel Ten news like hers. When she spoke to Clark there was a delay, but the transmission on her mother's set came in perfect synchronicity.

Marie said, 'You didn't want this did you.'

'I finally get the promotion I've been working towards for years, I bodge a big job. Now this.'

'It's not your fault, Blanche. Now listen. What are you going to do?'

'I don't know. Hugh wants it.' *It*, she thought. This thing in her body. This replicating cell that her husband wanted, as something of his. And it *was* partly his. The simple biological imperative of reproduction — a part of one organism entering another to make something new — seemed preposterous.

'Of course Hugh wants it. You're thirty-seven, Blanche. Do you want children?'

'I don't want to have another abortion.' Blanche's voice trembled. 'I couldn't stand it. And I do want to have kids but I'm not sure if I'm ready.'

'I'm sure abortions are less traumatic these days.'

'No, they're not; the procedure hasn't changed at all, we're just older. But that can make it worse!'

'Try not to get worked up. You're not going to do anything you don't want to do.'

As she soothed Blanche, Marie wondered if she had sounded as though she was encouraging her to have an abortion. She didn't want that. She would have loved another grandchild. The mere idea of holding a little baby made her glow and Blanche in her opinion was leaving it too late. At the same time she was afraid that encouraging her to have the child would be seen as disregarding her career. Imagining Blanche in labour, Marie felt her blood rush towards her daughter in empathy. Helping Blanche through her abortion was, paradoxically enough, a happy memory for Marie.

It was the beginning of the HSC. An end-of-school drunken-night pregnancy, no doubt. Marie knew the boy, John Reid, and thought he was nice, but just nice, nothing else. He and Blanche weren't in love. She remembered Blanche haemorrhaging. Marie had bundled up the bloody sheets and gone down through the rumpus room to the laundry to avoid Ross. Instead she walked right by him, because he had taken his coffee with the weekend papers to the bottom garden.

He lifted his head as she passed. 'Blanche still in bed?'

'I don't know.' Marie went into the laundry and ran the tap.

'It's midday.' His voice approached. 'She's got a Maths exam on Monday.'

'She's also got the flu.'

He stood behind Marie in the doorway. Always the dandy, he was dressed in bone linen trousers and a salmon silk shirt. He watched her press the sheets into the tub. She angled her body to hide the bloodstains but it was too late. 'She got her periods?'

'Yes.'

'Well, she can clean up after herself, can't she? We're due at the Tottis' at one.'

'She has the flu, and she has studying to do. I'll be ready in time, Ross.'

Ross went upstairs. Marie could hear him moving through the rooms above. He was tyrannical with all the children when they did their HSC, reminding them constantly, *Your mother and I weren't lucky enough to get a private-school education.*

Marie never knew how Ross had found out: if he had found the papers from the Family Planning clinic or if he had found Blanche in a weak moment, easy enough as she had spent two days in bed crying and bleeding. By the time Marie had gone back up to the kitchen, Ross was fuming in Blanche's bedroom above. *This isn't the time to be slutting around.*

She sat with Blanche later that night, forcing her to drink tea, rubbing her back, thinking a mantra, *Don't turn out like me, my baby.* Get a great mark, get a degree, don't have children so young, Blanche, *don't turn out like me.* And she was happy in that moment. She felt strong. Her daughter needed her. Marie knew that part of Ross's rage was due to this mother–daughter bond; he was also threatened by the burgeoning independence of his princess. But together, she felt her and Blanche to be invincible. She was proud of her daughter's sexuality and of her support of it. But even as she congratulated herself, an atavistic thought rose from the back of her mind, enjoying the price that Blanche was paying: *Well, you have choices now, don't you?*

Blanche almost failed her Maths exam but passed her HSC with a good enough mark to get into art school. She didn't turn out like her mother at all. She turned out like her father: moody, ambitious, demanding. As demanding of herself as she was of others.

'I've never wanted to have an abortion,' Blanche was saying. 'I've just *had* to. It's never been my intention. Does anyone ever *plan* an abortion?'

Marie had only been thinking of that first one but she wondered now how many Blanche had had. And where she, Marie, had been. She knew why she held her at arm's length: getting involved in her daughter's life brought with it so much responsibility. All that love she would have to give, which she didn't feel she had.

'Of course not.'

'Did you want all of us?'

'I suppose I might have had an abortion with Clark if it had been available. I was barely nineteen. I had to give up uni as you know. I considered giving the baby up for adoption but Ross wanted him. So we got married. I've never said this to Clark and I don't think you should either. Of course I fell madly in love with him when he was born ... I had an abortion when I was in my late thirties.'

'What? Why didn't you tell me?'

'Blanche, you were too young.'

'Was it before mine or after?'

'Before. I remember Leon was twelve because I remember thinking I can't have a child thirteen years younger than his brothers and sisters.'

'Was Dad supportive?'

'He picked me up from the clinic, made me a cup of tea. You know we didn't expect the same things from our husbands then. They didn't necessarily come to the births, for instance. And I don't think I wanted him there, to be honest.'

'Why not? Wouldn't you want the comfort?'

'I didn't want him to see me like that. Screaming in agony. All that mess. My body like that. I just wanted to get it over with.'

Blanche went silent. Louise Jones had told her she had split half her perineum, and that it hurt so much she nearly passed out. There was blood everywhere; she had to have a drip afterwards. Seventeen stitches. And her husband saw everything. God, it was barbaric the things that nature put women through. Blanche could hardly bear to think about it. 'Were you okay afterwards?'

'You just forget. You have your beautiful baby, and that's that.'

'I mean after the abortion.'

'It was a horrible experience. I didn't feel liberated, just robbed of something I hadn't wanted in the first place. As contradictory as that may sound.'

'So there might have been four of us.'

'Five. I had a miscarriage a few years earlier.'

Her mother's voice began to fade. She must have been exhausted. Chemotherapy had been offered as a means to reduce the tumours and, along with them, the pain, but nobody suggested it would cure her.

'Are you going in tomorrow?' Blanche asked her.

'Yes. I'm going to see my medicine woman too.'

'The tattoo woman?'

'Yes.'

'God, Mum, don't get any more tattoos!'

'Why not?'

'Haven't you got enough? Isn't it a bit ex*cessive*?'

'The picture isn't finished yet, Blanche.'

Blanche put the phone down in an even more acute state of distress. Such rare intimacy, then back to the schism. She flung herself onto her bed. Loud disco came through the window. She had seen André and a woman dancing when arriving home that evening. Through a gap in the blinds, two pairs of feet bounced across the parquet to KC and the Sunshine Band. André's new Nikes and a woman's sandals, to and fro like birds in a mating dance, the sandals tapping on the spot, a trainer insinuating itself in between. The entire place seemed to be shaking with the honeymooners.

Was it an age or only yesterday that she and Hugh were dancing their own celebration at finding this house? Hadn't they also been that happy and danced in their living room on a weeknight just for the hell of it? She had taken it all for granted: the initial daily lovemaking, the comfort, the euphoria. Five years ago, she and Hugh were the couple downstairs and André was her now, fighting with his ex-wife. And so it continued, the endless circle.

But she could idealise her own life as easily as the lives of others. Like her mother, she had fallen pregnant only a few months after she and Hugh got together. She was thirty and working seventy hours a week at Huston Alwick and loving every minute of it. She had presented Hugh with her decision to have an abortion as a fait accompli and though he accepted it, his grief had niggled her. On her way into the clinic, she had been surrounded by people with placards chanting, *Murder, murder.* She didn't haemorrhage as she had when she was eighteen, but the procedure drained a joy from her life and marriage that took a long time to refill. To this day the sight of right-to-lifers made her tremble.

She went into the kitchen and moved Hugh's present, an electric hot-chocolate maker, off the counter. He came in and wrapped himself around her. 'Why don't we try it out?' He was attempting to suppress his jubilation at her pregnancy, unsuccessfully.

'We don't even drink hot chocolate, Hugh.'

'That's why I got it.'

'There's no room for it.' Blanche indicated the benchtop, crammed with a barista kit, toaster, jaffle maker, juicer, food processor and microwave. The cupboards were stuffed with gadgets for everything from stopping bottles to opening them. Blanche poured herself a glass of Evian. 'I'm going to bed. Okay?'

'Okay.'

The hiss of the new machine travelled up the hall, then the nauseating smell of hot milk. A few nights ago it had been the smell of white wine and peanuts tormenting her. She could hear Hugh walking down the hall, bearing a gift she would refuse. 'I can't do it,' she said when he came into the bedroom.

He put down the tray. 'You mean this is making you sick too?'

'I'm sorry, Hugh, but I can't even handle the smell.'

Hugh picked up the tray and made his faltering way back to the living room. She heard the television go on. An English football match. Did you hear me, Hugh? She lay there desperately thinking, *I can't do it.*

He returned half an hour later. Blanche said again, 'I can't do it, Hugh.'

He lifted the covers and climbed in beside her. 'You're not going to have another abortion, are you, pooky? How could you even con*sider* having a third abortion?'

'Jesus, Hugh! You know how hard it was! Do you think I want to? And how can you talk about what I did when I was barely eighteen in the same breath? It's easy for you.'

'It's not that easy. I didn't find it easy at all!'

'Stop shouting at me!'

'You're shouting at *me*.'

Blanche grabbed at something. 'We'll have to sell Ultimo.'

'No we won't. Child endowment isn't means-tested. And we'll get the baby bonus.'

'Hugh, I *want* to work.'

'We've always said we wanted kids and you're in your late thirties. The agency will have you back.'

'The way things are now they'll be thrilled to have an excuse for my permanent departure.'

'No, they won't. I believe in you, pooky.' Hugh wrapped himself around her.

She dreamt all of the usual dreams. A helpless expulsion then innocent tears over the red toilet bowl. She dreamt of a family barbecue where her baby slept peacefully in a pram, her husband was ten kilos lighter, and everybody got on. She dreamt of Hugh announcing he was leaving, taking with him all responsibility for their separation; or falling ill and she nursing him through to his demise, her loss, her grieving legitimised. But what would it really mean, death, the ultimate absence? Mothers were different. Husbands could come and go but mothers were unique, mothers were forever. The death of her mother was a wound gaping invisible beneath the path ahead. All through the night she crashed through the jungle of her uncertain future.

The next morning Blanche made an appointment with the abortion clinic. In the afternoon she cancelled. The following day she made an appointment again.

All week Marie concentrated on the new arrangements, organising Fatima to come more often, giving Mopoke her medication, taking her own. How unreal her life seemed. She didn't realise until now how much one lived in the future: perusing university courses online, buying a new house, even reading the news seemed pointless. The relief at not having to house hunt was so great that Marie found herself smiling at the mere thought of it. She would not even have to do her own packing. The only household chore she retained was washing her clothes. Leon had a limited cooking repertoire — pumpkin soup, salade niçoise, steak, pesto — but Marie's tastes had become austere, so this didn't bother her. Susan had asked Leon to come and work in her garden and, having no income, Leon accepted.

Walking down to the cove with a towel over her shoulders, every little step felt like a victory. She walked into the water and breast-stroked out as far as she could, knowing she wouldn't be back here for at least a fortnight.

She parted the cottonwool of memory and codeine to peer again at her conversation with Blanche. She was amazed she hadn't mentioned the possibility of Blanche carrying the baby. Was she too focused on death? No, no, she wasn't going to die, Dr Wroblewski would have more news for her today. As she stepped from the shower into her wardrobe, Marie thought of her own lost children. Her abortion would now be a teenager, her miscarriage twenty-five. Their ghosts drifted around the house, wearing her clothes, watching television, leaving dirty plates lying around.

'I have your ultrasounds here.' Dr Wroblewski went over to the wall of light boxes. He flicked the switch and her insides were illuminated in black and white. They looked eerie and somehow distant, like meteorological satellite photos. Marie could discern nothing but two large concentric shapes that she assumed were her lungs. Where in those clouds and rushing black oceans was the storm that was coming to destroy her? Dr Wroblewski used a pen to indicate her organs. Then he pointed to a spot below the lungs. 'This is one tumour. This is another. And this patch here needs to be watched.'

He switched off the light and bade her sit on his couch. The cool disc of stethoscope moved across her back. 'Breathe in? Breathe out. Breathe in?' Dr Wroblewski moved around to Marie's side. 'Lean back. Unbutton your shirt, please.'

Marie obeyed. He cleared his throat, and looking up inserted the stethoscope beneath her shirt. He repeated the breathing commands then walked back to his desk.

'Can I get dressed now?' Marie asked.

'Right,' he said when she was seated opposite. 'What we're aiming to do is prevent this tumour from penetrating the stomach wall and reaching your pancreas.'

'What will happen if it does?'

'Your indigestion will worsen.' He scribbled something on a pad. 'I'm going to prescribe you more painkillers, stronger ones.'

'Is there much point to this chemotherapy?' Marie said to the top of his head.

'It will shrink the tumours. Your heart's sounding strong. Blood pressure's good. I think you'll cope fine with a course of chemo.'

Marie grinned. 'Well, yes, I am feeling good. I had a swim this morning. I'm eating well.' She looked at a painting on the wall of a red fish with a spiny outline and one blue eye, signed *Anna* with a child's hand. 'Is that painting by your daughter?'

'Yes.'

'It's gorgeous. How old is she?'

'She did that when she was seven.'

'It's very good for a seven-year-old.'

'Actually, she copied it from a book.'

Marie took the script. 'So the chemotherapy will get rid of the tumours?'

'The idea is to give you a little more time.'

The coldness of his tone landed like a punch in her stomach. She stared at him, willing him to make eye contact. 'How long have I got? Is it really only six months?'

'Well, I wouldn't plan my Christmas holidays.' Dr Wroblewski pressed his lips together in a polite smile. 'I wouldn't plan any more tattoos.'

Marie took her leave. When she turned at the door she found his grey eyes staring at her.

'This is going to be a very painful tattoo, Marie,' Rhys said to her an hour later. 'You're going across ribs and lower back. And I'm going to be using a lot of needles for that colour.'

'I trust you.'

Rhys unrolled the design. The angophora was to begin on the top of Marie's left thigh, one branch reaching up her ribs, another across her lower back. Its foliage would support the moth like a nest; on the side it brushed against the flames. The differing perspectives melded perfectly, like a Japanese woodcut, but the picture had more light, the usual spaces of Rhys's work opening around bare skin. 'I think I could do the outline in a couple of long sessions, maybe less.'

While Rhys drew up a stencil, Marie pushed down her trousers, lay on the couch and looked around the room. Nothing had changed in here.

With the first prick of needles her glands opened, releasing moisture from her armpits. She pressed her face to the pillow. The iron felt like a hot knife cutting into her flesh: it was the most extreme pain she had ever known. She asked Rhys for something to bite on. Rhys rolled a hand towel into a tight tube, and Marie clenched it between her teeth; Rhys also gave her a pillow to hold. Panic surfed high in Marie's chest and she began to pant.

'Breathe.' Rhys paused. 'Just breathe.'

Marie removed the towel from between her teeth. 'I'm cheating today. I'm on painkillers.'

'That's not like you. Are they making a difference?'

'No. They're strong ones too.'

'I could have told you that.' Rhys's tone was disapproving. 'It's nerve pain I'm hitting you with.'

'I need to tell you something, Rhys. I've got stomach cancer.'

Rhys sent Marie a startled look and put down the iron. 'God,' she said. 'I'm sorry.'

'That's what the painkillers are for.'

Marie kept her eyes shut, face pressed to the pillow. She could hear the creak of Rhys's chair.

'You knew last time you were here, didn't you.'

'I'd just found out. I couldn't speak about it.'

'Fair enough. Jesus, Marie, I'm really sorry. Are you starting treatment soon?'

'Chemotherapy next week.'

'Is the pain bad?'

'It's getting worse.'

'But it's benign, isn't it? That's what the chemo —'

'It's malignant. I have six months. Five and a half now, to be exact.' Marie looked straight ahead at Rhys's knees, clothed by green Bermuda shorts. A fly had landed on the left one and was busily rubbing its forearms together. Marie was astonished by the clarity of her sight, and the urgency of the fly's task. A surge of respect for the tiny insects in all their profligate industry moved through her like grief. She was surprised also at the brutal truth she was giving to Rhys: everybody else's versions had been edited. She wanted to say all of this: the fly, the eyesight (what a waste; why couldn't she bequest this remarkable gift to someone who would need it?), the varieties of prognosis. But she couldn't speak.

Rhys sprayed a paper towel with antibacterial and pressed it to Marie's back. 'Is there anything I can do, Marie? What can I do?'

'I want you to keep tattooing me.'

Rhys threw the towel into the bin, looking upset. 'Do you realise how much energy you're going through dealing with this? Don't you want to save it to fight the pain? Do you really want to exhaust yourself getting tattooed considering the ordeal you'll be going through in a few days?'

'Please, Rhys.'

Rhys lifted her glasses and rubbed the heels of her hands into her eyes. 'Okay. But with a short cut.'

'What do you mean?'

'Only one branch. I have to stop after this session, Marie. You have to rest.'

'I will. I promise.'

'Good. I need you to turn onto your side. Further. That's right. Are you comfortable?'

'Yes.'

Looking down, Marie could see the colour travel across her flank. She watched her body move with her breath, the rise of blood and ink, the trunk feeding into branches, and all of it seemed like a miracle. 'I can't believe I won't be coming here anymore.'

'You can still come and visit us,' said Rhys. 'You're always welcome here.'

He remembered walking home down these shady streets, schoolbag whacking against his legs. He wore a helmet of cicadas beneath the brushbox. The blazing sound was almost unbearable, but at night when his parents began to drink and fight, Leon longed for it again. He still loved the secrecy of the cove, its steep twisting roads and fairytale names. Mistral Avenue, Kallaroo Street, Magic Grove.

He remembered Blanche's stories of her piano teacher there. She used to smack Blanche's hands with a ruler when she made mistakes; she made her hot chocolate with water. Blanche only lasted a few months. Leon drove up the hill with the window down, looking out at the suburb. The cicadas still rang, the walls were taller and, in place of the rambling Federations or mock Tudors, every second house was new, built to the boundary with surveillance cameras and intercoms.

He braved the heat to drive to Richmond for nursery supplies. On the plains it was ten degrees hotter than by the harbour. He bought up big, as though he were working full-time. He even dropped in on his old rose grower for Susan's sake. One week back here and his skin was itching, his lips cracked. He was looking forward to working in Susan's garden in spite of himself. He was completely over roses, a native purist now, but he would humour her. He didn't care whose place he was working in; he just wanted to lose himself in earth, seed and mineral. To submit to cycles and species other than human.

Clark and Nell were due at the house around lunchtime. On his return from Richmond, Leon felt like a stroll in the garden, so he made himself a sandwich and went outside.

His mother must have been in denial about her health for some time — so many things had been neglected. She had become territorial and, apart from the lawn man, hadn't hired a professional gardener in years. And yet there were changes Leon hadn't noticed at Christmas. Clumps of kangaroo paws, and the native mint he had purloined on a camping trip to the other side of the Great Dividing Range had completely taken off. It smelt fantastic. The lilly pilly was fruiting. He plucked one and ate it, a sweet vinegar bomb frightening his mouth. He set to pruning the birds of paradise. He heard a noise. Nell was outside the rumpus room staring down at him. 'Hallo, Nell!'

She twisted shyly and looked up behind her at the house. Leon saw Clark at the window encouraging her to go to her uncle. 'How are you, Nell? Come and say hallo.'

Nell paused, then set off down the path towards him.

'When did you get here?' Leon grinned. 'D'you just fly in on your broom, did you?'

Nell looked up at him blankly. 'Daddy's upstairs. Daddy's thirsty.'

Leon crouched and held out his arms. 'Do I get a hug?'

'No.' Nell rounded her mouth as though considering something, or hiding a smile.

'Gee, that's a bit tough. You're a tough lady, Nell.'

Nell studied him for a while, then putting both hands to her cheeks announced, 'You're not Leo.'

'Yes, I am. I've grown a beard, Nell.'

She reached out and touched his face then sprang her hand back and looked at it and laughed. Leon returned to his pruning.

Nell watched him. 'Leo, why you doing that? You're not allowed.'

He loved the way she changed his name. 'I'm helping Mum. I'm a gardener, Nell.'

'Where's your garden, Leo?'

'In Brisbane. Way up north. A long drive.'

'Why aren't you in your garden?'

'Because I'm here.'

'Why?'

Her questions were like little taps on the knee, prompting reflex answers but his kicks could be dangerous. Leon wondered whether or not Nell knew her grandmother was ill. 'I'm here to see Mum. I'm here to help her in the garden.'

'Where's your mum and dad?'

'Mum's in town and I don't know where Dad is.'

'Why not?'

'Because I haven't heard from him in years.'

'Why?'

Leon stopped his work. 'Good question, Nell. I can't answer that one.'

'Why don't you ring your dad, Leo?'

'Cos I don't have his number.' Leon was surprised to feel himself smarting. He changed course. 'You know my dad's the same as your dad's dad? He's your grandad.'

Nell stared at him and Leon immediately regretted his words: what if she started wanting to see Ross and Clark didn't want her to see him or, worse, Ross himself didn't want to see her. Fucken hell, one innocent conversation with a child and he was in a minefield. Nell bombarded him with more questions about his parents and he tried to explain the tracery of relations in a family, how one person was a different entity to each member, and Nell grew bored, taking her hat off, trailing it along the ground.

'Put your hat on, Nellie.'

She obeyed with alacrity. 'I like my hat,' she pronounced it *hate*. 'Daddy had cancer.'

Leon looked down at the warped yellow canvas of Nell's head. 'Did he?'

'Yeh, he had cancer.' Nell squinted upwards. 'Here.' She touched her temple, then pulled her hat deeper over her head. 'Then he got it burnt off.'

Leon cleared the dead vegetation, Nell picking up a branch behind him. He hadn't seen her for over a year, and in that time she had transformed from a chubby toddler to a disturbingly overweight little girl with a perfect bob and the vigilant nature of her father. Leon felt angry with her parents for allowing her to overeat. All the obese kids these days, the selfish parents who treated their children like another possession, not looking after them properly but ashamed when they didn't come up to scratch. As he walked up the path with her, Nell reached out for his hand and Leon was so touched by this easy intimacy that he couldn't speak.

They walked into the kitchen hand in hand, and Clark beamed at them. Nell went into the living room and picked up her computer game, and Clark asked Leon what she had said during their garden stroll. He wanted to know everything, nodding vigorously as Leon recounted. 'Yeah, she's obsessed with mummies and daddies at the moment. She's *where's your mum this*, *where's your dad that*, she's obsessed with gender.'

'She sure puts herself forward. She's a real cutie.'

'She wants everything in its place. She's even like that with her toys, she lines them up: girl, boy, girl, boy, it's relentless.'

Leon thought, Like father like daughter.

'Juice!' Nell called from the living room.

Clark poured three glasses of apple juice and handed one to Leon. 'I know, Leon, you're giving me that look. You're thinking mummy and mummy, daddy and daddy.'

'Huh?'

Clark took a glass of juice into his daughter. Mopoke came into the kitchen. She looked up at Leon then lowered her shoulders and raised her hips in a long yogic stretch. Leon placed his foot beneath her back legs and nudged her out the door. Clark nearly tripped over her on his way back in. 'Shit. Bloody cat. So how d'you think Mum is?'

Seeing Clark so discombobulated, Leon was seized with a juvenile desire to snigger. He bit his lip. 'She seems alright, all things considered.'

'I think it's good you've come back to Sydney.'

'I don't know if I've come back permanently.'

'But you've got a job working for Susan Jones.'

'To tie me over. There's nothing much to do in her garden, you know.'

'Digging holes and filling 'em in again, hey?'

'Story of my life. I think Susan wants me there partly to keep the line open. Her and Mum've been fighting.'

'Really?' Clark's face brightened.

He looked good when he smiled, thought Leon. In a boyish, slightly nerdy way. His hair, still thick, was greying on the sides. When Clark moved back to the fridge, Leon caught a glint in his eyes that he couldn't quite read. He said, 'I'm still trying to figure out why Mum is so important to Susan.'

'They go way back.'

'I always thought Susan was a bit of a bitch to her.'

'That went both ways, you know, that little dalliance.'

'I know.' Leon was trying to think of the other friend, the dark-haired one that he had always preferred, but he couldn't remember her name.

Clark said ruefully, 'Mum's still seeing that bloody tattoo artist.'

'I've been reading about cancer on the net. There are changes you can make to your diet. There are people who've gone into remission indefinitely. Meditation seems to play a big part. Mum told me she meditated when she got tattooed.'

'Of course, I can see now what it was all about,' Clark said sententiously. 'It was a cry for help.'

'I thought she seemed really well at Christmas.' Leon had sworn off default positions but the family dynamic was bigger than him. He felt like a canoe on rapids: his older brother in the absence of their father would take on the role of patriarch, even patronising their mother in the process, and he would step in to defend her. How could it be otherwise?

'So did I. Until Blanche told me she'd been on ulcer pills.'

'Really?'

Nell switched on the television and called out, 'I want more juice, Daddy!'

They spoke more easily with the blare of cartoons behind them. 'I think her generation's very good at covering up,' said Clark. 'God, I shouldn't give Nell so much juice.'

'Well, give her water then.'

'Juice, Daddy! Daddy, juice! JUICE!'

'You want to deal with the tantrum?' Clark ferried the next glass out, muttering, 'I'm killing my child with sugar and television.' Leon heard him say to Nell, 'What do you say?' To which Nell replied with a big raspberry.

Again Leon wanted to snigger. 'Anyway,' he said placatingly when Clark came back into the kitchen, 'we survived alright.'

'You reckon?' Clark picked up the paperweight from the message pad and held it in his hands. 'It's weird, isn't it, being in the house now. It's not ours anymore.'

'But it so still is. That's what's weird.'

'It's like the anchor's been pulled and we're just floating. I'm cooking dinner here tonight. Will you be around?'

'I don't know. I'm waiting to hear from George. Has anyone contacted Dad?'

'Blanche was in touch with him about the sale of the house. He tried to get your contacts from me a while back, you know.'

Leon narrowed his eyes, the glass at his mouth. 'You didn't, did you?'

'Nooo. I wish you wouldn't be so paranoid, Leon. Maybe he's changed his tune.'

'He can't have been that keen. Like I'm not in the phone book.'

'You did fritter it all away, Leon.'

'He doesn't know what I did. And it isn't his business anyway. I'm an adult.'

'I suppose I should ring him. I haven't spoken to him for months.'

'D'you ever see him with Nell? Is he interested in her?'

'Yeah, but he won't put himself out. Besides which I'm not that inclined to waste my precious days with her dancing around Dad's schedule, you know what I mean?'

'Sure. Does he call you or d'you call him?'

'He sent me a cheque for my last birthday.' Clark smiled cryptically. 'I banked it.'

Leon wished briefly he'd traded a fraught or fake phone call for a cheque. Lacing himself into the pious triumph of the dieter didn't stop him salivating.

As though reading his mind, Clark said, 'You'll be well off when Mum dies, you know. We all will. You can still buy a property.'

'You're completely writing off her going into remission?'

Clark did not write this off in conversation to Blanche. He said to Leon, 'I'm just going by what she told me.'

'It's not how she put it to me.'

Clark assumed that his mother hadn't told Leon the truth because she thought he couldn't handle it. But he would have to find out somehow.

Leon watched Clark stacking his glass and again caught that strange glint in his eyes, like a window on the other side of the harbour winking in the sun. Something like the way he looked at his daughter. A fondness. Clark seemed taller too. He held himself differently. There was ease in his gestures, his back was straight. 'You look really well,' Leon said.

'I am well. I'm fit. I've got an income — a pittance — but at least I'm working. I'm happy in spite of everything with Mum.'

Suddenly it dawned on Leon. 'You've met someone, haven't you!'

'Ye-up.'

'Do tell.'

'Oh, you know. Beautiful, smart, sexy as all hell.'

For all his gripes with his brother, Leon loved seeing him this soft. He was also delighted at his acuity about Clark's emotions, and to have the opportunity to trade stories about relationships. 'So,' he said and grinned, 'when's the wedding?'

'Actually, ah, she's already married.'

'So what's the state of play?'

'One week we're on, the next we're off. I'm just here, waiting.' Clark looked at the floor, more vulnerable than anything.

'Be careful, mate. You might just be therapy for a marriage glitch. I've been through that one.'

Clark's eyes widened. 'You had an affair with a *married* man?'

'George. We were together for years, on and off. Remember? While he was still with his long-term partner, on and off, who he went back to in the end. I brought him over here twice. You don't remember?'

'Oh yeah.' Clark looked nonplussed. 'George.'

Jesus, it was useless. Leon stacked his glass in the dishwasher. He wouldn't have minded sharing, empathising, but Clark just didn't register. 'I'm going back out to the garden.'

He turned at the door and asked his brother something that had been on his mind since the first morning back home. 'Hey, Clark, do you know much about our ancestry?'

'We're mostly Irish on Mum's side. On Dad's mostly English. But there are some missing links on Dad's side and they might be Jewish. Or even Aboriginal. Like half this country,' he added with an opaque facetiousness.

'Really?' Leon was excited by the thought that his white blood might be tainted. It mollified the worry that his armband had been a mistake.

After finishing in the garden, Leon brought some flowers up to the house and placed them in a vase on the coffee table. He had left George a message two days ago but George still hadn't got back to him. He wondered if the reception here was dodgy. He rang his mobile from the home phone to check: no, all clear. Besides which, he knew very well he had four bars on his phone. He was disgusted with himself, acting like a desperate girl, gardening with his mobile in his pocket, willing the man to call. He longed for somebody to vent to. Clark sure wasn't interested. And how about that stupid remark about mummies and daddies? Fuck that for a joke. Leon peeled off his dirty clothes and walked into the shower. For a smart guy, Clark sure was a dumb cunt. Leon didn't want to be here tonight. He didn't want to be alone either.

Crossing the landing to his bedroom, looking down at the open plan empty of all life but the flowers he had cut that afternoon, Leon longed for company. Even with Clark banging away in the kitchen, the house at dusk seemed a cavernous lonely place. Leon had never thought of it as it had truly been these past eighteen months — a single-occupant residence, the occupant not much of an entertainer. In his mind, it remained in the past. His strongest memories were of the parties.

He loved the advertising parties. The music, the shouting and dancing. The tropical cocktails decorated so heavily it was a wonder they stood upright, the extravagant vases of vivid, sadistic flowers and the swirl of people in the open plan. For the first hour, the children were allowed to pass hors d'oeuvres. The women were so glamorous with their year-round tans, high shoes and flimsy dresses, their mouths filled with laughter and cigarette smoke. After being sent to bed, Leon would watch the parties with his siblings from the landing. There was a sense of unravelling in the late hours, of the illicit. It was better than television.

'Which one do you like?' Clark asked him one night. He meant the women.

'Dunno,' Leon replied nervously.

'Who's down there now?' Blanche came and went from their vantage point like a referee. Three years younger than Clark, almost twelve, Blanche assumed authority over both her brothers. Clark resented this usurpation but at the same time was in thrall to her burgeoning femininity. Whenever he asserted himself, Blanche only laughed at him. Leon crouched beneath their tension.

'Come on, Leon,' Clark scoffed. 'There must be one. I'll take Susan.'

'God, Clark. She's like a hundred years old or something.' Blanche spoke into the comic book she had brought out of her bedroom in case the boys thought she was taking all of this seriously. 'And Leon's *nine.*'

'Which Susan?' Leon asked.

'Mrs Jones, you idiot. On the couch next to Mum.'

Leon leant forward to inspect the tall blonde in a strapless dress and matching shoes, a clatter of bangles along her brown arms. He imagined grappling with her and her folding and breaking like a stick insect. He was always the last to retire from this game into his and Clark's room, a constantly disputed territory of disappearing assets and broken ceasefires. The delay in the completion of Clark's attic had made him even more aggressive than usual. Leon's eyes followed the path of a brunette across the living room, her undulating breasts, black swallow brows and crimson mouth. He admired the darkness of her. Her difference. 'I'll take her.' He pointed with confidence.

'Gina Totti? She's a bitch.'

'Why?' Leon protested. He had fallen into the trap again. He knew how important a man's taste in women was, but the correct one still eluded him and Clark as usual was ahead. Even Blanche snorted loudly. Leon sat morosely in a fug of humiliation.

Clark looked down at the brunette with disapproval. 'I hate wogs.'

'Don't be such a racist, Clark,' Blanche admonished. 'It's so uncool.'

Leon watched Susan walk into the chink of passage below then disappear. She wasn't nearly as spunky as his brunette, who was walking towards the kitchen behind her. A man emerged from the kitchen and Gina stopped. He was dressed in white linen, like so many others at the party. He and Gina stood very close, talking urgently. 'Look.' Leon sniggered as the brunette was pressed up against the wall by the man. His excitement increased knowing that nobody in the living room could see this couple. Then he recognised the white linen shoulders as his father's and regretted drawing attention to them. His brother and sister regarded the scene below with prim mouths. One of their father's fingers slid beneath the strap of Gina's dress like a witchetty grub. Leon could smell his brother's breath as he cursed over the banister. Their mother was now heading for the passage from the living room with a handful of dirty glasses. Susan exited the kitchen, saw Gina and their father, then walked down the passage, colliding with their mother at the other end. Something spilt on Marie's dress and, with Susan steering her out of the passage, she abandoned the glasses and began to mount the stairs, head down, not noticing the children until she was level with them. 'Go to bed *now*.' She went into her bedroom and slammed the door.

Clark's eyes were glittering. 'Say, Blanche. You know we got rats in the cellar?'

But did Clark really say that? Leon wondered as he walked down the stairs to join him in the kitchen. Hadn't he — Leon — followed his mother into the bedroom, to help her pick out another dress? He remembered picking his favourite Marimekko. In which case he wouldn't have seen let alone heard Clark say anything to Blanche. But the dress memory could have been from another time. Still, the glittering eyes of Clark remained etched in his mind, and the cut of the remark. Then there was the liaison of his father and Gina Totti. Yes, Gina, that was her name. Gina had been Leon's first attraction, the premier signal of his tastes, even if the gender had been wrong. He wondered what had become of her.

During those first weeks, Marie sometimes woke in the middle of the night and remembered she had cancer. She lay there thinking of all the possible reasons the disease had chosen to occupy her body. She examined her family first of all. One grandfather had died of

Parkinson's disease, one grandmother of a stroke. Her sister Judy in Tasmania had died in a car accident aged sixty-one. Could she have taken to her early grave the guilty gene? Or the other grandparents who had died before Marie was born, of what she didn't know: was it from them? Or, most likely, her mother with those mysterious gynaecological problems that hadn't actually killed her. But might have.

She thought about her diet. The white bread and chocolate biscuits; tinned corn, peas, beetroot and tomatoes; the takeaways and battery chickens year after year. All those chemicals and hormones; and had she fed cancer to her children as well?

She began to see cancer everywhere. Reports on new treatments, new research and funding proliferated. The spiralling figures, the death toll. Her pulse raced at every news item as though she were seeing excerpts from her diary on the front page.

Was it in the packaging? One program suggested that fire retardants, now worked into every household product from telephones to couches, were responsible. Was it pesticides? How many apples had she eaten without washing? Flea treatment, cockroach baits, toxic honey for ants in the kitchen. And how many clouds of insect repellent on how many summer nights had drifted back down, cool and deadly, onto her sleepy face. *Short of living in a tree*, said an environmental scientist with breast cancer on TV, *I don't think we can avoid it.*

Then there was the drinking. Year after year, hangover after hangover booming a warning she hadn't heeded. She couldn't remember a time when she hadn't had indigestion. She felt ashamed at how much she had abused herself, as she lay with her hand on the sleeping cat, looking through the bay window at the night sky.

And yet, even then, why should she at the age of fifty-nine and a half have absorbed more toxins than Susan, for instance, who was five years older? More pertinently, Ross and Jonesy, intermittent alcoholic and chronic workaholic, the entire thirty years that she had known them. Compared to those men, her own drinking was surely insignificant.

No. She had never lived next to an industrial area, she didn't drive in traffic every day, she didn't go near her mobile phone for days at a time, her diet was better than the diet of most. No.

For hours Marie lay there performing autopsies on every aspect of her life, searching for a clue. Why me? she thought as hands locked tighter around her throat. Why *me*?

'So what's happening with your mother?' Terry asked Blanche.

'She's going to die.'

Terry rolled his eyes. 'Well, we're all going to die, sweetie. What's going on?'

Blanche's heart began to thump in her chest. 'She's having chemotherapy this week.'

'Does that mean you're going to be leaving work early again?'

'No. Where shall we take Sean?'

Terry pursed his lips. 'I feel like seafood. Costa's.'

'Okay.' Blanche visualised baby octopi shrivelling on a barbecue and felt revolted. 'Sounds good.'

Terry pushed a sheaf of paper across his desk. 'This just came in.'

Blanche picked it up. It was for sanitary napkins. 'Great.'

'We've only got a couple of weeks.'

'That's fine. I've got an idea up my sleeve.'

She walked back to her office thinking, You're not going to die, Terry. I mean you look like shit, but you're not going to die in a few months' time. Sadly. And since when did I punch the clock every day in front of you? Seventy hours a week not enough, dickface? And all the hours thinking at home, the wheels constantly turning, in the bath, in the car. Sanitary napkins!

She was lying on the floor when Kate came into her office. She opened her eyes to find those excellent cowboy boots in her face and realised she wasn't thinking those things about Terry, but muttering them out loud. She let out a little scream.

'God, I'm sorry. The door was open, so I thought it was okay to come in.'

'It *is* okay.'

'Should I come back later?'

'No. I'm going to lunch with Terry and Sean.'

'Who's Sean?'

'The new guy from Konica.'

'Oh *him*. He's dishy.'

The word *lunch* made Blanche's stomach lurch. 'Come *in*, Kate!'

'We just need you to sign off on something.' Kate stood awkwardly looking down at her. 'Ya righ'?'

'Just resting my back.' Blanche stared up at the ceiling, hoping she looked cool and louche, rather than weird and sick, lying on the floor like this. She had lain here and stared at the ceiling every day this week and still couldn't find a single flaw in the expanse of white. She sat up slowly. Blood drained from her head. 'Have you ever been pregnant?'

'Ye-ah.' Kate eyed her warily. Blanche noticed the patterns on the cowboy boots were bucking broncos. Or flowers, or cacti. Maybe all three? The designs were ingenious. Oh god, why couldn't she look like that, why couldn't she have clothes like that?

'I was always so paranoid about being the kind of woman Neil French and his ilk go on about,' she said, staring at the boots.

'Oh stuff him, he's a dinosaur. He writes these three-thousand-word ads that nobody cares about. He's just a bloody Pom.' She grinned. 'Are you pregnant?'

'No, no.'

'But you're thinking about it? Lim was telling me a story recently about this boss in the US who was ringing her team right up until she started having contractions. And two days after having the baby she was back at work.'

'Wow, that's amazing.' Blanche thought that if she concentrated hard enough on the bucking bronco cacti flowers, she might be able to stand up without fainting. She could pass the pad ad on to Kate, call overload. *Pad ad*, a voice in her head snickered. The brittle, flippant mood that Blanche had brought to work that morning was having a field day. On the other hand, she could call Terry's bluff and do the best ad of the year with the most despised product on the planet. 'The reason I'm asking is that there's a pitch due for sanitary napkins.'

Kate made a face.

'I know. But listen. Urban scenarios, fast editing, a young female executive in a rush. At the end she reaches for her' — Blanche picked up the papers and searched for the name — 'Invisible.'

'I hate pads. I *never* wear them.'

'Neither do I. And then it's, *Thank god I'm not pregnant!* And a shot of her blissed out, holding the product against her heart, sort of thing.'

'You're joking, aren't you?'

'Well, we could change *god* to something else, so we don't alienate the Christians.'

'I'm a Christian.'

'*Thank heavens I'm not pregnant!* Or something.'

'That's not the problem.'

'Heaven is kinda the same, isn't it.'

'No, I'm a Christian, and that didn't occur to me.'

Blanche was horrified that Kate was a Christian. Maybe it was time for another Crusade. Hang on, an anti-Crusade, wouldn't that be? She said, 'I'd love to do an ad in the Level 41 toilets.'

Kate was tickled. 'You've got balls, Ms King. To be honest with you, I know loads of women who would love it but I don't know if it would get through.' She eyed the drawings propped on Blanche's whiteboard. 'What are they?'

'Roche,' Blanche lied. The drawings were of tunnels done in charcoal. Huge, tortured scrawls, the most satisfying, exciting things she had done all year. Just for the hell of it, for herself and not a client.

'Interesting. They remind me of early van Gogh. This is an avenue of trees, isn't it? They're so dark and, um, *European.*'

'Yeah.' Blanche was flattered. 'Have you been to the van Gogh museum in Amsterdam?'

'Oh, only about a hundred times. It's only one of my favourite places in the whole *world.*'

'Isn't it the best!'

'God, I love these drawings.'

Blanche got up slowly, a smile plastered over her throbbing nausea.

'It's heart medication, isn't it? Or cholesterol. It's blocked arteries. You could digitalise these and do something really amazing with them.'

'Well, they're not quite there yet,' Blanche said modestly.

Kate looked at her watch. 'Sorry to rush you.'

'Okay, I'll be in in two secs.' Blanche popped an anti-nausea tablet out of its blister pack. As soon as Kate left the office, she rang Clark. 'Clark, I need you to pick Mum up on Friday.'

'I can't. I'm getting Nell from school.'

'Well, it's Leon's day at Susan's and I can't leave work early this week. They're tightening the thumbscrews. Could you get her after Nell?'

Clark spoke in hushed tones. 'Look, I think it's a bit confronting for them to see each other when Mum's sick. I still haven't told Nell.'

'Why not?'

'Because she's *four*? They don't understand death at that age, Blanche. They've barely figured out life, you know.'

'Sure, but can't you tell her she's sick? Like, Granny's got a funny tummy?'

Clark said nothing. It occurred to Blanche that Clark might be worth asking about babies, but she resented the patronising, long-suffering tone he took with her whenever children were mentioned, as though she had no idea. She didn't want to give him an opportunity to lord it over her. She craved comfort and a listening ear, neither of which she would get from Clark. She wanted him to tell her not to have an abortion because having a baby was so fantastic. She said, 'Did you know she doesn't have private health cover?'

'I know. One of her cost-cutting measures last year. Look, I'm in the library. Can we talk about this later?'

'Just text me when you've made up your mind.'

Blanche went up the corridor to sign off on the job and found Lim alone.

He smiled broadly when she entered. 'Hey, lady, how is it?'

'Good!' Lim's computer was on YouTube playing a rap song. 'What are you watching?'

'One of the best ads I've seen in years.'

'Whose is it?' Blanche perched on the edge of his desk and watched the song unfurl on a beach, the singer a white guy in sunglasses, white zinc and white hoodie.

'These guys out west. It's a guerilla ad for the Cancer Council. They're in Parramatta.'

The ad did look sickeningly good. It featured a singing carcinoma on the main character's back. Blanche noted the title so she could go back and watch it in her office, over and over. She could see out the door across the hallway into Terry's office. Kate was in there. Terry had his hands behind his head and was laughing uproariously, looking Kate up and down.

'It's just so bold and funny. And they've had like five and a half thousand hits in less than two weeks, and someone's set up a fan page on facebook.'

'You're from Parramatta, aren't you?'

'Yeh, I'm a westie,' Lim said proudly. 'I went to school with one of these guys. They've just asked me to join them actually.'

Blanche widened her eyes. 'You'd go and work in *Parramatta?*'

'It's alright. It's the real centre of Sydney, when you look at a map. It's forty minutes on the RiverCat, which is quicker than most public transport in this city. Someone like me can afford to buy a house. It's really multicultural. My mum and dad are out there, you know.'

'You're abandoning me!' Blanche was only half joking.

'Look, I'm just thinking about it. I get to buy in as a partner and be creative director, which means I get to schedule my own hours, which means I'll have time to write my novel. Blanche, I *love* working with you but it's just too *corporate* here. I can't spread my wings.'

Everything that Lim said made perfect sense: it was a golden opportunity. 'I'm taking you for a drink after work, boy. I'm not letting you go as easily as that.'

'Sure.' Lim whispered as Kate came back in, 'Nobody knows!'

'Oh, while you're here,' said Kate to Blanche, 'these are just in from casting.'

Blanche went through the photos. 'No, too thin. No, he's just done Westpac.' She stopped at a photo of a handsome square-jawed man with perfect teeth. 'Who's this again?'

'He was in that cop show a few years back,' said Kate. 'He was really good.'

'Uh-huh.'

'I don't know why they sent his picture over,' Lim said. 'I mean, an Aboriginal in a car ad?'

'Yeah.' Blanche continued through the pile. She stopped at the last photo. 'He looks a bit like Beck, doesn't he.'

'He was our pick too.' Kate smiled.

'Okay, team, we're on the same page.' Blanche held up her index fingers, like a rap singer.

'See you at lunch,' Kate said.

'I can't, sorry, date with Tez.'

'I know. He's asked me to come along.'

'Oh. Oh great!'

Blanche went back to her office. Well, who would have thought. Kate and Terry. So it might be those cowboy boots rather than Lim's Merrells that would tramp right over the top of her the second she dropped the ball. She had fluked it from the art department herself; who said it couldn't happen again? This thought cleared Blanche's head and a flinty determination took hold. She might just have this baby, and keep her job at the same time. She might do the best ad for sanitary napkins that anyone had ever seen. And why not hope like her brothers that Marie's cancer would go into remission? Why not leave all options open? She might be dropping her baby off to her grandmother to be babysat in a year's time. For the next hour Blanche cut a swathe through her backlog of emails and phone calls. She spent ten minutes in the bathroom fixing her hair and make-up. She lowered her head, smiled up at herself through her vampish brows, then strode out to collect her colleagues for their lunch date.

Almost every chair in the chemotherapy ward was occupied. The first woman was young, reading the *Herald*, her enormous eyes

Wexford Public Library Service
Tel: 053 9196760
www.wexford.ie/library

Borrowed Items 09/11/2016 14:55
XXX4857

Item Title	Due Date
* The time is now / Pauline McLynn .	30/11/2016
* Indelible ink.	30/11/2016
* A closed and common orbit / Becky Chambers.	30/11/2016
* The devil's feast / M. J. Carter.	30/11/2016
* A city dreaming / Daniel Polansky.	30/11/2016

* Indicates items borrowed today
Thank you for using self service at
Wexford Library

saintly in her bald head. The next was slightly older than Marie, chatty and curious, like a beauty parlour client in her pink scarf tied turban-style. A couple of the alcoves had their curtains drawn. A woman with wavy auburn hair sat white-faced as the line went into her arm, a man who looked like her husband reading to her loudly as though addressing a classroom. Both of them stared at Marie's tattoos, then her face. There was a man adjacent with lush, pitted Islander features and volcanic eyes. He was reading a book called *Stalingrad*. A scorpion clung to the side of his scalp, a teardrop to his cheek.

The chatty woman on Marie's other side said, 'You've got the lime juice cordial. That's what I call it.'

'That's a nice way of putting it.' Marie had been thinking it resembled uranium juice, if there was such a thing. Liquid yellowcake.

'Well, we have to look on the bright side. I had it for my first bout. It didn't work for me.' She nodded after each sentence, pre-empting disagreement, her nose denting the air. 'But I'm sure it will for you.'

The woman with auburn hair glared at the chatty woman. Her husband read, '*Robert had a job teaching ...*'

A passing nurse said, 'You've all got your own special mixture.'

Marie was surprised to find herself content in here with the companionship of the ill. She considered this a brief stop-off. She watched the antivenom infuse, imagining it course through her blood straight to the tumour like weed-killer. She knew it would actually poison everything, but hopefully the right cells would regrow. She shifted to relieve the skin itching on her flank.

The chatty woman said, 'Is it breast?'

Marie panicked for a moment, thinking her bra must be showing. 'No. Stomach.'

'Most of us are breast, of course.'

From the auburn hair, a disapproving sigh.

From the Islander a cheerful, 'I'm not!'

The chatty woman ignored them. 'You're quite exotic,' she said to Marie. 'Especially with those things on your arms.'

Marie politely agreed, hoped the Islander would notice them.

'And this must be your son,' the woman went on. 'Isn't he handsome?'

Leon had returned from the cafeteria. He placed himself tactfully between the chatty woman and his mother. 'I got apple and blackcurrant fizzy drink, or organic orange juice. Take your pick.' He added in a wry whisper as he sat down, 'Compulsory Madonna lilies in the corner.'

The Islander was being infused with raspberry-coloured fluid. The pouch on his drip stand was nearly empty. Marie was aware of Leon's eyes continually on him and she looked steadfastly at her feet. She was terrified the Islander would realise Leon was gay. She didn't want him to register her curiosity either. She was angry with Leon for thinking he could just stare at a man in public like that, as though it didn't matter. Especially one of those Islanders, god knows you shouldn't provoke them. In a flash she imagined the Islander heaving himself up with a roar, ape-like, and crushing Leon between his fists. She collected herself and said to her son, 'How's it going in Susan's garden? What are you doing?'

'Digging holes and filling them in again.'

'Ha-ha.' She stared at Leon, willing him to look at her, not the Islander. 'What else?'

'She wants natives. She's got this awful row of agapanthus that I'm replacing. And I'm going to try some roses.'

'That's not like you.' Marie was barely registering what Leon was saying. Even with her head turned away from him, the presence of the Islander dominated her. When an intern arrived ten minutes later to remove the shunt from his arm, Marie began to relax. She and Leon watched him walk out of the room. Tall, big-boned, with a presumption of space, he would have once had the physique of a rugby player. He moved with the lumbering grace of someone unwilling to relinquish a fine suit that had grown too large for him.

'Impressive,' said Leon quietly.

Marie said nothing. She was enraged.

She began to feel sick towards the end of the hour. A flush had spread up her arm and the desire to scratch obsessed her. A spinning sensation moved over her brain every minute or so and she felt incapable of walking. They wheeled her into a ward to recover. She began to vomit. Leon stood by the bed with his hand over his mouth as an intern examined her. 'It's just a reaction to the chemotherapy. We're going to keep you overnight and Dr Wroblewski will see you in the morning.'

At night the hospital reduced to its elements of cheap furniture, white linen and stainless steel. Marie didn't want to be there. The bed was like a rack for objects, not humans; the others in the room coughing and groaning behind their curtains. She felt miserable in her gown, plastic vomit bowl by her side. She looked back on her fear and anger earlier in the day. You stupid bloody racist, she cursed herself. Stupid bloody homophobe. But there was something else in her anger with Leon that she didn't quite want to let go: rivalry. Even in this decaying body she desired, to the point that she wanted to fight for it. With lust racing through her blood, it was hard to believe she was sick let alone that she was going to die.

She saw the Islander on the verandah the next day, smoking in a chair down the end. The young woman with the beatific eyes was up the other end, holding the hand of a Chinese woman in a red jacket. It was hot out here and patients shuffled to and fro with their skinny limbs exposed. Marie settled into a chair not far from the Islander and dozed with *New Scientist* in her lap. Smoke from his cigarette rippled through the air elegant as silk.

'Hope you don't mind.' He glanced over. 'I only have a couple a day now.'

Marie's nostrils sought the aroma as a reassuring envoy from the outside world. 'I like the smell.'

'Most people complain it makes them sick.'

'I'll blame the chemo for that.'

'I'll blame liver cancer. Brian.' He held forth his hand. It was warm and dry.

'Marie.'

They went back to their reading. The air began to tighten like an inflating balloon. Marie could feel Brian's eyes on her arms. She had already taken in what she could of him. A spiderweb on the left elbow, little marks on the joints of each finger and other things too blurred to read from here.

'Designer tatts, eh?' he said with mild deprecation.

'Somebody designed yours too at some stage,' Marie shot back.

'Yeah. The gods.'

'I don't believe in God.'

Brian chuckled. 'Not mine you don't,' he affirmed.

Marie's eyes remained glued on the headline: *The rainfall and inflow crisis*. She couldn't decipher a single word.

Brian said, 'It's good work, eh. Passionflowers. Beautiful. Who did it?' He pronounced it *ut*.

'Someone called Rhys.'

'Rhys!'

'You know her?'

'She's a legend! I know a few blokes had work done by her. Her stuff's won competitions all over the world. Where's she working now?'

'In a studio in Surry Hills, in partnership with a man called Rob.'

'Oh yeah?' It was hard to tell how much of his pallor was jaundice; criss-crosses were weathered into his neck. He looked frail in that moment, with his head hung forward and lips parted inquisitively, the gaps where back teeth were missing visible. His eyebrows had fallen out. A look of anger crossed his face, intimidating Marie. 'She used to work at Skinned Alive, one of the Rickers outfits. That was years ago.'

Marie was still adjusting to his Pacific accent. 'The who?'

'The Wreckers?'

'Aren't they bikies?'

Brian smiled at her pityingly. 'Yes, ma'am.' He fiddled a cigarette out of his pack of Longbeach, then put it back in. 'Fucken racist cunts they are too. Scuse my French. Glad she's not working there anymore.'

'She's done almost everything I have,' Marie said proudly.

'I could never afford someone like Rhys,' said Brian, not without self-pity.

He chose the chair next to her that night in the television room. Everybody else had gone to bed. He sat down carefully, as though his body were precious cargo. Previously avoiding his gaze, Marie now watched his face constantly, for the battle of disparate elements that took place there — timidity, joy, confusion, anger, and the dazed non-expression of the sick and medicated.

'I got three others in my room, right? One of 'em coughs all night. Another fights with his missus till visiting hours are over. And the third one looks like he's gonna cark it any minute.'

'How depressing.'

'Yep. Can't wait to get out of this joint.'

Marie had been moved to a double room, the patient opposite recovering from surgery. She had come into the television room for solitude and a larger screen that she didn't have to crane her neck to see, but she welcomed Brian's presence. Each time he appeared she was struck by how frail he was, as though in his absence he inflated to an archetype that was increasingly irrelevant. Marie consulted the program. 'There's a James Bond movie on in half an hour. Do you like James Bond?'

'Yeah. I'll make a cuppa.'

Marie went to her room for the fruit her children had brought her, and cut up a mango. She could see now how much of Brian's irritation was with his ailing body. The demeanour he bore to the outside world seemed neutral. He wore a dressing-gown with a design of dull green checks. Part of an exposed thigh bore what looked like a Samoan tattoo that moved in semi-circles all the way down to his calf. She passed him a piece of fruit. 'If you eat some of this, it will help me eat too. I've lost too much weight.'

'What can you do?' Brian patted his thighs sadly. 'I used to be two hundred and ten.'

'I loved it at first, all the weight loss.'

'Don't like skinny women. All those diets and shit.'

'I've got an appetite tonight.'

The movie began with James Bond drinking a cocktail on a boat in the Caribbean. For the next fifteen minutes, he moved through an impossible world of colours, gadgets and superhuman strength.

It was exactly the sort of thing Marie was in the mood to watch. When the ad break came on, she asked Brian, 'Why do you think you got it?'

'I don't know. Maybe I was just unlucky.'

'Do you believe in all those theories about stress and anger?'

'All I know is that I've got it and I'm gonna beat it.'

Marie said something she hadn't wanted to say to anyone else: 'I think I might have got mine from drinking.'

Brian raised his eyebrows in polite enquiry. 'Oh yeah?'

James Bond got on a plane, looked at his watch and frowned.

Brian said, 'I'm hep C, eh. Got it in gaol.'

'Oh,' said Marie, more concerned by the gaol than the virus. 'I'm sorry.'

'Ah, you couldn't avoid it. At least I'm out now.'

The plane began to plummet. They watched the film in silence. Marie thought about Brian in gaol. She pictured a long room of stone floors, cells lining the walls, sartorial guards strolling up and down, truncheons swinging from their belts. An ordered, ascetic, masculine environment.

'I ran the heroin in Long Bay for a while. Too much of the good life,' Brian said airily. 'That's why I got it.'

'You took drugs in *gaol*?' Marie was suitably shocked.

'Anything you want, sister. The best smack in Darwin for years was sold out of the gaol.' This said to up the ante. 'I'm just waitin' for crystal meth to get a hold in the penitentiary system. Imagine the fucken riots then, eh? Ha. They'll be talking about the good old days of heroin. Don't worry, I'm more of a Jim Beam man these days.'

'Oh, really? I was a Chivas girl for a while there.'

They snickered as footsteps stopped in the corridor. The door opened, revealing the night supervisor. Brian turned down the TV. 'We're just hevving a cup of tea,' he said politely.

'We're watching James Bond,' said Marie with a touch of insolence.

The nurse regarded them suspiciously. 'Lights out in half an hour.'

When he was gone, Brian pulled out a joint, announcing, 'Best medication for cancer.' From the other pocket he pulled a hipflask.

'You're organised.'

'You on the wagon?'

'I have the occasional tipple.'

Brian sloshed some bourbon into their tea. 'Your *health*, madame,' he said in a posh voice.

The bourbon went down like fire, lighting up her whole body, as car after car exploded on television, and James Bond ran for his life.

Leon drove into the city along the winding back roads. The newsreader was saying an arsonist had been charged with lighting a bushfire in Ku-ring-gai Chase. Leon was dismayed by the obliteration of the land's natural contours by the new houses: Mosman was no longer a semi-feral foreshore, it was a luxury getaway, landscaped to within an inch of its life. God, he loathed this city, the pretension, the disregard, the wealth — the selfishness of the wealth. As he took the hill onto the bridge, he went into his mother's fantasy of a bushfire on the foreshore, consuming vegetation and houses alike. Then he was over the harbour, driving towards buildings sequinned with setting sun, and the beauty of it took his breath away. How he had missed it.

He was nervous about seeing George. He had avoided looking him up on previous visits and George eschewed online profiles so Leon couldn't check up on him. He had worn his memories like old polaroids into near blankness. George's misted form in the shower cubicle; his neck, his smell, as they kissed in the palm grove of the Botanical Gardens. The thick line of hair from navel to groin, George rolling onto his back and lifting his legs for him. Leon had moved up to Brisbane mainly because it seemed like a place that George would never visit, but he still found himself scouring the papers for an event that would entice him. Some days, walking down the street, every dark-haired man looked like George. Leon had rung him for his birthday in January and surmised from the screeching parrot in the background that George had moved in with Linus, but he didn't ask. He didn't want to know.

Leon admired himself in the shop windows, a naturally bulked six-foot silhouette with tawny bushy hair, in a faded wife-beater, low-slung Diesels and Cons. He arrived at the restaurant first and was sitting facing the window, chest puffed out, arms crossed in front, when George arrived. George greeted him with a kiss on the cheek and sat down opposite. He appraised Leon's body calmly then looked into his eyes. 'Long time no see. You look really well.'

'You too.' Leon felt nervous.

George ordered almost straightaway.

'So,' he cut to the chase, 'your mum. Which oncologist is she seeing?'

'This guy at the hospital.' Leon tried to pronounce his name. 'Do you know him?'

'Wroblewski? I know *of* him.'

'What's he like?'

'He's alright. Their new oncology floor's pretty good. Well equipped, well set out.' George made it sound like a theme park: *Scare yourselves silly on the new Oncology Ghost Train!* 'That hospital's also rife with staph.'

'Great.'

'Sign of the times, mate. We're sterilising ourselves to death. So what's her prognosis?'

'Stage four.' Leon handled the jargon like a new weapon, aware he still needed lessons, hoping nonetheless it looked powerful in his hands. 'Roe whatshisname's given her six months.'

'No surgery then?'

'Nope.'

Their food arrived and George paused while the waitress arranged it. It was a noisy restaurant, full of the hard shiny surfaces so prolific in Sydney now, and they had to raise their voices to be heard. The sides of Leon's face ached with the strain. They helped themselves to food.

George said, 'Listen, you don't need to worry about the staph. The main thing will be palliative care. If she has good palliative care, that's the best you can do.'

Leon kept his eyes on his Mussaman lamb curry. 'She reckons she can beat it.'

George said nothing.

'This food's amazing,' said Leon.

'Yeah, isn't it?'

George looked thinner, fitter and more serious. He had grown sideburns, the lines around his eyes were more pronounced, and his hair was quite grey, all of which Leon found painfully sexy. He feared and trusted George's professionalism. George had cut his teeth in Ward 17 at the height of the AIDS epidemic; now he was managing Triage. In Leon's eyes he had always carried the wounded glamour of the returned soldier. Leon had never known anyone with AIDS let alone anyone who had died, a fact that used to make him feel inadequate in the company of George's friends. All the older gay men's stories of the halcyon days of wild dance parties were laced with death, like Mexican festivals. To Leon, death seemed a higher truth, the only place where he would finally understand. But now that the possibility of it loomed, the questions only increased.

He felt himself yielding again, not to George who evidently didn't want him, but to an old desire that now floated beyond both of them. He wished George could have been seduced by him. He was like a hitch-hiker tired of waiting, hefting his bags onto the same old truck.

'Mum was looking quite well,' he said. 'Then she had a bad reaction to the chemo so they kept her in for a few days.'

'That's a bummer. Hopefully they'll get the mixture right next time.'

'So you don't reckon she can beat it?'

'I really can't say.'

'But generally what is it with stage-four stomach cancer?' Leon insisted.

George inclined his head sympathetically. 'Generally it's end game.'

Leon spooned more rice onto his plate. He wanted to swear or throw something. He could feel George watching him.

George said quietly, 'Are you moving back to Sydney?'

'Why's everybody think I'm moving back to Sydney?' Leon said with a bitchy lisp. 'This town's a dump.'

'Feel loved, matey.'

'I left too quickly to pack my stuff up.' Leon watched four guys at the next table pay their bill and leave. White, Arabic, Asian, all muscle-bound, short-haired, in designer t-shirts. George forked food into his mouth and looked up through his brows, nodding.

'What'd you do for Christmas?' Leon asked him.

'You won't believe it.' George grinned. 'I spent it in Villawood.'

'What?'

'My uncle's been chucked into Villawood. They want to deport him. He's been here since '69, married with three kids, but he never got it together to get proper papers.'

'Fuck that,' Leon fumed. 'This whole fucking *country*'s a dump. Poor bastard.'

'He's a bit of a fuckwit, actually. Homophobic Leb, you know. Which doesn't mean I don't feel sorry for him. We took loads of food in and had a pig-out Leb-style. We're getting a barrister for him, but apparently his chances aren't good. Most of the people in there are Chinese.'

'Oh yeah?'

George laughed again, partly to himself. 'Y'know, Leon, I hate to sound cheesy, but it's not such a dump as all that here. I mean, where else would you be? Jordan? Where they torture us?'

'I don't know. That's what I'm gonna figure out over the next while.' Leon reached for the water. George wasn't drinking: part of the fitness regime maybe. Leon was dying for a beer but didn't want to drink alone. 'Been going out much?'

'No.'

'Gettin' old, are ya?' Leon said in Strine.

'Ancient.' George smiled. He was forty-five, twelve years older than Leon for this half of the year, eleven years older when Leon turned thirty-four in August. 'It's pretty dead anyway. The sniffer dogs are everywhere and if I get caught with so much as one joint I can get struck off. You haven't missed anything being away, y'know.'

Leon wondered if George wasn't being a bit melodramatic. Those medicos were the biggest party animals he'd ever come across. Drug pigs, the lot of them. Hard to imagine them stopping just like that. 'I was thinking of going for a quick beer. You want to?'

'You go ahead. I have to turn in.'

They said goodbye out on the street. 'It's gonna be a long haul, mate.' George rubbed his back. 'If you need anything, just give me a ring. Okay?'

Leon walked down to Oxford Street alone. He felt like a tourist: disoriented, out of place, faintly excited. He went into a bar and ordered a beer, for which he was charged seven dollars. He stood against a wall watching the crowd. It seemed to be all clean-cut young men, fresh out of high school. He bitched to George in his head: *I felt like I'd stumbled into a Young Liberals convention.* The music was Cher on a video screen above the bar; there was no DJ booth. Leon wandered into the room adjacent and found two walls of poker machines attended by three people. He went back into the bar. A couple of preppy guys in the corner were eyeing him off, but Leon ignored them. It was cold beneath the air-conditioning so he moved along the wall and picked up a gay paper. There was a column about the scourge of gay bars titled *Female Arse Crack*, which made him laugh. He looked around the room and saw a couple of straight girls sipping cocktails, but they were standing, so he couldn't see their arse cracks. He couldn't see any safe-sex packs either. It all began to feel ominous: the shiny steel and pine finish, the expensive drinks, the loud hollow music. The young perfection. He probably just needed to have another beer and loosen up. He pulled all the coins out of his pocket and counted them. Not even enough for a middy. He left.

Up at Taylor Square he saw four cops on foot patrol. Their uniforms were baggy trousers, army boots and baseball caps. They looked like riot police or kids pretending to be. Moving away was supposed to cure the disappointment in what his home town had become. But sights like this still riled him.

Did his mother realise what lay ahead? he wondered as he walked the laneways to his ute. George had told him more tonight than he had learnt in weeks of conversation with his family. Had Dr Wroblewski been clear with Marie and told her everything she needed to know? If he had, why did she say she could beat the cancer? It seemed to Leon that all of them, let alone his mother, were sitting ducks, and he didn't have the strength to move out of the way. Indeed it felt right to receive the impact straight on. His two and a half weeks home seemed longer and more eventful than the two and a half years he had spent in Brisbane. He searched for a memorable incident during his time away and nothing came to mind. He realised that everything he had tried to escape — his family, George, his vexed relationship with Sydney — had never been more than cursorily buried. And that he had rushed down here not just for his mother but for himself. Even while writhing with hatred for the place, he couldn't keep away.

He was woken the next morning by a phone call from Clark.

'Are you picking up Mum on Sunday?'

'I thought you wanted to.'

'Something's come up. I can spend Monday with her instead. I'll bring groceries over and cook some meals and freeze them,' Clark said excitedly. 'I'll fix up the house.'

'Okay then, but give her a ring so she hears it direct from you. Oh, and Blanche has been looking for places for Mum. And she's emailed some links to us and we're supposed to check them out and get back to her.'

'Yep, will do.'

Clark put down the phone and punched the air. He danced into his bedroom to shadow-box the mirror. He let his heels fall to the floor and watched his flab wobble then pinched it. Not too bad. He kissed his mobile, containing Sylvia's latest text: *Sweetheart I'm free! All weekend! xo.* On Tuesday night, in Clark's car at Gordons Bay, they'd had two hours of amazing conversation followed by gut-wrenching laughter imitating the characters from *Summer Heights High*; then, completely unexpectedly for Clark, half an hour of loud, urgent sex squashed in the back seat. He went into his inbox again to look at Sylvia's message. He caressed the bruises on his knees.

They were back on.

He went down to Hall Street for food, candles, wine and flowers. Took the narrow walkways that ran between the streets, exulting in the pink frangipani and weathered paling. On the steep path above Forest Knoll, he heard a rustling and watched a blue-tongue lizard slink through a crack beneath the wall of a house. He hadn't seen one for about ten years. On his way back up the path forty minutes later, labouring beneath a backpack full of groceries, Clark opened his Opinel knife and cut two leaves from a copse of bananas then carried them carefully home.

He changed the sheets. He remembered Sylvia saying she hated cleaning so he left his flat dishevelled and went to the beach for a swim. He began to cook at four o'clock, listening to Nina Simone's *Baltimore*. He made cucumber raita with mint, and spinach raita with fenugreek, cumin and black mustard seeds. He made pappadams and a coconut, coriander and green chilli paste to dress the fish with. Sylvia arrived as he was wrapping the last piece in its banana-leaf packet. She had been at a conference at Macquarie Uni all day and her skin was hot and sticky from the drive. She gave him a bottle of wine and flopped into his arms.

'Mmm,' he said. 'Your neck's salty.'

'Can I have a shower?'

'Down the end of the corridor. There are towels in the cupboard.'

'Can I take my bag to your bedroom?' She looked at him shyly.

'Yeah. Second room, past the study.'

'Great flat, cheaptart,' she called back to him.

It comforted him to hear her moving through the rooms after she had showered. To know she was naked in his bedroom, drying herself on his towel, surrounded by his things. He had wine poured and candles lit when she returned in a clean singlet and sarong. Dusk had turned to night.

Sylvia shook out her wet hair. 'It's gorgeous being in a house full of books.'

'You don't have any?'

'Yeah, but most of them are in my office.'

'My mother's coming out of hospital tomorrow.'

'Great. How is she?'

'Not so great.'

'I'm sorry. Are you picking her up?'

'No, Leon will.' Clark placed the pappadams before her. 'I've kept the weekend for us.'

'Good. So have I. Yuuuum.'

He felt her watching him as she ate; he felt like a god in his shorts and t-shirt, crossing the worn lino to the refrigerator. 'Did you have a good week?'

'Oh, the usual.'

'Do you actually *like* your job?'

'Am I being a whinging academic?'

'Not necessarily. I'm curious.'

'Well, yeah, I like my job. I choose to do it. I'm lucky, really.' She took another pappadam. 'But sometimes I think I've become a boring old fart. You know, teaching north shore brats How to Steal Legally.'

'I thought you taught Law Reform.'

'And other lofty subjects like Contracts.' She looked around the room. 'You're so *neat*. You'd go mad living with me. I'm a total slob.'

'I didn't clean especially for you.'

Sylvia hugged him while he continued his chopping. 'You're so sweet. What are you making?'

'Fish steamed in banana leaves.'

'Have you been chopping up chilli?' She pulled up her singlet and placed his fingertips on her nipples.

Clark immediately moved one hand down, into her knickers. 'Do you miss your old job?'

Sylvia slapped him away playfully. 'I don't know. Sometimes, I guess.' She walked back into the living room. 'You always go back to that one, don't you, y'bloody perv.'

Clark grinned at the chopping board. 'How long's it been? Since you married Franco?'

'Pretty much.' She was out of sight, crunching on a pappadam. He heard her sifting through his music. 'Can I put something on?'

'Please.'

'I love you, you know that?' She said it almost absent-mindedly. Then Tom Waits strode out of the speaker.

'*Orphans*,' Clark exclaimed. 'Perfect!'

'I've never heard it.'

Clark brought the food out and pulled back a chair for her. She placed her hands on the back of his neck and kissed him on the lips. 'I trust you, you know. Why's that?'

'Because I trust you.'

'Okay then, so I have done a couple of jobs since I got married. A few years ago an old client rang me. He'd just been diagnosed with cancer and wanted to have a good time before starting treatment.' Sylvia ate while she talked. 'This is delicious.'

'I admire his taste,' Clark said judiciously, fighting a flash of jealousy. 'Gives new meaning to the phrase *mercy fuck*.'

'I wasn't being kind. He was offering me a lot. Franco and I were going overseas and I was sick of always having less money than him so I agreed to see this guy. I really liked him, you know. He was one of my best regulars. A real gentleman and a generous tipper.'

'And how was it?'

'It was a hoot.' Sylvia's face lit up. 'We had room service, French champagne, and he had a dominatrix come in on it.'

'*Really?* Did she whip him?'

'Nooo. She supervised me scrubbing him down in the spa. She was amazing, all in latex. I was like the fluffer. We were in hysterics the whole time. She fucked him with a strap-on. It was like *Satyricon* meets Benny Hill.'

Clark groaned. 'Not for me, thanks.'

Sylvia said nothing.

'Obviously his cancer didn't get in the way.'

Sylvia concentrated on unwrapping her second piece of fish, hooking her little fingers out of the way. 'It was melanoma. He was in a bit of pain. I think it was spreading.'

'Did he recover?'

'I don't know. I never heard from him again.' Sylvia looked

uncomfortable. 'Sorry, Clark. This isn't really the best topic of conversation right now, is it?'

'Did you tell Franco?'

'No.'

'Why not?'

Sylvia looked up sharply. 'I just wanted to do something for myself. Anyway, I'm telling you now. Look at us sitting here eating dinner in our underwear. Don't you love hot nights? I wear nothing at home in summer.'

Clark rued the judgement in his voice. Impulses and feelings speared from him like darts, too fast to rein in. He wanted to bless and curse Sylvia at the same time. 'If my life was cut short, I'd pay every last cent just to have one night with you.'

'It's not the same, sweetheart.'

Why couldn't he say anything right? Eyes vague, Sylvia shook her head as though trying to rid herself of something. Clark saw this gesture increasingly often and it made him uneasy. She had eaten everything on her plate and when he served her more, calmly took up her cutlery again. 'I love your appetite,' he said.

'I love your food.' Tom began half singing half talking about his first kiss in a gravelly voice. Sylvia wrinkled her nose. 'This is getting boring.'

'I'm going to the toilet. You can change it if you like.'

The sight of the seat down warmed him. Out the window a crescent moon had risen behind the she-oak, a dense black scribble on Prussian blue. Clark flicked the seat up, sank his chin to his chest and let the piss flow from his body. Sometimes when Sylvia spoke about clients with her pragmatic compassion, he was filled with admiration in the same way he was for field workers with the disadvantaged. He focused on this feeling, but the insecurity began to leak again.

He could smell tobacco and, when he returned to the living room, found Sylvia hunched in a corner of the couch, cigarette in hand. 'You started me smoking again,' he said with good-natured accusation, filching one of her Stuyvesants.

'More like the other way around.'

'No, it wasn't.'

'It was! You had a packet with you the last two times we saw each other.'

'Yeah, but you had them *before* then. And I never have them in the house.'

'Neither do I.'

'You do in mine.' Clark inhaled deeply. 'Does —'

Sylvia looked at him expectantly.

He was going to ask her if Franco smoked but stopped himself in time. He blew a plume over her head and said huskily, 'Nicotine's an intellectual stimulant.'

She lit another cigarette and blew the smoke straight in his face. The photo on the packet showed yellow and black rotting teeth and the sentence SMOKING CAUSES CANCER. 'We'll have to get them to change their picture,' she said. 'Clark in the library.'

Sylvia never spoke about her husband, and Clark took this as evidence of her inevitable move towards him. By blocking Franco, Clark also kept a portion of Sylvia's feelings at bay. Yet looking at her now, returning to her inward preoccupations as she smoked greedily, he remembered that she was a married woman with a full-time job under enormous emotional strain. He sat sideways and embraced her with all four limbs, like a crab. He saw his watch over her shoulder. Ten past ten. He had forgotten to check Blanche's links of places for his mother. Worse, he had forgotten to ring his mother. What a selfish cunt he was. The truth was he was terrified of hospitals, and to imagine his mother in that sterile blue light was to imagine a sort of static decay, like an old daguerreotype eaten by silverfish. He felt sick just thinking about it. He cinched his arms around Sylvia's wracked form. 'We'll be okay, cheaptart. We'll be fine.'

Here she was at last in his bed, her total nakedness. He stretched against her, wanting every millimetre of her skin to imprint his. With the whole night ahead they still fucked like thieves, quietly and quickly, muffling each other's orgasms. Afterwards, she curled into him and Clark drew the room tight around them like a pouch. 'Isn't it incredible, sweetheart? This moment?'

'Hmm?'

'Our bodies, our health. *Isn't it?*' He squeezed an affirmative sound out of her. 'I feel so safe with you. My body feels happy, like it's losing its old fears.'

'Safety,' she mused. 'We long for it. Then it suffocates us.'

He woke with her clinging to him. Moving his arm from beneath her, he saw she was awake. The clock on the dresser said one a.m. 'Why don't we just drive off a cliff together?' he said.

'I've thought of that. It would make things a lot easier.'

He watched the blink of her eyelashes. 'What do you get from him?' He felt as though he had just removed his shoes on a bitumen road in forty-five-degree heat.

Sylvia thought for a while. 'A good home. Franco's practical. I like that because I'm not. He's a good cook, knows how to run things. I'm hopeless at all that stuff, Clark.'

'I can cook.'

'You're a great cook.'

'But you'd have to help with the shopping.'

'Okay.'

'And cleaning.'

'I'll hire someone.'

'What else?'

'What?'

'Keeps you in the marriage.'

Sylvia took his face in her hands. 'I hate talking about this, Clark. I hate hurting you.'

'We have to face this.'

'Franco champions me in my career. He's unwavering in his commitment.'

'Are you?'

'Obviously not,' she almost snapped.

'Sorry.' In the flat adjacent, a door creaked. There was the pad of footsteps then a tap turned on. 'Do you want to have children?'

Sylvia paused for so long that Clark thought she was falling back to sleep. 'Yes, I think so. I know I've left it ridiculously late but I'm really healthy and I have a friend who had a beautiful baby at forty-two. We've been together for ten years.'

It was himself he had envisioned in the role of father, not fucking Franco. Every word she spoke cut a little slice from his heart. 'He's wealthy, isn't he.'

'I know I've been spoilt.'

'Do you love him?'

'I love my life with him, we get on really well, hardly even fight. But when I'm having dinner with him, I'm talking to you in my head. And when I'm in bed with him, it's you my body wants. Just you.'

Sylvia's breathing deepened.

'Do you like Nell?'

'I *love* Nell. And I love how you are with her. Seeing you two together. It's gorgeous.'

She shifted onto her side and looped an arm back to take Clark's hand. He watched her fall asleep then walked the long snaking corridors of his mind. He saw Sylvia in a room with his mother, a little party by her sickbed except Marie didn't seem sick, just tired and enjoying the attention. Sylvia was elegant and capable, delighting the whole family. He saw her in this bed beside him in the morning; he saw her pregnant, his ear pressed to her swollen belly, Nell cooing. He lifted Sylvia's hair and kissed her nape. He saw her in fishnets and a miniskirt, strolling through the foyer of a ritzy hotel, men's eyes following her. Then an Albert Tucker tart was leering from a painterly alleyway, Blanche muttering *whore* under her breath, and Clark was protesting righteously: *Don't you dare call her that!* Sylvia sauntered on, conferring with some bitch in high heels brandishing a bullwhip ... *I wanted to do something for myself.*

How could he stop that? It was a perfectly sound doctrine when looked at objectively (and god knows provided him with rich fodder for masturbation). It also made him want to pluck out his hair strand by strand. Why wouldn't she go behind his back as well, and what could he offer her in recompense? He had the detritus of a failed marriage behind him, his income was negligible, he had no career, and by the time he had finished his PhD the university system would probably be so diminished that an academic path would have closed off as well. Besides which, did he really want to teach? As for the party by the sickbed, get real, Clark. His family was a total disaster zone.

Meanwhile his mother was lying in hospital battling cancer while he lay here gazing at his navel, thinking about his dick. He looked at the clock. Twenty-five past two.

The tick of each second swelled and filled the room so that time seemed to be a mass of mercury, slowly pulsing. He had not a shred of hope left that his mother would go into remission. Thinking of the inheritance and the house it would buy — and the holiday it would give him and his daughter — opened a light inside Clark as though he were walking into that actual house, sinking his full weight into an actual couch. He could buy Sylvia perfume. He could pay for the cleaner.

He couldn't sleep. It was possible he didn't want to, that he wanted to remember this entire night with Sylvia. In the dimness her back was like a cello, rising and falling with breath. He stroked her, moved the sheet to reveal the curve of hip, moved his body closer. He ran his finger down the cleft of her arse, found her cunt still warm and moist from sex. He could slide right into her from here, he had never fucked her from behind. His cock thickened as he thought of the dominatrix and the client. He wanted to spread Sylvia's arse cheeks and plunge inside her. They always used condoms but it felt so good to rest the head of his cock in her crack like this, drooling on her. He imagined spraying cum inside her. He'd never found a woman who'd let him fuck her up the arse. Sylvia would surely: she had been, in her own words, *such a good whore*. He clenched his teeth, wanting to laugh and bite her at the same time. He imagined her groaning, pinned beneath him, opening to his thrusts. He pushed against her sphincter and she twitched and made an irritable noise. Fuck you, bitch, I'm gonna fuck you right up your arse; he pushed again, harder, she twisted away. He heard her mutter something like ... *you doing?* She squeezed his hand then her hand flopped straight back to sleep. Clark lay back mortified. What *was* he doing? Jesus! He gripped his treacherous erection so hard it hurt. He lifted the sheet gently back over Sylvia. The desire to fuck, hard and angry, churned through him, along with self-hatred.

It was past three, and in twenty-four hours Sylvia would be lying in her bed and he would be here alone. He wasn't sure whether Franco was coming home early Monday morning or Sunday night, but the mere fact that she would be in bed with another man soon struck him as outrageous. He had put up with this for two months now. How would she feel if she was in his shoes? He hadn't so much as shed a tear over it in front of her. Sure, he had told her he loved her, but that was kind of the opposite, wasn't it? God, if it was her, there'd probably be weeping and wailing every night. Sylvia had said she'd never had so much as a one-night stand before, but since her anecdote tonight, Clark decided he couldn't trust her. He remembered what Leon had said in their mother's kitchen. He had dismissed it at the time, but now it occurred to him that he was being used, and this made him angry. No wonder he'd nearly raped her a minute ago. Not that it was exactly rape. No need to exaggerate. Tension flickered through his body like an electrical current.

He stretched his limbs. He'd found Franco on Google. He was an executive at Sony, generic wog-looking, smug businessman. Handsome, Clark supposed, but he couldn't tell with men. The possibility that Franco had a bigger dick than him brought another tidal wave of insecurity over him. Yeah, Sylvia was insensitive about his position. That casual mention of her summer nakedness. Who did she think was there to see? Franco, of course. Nice work if you can get it. It was all very well to act as though Franco didn't exist, it made for more peaceful loving, but it was really *him* who didn't exist: Clark was the bit on the side. Maybe he was no threat to Franco. God knows, Sylvia never mentioned the elephant in the room.

Hadn't he known this all along?

On the other hand, once he had prodded Sylvia with all the subtlety of a red-hot poker, she had offered some pretty devastating information about Franco. About *them*.

Them, them, there was always them.

Well, you just wait, Franco. I'll come in guns blazing, and you won't know what's hit you. Cuckold, Franco, *I'm fucking your wife, and she loves me!* How big is it, Franco? Pistols at dawn.

Clark honed in, and Franco shrivelled in the oven of his mind. When it boiled down to it, Franco was an unknown quantity, but what Clark did know was this woman beside him and for all he knew she was going to leave him and he was just another one of those things she *needed to do for herself*. He would have to learn how to unlove her. The clock said five to four.

Her mouth was too small, her breasts as well. She flirted with waiters. She burped out loud, followed by a pathetic *Excuse me*. She buried her tampons in pot plants. She spat in the gutter, casually, like a man, while Clark stiffened in outrage beside her. She never had any qualms about giving her opinion or pulling him up on things — come to think of it, she could be a real shrew. She couldn't cook and sounded *proud* she couldn't like it was some grand feminist statement or something, like saying she was a slob. She'd left her wet towel on his bed tonight and the sheets were still damp. He looked at her in the pre-dawn light. She was actually snoring faintly. He lay along the far side of the bed. And woke with her above him, leaning on one elbow, drinking water, smiling down. 'Hallo, lover.' He parted his lips to receive the cool liquid, then her kisses. 'I want you inside me.' She ran her fingers down the cleft of his arse and he came alive. The night burnt to ash behind him. Where am I? he thought as she climbed on top of him. Who are you, who are you?

Marie was dressed and sitting on the verandah when Blanche arrived. She was waiting to say goodbye to Brian. She had glimpsed him that morning through his door, sleeping the dead, unnerving sleep of the very ill. He didn't appear on the verandah and, after leaving a note for him, Marie walked to the lift on her daughter's arm. A wardsman wheeled a gurney past them, the patient's face blending into the pillows. Marie was relieved to be departing, the hospital now irrevocably a place of sickness not cure, the past days an eternity. But she fretted about Brian and didn't want to leave him. Blanche's body beside her felt so young and firm.

'Are you feeling a bit better?'

'My medicine woman rang me this morning, so that cheered me up. She wanted to come and visit, but because I was being discharged I said we'd go and visit her.'

'You're not getting another tattoo, Mum.'

'No, unfortunately. I think you should meet Rhys. She's the same age as Clark.'

Blanche watched the numbers over the door go down one by one. The nurse beside her looked at the floor, a smile flickering on his lips. 'You look exhausted. Why don't I just drive you straight home?'

'I want to go and see Rhys,' Marie said plaintively.

They emerged from the cinema of hospital into daylight, all around them people, cars, trees, noise.

'Mum, you're sick. Can't she come and visit you? Tomorrow or something?'

'She's going camping tonight and I want to say goodbye. If you don't want to come, you can drop me off and I'll get a taxi home.'

'Don't be ridiculous. I'll take you.'

Inside the car, Marie sat forward. Bepanthen was what she needed more than anything right now. She was learning to adjust her desires to the small increments of days and hours. Blanche followed her directions and parked the car opposite the studio. 'I'll wait for you here.'

'Suit yourself.'

The walk across the road was a trek through a wilderness. How could she have lived in the world all these years, where had she found the energy for all this speed and stimulation? A can clattered along the gutter; there were shouts down an alley, the blare of music from a passing car. She reached the oasis of the studio. There was a faint smell of burnt rubber and across the footpath a black smudge as though somebody had lit a fire.

Stew came out. 'Queen King!' He embraced her, his funky sweat overpowering. 'You've been doing it rough, I hear.'

'Yes. Just a bit.'

'Are they making you better?'

'They seem to be trying.'

Stew took his phone out. 'I'm in a bit of a hurry but can I get your number? We'll catch up soon, okay?'

The studio was surprisingly empty. Rhys took Marie straight through to the kitchen. 'Welcome home, trooper. What can I get you?'

'My back's on fire.' Marie sank into a chair. 'Where is everybody?'

'It's my day off.'

She began to relax in the oddly shaped room with its flaking cupboards and worn chequered lino, relics of the mid-twentieth century. On the table stood a vase of orchids, flared and downcast, like reaching hands. There were empty takeaway containers on the sink and groceries in a bag: camping paraphernalia was stacked in the corner. Rhys fetched a stainless-steel bowl and a bottle of tincture. She filled the bowl with kettle water then dropped some tincture into it. 'I'm going to go over the area with some calendula first. Can you lift your shirt for me?'

Rob appeared in the doorway. 'Hey, Marie, great to see you.'

Blanche had watched her mother cross the road, a small determined figure in a blue silk shirt, hair blowing in the breeze thick as a wad. Didn't your hair fall out with chemotherapy? Her mother's hair, strong and lively, was one of her best features. Was it that strong that it would hang on? She watched the boy in stovepipes emerge and greet Marie. In their blithe, conferring figures, Blanche glimpsed the other life her mother had been living. She was intrigued, moved and resentful — and ashamed of her resentment. Her stomach began to heave. She opened the door and walked a little way to throw up in the gutter. There was something liberating about vomiting in the Indian summer dusk as though she had relinquished control in a glorious hedonistic arc, or delivered a timely message to the hateful tattooist across the road.

She went to the corner shop for a bottle of water and a packet of mints, then got back inside her BMW. The car was a cosy vinyl-smelling world in the unfamiliar street with that tattoo parlour whose innocuous front gave nothing away. Blanche watched it like a private detective, alert, suspicious. She wondered about the lick of black on the footpath. She flicked the key and the radio came on to Skyhooks' 'Horror Movie'. She was back in the 1970s with Clark in the rumpus room, in Joke Shop masks miming to the song, each trying to outscare the other; Clark too old to withstand the game long so that Blanche's final bound from behind the couch crumpled before his freshly revealed, disdainful face. Where was he now? Off fucking his married woman while she was again the ambulance driver. In order to be here today, Blanche had cancelled a meeting with Kate to workshop the sanitary napkins, but this was as much escape as sacrifice as she still had no ideas beyond the unsuitable one she had told to Kate a week ago. The songs on the radio degenerated and she went to the ABC. *There is no government push to change existing legislation surrounding abortion,* said the prime minister. *But that doesn't rule out a private member's bill.* Blanche crunched the mint between her molars. This morning she had made a second appointment for an abortion. 'Rush now while stocks last,' she snarled at the radio.

The boy in stovepipes was walking across the road. For a second Blanche panicked, thinking her mother had sent him this way but she realised as his face came into focus, morose and preoccupied, that he was oblivious to her. He looked much older this close, the same age as Hugh, his arms bright with tattoos. Two men holding hands, dressed in army trousers, walked the other way. Blanche placed her hands on her belly. Do you attest that your mental health will be jeopardised by the birth of this child? *Yes,* she had ticked. *Yes, yes, yes,* all the way down. Why couldn't she be like the women in magazines? *I'm so thrilled! We've been trying for ages!* She was a devil woman, crouched by the fire, sharpening her instruments ready for the kill.

Half an hour later, stiff and impatient, Blanche got out of the car and crossed the road to the tattoo parlour. Past the reception desk, Blanche saw her mother from behind. She was straddling a chair, clasping its frame to her body. Her back was bare, beside her a woman with a tube in her hand. Blanche was dazzled by the colourful gloss of her mother's skin, some of it tattoos, some rashes. She stopped in the doorway, gripped by prudish jealousy. The woman turned. 'Hi. You must be Blanche.' She extended then retracted her hand. 'Sorry, I'm covered in cream.'

Marie twisted around. 'This is Rhys. My daughter, Blanche. I've been dying of itchiness the last few days.'

'I could have done that for you.'

'I didn't take any cream in with me. I didn't think they'd keep me in that long.'

'There's some tea in the pot, Blanche. Cups are up there. Help yourself.'

'Thank you.' Blanche walked over and mechanically poured. She sat at the table, which was covered in papers, a vase of purple orchids, toys. Sit still, she silently admonished her stomach. 'Do you tattoo in here?' she enquired.

'No.' Rhys laughed. 'This is my kitchen.'

Sorry for asking a polite question, thought Blanche.

'The moth's not too itchy, is it?' Rhys said to Marie.

'It's calmed right down.' Marie tried to move a toy truck near her elbow but it was stuck to the table. An orchid landed on the telephone bill with a loud clack. Sap had dripped everywhere, adhering Travis's truck to the table and, it now appeared, Blanche's teacup. The room was electric with Blanche's embarrassment.

Rhys floated the shirt back over Marie's body. 'Has he had his dinner?' she enquired.

Travis had walked into the kitchen. Barefoot, he was cradling a guinea pig in his thin arms. 'He's had lettuce and carrot,' he replied. He squatted to release the animal then, staring at Blanche, caught it again. Rhys introduced them and he walked over. 'This is Ted.'

'Hi, Ted.' Blanche was hypnotised by the child, the green-golden of his eyes. He was like a creature from a forest.

'Rob gave him to me.'

'He's cute.'

'Wanna hold him?'

'Um. Okay.' Blanche took the guinea pig onto her lap. He

skittered off, half shimmying down her leg, half falling to the floor.

Travis giggled then picked up Ted and took him to Marie. Ted sat on Marie's lap twitching his nose. Between her fingers Marie noticed some strands of her hair. She discreetly released it onto the floor. 'I met some interesting people in hospital, one of whom is a fan of your work.'

'Oh, really?'

'I'm sorry we couldn't get you into private care, Mum,' said Blanche.

'I like it in there. As much as I'm able. A jailbird called Brian, who said your work has won competitions all over the world.'

'Yeah, I've done a few of those blokes. Pussycats mostly. At least with me.'

Rhys and Marie began to discuss prison tattoos. Marie had a bit of a smarmy look, Blanche noticed. She said to Travis, 'I hear you're going camping.'

'Yep. We're gonna see parrots. Green and red and um … We're gonna go swimming.' He pressed against Marie's leg and fondled the guinea pig, and when Marie placed her hand on his head she felt a circle of warmth complete itself through her body, lighting a possessive yearning. She wished he were hers, along with Rhys, and the whole room seemed fluorescent with this treacherous display.

'That must be fun,' said Blanche to Travis.

'Yep. There's fire.'

'Do you ever go to those tattoo conventions?' Marie said to Rhys.

'Nah.'

'Why not?'

'Tattoo artists are totally insane. I couldn't stand it.'

'You saw a bushfire?'

'Naooo, we have a campfire. For marshmallows. We do dances.' He moved into the centre of the room to demonstrate.

'Travis goes feral,' Rhys quipped.

'Dad's coming too.'

Marie looked questioningly at Rhys.

'We're good mates,' Rhys explained. 'We go way back. You

might've seen him at FAST? In his Osama bin Laden t-shirt?' She made a wry face.

Blanche was running along behind the conversation, trying to catch up.

Travis stood on his toes, peered across the tabletop and wrenched his truck from its ooze of dying flowers. He licked the wheels experimentally. 'It's sweet!' To her mortification, Marie saw her hair had also travelled to the truck. She felt a comforting warmth spread across her lap then Travis was leaning against her, squealing, 'Ted's done a wee, Mum!'

'Okay, Trav.'

'He's done a wee, he's done a wee!'

'God, Marie, I am so sorry.'

'That's alright.'

Blanche seemed about to say something, or get up.

'My hair's started to fall out,' Marie said with false gaiety. She handed the guinea pig to Travis, then went to the outdoor toilet.

In the kitchen, Blanche told Rhys that Marie had responded badly to chemotherapy and nobody seemed to know what the next step was. She spoke from inside a tender, taut place, like a pustule ready to burst. Rhys listened as Travis climbed into her lap. Blanche wanted answers. Four large hazel eyes stared at her.

'I'm sorry,' said Rhys. 'It's awful. I wish there was a cure.'

'Well, she calls you her medicine woman.'

Rhys smiled.

'Why did she come here?' Blanche said fiercely. 'Why did she do this?'

'Because she wanted to.'

'Yeah, and sometimes I want to commit murder.'

Rhys's head flicked back as though she had been hit.

'You don't like me, do you,' said Blanche.

'I don't know you. But I do like your mother. I have a huge respect for her. We've become friends.'

Respect. The word inflamed Blanche. 'Well, why then? *Why?*'

'I guess she wanted to do something independent. She wanted a change and this was a big part of that. She loved being tattooed.

She wasn't one of those people who just likes adornments. Every design meant so much to her. I mean *means*. She could tell you better than I can. Why don't you ask her?'

Blanche glared at Rhys. Those mutilated hands, her scrawny son hearing all this stuff about prisons and tattoos, the dirty soles of his feet facing her like two shut doors. He was humming loudly, running his truck down his mother's thigh. 'Do you just tattoo anything on anyone that walks in here? Take the money and mark them for life. Is that it?'

'I tattoo consenting adults with designs of their choice.'

'Mum would've consented to anything after a drink or ten.'

Rhys tightened her mouth. 'Nobody gets past reception with so much as two beers under their belt. I've never seen your mother drunk. She was — is — one of my best clients. If not *the* best.'

'I can see that. You must've made thousands from her. A real cash cow.'

Rhys shifted Travis. He crouched on the floor and began to zoom his truck up and down with great crashing sound effects. 'Go upstairs, darling.' Travis left the room and Rhys looked at Blanche with glittering eyes. 'I was going to give you the card of my acupuncturist —'

'More needles. Great!'

'Will you at least take this one? All my details are there. I'll be out of range some of the time but I can pick up messages. Can you let me know if anything goes wrong?'

'What more could go wrong?'

Marie was coming through the door. 'Shall we go?'

Rhys handed the acupuncturist's card to her. 'Apparently it helps with the side effects of chemotherapy.'

Blanche looked away as her mother and Rhys embraced.

'What's FAST?' she said when they were in the car. 'Did she mean drugs?'

'It was a sort of party I went to with her. A cabaret.'

'You haven't been taking drugs with her, have you?'

Marie wanted to laugh but was afraid of upsetting Blanche. 'I think I've taken more drugs this past month than in the rest of my life put together. I've had codeine or pethidine every day. I suppose I'm becoming a junkie.'

'You said she was a single mother.'

'She is.'

'But Daddy's going camping.'

'She's not in a relationship with him.'

'I would have said she was a lesbian, actually.'

'Really?' Marie was partly defensive, partly impressed.

'Yeah. She's got a toughness about her. That job. You'd have to be tough, the people you deal with.'

'You're tough, Blanche.' Marie looked over. 'And it isn't an insult.'

Driving through the city, the oval of her daughter's face clung like a tear in the corner of Marie's eye. She couldn't blink it away. She thought about the child Blanche was carrying. Would it be close to its mother? Would it even *be* at all? And if Blanche kept it, would she, Marie, live to know it? She thought about the miracle of a newborn, the family crowding around with conjectures of who the tiny, squashed creature resembled. How narcissistic we are, wanting our children to be both replicas and advancements. Surreptitiously, all the way home, Marie studied the profile of the distressed, self-possessed woman beside her. The pain was almost unbearable.

'Are you happy for us to decide on a place for you?' Blanche asked ten minutes later, looping through Cremorne. 'I've got a shortlist, and Clark and Leon said they'd come with us too.'

'I'll come if I have the energy.'

'We'll get you somewhere simple and comfortable. You won't have to worry about a thing.'

'Thanks, that'd be lovely.'

A relieved silence settled between them.

Susan's car was parked out the front of the house. 'I didn't think she'd still be here,' Blanche muttered as she pulled in behind it.

'Oh no,' said Marie. 'I haven't been returning her calls.'

'I think you've got a pretty good excuse, Mum. God, listen to us. In thrall to the old dragon.' Blanche reached for her mother's bag then helped her out of the car. Together, they walked down the path.

Marie went straight into the kitchen and took two Panadeine Fortes. The five-degree drop from inner-city heat to harbour cool stroked her body. Susan was sitting at the dining room table with Leon. Marie settled on the couch with Mopoke, a reassuring bolster against the three pairs of eyes watching her. Susan's looked red. 'I've brought you some macaroni cheese,' she said.

'Thank you,' Marie replied, her agglutinated stomach throbbing balefully.

The room stirred into activity. Blanche said she had to go to the bathroom, Leon to the kitchen. 'And a book.' Susan passed Marie a large novel. 'It's won a swag of prizes.'

The cover showed a parched Australian landscape. Prize stickers like UFOs floated across the red sky. A skeletal tree stood in the foreground. Marie thought of her unfinished angophora and, looking at the arid jacket design, had an unpatriotic pang. She clung to it as distraction from the spear embedded in her stomach. Gradually, with the opiates blooming and her hand in Mopoke's fur, she began to relax.

'Leon's doing a marvellous job in the garden. You must be pleased to have him back. Is he going to stay when you get out of hospital?'

'I am out of hospital.' A strange high note emerged from Marie's stomach. She hoped Susan would be offended or uncomfortable.

Susan looked away from the sound. 'I mean when your treatment's over.'

'There's very little treatment, really. I might have already done my dash.'

The quiet counterpoint of Blanche and Leon in the kitchen was suddenly audible, Blanche saying ... *like I've got an alien growing inside me* ... Mopoke wrapped her legs around Marie's forearm. 'Beautiful puss. And how are Louise, and the little one?'

'They're doing very well. Is she pregnant?' Susan swung her eyes towards the kitchen.

Marie shrugged. She didn't know whether or not Blanche was going to keep the baby, and she didn't want to discuss it with Susan. 'And Jonesy?'

'He's finally got onto the board of trustees at the Art Gallery, and a good thing too. He's going to shake them up. He's had two requests from artists to paint his portrait for the Archi.'

'Yes. They favour big heads in that prize.'

Susan crinkled her eyes indulgently, like a mother whose child had thrown food on the floor in front of guests. Marie felt a sadistic thrill. Funny how being decrepit, diseased and sentenced to death gave you so much power. She couldn't go to Morocco nor even drive herself into town. She could hardly move off the couch. But she could say whatever she wanted: she had bitch licence.

'He wants to come and see you, but we thought I should come on my own first.'

Leon arrived with cold drinks and fruit. 'Oh, how sweet.' Marie smiled at him.

He gave Susan an envelope. 'Boil 'em before you plant. Or get some sandpaper and give 'em a rub or something, to help them open. I'm giving Susan some seeds from your wattle trees, Mum.'

'Lovely.'

'What about burning them, Leon? You used to barbecue seeds first, didn't you, Marie? Shouldn't they be burnt?'

'Nah, the pods not the seeds. Anyhow it might also be the flavonoids that help them open. I don't know. Right. I'll leave you ladies to it. Blanche and me are outside if you need us.'

'Oh, the lovely house,' said Susan when they were alone. 'What dreadful timing, Marie. How long have you got?'

'To live in general? Or just here.'

'I meant in the house.'

'Two more months. We extended the settlement.'

'Louise knows the couple who bought. She says they're very nice. Second-generation Mosmanians.'

'Blanche says they're going to build a four-car garage and a swimming pool and take out most of the garden.'

'Well, it's a good thing you're leaving then.'

Marie thought angrily, obviously they wouldn't be doing any of this if she *wasn't* leaving, but Susan's insensitivity to the sequence of events had her confused as well, so she said nothing. She frowned at the view to communicate boredom and disgruntlement.

'Where are you going to go?' Susan asked politely.

'The children are looking for somewhere for me to rent. Somewhere for me to go and die.'

'I can't believe it.' Susan looked away, blinking. 'And you look so good.'

'Yes. It is hard to believe.'

'And you're being so brave.'

It was hard to talk as well, the effort provoked the sort of feeling you got when you stood up too quickly, though Marie knew she wasn't going to faint or even fall. She hoisted herself to an angle that enabled her to drink. The movement sent dizziness pulsing down her limbs.

'There was a record king tide when you were in hospital. It came right over the sea wall and hit the old Deco apartments at Neutral Bay.'

Marie didn't know what to say. She wished she had seen it. She was tired of squeezing her buttocks together to restrain farts; she had given up the idea of shitting. She sat stewing in her bitterness.

'I saw Gina the other day,' Susan went on. 'She wants to bring you communion. I don't understand any of that, but that's what she said.'

Marie thought, Well, Gina can come and say it to my face. She said, with the weariness of a luminary who'd been too busy to carry out a task the world had been waiting for, 'I haven't made my confession in so long, Susan. I don't think God would approve.'

Susan looked at Marie, bright-eyed, questioning. 'I always thought it would be a comfort, having such a strong religion.'

'More like a torture. That's why I don't have it anymore.'

Susan watched her respectfully. Marie was getting tired of kicking her: Susan's indulgence provided no resistance, no satisfaction. It was like picking a scab: Marie couldn't stop herself going to the root, regardless of the pain. 'I mean, we need to believe in more than just comfort, don't we?'

'I believe in God,' Susan said.

'Really? You never told me that.'

'It never came up in conversation before, it was never relevant.'

'Why is God only relevant when someone's dying?'

Susan looked uncomfortable.

Marie persisted: 'You never go to mass.'

'I just don't believe it's all for nothing. There has to be something there. Don't you think?'

'That's there.' Marie jerked her head at the view. 'That's enough, isn't it?'

'But I mean more than that.'

'Isn't that enough? I mean *look* at it. It's a universe.'

'Well, yes, it's beautiful. But it has to *mean* something.'

'It means a million things.'

'Like what?'

'I don't know! The tides, photosynthesis. Developers ... Murder.' She twisted her mouth.

'I don't understand.'

'Why should we? Life isn't a formula, is it?'

Susan looked frightened, and Marie felt again a combination of disdain and guilt. She shut her eyes to gain her balance. The clocks were changing back in a few weeks, the paperbarks were in flower. Marie sensed the garden stirring outside. Just weeks ago she was working through those corridors and rooms of vegetation, in her head the ever-changing list of things to be done, but now she had no idea what was going on down there. Chaos, growing over her.

Susan was blinking away tears. 'I always admired you for your independence, Marie. I never went to university, I never did anything. I couldn't even garden.'

'I was a housewife with three children, Susan.'

'No, you weren't. You were always a bit different, not like the other Mosman mums. That's why I liked you; I was never bored with you.'

'How so?' Marie sniffed the air for a compliment.

'I never knew what your opinion would be; I never knew what you were going to wear; you were very forgiving of me and Gina. I don't know!'

What she had meant was, How was I different? But Susan hadn't understood and Marie was too exhausted to clarify. She was sick of these ritualistic meetings where her illness was bowed to, and the talk was of herself in the past tense. How compact and romantic the Last Supper seemed. Everybody gathered at the one meal, all elegy, accusation and grieving over and done with in one go. Not this endless reminiscing and whinging. Seeing Susan hurt made Marie's mettle retract. What was to forgive, at the end of the day? Nothing much. Gina had always been impermeable. Susan's infidelity had been repaid. Amazing how you nearly die of passion, shame, loss, betrayal, only to find the source of anguish desiccate, if not vanish altogether.

But vanity persisted. She did look good, she saw in the hall mirror after she had said goodbye to Susan. Chemotherapy was like a crash course in exfoliation. She looked luminous. Not that her hair would last much longer. Funny how the most unnecessary body parts — hair and nails — continued growing after death. Maybe it was the important things that one let go of first, because they were so difficult.

And why did everyone call it *brave*. Did they think she knew what was happening and was mounting a coherent defence? She wasn't brave, she was terrified. She was heading straight for death and she knew nothing about it.

On Sunday Blanche went to visit her father to discuss a matter that he hadn't wanted to go into on the phone. She was also going to tell him she was having a baby. Pulling up in his steep Seaforth driveway, she wondered if the two things weren't in fact the same. He could have found out about the pregnancy through any number of channels, and he could be going to offer her something for it. Maybe the house in Berri: he never used that house. How exciting.

Entering his property, you assumed a mansion: the small funicular railway through an almost vertical garden arranged among rocks as big as cows, the long terracotta roof, Middle Harbour below, busy with boats. The house clung like an oyster to the cliff facing Beauty Point, the rooms strung in a row with a cavern beneath that Ross used as a study. It was less cluttered now Traci had moved in. The antiques had been whittled down. Just inside the door was a large pair of cloisonné vases on a rosewood table with intricately carved dragons coiled around the legs. Above them, an ancestor scroll depicted a nobleman seated in a crimson robe, his wife in black standing behind him. Pale Chinese rugs with red and blue borders covered the floor, and other statues posed around the fireplace in the middle of the room, below a flue. The place was neat as a pin. Classical piano tinkled from the speakers.

Blanche hadn't seen her father for almost a year and was surprised by the man at the door in chinos, boating shoes and a fawn silk shirt not distended by stomach. He looked so much smaller and younger without the girth he had carried throughout her childhood. He had been clean shaven for two years now, but Blanche was still not used to it.

He gave her a hug. 'Princess! You've lost weight.'

Blanche knew she hadn't. She had put it on.

'Hi, Dad. So have you.' But she meant it.

'I'm still on my special diet. Have to watch the blood pressure and diabetes.'

'It's always so much more intimate, once you're inside this house,' Blanche said warmly, following him to the kitchen.

'Oh yes, it's not a big house. It's perfectly manageable.' Ross took from the fridge two white plates covered in clingwrap. 'And only one room without a view — the bathroom.'

'You've made lunch?'

'I'm a sushi chef now, don't you know.' On each plate, neatly arranged, were four prawns, four pieces of shop-made sushi and a handful of green salad. He carried them out to the terrace and opened the sun umbrella over the table. A bottle of Verdelho was cooling in an ice bucket. 'Are you drinking, Blanchie?'

'No, thanks. I'm driving.' Blanche lowered her glasses against the glare.

'So what are you working on?' her father asked. He didn't know or he was being coy, stringing her along. God, he was good.

'Don't ask. Sanitary napkins.'

'A good product. I'm not taking the piss. It's one of the most fundamental products there is. Look at an old magazine, half the stuff we used to sell is obsolete now. Not sanitary napkins.'

'I s'pose so. Listen, I'm not handling eating very well either, so don't be offended if I can't finish this. I'm pregnant, Dad. I'm going to have a baby.'

Ross whooped and Blanche found herself grinning from ear to ear in a way she hadn't for a long time, let alone in the vexed period since falling pregnant. 'We have to drink to that!' He got up excitedly. Blanche shook her head. 'Just a little glass of Moët, go on, princess. Just a half-bottle.'

'I honestly couldn't manage more than a sip, Dad. Be a shame to waste it.'

'I'll cork it. Traci's coming home later. She'll help me.' He fetched another ice bucket and the champagne and glasses. 'I'm superstitious when it comes to celebration, Blanche. If it's gonna be great, it's gotta be Moët — and it's gonna be great.'

The champagne danced on her tongue, fresh and tangy. It tasted like the first swim of summer. She ate some sushi and didn't feel nauseous. 'It's lovely being here, Dad. Thank you for all this.'

'It's lovely having you here.'

'That's amazing.' Blanche indicated a giant Buddha's head in the corner of the terrace, looking out to the Spit.

'It's Traci's. She's a Buddhist. You knew that, didn't you?'

'Where is it from?' She reached out to pat the cool stone.

'Laos, eighteenth century. No' — Ross struck his forehead — 'Cambodia. Yes, Cambodia. Have you been there?'

'No, just Hong Kong and Bali.'

'It's past its prime, sadly. I don't mean the piece, it's a magnificent piece. But I don't think Cambodia ever recovered from the communists. Bit of a dump, really. The people aren't as friendly as they are in Thailand.'

'That's what I always hear. Hugh and I are the only Australians who've never been to Thailand,' Blanche said with a mixture of pride and wistfulness.

'I got the Buddha for Traci on our anniversary.'

Anniversary. Why did that hurt her, after all this time? They all knew that Traci had been around before Ross had left Marie. Blanche comforted herself with the champagne. It tasted like a magical elixir from a fairy tale. She unpeeled a prawn and dipped it into the tartare sauce. She hadn't eaten so much without feeling uncomfortable, either. The tides are turning, Blanche, she told herself. She had been glad, when coming today, knowing that Traci wouldn't be here. Traci, a groomed, astute, independently wealthy woman who had studied feng shui in New York and incorporated it into her interior design. She looked you in the eye when you spoke, attending to every word. Traci also had a habit of winking at Blanche whenever Ross was looking elsewhere. Blanche interpreted these winks as fatuous messages of feminine solidarity, but sitting here with her father in such good form, she wouldn't have minded Traci's presence. It was time she got over her childish resentment. Traci, even from the other side of the room, commanded Ross's attention. He softened around her. There was something in that. Ross offered her more champagne, but Blanche refused so he poured the rest into his glass.

'Make a wish,' Blanche said as the final drips emerged.

'I wish for a happy and healthy son for my beautiful daughter.'

'We'd be just as happy with a girl, Dad.'

'I've got a granddaughter already. I was being selfish. I was being *democratic*. And your mother,' Ross looked at her, 'how is she?'

'Pretty sick. Keeping her spirits up.' Blanche spared him the details, that if Marie's chronic constipation didn't ease, she would be hospitalised.

'Clark told me she had a rough trot with the chemotherapy.'

'She's picked up a bit since coming home. She walked down to the cove the other day.'

What was noticeable about this house, particularly the terrace, was the lack of birds, apart from the occasional pelican gliding over Clontarf in the distance. It felt so exposed here on the cliff.

Just the elements of air and water, no animals, no trees. Spit Bridge was open, like two TimTams at forty-five-degree angles. Weird how something so ugly could look so beautiful. One after another, boats passed through the channel. Blanche felt muffled by her sunglasses: she pushed them back up onto her head.

'Are you all coping?'

'I guess so.'

'The medical bills covered?'

'She'd stopped her insurance, Dad. Everything's being paid for with the estate, via Hugh's chequebook.'

'I knew you and Hugh could be trusted to look after things. You doing okay?'

He didn't seem the slightest bit fazed at the debts Marie had incurred. Blanche wasn't sure if that was a good thing. 'Yeah. Except Hugh bought a property in Ultimo that I don't, um, agree with.'

'But you're secure in your own place, and you've still got that flat in Neutral Bay?'

'We own Lavender outright, and Neutral pays its way.'

'Good. Excellent. You've done well. I'm proud of you. You've been good to your mother, you know. Very good with all of this.'

'You just do what you've got to do, don't you?'

He listened and spoke with his head inclined towards her, his tone insistently gentle, brow furrowed. 'Well, I'm really very sorry. It's very tough. It's tough on all of you.'

'Are you going to visit her? Have you rung her?'

Ross moved his tongue around his teeth and gazed at the view. What had happened to her gruff, macho father? Was it just a memory-versus-actuality disjunction, like the dining room table that had loomed over her as a child and remained fixed in those proportions in her mind through all the years of looming over it in turn as an adult? All his brutalities now seemed petty, the blunderings of a man uneducated, like most, in the ways of parenthood. Even the philandering could be seen in context: a 1970s advertising executive flush with success who'd married too young. And her mother had had her bit, and her mother had drunk hard too.

Ross made a gesture of helplessness. 'I've been thinking about your mother a lot, you know. But I don't want to upset her while she's going through this.'

'Dad, when she finishes going through this, she'll be dead. You're going to have to see her at some stage.'

'Yes.' He moved his plate away, lining his knife and fork neatly across it. 'I know I am. I want to choose the right time. It's the drinking, isn't it. Geez, what a comeuppance.'

Blanche wanted to change the subject. 'Do you get out much in your boat?'

The boat was at the bottom of the cliff, down a twisting staircase of wooden slats and steps carved into rock. Moored to an oyster-encrusted jetty, it was equipped to fit eight but rarely went out with more than one or two.

'I'm fixing it at the moment. Climbing up and down those stairs every day, believe it or not. That's where this has disappeared.' He patted his stomach proudly then uncorked the Verdelho.

'I used to love coming here in Jonesy's yacht,' Blanche reminisced.

'Oh yes, those were the days. Of course Jonesy's riddled with arthritis now from all that sailing. And he can't *give* that old hulk away.'

'Do you see much of them? Or the Tottis?'

'We went to Adelaide together to see *The Ring Cycle* in February.'

'How was that?'

'A bit bloody boring to tell you the truth. But Traci likes that sort of thing. She's educating me in classical music. She got me this one playing.' He indicated a box set of David Helfgott open on the couch just inside the door. 'Do you like it?'

'It's beautiful.'

'Anyway I'm sticking with the plain old motor boat. It's more independent. I don't have to rely on a bunch of ugly blokes to help get me onto the harbour.'

Blanche walked to the edge of the terrace in order to see the sapphire water of Quakers Hat Bay. 'God, it looks tempting. I'd love a swim.'

'No, you wouldn't. Saw a bull shark down there in December, near the bridge.'

'No.'

'Oh yes. Sharks are back. We're victims of our success in cleaning up the waterways. Don't you move. I'm bringing us dessert. Tea or coffee?'

'No, thanks.'

Blanche got out her mobile and texted her team. *How was lunch? What did Sean think of the pitch?* Ross returned with fruit tarts and cake forks. She had never seen her father take responsibility for an entire meal. All her childhood he had never lifted a finger. She smiled at his careful serving. She felt a rush of affection for this calmer, smaller person, and simultaneously nostalgia for the big father of her past, a longing to curl up in his lap. In the living room, David Helfgott thundered down the ivories and rumbled menacingly among the bass notes.

'So. What did you want to talk to me about, Dad?'

'Business.'

Blanche tried not to smile.

'It's not good news, I'm afraid. I'm going to have to claim half of the estate.'

Blanche felt her jaw literally drop.

'I've lost a shitload of money lately, Blanche. I can't tell you how much on the stockmarket. Numbers are down at the resort. I'll probably have to sell it.'

Blanche spoke with disbelief. 'I find all this recession talk *sooo* exaggerated. We're still working day and night at HA.'

'Your clients still paying on time? Mine aren't.'

Blanche thought spitefully, Cos your ads are shit. 'You can't claim the estate, Dad. That's outrageous. Mum got the house in the settlement. You had the resort and other properties and your business and shares.' Her voice began to rise, along with her gorge. 'It's il*legal*.'

'It's perfectly legal. We settled out of court. Without the imprimatur of the court, the property is hers by my goodwill. It was a gift.'

'So you'd be doing this even if she was going to live?'

'Well, yes. Half the estate is still a decent amount of money. Besides which, you told me she was going back to university and wanted to get a job.'

'She's fifty-nine and she's been a housewife her whole life, Dad!'

'Blanche. I had a three-hour meeting with my accountant last week and I have no choice. I have to make a claim.'

'As if you have no choice. Look at this house! What about us? That's not fair!'

A steely expression came over Ross's face. 'Right now, it's your mother's property, not yours —'

'And she's dying.'

'— and all of you children received money from me to buy your own properties when you were twenty-five which is more than what 99.9 percent of the people in this world get.'

'*You* chose to give us that money!'

Ross's face darkened and he became her childhood father again, hard, callous. 'I left school at fifteen years of age and worked my fingers to the bone for another fifteen before I was able to buy a property! Rabbit once a month was a treat in my childhood. Do you have any idea?'

'I work hard too! And what about your grandchildren? *Plural* now, Dad.'

Ross sighed. The smell of fermented grapes washed over her. 'Princess, please. I know you have a lot on your plate. I've been dreading telling you this. I'm not going to do anything now, but when your mother dies, half the estate is going to come to me, and that's final.'

Blanche shook off his hand, left the table and ran the length of the light-filled house to the bathroom.

Parked in the shade on the esplanade above her father's house, Blanche tried to recover. How dense and beautiful the foreshore of Quakers Hat Bay looked, and the water all around rippling in the sun. There was the clatter of wings against foliage then two currawongs burst forth carolling loudly. More than Sirius Cove, this was the place that Blanche had associated with that trio of couples — her parents, the Joneses and the Tottis — no doubt from those sailing trips.

She didn't know what had possessed her an hour before, reducing her father to an innocent like that. She thought of her mother at her own age and was staggered by the differences. Although she never had time to even cook proper dinners, Blanche's life seemed so simple. Just her and her husband and her work. She hadn't even had her first child. Her mother, on the other hand, at the age of thirty-seven had three children almost grown, with a husband who never lifted a finger around the house, and that house was enormous. Imagine the endless toil. And the way she and her brothers were at that time. The fights that blazed through the house. Ross shouting, Marie crying.

But the worst was the infidelity. Not only did he not help at home, he had also fucked Marie's two best friends. Imagine how full-on that must have been. Blanche would have cut his balls off if he'd been her husband. Still, she wasn't sure her mother knew about Gina back then, nor even later. She wasn't even sure if Gina's rejection of Ross that she and her brothers had witnessed at that advertising party had been of an initial advance or a request for more. Susan seemed to know everything and was trying to shield Marie. She must have still felt guilty about her and Ross. All of this before Marie had taken her revenge with Jonesy. Susan did not maintain that deference and apology. Nor Marie her hurt. So, revenge paid off.

Blanche also remembered how much her mother had admired Pat Hammet for working, and how Gina had held herself above Marie and Susan because of her job in Mosmania. Blanche had been so contemptuous of all of them, so sure that what she had planned for herself was better. She wasn't going to settle for a job in a dumb homewares shop let alone be a housewife. Yet even she had compromised in choosing advertising over art. And speaking of compromises, the baby wasn't even born yet. Sitting by the harbour always lulled Blanche. Time stood still; she came right into the moment. But today the movement to a finish line was ineffable. Marie would never fulfil her desire to work. She could have gone back to study if she hadn't got cancer. Blanche wondered if she would have been able to get a job. Would she have had fulfilment from that, or did psychologists become wage slaves too, and get poisoned by their jobs like advertising executives? And what could you take with you at the end of the day whether you liked your job or not? Yachts? Houses? Your hair and skin. Maybe not the former, if you'd had chemotherapy ...

A text from Kate came through. *All's well, boss, take a load off. x* Blanche's head pounded. She had finished the bottle of water in her car, but her mouth was still dry. She was stuck to the seat with perspiration. She put the key into the ignition, but her hand began to tremble so violently she couldn't turn it. She could barely dial Hugh's number. When he answered she began to cry. 'Can you come and pick me up, Hughie?'

'Has the car broken down?'

'No. I kind of have. I'm really sick. I can't drive.'

'Sit tight, pooky. I'll be there as soon as I can.'

Blanche looked down at the harbour and ached with longing. Even if she couldn't take it with her, she still wanted her house by the water. Beneath her righteous anger with her father for stealing from her mother burnt the flame of her ambition. More than a million dollars that had been coming to her had done a U-turn right before her eyes, just when she was about to have a baby. That she was well-off even without this sum was irrelevant.

Blanche flipped down the visor and dabbed her eyes in the mirror. At the age of thirty-seven, she was distraught to discover a deep line down the middle of her forehead and one either side of her mouth. She sat waiting for Hugh, amazed at the sight of these lines, wondering where she had been and what she had done.

Clark waited for Sylvia in front of the university. The wind cut through his jacket, and he stepped from side to side to keep warm. Looking around the forecourt, he imagined Sylvia appearing in every item of clothing he had ever seen her wear. Her jeans with the small hole in the knee, the red silk scarf, blue trainers. The way her face lit up when she saw him. All his past lovers had chastised him for his disregard of clothing, but with Sylvia he noticed and remembered everything. Then she was there, in a beanie. She looked like Annie Hall.

They wrapped themselves around each other. 'Come inside,' Clark said. 'I want to find somewhere we can be alone.'

They walked into the dim interior holding hands. Sylvia let go of his to move her hair out of her eyes and Clark felt as though he would die until he took her hand again, but she kept it to herself. 'We shouldn't be like this in public,' she cautioned. They walked rapidly past the cafeteria, a boy handing them leaflets for a rally. They took a lift to lower ground and walked outside.

They were alone. They stopped to kiss. 'I'm wet,' she said. He leant into her. She was older than him, taller than him, she was possibly even stronger, he loved that, he loved her. A delivery man appeared, wheeling a trolley loaded with cartons. Clark took Sylvia's hand and led the way around a corner until they were in a narrow passage beneath an air-conditioning duct, the forecourt just above eye level. Sylvia stood with her back to the wall watching Clark light a cigarette.

'Can I have some?'

He passed the cigarette to her.

'How is she?'

'Who?'

'Who do you think?' She passed the cigarette back.

Clark took a drag. 'My sister's just gone into hospital.'

'Oh god.'

'Hopefully not serious. It's to do with her pregnancy.'

'And your mother?'

'Back in on Friday.'

'Is she in pain?'

'All the time, I guess.' Clark inhaled till he was dizzy, the filter soggy between his lips. 'I can't have any more.' He gave the cigarette back to Sylvia. She shook her head and he dropped it, then pulled her towards him. 'I wish you could have met my mother, Sylvia. Maybe you still could.'

'Oh, babe.'

'I want you. I want you to leave him. I'm serious, Sylvia.'

'I know you are. And I am too. And I'm working on it.' She pressed her mouth to his.

The wall was cold against his back. A drip from the air-conditioning duct struck his scalp through his hair. 'Touch me, please.' Legs moved across the forecourt then stopped, a butt landed and was ground by a shoe, Sylvia's hand on his fly burrowing inside cupping his balls. 'Oh god, I feel like I could come right now.' He sank his fingers into her wetness, muttering insanely into her hair.

'What?' she said.

'You're mine.' He pushed into her hand. 'You're mine, say you're mine. You're mine, you're *mine*.'

Blanche decided not to tell her brothers about their father's intentions until she was out of hospital. They had put her on a drip immediately when she arrived, and by the following evening, with Leon there, she felt rested. Leon had brought some grevillea flowers and arranged them in a jug from the nurses' kitchen. Blanche was touched.

'Geez, Louise,' he said cheerfully. 'I was having a week off the hos', now you've dragged me back in.'

'Sorry.'

'I should hire myself out as a professional visitor. Clark sends his love.'

'Yeah, he texted me.'

'And Mum, of course.'

'You're all being really sweet.' Blanche thought how ironic it was that only a day ago, when on the verge of collapse, she had been remembering their fights in vivid detail. 'Remember that time you tried to cut my head off?' She smirked.

Leon was about to reply when the nurse came in and replaced the empty bag on the drip stand with a full one. 'An*other* one?' said Blanche.

'Yeah, we keep 'em coming.'

'What's in them?' asked Leon.

'Bit of a cocktail. Mainly saline. Most of your condition is caused by dehydration, Blanche. We'll be feeding you these every day till you're better.'

'She looks a lot better already,' said Leon.

Blanche had stopped vomiting and her brief stay in hospital was having a placatory effect on the family, as though they could now imagine any of them, including Marie, moving through these ominous white tombs as easily as through hotels. Leon was struck by how soft and dreamy his sister looked against the pillows. He had brought her a chocolate bilby for Easter, which she consumed enthusiastically. *Hyperemesis gravidarum*, said the clipboard at the end of her bed. A condition, Blanche told Leon, that their mother had suffered through her own pregnancies.

He returned to their conversation when the nurse had gone.

'It seemed perfectly logical at the time. You were like, *Go on*. You threw back your head. Like this.'

'What a martyr. I should have been a Catholic.'

'We were so calm, weren't we? There I was, sawing away at your neck with the breadknife, wondering why nothing was happening. Afterwards you broke your hairbrush on my head.'

'God, that was satisfying.'

'Poor Mum. Hosing us down in the garden.'

'I always got the blame.'

'You were older.'

'But you were a big boofy boy!' Forgetting the line feed, Blanche moved her hand then winced. 'I don't want her visiting me, Leon. She's got enough on her plate.'

'She's quite good today. Pottering around the garden. She's thrilled you're keeping the baby. What convinced you in the end?'

'Hugh. We can take out another loan.'

Leon looked perplexed. 'You guys are set for life, aren't you?'

'Hugh thinks it's best if we do. Look, I know Hugh can be a boofhead. He's much more conservative than me.' Blanche spoke hastily, as though afraid of being overtaken by further vomiting, or contradiction. 'But he's so supportive. He literally got down on his knees and begged me to have this baby and promised to do everything he could for us. It's one of the main reasons I'm keeping it. Because he meant it, and I trust him. Even if he is a crap housekeeper.'

'I guess you're not much better.'

'Thank you.'

'I'm even worse. But you've got Fatima.'

'Every single day Hugh tells me he loves me. And I need that. I'm probably very insecure.'

'I think we all are. I think it's a family illness.'

'Or a national one.'

'Clark's a good housekeeper, you know. Not a speck of dust.'

'That's Dad. He's got Dad's fastidiousness.'

Leon was about to point out that it was their mother who had done everything around the house when Hugh arrived in a blaze of lilies, with Blanche's laptop and more chocolate. Blanche grabbed it greedily. 'Narva!' she cried. 'Was it easy to find?'

'I got it in Paddington.'

'Jesus, are you serious? That far?' Blanche tore the packet open. 'Did you try our local?'

'I tried just about everywhere.'

'Bloody hell! It should be *everywhere*.'

'Don't stress, pooky. Don't think about work.'

Leon went to find a vase. When he returned, Blanche and Hugh were holding hands and discussing names for the baby. Leon felt jubilant without knowing why.

'This little terror,' said Blanche, 'has made me aware every second of its existence. It's been trying to tell me something. So I want something kind of feisty. What do you think, Leon?'

Names, thought Leon. Signifiers or red herrings? Their names had been plucked out of a hat, Clark and Blanche from the Hollywood hat, his own he didn't know. He liked it — Leon King — a big name, masculine. He knew people who had changed their names, one with whom he had studied horticulture going from Sharon to Fern in second year, everybody continuing to call her Sharon behind her back, pronouncing *Fern* with a mocking American accent. 'Well, we have Celtic ancestry.'

Blanche looked nonplussed. 'Clark would know about that.'

'I do too,' said Hugh. 'Welsh.'

'My name's kinda Jewish, isn't it?' said Leon. 'Clark said there's a few missing links in our family tree. He said it could even be Aboriginal.'

'Aboriginal?' Hugh pulled a face. 'I doubt it.'

'Why not?'

'Well, you hardly look it. I mean, you're *white*.'

'We could still have a bit. I wouldn't mind. Anything'd be better than boring bloody Pom.'

'I've got English blood and I'm proud of it.'

'Look, we're just white trash,' Blanche said in a conciliatory tone. 'So come on, Leon, any suggestions?'

'How about Kylie?' Leon minced.

Blanche and Hugh stared at him.

Leon lifted his shoulders up to his ears. 'I didn't mean it like that.'

'Like what?' said Blanche. 'Sorry. I just don't get it.'

'Kylie's an Aboriginal word, isn't it?' said Hugh. 'Is that what you meant?'

Why had he said Kylie, why had he spoken like that? Was he trying to mock the poofter he thought they thought he was? Subliminally channelling a cancer joke? Maybe it was just the family habit of pissing on anything remotely sentimental for fear of feeling. He didn't believe Hugh that Kylie was an Aboriginal word, but a quick google when he got back to Sirius Cove proved he was right — it was a West Australian word for a type of boomerang.

By Blanche and his mother's hospital beds, the sense of his physical strength had felt heretical to Leon. He *had* been a big boofy boy, stronger than his sister for as long as he could remember, stronger soon enough even than Clark, much to Clark's chagrin, yet he had always assumed that as the youngest and the one picked on most by his father, concessions were his due. His homosexuality reinforced this. He knew there was hurt beneath Blanche's joking reminiscences but he had been so preoccupied by his own wounds, so convinced of his inferiority, that it hadn't occurred to Leon that he might have wounded others. Blanche was right, his mother did favour him. He shut this out in order to breathe. He also needed to keep the idea of privilege foreign: to admit to it would be to admit that he in turn owed concessions. It was a logic with infinite implications. When applied across the board, the debts were never-ending. An entire people could owe another, in perpetuity, and that was just preposterous. It was impossible to even contemplate.

He had noticed the cockatoo in the angophora early that morning as he drank coffee on the deck. It was clambering up the trunk with beak and claw, crest half open like a budding flower. From the depths of the house as he washed and dressed, Leon was aware of shrill cries over the phatic noise of the day, and when he entered the garden he saw a group of mynas attacking the cockatoo. The large muscly parrot stood its ground, lifting a leg to scratch behind its ear then hopping further along the branch. Standing below the great shirring tree, Leon saw it was joining its injured mate.

Inside the shed, he rummaged through the tools on the wall till he found a tomahawk. Lifting it revealed a child's handprint on the brickwork and below that a crude drawing of a warship. All along the wall a line of black warships steamed towards the door with autistic precision. This was his artwork. He couldn't remember a childhood fascination with war. Maybe it was just a desire to get away. Leon hesitated in the gloom, running his thumb along the axe blade, trying to remember. His mind retrieved nothing. It kept returning to sex.

He had seen the American warship come across the harbour at dawn, so big it nearly closed the gap between Curraghbeena and Sirius points, a sliding wall of gunmetal grey hefting its mass around to weigh anchor in Woolloomooloo Bay. Its arrival had dominated the news for days: the dock would be swarming with cameras by now. And the Prime Minister would be waiting with his television rictus, and all across the indentured suburbs girls would be primping themselves for the US Navy, Potts Point poofters hoping for some run-off. Oh yes, it would be a good time to hit the beats. Maybe later, when he had finished work. The sound of the bird war, even here in the shed, was all-pervasive and shook Leon out of his reverie.

He picked up the tools and left the shed cursing the mynas. In just a few years, the little bastards seemed to have taken over the entire city. The cockatoos were waiting it out, two white dabs high in the tree. Monogamous animals, parrots. Leon found that unaccountably romantic. As the temperature rose, Leon packed his ute then drove to work at the Joneses'.

The good thing about being a gardener was that you didn't have to check in with your employer like an office worker arriving to start the day. The best jobs even gave you mastery of the domain; you could walk right in and start without seeing anyone. Unless your employer lived behind high walls, with cameras and intercom. If you were buzzed in with nobody appearing, as Leon was today, you knew it was one of the hired help, and the owner wasn't home. Leon felt lighter for that: he drove in and parked behind a blue Mazda then took himself down to the garden. Susan, unfortunately, was there. 'What are we going to do today?' she said brightly.

The Joneses' garden was neat as a toy farm. Even the section of broken marble at the end of the path seemed just a manufacturing fillip, like a bleed of plastic from the seam of the mould. Leon had probably reinforced the perfection with his arrangement of rose bushes, but he'd hardly had a choice. There wasn't much to do now except find a spot for the wattle once it had sprouted, and germinating those seeds was Susan's little home-science project so he would have to wait. He scanned the garden. 'Bananas could do with thinning. I'll chop that one down and wrap the bunch so it can ripen.'

'Terrific.'

The banana palms did look terrible and Leon was pleased to have found a necessary task, rather than just trimming the plastic bleed. While he fetched tools from his ute, Susan went to the kitchen for watermelon. Leon knew that part of his job was to talk to her, and he walked back up to meet her on the terrace.

She lifted the brim of her hat. 'So Marie has gone back into hospital.'

'Two days ago. She's doing another course of chemo.'

'And how's it going?'

'They haven't started it yet. She's doing tests first or something.'

The harbour shimmered all around them, here in the toy farm, raised and perfect on the bluff. Middle Harbour was a mystery to Leon. He associated it with sharks therefore wildness, and at the same time a more secluded sort of luxury. Also, of course, his father, whose house was further in, beyond Spit Bridge. He associated it with childhood in general, as he did the Joneses. The lines on Susan's face still had the capacity to surprise him, like the picture of Dorian Gray.

'Your mother was talking about religion the other day,' she said.

'Really?' Leon took the largest slice of watermelon and chomped into it.

'They say a lot of people go back to it.'

'She hasn't mentioned it. She doesn't believe in God.'

'Do you?'

Leon put down his rind in surprise. 'No.'

'I keep looking at properties for her on *Domain*,' said Susan, changing tack. 'There's a semi in Avenue Road for just under three million, there's a gorgeous three-bedroom flat in Mosman Bay for even less.'

Leon felt guilty that he hadn't looked at the listings that Blanche had sent him. He had never lived with such a definite prediction, nor at the same time so in the moment. 'We're just looking at stuff for her to rent for the time being, Susan, because we don't know how this thing will play out.'

'She said to me that she had less than six months.'

Leon said nothing.

'And here I am looking for houses for her to buy. There's no point, is there? I don't know what we're going to do without her.'

Leon also felt nothing. He said, 'I'd better get to work.'

'Well, I'm going out soon. So you just help yourself to anything in the kitchen when you have a break. Okay?'

Leon walked down to the banana palms. They made him miss his Queenslander with its shambolic garden and scaly-breasted lorikeets. The tomahawk was blunt. He missed his own tools too, even the half-life he had left behind in Brisbane. As the cicadas swelled, his irritation grew at the massive inconvenience of his mother's illness. Was it really as hard for them as Susan said? There was something so easy about it as well: it nominated priority and obviated choice. All the same, Leon couldn't project beyond each day. He was positive his mother didn't believe in God, any more than he did. Which meant that in a few months she would be in the ground, mineral and bone — was that the words to a song? — for the worms. He didn't know what to feel about it.

He blazed through the copse of banana palms for the next two hours, removing those going to seed and the one with a ripening bunch. He threw his whole weight into each blow, enjoying the violence of blade through fibre. His t-shirt became drenched in thin sticky sap and he removed it, enjoying the sun on his bare skin. He dragged the oozing trunks to the side fence then wrapped the green bunch in a plastic bag. He wandered around the garden poking a stick into the beds. In places sand was emerging. No matter how much compost and mulch was laid down, the sand was always rising.

He was standing in the kitchen drinking water when the vacuum cleaner started up in the hall. He leapt with fright, then realised it must have been Fatima. He went out to greet her, but she had her back to him and couldn't hear. When she turned and saw him, she screamed.

'Sorry!' Leon realised he still didn't have a shirt on. 'Didn't you know I was working here?'

'No.' Fatima stood there with her hand on her chest, then she laughed. 'You give me fright.'

Leon climbed into his t-shirt. 'I do the garden here. I'm a gardener by profession.'

'You are good to help your mother.'

'Yeah. That's for love. This is for money.' He spread his lips in a smile.

Fatima nodded politely. On the one hand, Leon wanted to put her at ease and let her know he didn't think he was any better than her because he was the son of the woman who owned a mansion she cleaned. On the other hand, he didn't want her to think he was just more hired help. He usually stayed out of her way when she cleaned his mother's house. She had always struck him as a bit false in her perfect clothes and heavy make-up. Now he saw her skin was fresh, the black curve of her eyebrows quite natural. She was proud, and she was also shy.

'Are you due at Sirius Cove tomorrow?'

'Yes.'

'Because Mum's back in hospital. But I'll be there.'

A look of concern crossed Fatima's face. There wasn't a single line on it, but Leon felt somehow younger than her. 'She said chemotherapy was bad. She look terrible last time.'

'Yes, but they're giving her a new mixture. It'll be different this time.'

'Yes, it cured my sister.' Fatima propped the vacuum hose against the wall. She nodded thoughtfully. 'My sister have cancer. She was very sick in beginning, but now it's all gone.'

She smiled at Leon encouragingly. Leon felt a bit queasy.

'The chemo's just to shrink the tumours, Fatima. It's not going to save her.'

Fatima looked startled. Her face jutted forward. 'She said she get better.'

Leon said nothing, just shook his head. Fatima's eyes darted around nervously.

'Will you keep cleaning for us?' said Leon. 'Like when my mother moves house, when she gets really sick?'

'Of course.' Fatima crimped her mouth. She shook her head then looked back at him with emotion. 'I'm sorry.' She picked up the vacuum cleaner and went into the living room.

Saying it out loud was like learning it afresh. Leon felt terrible when he left the Joneses' later that afternoon. He still burnt with energy at Sirius Cove so he worked in his mother's garden for another hour. He knew he was only tending to what would be destroyed. A garden was like a child: you could convince yourself it was for the common good and that you served it, but really it was the other way around. It was there to serve you. It was your therapy and your sustenance. When Leon walked through it after his swim, he felt happy seeing the evidence of his work. Then he noticed the xanthorrhea had scale. He pressed a spear between thumb and forefinger, feeling the squish. Christ, they were rampant. A breeze came over the headland and he turned in it to relieve his sunburn. He knew he would be spending another night at home. Sailors or no sailors, the drive into town was just too far.

Marie's last request to him before she returned to hospital was a complicated regime of pills and food for Mopoke. She had fixed him with her drugged blue eyes and exhorted him to be nice to her. The cat had grown more miserable each day and was howling outside Marie's bedroom when he went upstairs. And she had pissed on the landing again.

'Shut up,' Leon cursed. 'Shut *up.*'

What the fuck am I doing here?

After lunch, Marie came out to the verandah. There was a patient sitting down the end in the spot she usually chose, obscured by a visitor. Marie drew the blanket close, angling her legs to draw warmth from the sun, thinking it ironic how tortured she had been by its heat only recently. Apart from a burning around her rectum after another enema, the pain wasn't too bad today, and she reclined in a pethidine dreaming, wanting nothing. Ten minutes after a shot, she could be sure of this blissful state of non-caring. The closest thing to it was the feeling of second trimester, after the sickness had worn off and before the weight had become uncomfortable.

Voices floated along the verandah, one female, one male ... *here a month and I'm still paying your bills ... I fucken tried ... your son not mine ...* The visitor beginning to cry, the patient's voice growling. Marie opened her eyes. The sun hurt. She could see the visitor's back, comb marks carved into her greasy bleached hair. *Jesus Christ, woman.* It was Brian's voice. *I just wanted us to have a nice afternoon together.*

Marie shut her eyes, feeling sympathy for the woman, who left soon after. Marie imagined Brian had left as well. She felt content out here in the fading light even though her lunch, a ham sandwich on white, was still boiling in her oesophagus. Eating it had been a marathon. She could smell cigarette smoke. A burp rasped out of her body then Brian was shuffling down the verandah.

'My son won't visit cos he thinks I'm a loser.' He snorted. 'He's probably right.'

He slumped into the chair beside her and his hand brushed hers and, though she had no energy to placate him, Marie opened her hand to his.

That night she found two miniature paperbacks of the Gospels in the bedside table, perfect for bite-size reading between nodding off. She had begun Susan's novel but every time she opened it forgot what was happening and had to reread the previous page again. She opened the Gospels. *Steps to becoming a Christian*, she read. *Admit to God that you have sinned.* She shut the book crossly. She shifted around, trying to get comfortable. Increasingly, the best position was flat on her back. Over and over, she stroked the memory of Brian's hand. Sleep eventually came.

The next afternoon when she came out to the verandah, Brian was in their spot at the far end, smoking and reading his book, *Stalingrad*. He was wearing boardshorts and a Cold Chisel t-shirt. Without the hospital gown he seemed so much healthier. Marie sat beside him. As soon as he finished his cigarette, Brian cleared the ashtray and returned with a jug of water and two cups.

'How sweet of you.' Marie tipped some water into the dehydrated gardenias.

'The least I can do.'

They sat looking out across the red-roofed suburb.

'Was that your wife who was here yesterday?' Marie asked him cautiously.

'My ex. My third ex. Ask any of the ladies I've been with, Marie, they'll all tell you I'm a bastard.' There was a note of pride in his voice, a sort of resentful challenge.

'I've always had a bit of a thing for bastards.'

Brian laughed.

Marie felt embarrassed. Why had she said that? But it had gone down well. 'It's pathetic really. How did your tests go yesterday?'

'I have to have another procedure.'

'What sort of procedure?'

'Dunno. Can't make sense of it anymore.' The sun was moving around the pylon, striking the terracotta tiling and making the whole verandah glow. 'Nearly finished my book. Those poor buggers didn't have a hope in hell. Freezing, starving. Doomed from the start.'

'Do you read many war books?'

'All the time.'

'Why?'

'War makes the world go round.'

'You think?'

'Well, what do you think does?'

Love and money occurred to Marie, but they sounded too human to give the full picture. 'Chaos?' she said.

'But that doesn't make sense.'

'No. Does war make sense?'

'Blokes attacking each other. Genocide.' Brian smiled, the black molars showing. 'People taking land. Yeah, it makes sense.'

'Rape,' said Marie.

Brian said nothing.

'I'm reading these.' Marie showed him the Gospels.

'Oh yeah? I read the Bible in gaol. Can't remember those bits. When're you having your next chemo?'

'Tomorrow. Doxorubicin.'

'That'll make your piss go red.'

'I'm glad you warned me.'

'They didn't warn me. I thought I was pissing blood when it first happened. I thought I was dying.'

'But you —' Marie stopped herself, just as the nurse named Carla appeared.

'There you are! Your afternoon tea is here.'

'This is the life, eh?' Brian hauled himself upright.

The tea for some reason was in proper crockery today. Marie listened to the chime of spoon in cup, Brian slurping. So sore and vague she couldn't speak. *But you* are *dying*, she had wanted to say. But what did it matter?

Next thing she knew, Clark was beside her. He had a bag of peaches. 'Sorry I'm late.' Marie opened her arms to her grandchild. Nell moved awkwardly into her embrace then reattached herself to her father's legs and stared at her grandmother. Marie introduced everybody, and Brian held out his hand to Clark. They shook firmly, looking one another in the eye.

'I saw Susan downstairs in the cafeteria. She's got a bunch of flowers this big.' Clark addressed them as a unit, explaining to Brian, 'Susan's Mum's best friend.'

Nell was staring at Brian. He caught her eye and winked, and she hid her face in Clark's jeans.'

'Hallo!' Susan came down the verandah rattling a plastic bag of fruit, garnering admiring looks along the way. Clark dragged a chair over and introduced her to Brian. There was a boyish naughtiness behind Clark's civility, Marie noticed, as though he were expecting scandal. It reminded her of David on their last date together and her eyes sharpened. Brian drew himself up: Susan gave his hand a quick shake and sat down, not knowing where to look.

'Marie's best friend, eh?' Brian said to her cheerily.

'Yes.' Susan was pleased. She noticed his book and looked at him differently. '*Stalingrad*. I've heard good things about that book. What's it like?'

'A bloodbath. The usual story. I was telling Marie.'

Clark took Nell's hand. 'We're going to find a knife to cut up these peaches.'

'I must read it. I took the liberty of arranging some flowers in your room, Marie. And I'm making you a little cap' — Susan pulled out some knitting — 'so you don't catch cold. Feel how soft it is.'

'That's a good idea,' said Brian.

Marie touched the wool. 'It's cashmere. Thank you.'

Clark returned with plates and a knife, Nell lugging another large bunch of flowers. Clark removed the card and handed it to Marie.

The Chinese woman wheeled her companion out and smiled over at them. 'Having a party?'

The card read: *Dearest Marie, All the best to you at this difficult time. Your bravery is inspiring. Thinking of you with much love, Gina and John.* 'The Tottis,' Marie said out loud.

'Good,' Susan said with satisfaction.

'That's a very impressive tattoo on your leg, Brian,' said Clark. 'I've seen them down at Bondi.'

'Oh yeah?' Brian shifted his leg as though he wanted to hide it. Marie stared at Clark.

'Yeah, lots. Saw one on this Brazilian guy the other day.'

'Like this?'

'Yeah. On his arm.'

'Brazil*ian*?' Brian made a face. 'You sure?'

'There are heaps of Brazilians in Bondi. The beach is a total tattoo gallery. *Everyone*'s got one. They're *every*where.'

Brian looked even more perplexed. 'Brazilian, eh?' He glared out at the red roofs.

He had the same effect on Clark as he had on Leon, Marie realised. They both wanted to impress him, even if differently motivated. And on her. A calm, even friendly authority, but not to be messed with. He must have been perfect running things in gaol. 'How are you Susan?' she said, changing the subject. 'How's the garden?'

'Lovely. I'm very happy. Leon is a master.'

Nell finally placed the flowers on the ground and let out a loud sigh.

'Oh, Nellie, you big strong thing, sorry.' Clark rescued them. 'So what does it mean?' he said to Brian.

'Eh?'

'Your tattoo.'

Brian's eyes slid over to Marie as though sharing a joke. 'It means I'm a sexy motherfucker.'

Clark and Susan laughed awkwardly. Marie gathered Nell in her arms and whispered, 'Why don't you be a good girl and put these in Brian's room with Daddy. I've got plenty. Ask the nurses where to go.' Clark and Nell left on their next mission.

'Aren't they lovely? It's always difficult buying flowers for Marie,'

Susan told Brian. 'She's the best gardener on the north shore.'

Brian returned to the conversation politely. 'Is thet right?'

'Oh, I have another present for you.' Susan passed Marie a package. Inside the tissue paper, Marie found a beautiful cloth printed with designs in black, brown and white. She remembered seeing a pile of them at David's place. She pocketed the card to read later.

Brian studied the cloth, frowning.

'Who's that from?' said Clark, reappearing with Nell.

'David Rosenthal. He gets them from Tonga.'

'Who's he?' Brian asked.

'A friend.' Marie spread the cloth across her knees.

Susan sent out a look full of innuendo. Clark caught it, with Brian's eyes upon him. He cut a peach into quarters and offered it to Brian.

'Thank you. Your boyfriend, eh?'

Susan opened her plastic bag. 'And these mangoes, I nearly forgot.'

'An embarrassment of riches,' said Marie.

'You're a dark horse, Mum,' Clark joked.

'Oh stop it. If he was my boyfriend, he'd be here, wouldn't he?'

Nell went to Marie's lap, and stroked the cloth. Marie kissed the top of her head. She longed to pull her into her arms but didn't have the strength. Clark handed the fruit around.

With a mangoey finger, Nell began to trace the vine on Marie's arm. When she reached the first flower, she turned her fingertip in a spiral. 'You're tickling me, Nellie! Press a little harder.'

'David's away,' Susan said, needles clicking. 'Look how big you are, Nellie. Are you going to big school yet?'

'No.' Nell leant against her grandmother and continued tracing up beneath her sleeve.

'She'll go next year.' Clark lit a cigarette, offering them to Brian. 'Is it alright to smoke out here?'

'You haven't smoked for about ten years,' said Marie.

The cigarette packet featured a child in a hospital bed staring miserably out from behind an oxygen mask.

'Stop smoking, Dad,' Nell said.

Brian took a cigarette and looked at Marie's present. 'It's from Samoa. Not Tonga.'

'It's very fast.' Susan showed off her knitting. 'I'm nearly finished. I'll make you a cap too, Brian, if you like.'

'Dad.' Nell stamped her foot. '*Stop* it.'

On Saturday Leon slept in then pored fruitlessly over the jobs and real-estate sections of the paper. In the afternoon he went for a swim and fiddled in the garden. After the evening news, he heated up some soup and ate it in front of the computer while he checked his emails. Two from friends, spam, invoices from suppliers in Brisbane. Political notices, which he opened mechanically. East Timorese resident for ten years to be deported. In Fiji, two men sentenced to imprisonment for homosexual sex. A petition against the collaboration of the CIA with Afghanistan warlords in the cultivation of poppy, a petition against whaling. Leon signed and forwarded them.

Leon watched the screensaver start up. What was the point in signing all these petitions anyway? There would always be a crisis going on somewhere. He touched the cursor and went to Gaydar. Then he decided to ring George. George picked up straightaway.

'Wanna go out for a drink?'

'I'm having a night at home, actually.'

'Same.'

'How's it all going?'

'Okay. I'm working a bit. Mum's back in for another chemo. What about you?'

'I've been studying. One exam to go.'

'You're such a hard worker.'

'I enjoy it.'

Leon wished George could be his mother's private nurse, but George was too much in love with his job running Triage. He didn't want to tell him about Blanche. He was sick of all the sickness and Blanche's didn't seem that important, relatively speaking. It was a hot musky night. A party had begun somewhere near the water, the shrieks of girls and chipmunk techno bouncing around the cove.

'Have you been out? Or just ensconced in the family stuff?'

'Just been here. Going a bit stir, actually.'

'Well, you're welcome to come over for a beer if you like. I'm having a break in an hour or so. Better here than some hideous expensive bar.'

What about the boyfriend? thought Leon as he showered, carefully cleaning his foreskin. Maybe he was there as well. Might be good to all hang out together, might help normalise things. Leon *wanted* him to be there, for the impediment to be a material thing, not a choice. He put on a black t-shirt and clean jeans. If it was tense, he could leave after one drink and check out the beat in Moore Park. He cleaned his teeth, pocketed keys, phone and wallet, told himself not to get so excited, and drove into town via the bottleshop.

George lived in a ground-floor flat at the back of Surry Hills. Leon remembered the couch but the chairs and table were unfamiliar. They must have belonged to the boyfriend, who didn't seem to be here. The living room was long enough for a dining room table as well, the kitchen full of implements. Mapplethorpe's self-portrait with bullwhip hung behind a set of turntables. There was a wall of CDs and records. Thom Yorke was playing softly. The place felt lived in and loved in.

'Cool pad.' Leon handed George a stubbie. 'You like living here?'

'Yeah. The shops are good and I'm close to work.'

Leon noticed a steamed-up pipe on the coffee table. Dread and excitement jabbed his bowel. 'So Mr Homebody's havin a smoko, eh?'

'Yee-up.'

'You're not one of those drug casualties in the new government ads, are you? One minute you're dancing, the next you're in a body bag?'

'There are no poofters in those ads. Nobody over twenty-five. Want a pipe?'

Leon hadn't had crystal for almost two years. He never sought it out. Nor could he ever say no when it was offered. Especially not to George. 'Sure.'

George went down the corridor into a room at the end and said, 'Yeah mate, I've got a friend here.' Startled, Leon turned to see a Russian Blue strolling purposefully up the hall towards him. Not taking its gaze from Leon, the cat jumped onto his lap and immediately began to purr. George laughed. 'You okay? Not allergic?'

'I'm fine.' Leon stayed stock still, remembering suddenly that he had forgotten to feed Mopoke and give her her medication, thinking it was always a good sign when their pets liked you. But what the fuck was that about, Leon? Tentatively, he placed his hand on the cat.

'That's Bruce.' George hunched over the table. 'Don't take it personally. He's a slut.' He tapped some crystals into the pipe then handed it to Leon.

Leon sucked in as much smoke as he could, held it and, as his heart began to race, said through tightened lips, 'My dad's firm made those ads, y'know.'

George roared with laughter, setting off Leon, the drug scouring his throat. The awkwardness between them melted. Leon remembered how much he *liked* this guy, what fun they used to have together.

'You seen him?' George asked.

Leon shook his head, watching Bruce rub his cheeks obsessively against his thighs. 'He's so *heavy*.'

'He's a Big. Strong. Boy.' George patted the cat with his cupped hand and Bruce stretched his paws ecstatically, the claws going through Leon's jeans. George got more beers and when he sat down again Leon caught a little puff of his body odour, like warm, yeasty bread.

They passed the pipe back and forth, pluming the air with dense white smoke. 'I never knew you liked cats,' said Leon.

'I didn't, until I met Bruce.' George reached over and stroked him, and Leon vanished the cat to imagine George's hand stroking his crotch. The icy, bitter beer tasted fantastic.

'So what were you planning on doing tonight? All revved up and nowhere to go?'

'Study. Cleaning. Maybe go on Gaydar later.' He grinned. 'You've got me on my first night off in a month.'

So he *was* on Gaydar. Maybe they could go on Gaydar together, and Leon could learn George's user name. God, he was getting horny. He wondered where the boyfriend was. Obviously not coming home soon. Unless they did Gaydar together. Imagine doing Gaydar, all three of them. Come off it, Leon. Fucking both of them. That might be interesting. No. No *way*. 'What are you studying?' He stared at George over a lungful of smoke.

'A pathology course. Just keeping my skills up to date.'

Leon gave Bruce a gentle push. The cat rolled obligingly onto the couch and Leon leant over to kiss George. Their hands began to roam.

'Hang on a sec.' George stood up. 'I want to show you something.' He crossed the room, discarding his shirt on the way.

'Nice,' said Leon to the hairy brown back.

'No, seriously. Come over here.' George removed the cover from a large tank in the corner. 'This is Lili, she's a diamond. She had a feed a couple of days ago so she's in a pretty good mood. Had a good sleep, babe?' The python stirred, lifting her head enquiringly. 'Wanna come out?' George placed his hand inside the tank. The snake's head hovered over his arm like a diviner. When she was halfway up, he grasped her in the middle and lifted her.

Heart racing, Leon watched her slide around George's body. He ran a finger along the scales. 'My god, she's quite big, isn't she?'

'She's a teenager. Beautiful girl,' George crooned, stroking her. 'Wanna say hallo to Leon? Take your shirt off, Mary.'

Leon obliged, enjoying George's eyes on his body.

He held his hand out to the snake. She began her ascent and every hair she touched responded. He shelved his arms and Lili drew around him, tongue flicking. He held his head away as the full weight of the python settled, her head probing the air near his shoulder, George's face wide with excitement. 'Isn't it in*sane*?'

'Can I walk around a bit?'

'Yeah, but not in the kitchen. She'll get into the top cupboards and stay there till Christmas.'

Leon walked slowly around the room enjoying the pain where the python tightened against his sunburn. Lili must also have belonged to the boyfriend, and Leon felt gratitude towards his rival. The CDs clicked over and old-school dirty house began to play. Leon turned his head to find right next to his eye the probing, delicate head of the snake. 'I've never been hugged so hard!' He felt delirious, he felt like dancing; for the first time since returning to Sydney he felt alive.

He began to talk and he couldn't stop. He told George about the green carpet snake he had seen as a child in the Sirius Cove house; he told him what it was like living back there. He talked about his mother and her tattoos.

George, who had a tattoo of a squid on his haunch, cocked his head. 'Come again?'

'Practically everywhere.'

'Well, who'd've thought! I remember your mother. I thought she was really sweet. Quite in thrall to your father.'

'They're actually pretty amazing once you get used to the idea. She said the oncologist is being horrible.'

'Oncologists are notoriously conservative. She probably freaked him out.'

'Don't doctors have a responsibility to their patients?' Leon demanded. 'You know, basic compassion?'

'Specialists are just technicians, Leon.'

'It's fucked.' Leon was trying not to sound desperate. Trying not to blame George for the medical profession's failings.

George came over. 'I know, Leon. I know it's shitty.'

'She's getting sicker. I was reading about Chinese medicine on the net, herbs and acupuncture, or unpasteurised goat's milk? D'you know much about that?' he gabbled, the breath catching in his throat, his mouth dry. 'I'm gonna take her breakfast tomorrow. The hospital food's crap.'

'Yeah.'

'What is it with that shit? I can't believe the shit they feed sick people. It's like great, let's make 'em sicker. I wanna find her another oncologist. D'you know any?'

'Nobody I'd recommend.' George held his hands out to Lili and she unwound. Leon's whole torso was stinging, and relieved of the weight of the snake he felt like he might bounce against the ceiling. He kept talking, becoming more emotional. George placed Lili in the tank, then took a joint off the table. He sat Leon on the couch, passed him the joint and held his hand. Bruce, curled up on Leon's other side, began to purr.

'D'you remember Mopoke?'

'She had a mopoke for a pet?'

'Her cat, called Mopoke. She's really old.' Leon let the air out in little bursts, passing the joint back to George.

'Oh, I *love* old cats.'

'She's got like a zillion things wrong with her — half every meal is medication; she pisses everywhere.'

'That often means they're upset.'

'I'm horrible to her, I forget to feed her. I don't like cats,' Leon said miserably. 'I can't help it: they should never have been introduced here, they kill birds.'

'Ssshh.' George rubbed his back.

Leon leant to his touch. The music was getting sexier, snaking through him. Leon put out the joint, took George's head in his hands and kissed him hard. He undid his fly, George pressed up against him, tongue searing his burnt nipples. 'Suck me,' said Leon hoarsely, leaning back, pushing down his jeans. George bent over and Leon felt the gentle scratch of his bristles, his lips.

Then George turned his head and lay it in Leon's lap in an attitude of comfort. He reached out and hugged Leon's knee. 'We can't.'

'Why not?'

'I just *can't.*'

'You were gonna go on Gaydar. Why not me?'

'You're not just a fuck.' George sat up.

'Look, I totally respect this.' Leon gestured to the room. 'I'm here for one night. Not even that.' He saw himself with his pants down, cock half hard, and felt vulnerable and compromised. He hitched up his jeans and reached for his beer. It was empty, so he went to the fridge for the last two.

'There are feelings.'

'You still have feelings for me?' Leon said quickly, immediately regretting his hopeful tone.

George sighed, head in hands.

'Why did you ask me over?' Leon said sullenly.

'Because you rang and I know you're going through a hard time.'

'A mercy mission?'

'No. I wanted to see you. I was going stir too and I wanted to hang out. I'm really sorry, Leon.'

Leon stood on the edge of the kitchen, drinking his beer. A stony heat was growing inside his head. He *knew* George was attracted to him. He found it unacceptable that he would say no. He read an interview recently with a writer who lived with his partner of thirty years and had another lover that he stayed with half the week, *and* he still had sex with other men. And he was happy and functional. Why couldn't he and George still have sex occasionally? Why the big drama?

'Want some more joint?' George said.

Leon came over and finished it, legs together, looking straight ahead. 'What time is it?'

'Nearly one.'

'What are you doing for the rest of the night?'

'D'you want to go out?'

'I feel a bit uncomfortable in this house, mate.'

George moved over and slung his arm around Leon's shoulders. 'I'm really fucking sorry, you know. I really fucking like you, and I want us to be friends.'

'We've always been *that*.'

They sat there in silence.

'Music's good,' said Leon.

'I think there's a party down at the cricket stands.'

'You going?'

'Nope. I've got a couple more hours of study and I have to work tomorrow. Here,' he said, stuffing the remaining drugs into Leon's pocket.

'No, it's okay. I might just go for a bevvy.'

'Honestly, you'd be doing me a favour. I've got a ten-hour shift. And here, have a Xanax too — you'll need to get some sleep at some stage.'

Leon walked down to Cleveland Street, enjoying the honeycomb sandstone walls and graffiti of the laneways. He jaywalked the big intersection into Moore Park, wondering what the name of the street he had parked his ute in was and how he would get it back to Mosman if he was out of it. Dance all night on water, mate. He didn't have much money on him but maybe if he saw someone he knew he could offload the drugs for a cab fare. Or else he could just drive across town and go to the hospital in the morning, straighten out that way. The lawns were dry underfoot; he sensed that in the daytime this area would still be showing the devastation of the heatwave. He walked deeper into vegetation, away from traffic noises. The sky was navy blue, pricked with stars. He could smell the chemicals exuding from his armpits. Energy sparkled off him; he felt good now, out here alone, night air cool on his skin. The world of duty, sickness and rejection receded. And, hey, there was a beat just up here. You watch, George, other guys'll want me, they always do.

He was also happy because the crystal wasn't burning a hole in his pocket. Once upon a time under these circumstances, when he was living in Redfern and ripping through his father's money, he would've thought nothing of cabbing it to the Cross to buy a pipe, finding a doorway away from the surveillance cameras, and smoking it straightaway. It would've seemed the most thrilling thing in the world to do. But now he didn't care. It was as though he had cured himself with a casual taste, like taking antivenom.

He walked towards the wooded area, past two guys leaning against the wide trunk of a Moreton Bay fig. He hadn't had sex since arriving back in Sydney over a month ago. It was a ridiculously long time to go without. In the deeper hush, he began to get excited. Silhouettes wandered across the grass. He walked past a dark guy, they looked at each other, then Leon set out with the man following. They moved into the shadows of a giant fig; he could see the guy's eyes, molten black, short black beard. The top buttons of his shirt were undone, he had his dick out. He was beautiful. Leon reached out to stroke his chest, then there was a flash and he was blinded. He saw a video camera, floodlights, and laughed at the man, thinking it was some kind of joke, feeling at the same time pissed off — how could anyone think they could just come in here and *make a movie* — but the man was panicking, looking left and right. Beneath his visored hand Leon made out police officers in a line, walking towards them, and other guys caught, some literally with their pants down. *What the fuck … ?* Somebody was running, a policeman pursuing; there were shouts, an American accent, sound of a dog panting, one of the police had a dog.

The line of police was abreast. They were in combat boots and caps, sleeves rolled up. One of them called out, 'Righto, sit down, please, hands behind your head.'

'You gotta be joking,' Leon said in what he thought was a low voice. His pick-up began to whimper and fumble with his crotch.

'No, we're not.' A brawny cop walked over. 'I said sit down.'

Leon and the man dropped to the ground.

'Hands behind your head.'

They obeyed.

Leon looked sideways and saw the man still unbuttoned and a wet patch on his jeans. Cheap Kmart jeans, cheap synthetic shirt and shoes, the man rigid with fear. Put your fucking dick away, mate, Leon thought with furious contempt. A female cop walked over with the dog and joined the male standing over them, two capped silhouettes with their legs apart, the light picking out a halo of red hair down the male cop's neck, bleached spikes on the woman's. Both of them wore blue latex gloves. 'Empty your pockets, please. Name and address?'

'What's going on?'

'Got any ID? All of your pockets, thanks.'

Leon was aware of similar interactions in the vicinity. There must have been about twenty police, standing over men who half an hour earlier had felt free and hidden from the world. Two with video cameras roamed around filming. Leon kept his head down. He had an unnerving intellectual lacuna, suddenly thinking homosexuality must be illegal, as though time had moved backwards and he were a criminal.

The male police officer had the dark man's mobile phone in his hand and was pressing buttons. 'Which one's your wife's number, should I call her?'

The dog was sitting right next to him, and Leon wanted to hug it for comfort. In a state of confusion, he worked his way through his jeans and jacket pockets. His fingers touched the little plastic bag of crystal, and the joint, and he wanted to laugh for the absurd bad luck of this night. He handed his wallet, phone and keys to the female cop, rattled off his mother's address.

'This is a Queensland licence. Can you explain that?'

'I live there.'

'So you're visiting Sydney?'

'Sort of. I'm not sure.'

'Ell-ah-ja.' The male cop was reading the dark man's ID. The man muttered back an Arabic word, chin to chest.

'You're not sure?' Light caught the edge of the cop's face. She looked barely twenty. Probably a dyke with that bleached cropped hair. Incredulous betrayal stabbed Leon. 'Any other pockets?'

His fingers touched the plastic bags again. The dog remained seated before him, gazing up faithfully. He loved dogs.

'This the only ID you've got, Ell-ah?'

'Can we see what's in there?'

Leon pulled the bags out. 'It's just dregs.'

She took them with her latex-gloved hands and showed them to her partner. He snorted knowingly. 'Where did you get this?'

'From a friend.'

'And who might he be? Or is it a she?'

Leon said nothing.

'Are you a citizen? Resident?' the male cop was saying to the Arab.

'You can say it here, and make it easier. Or we keep talking down at the station.'

Leon said nothing. The Arabic man hung his head also, the questions from both police continuing, and Leon felt briefly united with him, each feeding off the other's silence.

'Okay. You're coming with us.'

'You must be joking,' Leon said scornfully.

'No joke, mate. You have to come down to the station.'

Leon saw someone being led away by two police. The Arabic man was getting to his feet.

The female cop reached out for Leon. 'Stand up, please.'

'Get your fucking hands off me.' Leon slapped her away.

She stepped forward, grabbed his wrists and handcuffed him with unbelievable speed. Her grip was strong. The male cop glared at him. Leon's heart began to beat wildly, as though he'd just had two pipes in a row.

He walked slightly ahead of the female, trying to hide his face from the camera with his shoulder, but every time he hunched, her grip on his arm tightened. Fucking dyke bitch. Around the corner there was a paddy wagon. Another man was getting inside, next went the Arab. The female cop handed Leon to her partner and walked away with the dog. When they were alone, the male cop spoke out of the corner of his mouth, 'You blokes deserves AIDS, y'know. You take this crap then think you're God and spread it around. Then you expect taxpayers to look after you.'

Leon kept his head down as he climbed into the paddy wagon. It was too ridiculous; he just wanted to laugh. Inside, he wondered vaguely how the guys that got away had gotten away, because there sure were loads more men at the beat than in this van now. He should have just run. As they drove back onto the roadway, he looked around at his companions, silent, ignoring each other, a sorrier bunch of fuckers you couldn't find. The sorriest of all, his Arabic pick-up, huddled in the corner, blinking rapidly as if he was crying. It was pathetic.

The world viewed through mesh was surreal. People and buses and cars all moving with specific intent, carrying out their various tasks. And the traffic lights changing colour indefatigably all through the night, even when there was no one there. So much autonomy was dizzying. Leon could smell the sweat of every single person that had been locked up in this paddy wagon; he felt like he was somebody else and everything would slot back into place as soon as he had a chance to explain. He imagined telling the story over a beer at the party at the cricket stands, a circle of blokes looking at him in admiration.

They fingerprinted him then put him in a cell half the length of his body. He was painfully alert but wanted to lie down, but there wasn't enough room. The fluoro lighting felt like a chemical soup drowning him. Through the bars of his cell, he could see into two offices and part of the front counter — all the police going about their business.

The one who had arrested him eventually walked over. 'Ready to tell us where you got the stuff, and what you were doing there?'

'Can I have my phone back?'

The policeman smiled with mock sadness. 'No.'

'I'm allowed one phone call, aren't I?'

'You ready to talk to us?'

'I want my phone call.'

The policeman walked away, shaking his head in disgust.

Leon waited. He was dying for a leak. He saw one of the men that had been in the paddy wagon leave the station. There was someone in the cell adjacent making a lot of noise. The police looked over every so often, registering both him and the loud man, who they seemed to know. Leon could hear him muttering, *You fucking cunts didn't fucking tell me fucking bitch cunt.* He began to chew his nails. The policewoman walked over.

'Right, we're going to do a video interview.'

Leon panicked. 'No, I don't want to.'

'You'd make it easier for all of us including yourself if you talked.'

'I haven't got anything to say. I want my phone. I want my phone call.'

Leon was just mouthing words he had heard on television. He

didn't know if he was due a phone call, and if he was he didn't know who he would ring. George sprang to mind, but he cringed at the thought. Whereas Leon had always loved the unpredictability of beats and the sort of straight man you found there, George thought they were sleazy, desperate places for closets. Leon was ashamed he was now in a police cell next to a raving alcoholic.

The policewoman looked at her partner, who was laughing at the alcoholic. 'Shut the fuck up, Reg.'

Leon chewed his nails down to raw flesh. When he couldn't stand it any longer, he asked to be taken to the toilet. He found himself in a filthy room with one toilet seat in the corner, the urinal along the wall stinking. The policeman stood at the door watching him while he pissed.

The psychotic man was screaming when Leon went back to his cell: *Lemme out! Lemme out! Fucking cunts, cunts, CUNTS!*

The policeman picked up his baton and smashed it along the bars of the man's cell, silencing him. Leon sat down facing the wall. He tried to remember how much money he'd had in his wallet before they had taken it, what was in his phone that could incriminate him. Fuck, he had photos of George in there, naked, holding a hard-on. He realised how crucial his phone had become, as crucial as his wallet. Even clothed, he felt so naked divested of his possessions.

Daylight crept along the corridor. Leon stood and hung on the barred door until he had the attention of the male cop. 'Am I allowed my phone call? When are you going to let me out of here?'

'In due course.' The cop turned away.

'I have to visit my mother in hospital,' Leon called out, vexed.

'That's original.'

'Look her up! She's got cancer, she's in the RPA, and I have to go and see her this morning.'

The cop turned. 'Yeah, my mum's got cancer too.'

Again Leon had the sense of rough stony heat inside his forehead, pressing behind his eyes. He realised that he wanted to cry.

The police finally let him go at ten o'clock and Leon caught a taxi to his ute. Parking ticket, $179, great, *perfect*, icing on the cake. He drove to the hospital in a black mood, allayed somewhat by the fluke find of a free park near Missenden Road. He saw a paddy wagon near the hospital entrance and stiffened with anger. He went to the cafeteria for a coffee and muffin, then in the bathroom gave his armpits a cursory wash. In the lift a wave of exhaustion came over him. He fancied he could smell George in his beard, sought the scent like a drug, then lost it. He felt loose, rangy and combative as he strolled down the corridor. *Possession, indecent exposure, indecent language, resisting arrest.* His mother wasn't in her room. A Chinese woman told him she was on the verandah. Leon walked out and saw her down the end. He saw with a jolt that somebody was shaving her head and he almost shouted at her to stop, then remembered his mother talking about her intention to have this done. It was obviously the tattoo artist. He walked quickly towards them.

Marie smiled. 'Well, well, I hadn't expected to see you this early!'

Through the grey fuzz, Leon could see bald patches. And the bones in his mother's face, how her ears stuck out. She had aged so much in just one week. She looked like a prisoner, at once tough and fragile, her eyes enormous violets pooling the sky. Leon pulled up a chair as the clippering finished, and Marie introduced him to Rhys, who smiled as she flicked a soft brush over Marie's upturned face. 'How are things at Sirius Cove?'

'I haven't been in the garden much. I've been doing Susan's. But the xanthorrhea has scale.'

Marie looked crestfallen.

'I'm surprised you didn't notice it.' His remark seemed to float towards her in slow motion, like a missile. Now he had sat down, Leon felt unable to ever get up again, let alone make an attempt to retract this casual cruelty. 'It looks like it's been there for a while. I sprayed it with white oil, but it's pretty entrenched.'

Marie wondered what else she hadn't noticed. Rhys removed the sheet and the air bit her neck. Leon looked bad, unkempt. He even smelt bad. There was an irritable redness in his eyes that reminded Marie of Ross when he'd been drinking, and made her a little afraid. It seemed such a terrible portent that Leon's totem plant was diseased, the bugs multiplying under her nose all this time. He lolled in his chair stroking his beard, aware of his powerful good looks.

'I'm sure you can cure it. Leon's a gardener, Rhys. He's been a great help.'

'Yeah, I've heard a lot about you.'

Leon liked the look of Rhys, running a broom around their feet to collect his mother's hair.

'I've heard it's good to burn them,' she said. 'That's what Stew did with his.'

'Stew's a friend from the studio,' Marie explained. She felt exhausted. Willing a connection between Rhys and Leon. A sense of futility about that. Let alone the garden.

Rhys packed up her clippers. 'Well, I'll leave you to it.'

'You're not going? I thought we were having brunch together.'

Rhys hesitated, glanced at Leon. 'I can go and get you something and bring it back up.'

'It's alright. I'm about to go down,' Leon said, then remembered he had run out of money, and that the cafeteria was unlikely to have EFTPOS. He felt increasingly prickly and fragile.

'I really should get going,' said Rhys.

'Nice meeting you.'

Marie shivered and asked Leon to fetch a scarf from her room. 'And the blanket,' she called after him. 'It's on the chair.'

Getting up took an age, his thighs hurt with every step, there was a faint ache in his balls. He stopped in the bathroom to splash water on his eyes and drink from the tap. He draped the blanket around his mother's shoulders and helped tie the scarf around her head. He wanted to do these things for her, but he felt mechanical and knew it showed.

'I must look a bit of a fright,' Marie said.

'You look fine. But I thought you'd get that done at the hairdresser's or something.' Again the curt tone. At that moment, Leon hated himself.

'At Mosman Junction?' Marie gave him that unnerving violet stare. 'I wasn't game. I wanted to have it done by someone I trusted, in private.'

'It's not very private out here,' Leon said, indicating the Chinese woman he had spoken to earlier, settling her gaunt, bald companion at the end of the verandah.

'She doesn't care. She's dying of ovarian cancer,' Marie said coldly. 'And she's the same age as you.'

Leon looked at the ground. Marie wanted him to look at her. She was disgusted with her love for this selfish boy-man, and filled with a bitter pride at her deformities. She wanted him to look at her. 'Would you have shaved your mother's head, Leon?'

'Of course I would,' he said in a small voice.

'You can hardly bear to look at me. Is it because I'm sick? Or is it the tattoos? Or is it just because I'm a woman?'

When Leon finally lifted his eyes, she saw they were filled with tears.

Brian knocked after dinner to see if Marie wanted to come down to the television room. He was still in a ward with three others whereas Marie was now alone in a double room, her neighbour having left that day. She was hours after a pethidine shot, trying to last as long as possible, and more alert than she had been all day. She was watching the late news on her own television and invited Brian to join her. He had his hipflask, and into the little plastic cups he poured them a nip. He took out a joint.

'Next to the window,' said Marie, getting out of bed.

They smoked the joint in silence, looking out at the night sky. A half-moon was rising. Marie felt fuzzy when she went back to bed: a warm blanket had spread over the aches and pains and the nausea was gone. As Brian sat beside her, his gown rode up, revealing the leg tattoo. He saw her stealing glances at it.

'It's called a *pe'a*.' He pronounced the vowels distinct yet close as though separated by a pane of glass, then spelt it. 'They tep the ink in with chisels. You wanna see me other work?'

'Yes.'

He took off his gown and stood in his boxer shorts while she angled the light towards him. He was like an ancient tapestry, worn and embroidered over the decades. He pointed out different tattoos and told their stories. The first, from his adolescence in Auckland, was a whale rising murkily over the left pec. Around it were prison scratcher's lines and crosses. The names of his three wives were on his left arm, one after another. On his right arm and back were a skull, a dragon and a naked woman done by a favourite tattooist in Casula whenever he was free and Brian had the money. For his son, he'd had a carp tattooed on his stomach.

'The *pe'a* is my favourite,' said Marie, admiring what she could of the black organic shapes and fine gridding: unlike the other tattoos, Brian made no effort to show it. The left one rose in a curve over the hip, the right was much lower. Marie remarked on this.

'It's not finished,' Brian muttered.

'Why not?'

'I had to go back inside.' He looked ashamed.

Marie retreated from his private territory.

Brian sat in the chair and frowned. 'Fucken Brazilians, eh.' He had lost even more weight and in places his thighs seemed to be folding in on themselves. He grabbed himself in frustration. 'Sometimes I feel like a balloon after a party. You know, with the air come out?'

'My work's not finished either,' Marie said. 'Do you want to see it?'

'I'd love to.'

She parted her clothes to show him the vines; she was more protective of her belly and showed only a portion of the flames. 'They're so bright!' Brian exclaimed. She turned on her side to show him the moth. She felt the warmth of his gaze on her skin and drank it in like a plant. 'She really is the best,' Brian said after a while. He bent to her hip. 'What's this?'

'*Angophora costata*. My favourite tree in the world.'

'The unfinished one, eh?'

'Yes.'

'Frish, isn't it?'

She quivered at his touch. 'About four weeks old.'

'It's peeling a bit, y'know.'

Marie worried about her deterioration. She felt remiss, as though she had hung her most precious pictures on a soiled wall. They heard the night nurse passing and lowered their voices. 'Do they really look alright?'

'They're fucken awesome.'

'I'm itchy.'

'Where?'

'My back, right in the middle, where I can't reach.'

Brian gave her a gentle scratch between the shoulder blades. 'Your skin gets really dry in here, eh.'

'Oh yes, that's lovely, lower, yes, to the left to the left.'

They began to laugh. Footsteps passed again and they covered their mouths. The footsteps receded. 'I have some cream in that drawer,' said Marie.

Brian obliged, every movement quiet and careful like a thief. She could feel the blades of his fingertips through the cream. He went over her back with meditative strokes, then wiped his palms down his thighs. Then he began to squirm in his chair. 'You got me goin' now, I feel itchy everywhere.'

'Come up here. I'll do yours.'

'We're both so skinny we fit on these fucken log beds, eh,' he whispered as he lay alongside her. He glanced at the cloth folded on the end. '*Samoa*,' he affirmed. 'He was your boyfriend, eh?'

'No. We just went out a couple of times.' Marie squeezed cream into her palm.

He tensed initially at her touch, then began to relax. 'Oh?'

'I mean, his name wasn't worth tattooing on my arm.'

'And the flowers.' Brian gestured. 'You're loved, Marie.' He turned and gave her a sharp look. 'You put those flowers in my room?'

'I couldn't fit them on my table. I hope it's alright.'

Brian said nothing. He propped his head on his hand and looked out the window as Marie continued anointing him. His skin was fever hot, rough and cracked. He said quietly, 'I'd like to go back to

Rotorua when I get out of here. See the folks.'

'Maybe you could get your — what is it again? — tattoo finished?'

'*Pe'a*. No.'

'Why not?'

Again Marie felt a sense of trespass.

'The tattoo master I went to died,' said Brian after a while.

'Couldn't you see another one?'

'I'm too old. I hed my chance and I blew it.'

'Didn't we all.'

'What?'

'Blow it.'

'No, Marie,' he said harshly. 'We didn't all do fifteen years in the nick.'

'Sorry Brian.'

'Ah, don't worry about it.'

'There you are.'

'Thanks.' Brian turned and pecked her on the cheek. She looked at him in surprise. His eyes were sunken and bloodshot. He reached over and pulled another joint from his gown, then poured them more water. They didn't bother going to the window this time, just lay back smoking and watching TV. A meteorologist was showing maps of the receding icecaps. 'Us island people'll all drown with this business. My grandfather's place won't be there in twenny years.'

'Neither will we, Brian.'

'All this talk about refugees from the atolls. Like the Pacific wasn't already fucked, like we weren't already leaving.'

She took his hand. He looped his other arm around her shoulders. Her eyes were fiercely dry and when the news story finished she closed them for relief. She felt so lonely in her dying, she wanted to talk about it. She could hear every little sound in the room. Brian's breathing deepened, as though he were falling asleep. She opened her eyes to find him looking at her. He stroked her cheek. His skin was developing a yellow hue, his smell a faint pungency like the beginning of rot. She wondered which one of them would die first. Again came the answer: It doesn't matter.

They began to kiss, Marie's tongue tracing whiskey from his teeth. They moved closer, wincing at pressure on the sore spots. Her scarf fell off. Brian's fingers electric on her scalp. She knew the last of her hair would be scattering like iron filings. He smelt of medicine and dead skin. He slipped his hand inside her gown. 'Careful around my stomach, the tumours are just there.' He stroked it gently, moved to her breasts. 'These alright?' 'Yes.' They were smiling through their kiss. The miraculous throbbing in her cunt grew and she reached into his shorts. He lay back and let her touch him, sighing. His penis half hardened. 'I'm fucked.' He laughed softly. 'I'm too fucked to fuck.'

'We both are. Too sick, too old.'

'We're not too old. Just too sick.'

'How old are you?'

'Fifty-two.'

Marie hid her face in his neck. She would have said sixty-two.

'Fifty-three in four months. Gonna have a big party. You're invited.'

She wanted to slap him and make him face it. She wondered how she looked herself. Bald, emaciated. The extra decade sickness added would make her seventy. Dying, she thought, stroking Brian's cock, feeling it harden. He began to pant and felt for her cunt. She breathed in the smell of sweat and sickness and pulled till he cried out softly, drenching her wrist. 'Touch me, Brian.' She guided his hand until she came in a muted way. They fell asleep in front of the weather.

She was woken by Brian fumbling with the bedclothes. The light had been switched on and the night nurse was standing just inside the door. 'What's going on in here? And you've been smoking.'

Brian swung his legs over the side of the bed. 'I'm going.'

'I asked him in,' Marie avowed. She noticed one of her breasts had fallen out of her gown and pushed it back in. She was in a great deal of pain. The cramps were moving through her body, joined like carriages in one long train.

The nurse set his mouth. 'Just because you're sick doesn't mean you can get away with this.'

'What are you going to do?' said Marie. 'Kill us?'

The nurse waited for Brian to leave, then shut the door. All night Marie buzzed for pethidine, but nobody came.

The next morning she went into Brian's room to say goodbye before going down to chemotherapy. He was dozing and when woken needed a moment to focus, then he took her hand and wished her luck. He told her that in the old days when the chief underwent tattooing, his men were done alongside him to share his pain. The etiquette of the ritual forbade the tattooees to utter the smallest cry. At night there was dancing, feasting and wrestling matches, the ordeal and festivities lasting several weeks.

'Do the women get tattooed?'

'Yeah.' Brian wrinkled his brow in thought. 'There's a Samoan song about tattooing that says women grow up and give birth, men grow up and get tattooed.'

'Can we do both?'

'Sure.' Brian shrugged. 'I tell you what, Marie. When we get outta here, let's you and me go get a tatt together.'

'From Rhys.'

'Yeah. Listen. Why don't you look after my hooch tonight? In the drawer here. Don't trust the buggers around here.'

She decided to go to chemotherapy in a wheelchair, and to remain inside Brian's dream of a future for as long as possible. But the room now felt cold, each patient enclosed in a private pod of illness. The woman with ovarian cancer sat holding the hand of her Chinese girlfriend. The chatty woman in the scarf was gone. Marie never knew when somebody left whether they had gone into remission or died. The bald woman up the end was recognisable only by the husband reading aloud to her.

Marie watched the chemicals seep into her arm. She wished Brian was here. She thought of his stories of villagers dancing and feasting together. She remembered the dance floor at FAST, the centre like a molten core, the primeval soup, a blood vessel pumping with spirit and flesh. It was like another world; she could hardly believe she had been there.

Hugh was aware of Blanche uneasy beside him in the darkness.

'Hugh. Can you feel my breast? Here. I think there's a lump.'

'That's a novel excuse.' Hugh put down his magazine and rolled towards her.

'No, seriously, here, don't you think? It hurts.'

Hugh kneaded her left breast obediently. 'I can't feel any lumps. Do you want me to check the other one?'

'Yes.'

'Lie on your back.' Hugh probed.

'*Ouch.*' Blanche lay rigid.

'Absolutely beautiful, perfectly lump-free breasts. I'd stake my life on it. The most beautiful perfect breasts on the planet. You're pregnant, pooky, that's why your breasts are sore. They're supposed to be, a little bit, aren't they? Get some sleep.'

'I can't.'

'Read then.' He passed her *Harper's Bazaar.* 'God, that's a tome.'

'I can't concentrate.'

'Oh, Blanche, I don't know what to do with you when you're like this. I thought you said you were feeling better. You haven't thrown up for at least two weeks.'

'I am feeling better.'

On clear nights, they could hear the harbour from their bedroom. There was the swish of a boat passing McMahons Point. It *was* an excuse, in a way. Blanche wanted Hugh's hands back on her breasts, she wanted him to stroke her everywhere. Sex didn't have to stop when you were pregnant, did it? But she didn't want to stroke him in return: she didn't desire his body at all. She pushed away her sadness and guilt.

'Hugh?'

'Yes?'

'How long did your father take to die?'

'About two years.'

'So why did they only give Mum six months? She's only got four left you know. The second chemo is making her even worse.'

'My father had lung cancer and it went into remission then came back. Stomach cancer is usually aggressive. Blanche, a slow death isn't that great, believe me.'

'I've *never* trusted doctors. She looks terrible. You won't believe the changes when you next see her. She's lost *so* much weight.'

'Come here, darling. It's okay.'

Blanche moved into the crook of Hugh's arm. 'I think I'm going to get retrenched.'

'Bla-anche.'

'It's *true*. I was already on probation for the Diet Coke debacle. Kate did a fantastic job on the sanitary napkins when I was in hospital. Terry wants to sleep with her. My pregnancy will start showing in a month or so. I can see where it's all headed.'

'One thing at a time, okay? You've got enough going on already. Don't *think* about it.'

'Why do they say retrenched? Whatever happened to good old *fired*.'

'Blanche King,' said Hugh, stentorian, 'we're giving you *the sack*.'

'I never got that actually. I always saw someone with a sack over their head being marched outside.'

'Exactly.'

'It might be a good thing. I think I'm over it. I'm over the industry and I'm over being overworked. I'm going to make art.'

Hugh stroked her hair. 'Great idea.'

Blanche smiled. She felt relief, excitement, and a blast of strength. 'Yeah, that's exactly what I'm going to do. And I'll exit HA elegantly, not give Terry the pleasure of making me exit.'

The sound of André and his girlfriend's lovemaking leaked up through the floor.

'It's genetic, you know, Hugh,' Blanche said quietly. 'We're going to give our baby a double dose. Did you ever think of that?'

'It's midnight.' Hugh shut his magazine. 'I'm turning out the light.'

Neither of them could sleep. Hugh said, 'I thought of a place for your mother to move to.'

'Me and Clark are going to look on Saturday. I'm telling the boys about Dad and the estate then too.'

'Why don't we just put her in Neutral Bay?'

'Because we've got tenants there?'

'The lease expired ages ago.'

'They're great tenants, Hugh. They've been there five years, they painted it and they always pay on time.' But Blanche's defence sounded cursory. She turned so she was facing him. 'Me and the boys are still arguing over where to put Mum, you know. And Mum's no help — she's beyond caring.' Blanche thought to herself, not for the first time, how much more convenient it would be if her mother died sooner, but she felt too guilty to say it. The only advantage of dying later was the delay on her father getting his hands on the estate. She was surprised at how quickly she had adjusted to her mother dying, and overwhelmed by how much there was to *do*. Nobody warned you that death was an administrative nightmare; the stories were all about the emotional side.

'We can give them a month's notice,' said Hugh. 'That's fair. And after your mother goes we can do a few things in the kitchen and bathroom and put the rent up. The rental market is the best place at the moment. We need to be making a profit from Neutral, now we can't count on the estate, otherwise I'll have to sell Ultimo.'

'I know, and this three-month settlement stretches us too.'

'It's okay, I'm keeping track of the interest. But if I sell Ultimo now I'll be selling at a loss, which I don't want to do. Not now we're having a baby.' Hugh shifted so Blanche's ear was over his sternum. She listened to his voice in stereo. What he was saying made perfect sense, and she began to feel relieved.

'I really need some cowboy boots,' she said when he had finished talking.

'A propos nothing.'

'It's a pregnancy present!'

'Where will you put them? You've already got about ten pairs of boots.'

'Not cowboy boots, though. They're so versatile. If I get cowboy boots I can throw out all the others. I've found these ones online made by this guy in Arizona. They're amazing, they are pure art. I *need* them, Hugh.'

'I fully agree you need a pregnancy present, pooky.'

She squeezed his hand and fell asleep like that, lulled by his voice and the inner workings of his body, and the knowledge that, no matter what, he was there behind her.

When Blanche told them about their father's intentions to claim half the estate, Clark's first reaction was laughter. They were sitting on the deck: he had gone over to the north shore to house hunt and instead found himself drinking Diet Coke, receiving the news about Neutral Bay and the estate in virtually the same sentence. The move to Neutral Bay was immediately forgotten.

'I knew it,' Leon declared with heavy fatalism.

'*I* didn't.' Clark laughed. 'I can't believe it.'

'He's a prick. It's exactly the sort of thing he'd do.'

'But how can it be legal? They had a settlement, didn't they?'

'Out of court. Hugh and I have looked into it and there's nothing we can do.'

'What's Hugh got to do with this?' Leon said belligerently.

'He has a good lawyer. The same guy who took care of things when his father died.'

'Oh, *right*,' said Clark. 'So how long have you known? When did you see Dad?'

Hands clasped over her abdomen, Blanche looked from one brother to the other. 'About two weeks ago.'

'So Hugh's known longer than us,' said Leon. '*Oh-kaaay.*'

'I found out the day I went into hospital, okay? And I didn't tell you then because I was *sick* and I *knew* you'd react like this. And of course I'd tell Hugh straightaway.'

'Like what?' Clark raised his arms. 'How are we reacting?'

'Blaming me.'

'Who's blaming you?'

'Well, you're being pretty bloody hostile, Leon.'

'I'm just curious about Hugh *looking into this situation* for us.' Leon clawed inverted commas into the air for the last noun, looking to Clark for support.

'Well, have *you* got a lawyer, Leon? What are you going to do about it?'

Leon raised his arms helplessly as Clark had done, turning down the corners of his mouth. For a second, Clark thought he looked like Paulie from *The Sopranos* and he wanted to laugh. The relief of not having to house hunt for his mother had lifted his mood in spite of the news about the estate. He looked at the pile of mail he had collected from the kitchen table. The letter opener was a brass knife that had belonged to their mother's mother. It was one of the things he wanted when his mother died. He considered slipping it into his pocket when the others weren't looking. They didn't appreciate it in the way he did. He shuffled the personal mail to the back and began opening the envelopes with plastic windows, smoothing the letters on the table in front of him as he read out. '$1067 from the vet. $256 Sydney Water, final notice. $153 gas. Overdue. $1534 from the vet, overdue as well.'

'Ignore that. Hugh's paid the vet.'

'He pays Mum's bills as well, does he?'

'As a matter of fact, *yes*, Leon, Hugh pays with my and his money, since before she sold she was in debt and her cheques to Fatima were bouncing.'

'The house is sold now. Mum can pay you back.'

'Not till settlement.'

Clark felt light-headed. There was still a strange novelty in these meetings: he and his siblings hadn't seen one another this often since they were children. He was pleased that the main conflict as usual was between Leon and Blanche, and annoyed that he had again driven all the way across the bridge for a meeting that could just have as easily taken place at his house, if only they would come to him for once. He was avoiding Leon's gaze: there was a neediness and anger in it that made him want to run. He knew that losing their mother would be harder for Leon than any of them; too bad, Leon would just have to cut the umbilical cord.

He said: 'Well, obviously we whack every bill we have in here and use up as much of this estate as possible before Dad gets his hands on it. That makes sense, doesn't it, Blanche? We could take it to the wall: get yourself enough fertiliser for the next year, Leon; I'll do a big book shop; we'll charge it to the estate.'

'I'll get arrested for terrorism.' Leon laughed. 'I don't have anywhere to store it.'

'We have to go through the house things too, at some stage,' said Blanche. 'I was thinking of Sunday if that suits you two.'

'I wouldn't mind the dining room table. And this letter opener.'

'You haven't got enough room for the dining room table in Bondi, have you?'

'I'll be getting somewhere bigger.'

'What with?'

Clark looked up. 'Whoops! I suppose the table is yours after all, Blanche.' He felt furious.

'I might not want it. I might have the lounge suite instead. Leon, when you move back, you could set yourself up really well. TV, stereo, fully equipped kitchen. Clark doesn't need any of that, do you?'

Listen to her, thought Clark, the tiniest crack and she's in there organising, dominating. 'Ah, *sure*. It's all yours!'

'I can't think about that stuff now. I don't want anything.'

'Leon, we have to deal with it. And sooner rather than later. This pregnancy will start slowing me down soon.' She wanted to tell them she was leaving work to become not just a mother but also an artist, and how happy she was about that, but their hostility was still palpable.

Clark opened another bill. 'Dr Wroblewski. $2830.'

Out of the blue, Leon said, 'I have to go to court in a month and I can't get legal aid cos I'm not on the dole but I can't afford a barrister because my wages aren't big enough.'

'What are you talking about?'

'You buying too much fertiliser, mate?'

'For being a homosexual on the loose.' Leon began the sentence in one of his accents, the camp lisping one.

'Oh, right,' said Blanche.

'What happened?' said Clark.

Leon was embarrassed. He shouldn't have used that dumb accent: he would give away the stuff about the beat. 'I got busted for having a joint in my pocket.'

'You're kidding,' said Blanche.

'No, I'm serious.' Leon sat up straight and Clark could see he was telling the truth.

'Sniffer dogs?' said Clark.

'Yep.'

'What were you doing walking around with a joint in your pocket?' asked Blanche.

'I forgot it was there. I was going to a party. They were out doing raids.'

'What's being a homosexual got to do with it?' said Clark.

'They were really homophobic.'

'Where were you?' said Blanche. 'This didn't happen around here, did it?'

'I was going to a party in Moore Park. I'd been at George's.'

Clark watched Leon closely, thinking now that he wasn't telling the truth. He looked rattled. His eyes were red.

'Gee,' said Blanche. 'That's really awful, Leon.'

'I get a criminal record, stuffs up my business. Can't leave the country.'

'Well, there'll be enough money to cover your costs,' said Blanche. 'It's not like we're going to inherit *nothing*. Come to think of it, you could even pay me back that loan, Leon.'

Leon ignored her.

'So I could still get a bigger place, big enough for the dining room table.'

Blanche ignored Clark. 'Have you got a lawyer? Is he any good?'

'No.'

'*Leon*. You have to get a lawyer!'

'I didn't know where to begin. I'm still just processing it.'

'I know someone who could advise you.'

'Are you still seeing that woman?' Blanche said.

Clark laughed, properly now. He wanted to rip up the bills and throw them in the air like paper money. 'Oh the merry-go-round of life!' he sang and waved the bills around. His armpits stank and he didn't understand why — he hadn't had a drink in days, not even a coffee; he hoped his siblings couldn't smell them. Blanche sent him a weird look. Leon snorted in assent, but he was shaking his head at the same time. Clark couldn't wait to text Sylvia the news about the lost estate. He couldn't wait for her sympathy, her outrage, and her rescue.

For weeks now he had hardly done any work. Initially Sylvia was the source of distraction but, since the night she had stayed at his house, contact had ebbed. Clark had stated his position at the university: now it was a waiting game. Nell had chastised him on the weekend for his vagueness, and Clark realised that, as much as he tried to shrug it off, the impending loss of his mother's estate had rattled him to the core. At night in bed, his mind returned to the anxieties of finance and career; without the extra money he also imagined himself to be less attractive to Sylvia. The other thing to worry about was Leon. He seemed paralysed, paranoid, so Clark had taken it upon himself to organise a barrister. Then there was illness. There would be death. Reading had become impossible; only the strongest images had the capacity to keep Clark's attention. So when he was granted three days' access to photographic archives, he got there early. He sank into the chair with relief, as though he had arrived at the cinema after rushing around all day.

He clicked on the light and pushed his face inside the safety of history. The pictures weren't arranged in any particular order and, as much as he hoped for the north shore, most of them again were of the inner city. He lingered over crime scenes, nostalgic for a squalor he had never known. The dead seemed so exalted, as though this moment were their apogee. He felt like the camera — disrespectful, intrusive — but had no desire to stop. He didn't even have a toilet break. He wasn't the first to see these pictures, yet so few had gone before him that their tracks were visible across the sand. He was Captain Cook in a new land. These were *his* dead.

At two o'clock when he could hold on no longer, Clark went to the toilet. He bought a sandwich and bottle of juice and ate lunch in the gardens. It was a warm day; lorikeets squealed in the trees around him. He had asked Leon if he was able to concentrate on work and Leon had replied that his work was respite: in fact he craved getting into a garden, dealing with solid matter and helping things grow. Blanche on the other hand admitted she was having trouble but she had her pregnancy and was leaving anyway. Clark was so glad she was quitting advertising: it made her more human in his eyes. It was almost four o'clock and the sandwich dissolved immediately in the acid of his stomach. He rang his mother and left a message on her voicemail. He didn't text Sylvia till five nor had she texted him. She had responded with alacrity to his inquiry about a barrister, both of them almost grateful for the distraction of somebody else's problems. Clark read James Ellroy when he got home. He spoke to no one, and by the next morning his dreams of a brilliant thesis began to grow again.

He set to work on the remaining archives as soon as he arrived. He wondered what it was that made someone resemble their era. Some of the people in these photographs looked so contemporary; others were typecast to perfection. Sylvia would have suited that dress, he thought, gazing at a Depression-era prostitute. He pressed onwards, rueing his slide back into Sylvia-land. And then he found the picture he didn't know he was looking for: a murder-suicide in Mosman Bay. In a street not fifteen minutes from his childhood house, a psychiatrist had come home from work and shot his wife, two children, then himself. Clark's pulse increased. He moved the photos around, returning to the overhead shot. The corpse of the wife was framed by the foreshortened legs of a tripod, increasing his claustrophobic sense of voyeurism as though the final wretchedness of this woman were literally caught between his legs. Clark reeled: he had suddenly changed places and instead of being the camera had become the woman herself.

He packed up his things and walked out to catch a bus to the hospital. He had reached middle age with violence and disease at a safe distance, but today when he emerged into the bright sunlight he felt pixellated by death and loss, the mark of every twisted neck, every pool of blood and violated room still upon him. He couldn't be Cook: he couldn't write the stories as though they belonged to him. They could only be written as though he belonged to them. It wasn't an act of control so much as one of submission. Nothing, in fact, was within his control. He stared out the bus window, miserable in the fug of his terrible BO.

Looking through the doorway at his sleeping mother, Clark fumed over his father's behaviour. The financial ramifications were just the surface evidence of a deeper injury he was inflicting on all of them. Instead of watching his siblings from afar, satisfied with his cool, Clark felt pulled right into the centre. His armpits smelt like nothing less than fear and anxiety. He envied Blanche and Leon their freer emotional expression. He couldn't fault Blanche's idea of Marie moving to Neutral Bay. He vowed to take Nell to Sirius on the weekend, stay the night, go for a bushwalk or something. He wanted to *connect*.

He didn't want to wake Marie so he went down to the hospital pharmacy with the script the nurse gave him. He had been here before. The long, low-ceilinged corridors with their tracks of exposed wiring, the masonite walls. It was oppressive. He walked the slope past an intern wearing a surgical bonnet then into a new section, pristine white with fluoro lighting. Through a large window to the right he glimpsed a walkway, a nurse hurrying across it to the building adjacent.

He turned and found himself back in an old section, all worn lino and raw brickwork. Nobody was around. He turned another corner. He was lost. Can somebody help me? The hospital seemed the perennial nightmare of this city of shifting sands, always being destroyed and rebuilt. Every corridor sloped downwards, drawing him deeper into the bowels of the building.

Down he went, into the second circle, past a sepia remnant of men cutting sandstone for the building's foundations, then the Victorian days of starched matrons and coppers boiling infection from tubercular sheets. Plague hospital, lunatic asylum; did they haunt the sick of today, those returned soldiers peering gauntly from their beds? The dead rose up around him. The air-conditioning hummed in his ears, huge silver ducts snaking overhead. What did they keep down here? Maybe around the next corner he would find someone stirring a cauldron. He passed two nurses wheeling a gurney, the patient sprouting tubes. He saw a sign to the pharmacy and followed it to the end of the corridor. At last. He handed the script over and the pharmacist returned with two bags of medication.

Clark passed the nurses and their patient again on his way back to the ninth floor. A small screen with red and green wavy lines was propped on the end of the gurney. The nurses joked as they hefted it towards the lift. 'We're taking you on a magical mystery tour.' The patient was motionless, face covered by an oxygen mask. Clark saw the name on the gurney. *Brian Va'a.*

It was his mother's Brian. My god, did she know the state he was in? She had made light of coming back to hospital, saying how much she enjoyed his company, and Clark had fantasised a romance between them, which of course was ridiculous. Was Brian alright? Had Marie seen him? The gurney caught up with Clark at the lifts, and he stared at Brian who was oblivious to the singing nurses. Clark wanted to rip out the tubes and shake him awake. The female nurse pulled her ponytail from beneath her surgical gown and pressed the lift button, humming under her breath.

Blanche went back to Sirius Cove the next Sunday. The house seemed empty. She could smell stale cat food from the kitchen and in the laundry found the plate shifting with ants. She hadn't had any time with Mopoke on her last visit and felt bad about that. She had almost considered bringing the cat to stay with her. She threw the old food out, cleaned the meal mat, then followed the sound of the television down to the rumpus room. Clark, Nell and Leon were there, eating pizza. 'Hi,' said Blanche from the doorway.

'Hi,' they replied, eyes on the screen.

'Does anyone know where Mopoke is?'

'No. Haven't seen her.'

'Me and Nell fed her yesterday but I don't think she ate it,' said Clark.

'Yeah, we fed her.'

'The food was full of ants. Did you give her her medicine?'

'Of course,' said Leon.

'What medicine?' said Clark.

They shifted irritably in their seats. Clark turned down the television, saying with a helpful tone, 'We've made a start on things, we've got a list here.'

'Okay, great. I just want to find Mopoke to say hallo.'

She began in the laundry, checking the cupboard then behind the washing machine. What about the dirty clothes basket? But Mopoke hadn't been able to jump into the basket for over a year now. Blanche searched in the study then crouched in the living room and looked beneath the couches. 'Mopoke, Mopoke!' She went upstairs, thinking Mopoke could no longer climb them easily so if she was up here she hadn't eaten for a while, and if she wasn't she must be in the garden or even, ironically, somewhere in the rumpus room. She walked along the landing calling her and went into Leon's bedroom, which smelt of dirty trainers and unwashed hair. What a pig. Mopoke wouldn't be in here; she had never liked Leon much more than he had liked her. Up in Clark's attic room? But no — more stairs. Blanche stopped in the bathroom to look at herself in the mirror. She looked terrible: fierce and drawn. She sat on the toilet and peed, head in hands. Her cunt smelt different and she took solace in her body's animal changes, fate turning its wheel without her having to do anything. She remembered Mopoke's arrival when she was a teenager. She was a water cat, tightrope-walking the bath's edge while Blanche lay beneath a doona of bubbles. Oh, how she loved that cat. 'Mo-ey, where-are-you?' Blanche went into her mother's room.

She registered the painted boxes from Austria in which her mother kept her jewellery, all of which would naturally be hers; the antique card table would also go on her list. She opened the cupboards, releasing scents and memories, finding no cat. She looked under the bed and there was Mopoke sleeping in her mother's blue silk shirt. 'Moey! *Here* you are.' Blanche felt a strange hardness through the fur and quickly pulled the cat out. 'Oh no, Mopoke.' Her eyes were half open, her teeth bared, her entire body stiff. She was dead. Blanche picked her up and began to cry. The smell was terrible. She tried to close Mopoke's eyes and mouth but they sprang back open in a leer. She stroked the fur, receiving a strange crackling sensation from the flesh beneath. 'When did you die, darling puss? Did it hurt?' She noticed a small turd at the base of Mopoke's tail. Fluid came from her mouth as well. Blanche went into the ensuite for toilet paper and cleaned her orifices, weeping copiously. She wrapped Mopoke in the blue silk shirt, and took her onto the balcony.

The harbour at dusk. Everything was luminous. Purple storm clouds swelled on the horizon. The water was smoky lilac and the foliage in the garden polished lime. An eerie absence opened in the house behind her, and the loneliness of losing this place and her mother was never clearer. Blanche sat there crying with Mopoke on her lap while night seeped into the garden.

Leon was at the sink when she went down to the kitchen. She placed the silk bundle on the counter, her swollen eyes looming. 'Want a cup of tea?' he offered.

'No, thanks.'

Leon placed a cup on the counter. 'What's that smell?'

'It's Mopoke. She's dead. I found her under Mum's bed curled up in this shirt.'

'Jesus Christ, take it off the counter!' He withdrew his cup. 'We eat from there!'

'She's wrapped up and I cleaned her. Where are the bin liners?' Blanche calmly began to open and shut drawers. 'Have you changed things around?'

'I haven't touched a thing. What are you doing? How long's it been dead?'

'How would I know? You're the ones who've been here. I'm going to bury her.'

'*Bury* her? How d'you think the new owners will feel when they dig up a rotten cat in two months.'

'Stuff the new owners! This is still Moey's house!'

'It's pitch black out there.'

'Look, Leon, I know you hated Mopoke, but Mum loved her, alright? I'm going to bury her in the morning.' Grimly Blanche continued down the row of drawers. 'Why can't I find anything in the house I grew up in?'

'I didn't *hate* her.'

'I remember you hitting her.'

'I did not!'

'You did. For killing a bird or something.'

'Oh god, Blanche, I was like ten or something.'

'Crap, Leon. We didn't get her till you were thirteen and it was years after that and you hit her really hard. You were foul.'

'Have you kept tabs have you?'

'What's going on?' Clark appeared in the doorway.

'The cat's dead.'

'When? Where? What happened?'

'There.' Leon pointed, adding accusingly, 'That's a good shirt of Mum's, isn't it, Blanche?'

Blanche had found the bin liners. Clark began to babble. 'How long's it been dead? Whose shirt is it? It's Mum's, isn't it? Christ, Blanche, what are you doing?'

'I'm putting her in a bag so I can put her in the freezer and bury her in the morning.'

'Oh no, not in the freezer!'

'What are you doing with Mum's shirt? Blanche!'

'I'm burying her in the garden in Mum's shirt and I'm putting her in the freezer now because you guys are so thick you didn't notice she was dead and you're so cruel you don't care. Here' — Blanche yanked at the packet — 'I'll double bag her.'

Nell was standing in the doorway, just behind her father.

'You are not putting *that* into the freezer.' Clark marched over.

'Why not? You put dead cow in there all the time.'

'It'll smell the whole thing out. It'll contaminate everything.'

'Try your bedroom for smell, Leon.'

'We'll take it to the cat morgue.' Clark began to panic.

'In fact, she probably *died* from your smell.'

Leon laughed. Eyes on the bundle, Nell's mouth crumpled. Her father still hadn't seen her. 'There's some kind of pet morgue, isn't there? They've got ways of disposing of animals, don't they? Doesn't Mum have a vet? Where's that bill? Where's her address book?' He strode around the kitchen, rapping out demands. 'She can't be told about this, okay? We'll take it to the morgue now.'

'What's this *it* bullshit?' Blanche opened the freezer and began to move things. 'She's a *she* and she's called Mopoke and she's only lived here about twenty years, which is almost as long as most of us.'

'Blanche.' Clark took her by the elbow. She shook him off and dropped the bag containing Mopoke. Clark seized it and went to the door, eyeing his sister warily. 'We're taking it to the morgue. *Nellie.*'

'Daddy.'

'I'm doing what Mum would have done, you arseholes!' Blanche began to scream. 'She would've buried Mopoke in a fucking mink coat if she'd had one!'

'Nellie, go and watch TV. Now!'

'We can take the ute.'

'No way!'

Clark wagged his finger. 'Listen, you self-righteous little harridan, it's just a cat, so get over it.'

Blanche flew at him, Clark raised his arms in front of his face and the package containing Mopoke clattered into the hall. Nell disappeared. Leon came over and tried to restrain Blanche, everybody yelling, Blanche's limbs flying. 'I'm pregnant!' she screamed. She kicked and punched her brothers, then charged into the hall and grabbed Mopoke, Leon pursuing her but she was out the door and at the front gate, her voice ringing out through the night. 'I hope somebody disposes of *you* when you die! I can't *wait.*'

Hugh was eating dinner when she arrived home. 'What's that you've got there?'

'Tomatoes.'

'Looks like enough to feed an army. We bought some yesterday.'

'They're from my mother's garden,' Blanche explained, opening the freezer and placing Mopoke beside the ice trays.

'Oh. I didn't know she grew them.'

'She grows everything, you know, Hugh.'

Early in the morning, Leon heard the creak of the shed door. He had barely slept. He went to the window. Seven a.m., drizzling, Blanche's black-garbed figure moving across the lawn. She had a garbage bag in one hand, a shovel in the other. She glanced up at the house and for a second looked so much like their mother that Leon almost panicked. He dressed quickly and went downstairs to the hall cupboard for his Driza-Bone. He pulled out one of his mother's raincoats then went into the garden.

Blanche turned her back on him. The rain began to fall more heavily.

'Here, put this on.' Leon helped her into the raincoat. She picked up the shovel and wandered from bed to bed, Leon following.

'What about here?'

'You'll hit the root system of the grevillea.'

'Next to the black bamboo?'

'I think we should find a tree, maybe the lime. I'll dig the hole if you like.'

Blanche handed him the shovel.

Leon found a spot and dug a hole. Blanche emptied the bags. Her manicured hands with their angular, silver rings had no qualms pressing the silk package to her face then placing it in the hole. She threw a handful of dirt on top. The rain began to pour. Leon shovelled dirt over the grave.

'Hang on a sec.' Blanche went down to the rockery where they had accumulated a collection of fossil ferns in their childhood and picked some wattle. Leon patted down the earth then Blanche placed the remaining wattle on top, pinning it down with a fossil fern as headstone.

Leon watched her crying. He couldn't understand this outpouring of emotion for a cat. He remembered the wattle in bloom like a wall of fire along the northern side of the garden, Blanche in front of it grinning into the sun. Or was this a photo that his memory had scanned and reproduced as its own issue? After Blanche had stormed out last night, Clark had put Nell to bed then returned to the rumpus room where they had watched *Law & Order* and compared bruises. Clark claimed his shoulder killed, but there was no mark on it. Blanche had been right about Leon hitting the cat. Almost two decades ago. Mopoke had brought in a spotted pardalote and dropped it on the floor before him. Leon had picked up the beautiful, tiny bird and watched it die in his hand. In a rage, he had fetched the cat a great whack on her rump. He had never seen a pardalote since and still blamed the cat for this. He looked at Blanche crouched by the grave, curvy, feminine, vulnerable. A scary fighter. They had all thought she would be an artist, then they had thought she would be the most successful female advertising executive in the country. Now she was leaving the agency. She looked so tired and beaten, and she was pregnant, which in Leon's mind erased everything else. He was bamboozled by how she stayed with that dolt Hugh. He couldn't imagine her being an artist. He stared at the back of her head, wondering what really drove her.

Shortly after Carla told her that Brian had died, Dr Wroblewski came to see Marie. For a second Marie hoped for good news, but all he had to offer her was the ritual of examination, this dance of the western shaman. With fingers gathered into a beak he tapped all around her abdomen. She listened to the different percussions and wondered what her body was telling him. Again, the flare of hope rose within her, despite the fact that everywhere hurt. Marie bore the examination silently until Dr Wroblewski reached a place that made her cry out. He withdrew and she gathered the covers back to her chin.

'Right. We won't be able to let you go home yet. The tumour appears to have reached your liver. It may start bleeding.'

'Please don't give me any more chemotherapy. I keep vomiting.'

'That's the illness as well.' He stretched his mouth into an apologetic smile. 'The tumour in your oesophagus is spreading too.'

'What are my options?'

'Radiotherapy. But it could prove difficult marking you up with all those tattoos, and we can't guarantee results.'

'What would you recommend I do?'

'I can't make that decision for you, Mrs King.' He looked at his watch. 'Right. Must run. Think about what you want to do, and let us know.'

'Please, Doctor,' she said to his departing figure.

He turned and gave her a harried look.

'I need some morphine.'

Ten minutes later Carla arrived. She turned Marie over and gave her a shot. Marie's haunches were becoming bruised from the needles. Carla noticed how dry her skin was and offered to rub cream into it. Marie lay on her side waiting for the drug's warm light to part the clouds as Carla chatted and anointed her. She left two morphine pills by the bed. 'If you can't hold them down, we'll give you a fentanyl patch.'

'There isn't much point in any of this, is there?'

Carla sat on the edge of the bed. 'In what?'

'Chemotherapy, radiotherapy. Hospital in general.'

'Well, the advantage of being in hospital is that when and if something goes wrong, you get instant help. In that sense you're better off here. If you want to go home, we can send someone in to discuss palliative care at home.'

Marie felt her eyes closing. She liked the sound of Carla's voice. 'I wish I could just fade away; feel like such a nuisance.'

'It's hard, but don't worry about us — our job is to help you. Just think about what would be best for you.'

In the unearthly light of the shuttered room, Marie gradually entered reality. A figure was sitting by the bed. Difficult to make out his features. 'Brian,' she said.

'Hey, Mum, how are you?' It was Leon.

Marie struggled to prop herself upright and Leon came over to help. The pain was back. She reached for the pills. 'Water, please.' She drank them down. 'The blinds. So we can see each other.'

The sun poured in and, when Marie's eyes adjusted, she saw Leon, glowing with health. 'Brian died.'

'Oh, Mum, I'm sorry.' Leon took her hand. 'We're taking you home as soon as possible. Are you happy about that?'

Marie nodded. Home. The garden. Harbour. Cat. Home, how she longed for it. Then she remembered that she had to move house, and began to fret. Mopoke, how would Mopoke cope? She licked her lips, a slow awkward manoeuvre, and formed the words. 'How is Mo?'

'She died, Mum. Two days ago. Blanche found her.'

Marie stared. Leon seemed to be talking on a distant stage. A bark emerged from her throat, half sob half protest. 'Oh, how *could* she.'

'Blanche didn't do anything, Mum. She just found her under your bed in one of your shirts. Me and Clark were downstairs, we didn't know, we didn't want to tell you straightaway because you were in treatment, we tried to give her a good funeral. Blanche buried her in your blue silk shirt, I hope that's okay. She's under the lime tree. I'm sorry, Mum.'

Marie withdrew her hand and shut her eyes. Brian. Mopoke. Too much. She was aware of Leon getting up and leaving. Her gorge rose and she tipped forward to vomit on the bedcovers. There was the sound of running water then Leon coming out of the bathroom. 'Oh god. It's black.' He grabbed some paper towels and cleaned it up. He disappeared into the bathroom then returned with a damp towel and pressed it to her face and hands. 'We're taking you home tomorrow, Mum. We'll get you better.'

'I'm not going to get better, Leon. I'm dying.'

'I know.' It was the first time Leon had been able to say it, and he felt vastly relieved.

He lay a fresh towel on the bedcovers and stayed with his mother until she fell asleep. 'It's raining,' he said at one stage. 'We've had three days' worth.'

Later, she was alone in the dim room. Was it dusk or dawn? The window glaucous, *rat-tat-tat* of rain, overcast light inside and out. There was a fresh bedcover and Carla was hooking her up to a drip.

'You're dehydrated, Marie. We're going to give you at least two bags before we let you go.'

The clock said twenty past eleven and Marie realised it was morning. She wasn't sure if it was the day that Leon had visited or the following, meaning the day she would be going home. She didn't want to reveal her disorientation by asking. What difference did it make anyway? She extended her arm to Carla, then her haunch. Carla did her job and left. And the morphine fever, the pain burning through, and on her cracked lips the taste of blood. She managed to pull the covers up and fell into a light sleep.

The next time Marie woke, she felt refreshed, even jubilant. Carla had left the window ajar, and from the bed Marie could see clouds in procession moving over the city. They were soothing and fascinating to watch, like waves. As the drug receded and her body hydrated, Marie became alert. Again, the thought of her impending move from Sirius Cove assailed her and she sighed in vexation. She squeezed some paw-paw cream onto her lips. She realised that her jubilation had come from the simple fact of waking and having a clear head. She no longer expected to live beyond the next day. This was it. The final sickness. The ultimate threshold.

Still there were little pleasures and necessities. When Carla released her from the drip, Marie got out of bed and stretched. She washed herself cursorily at the basin and rubbed cream into her skin. The tattoos consoled her, like the company of friends. She chose the spotted silk pyjamas that Blanche had bought her, saying out loud, 'Dear Blanche, aren't they gorgeous.' She dressed, brushed her teeth and hair, put on a little eyeliner, then returned to bed.

Just as she was finishing lunch, there was a knock on the door. Marie called out and a man in a tweed jacket appeared.

'Hallo, I'm Father Dwyer,' he said cheerfully. 'Carla said you might want to see me.'

Marie sat up confused but not displeased. 'Come in.'

The priest came in and sat in the visitor's chair. He was about her age, with a florid complexion and receding hair that lifted off his scalp in comical wisps. His eyebrows were similarly scattered, his collar rumpled, giving him an air of having just woken. Marie discerned a tiny gold crucifix buried in his lapel. She felt an immediate tribal bond. She was glad she had washed and was wearing her best pyjamas.

'How are you today, Marie?' Father Dwyer asked.

'I've perked up a bit.'

'You're looking good. Are they taking good care of you?'

'Carla's been very kind.'

'She's an excellent nurse, isn't she? I had her when I was sick.'

'What was wrong with you? Were you in here?'

'I was just across the hall. I had bowel cancer four years ago.'

'And look how well you are.'

'I'm a very lucky man.'

A flutter of hope passed through Marie. Then fatalism, tinged with jealousy. 'Father, I'm not going to recover, you know.'

'I know.' His expression remained utterly unsentimental. 'I see you've been reading the Gospels.'

'Yes, they were in the drawer. When I'm not too out of it, I read.'

'How are you finding them?'

'The Bible is a beautiful book.'

'Isn't it? Never dates, never tires.'

'Some of it does. All that preaching in the New Testament against the laws of the Old.'

'Yes, a lot of those early writings needn't be taken literally.' The priest examined a spot on the blanket, his eyebrows rising as he warmed to his topic. 'But you know, I saw an interesting documentary about a man going around the Middle East looking for archaeological evidence of the floods and fires and so on. I'm not a creationist, Marie, but what this man unearths is really quite extraordinary.'

'There's a source for every story. And all that non-attachment, the relinquishing of things. Even family. Jesus is like Buddha in some ways.'

'That's right, in many ways, actually.'

'The discipline of prayer.'

'Yes, it is a discipline. It's a pleasure too.'

'People talk about meditation in that way. I've heard of people beating cancer with meditation.'

'Is that right?'

'I was never good at it, Father.'

'What?'

'Discipline, prayer. I haven't prayed in decades. I thought I might try meditation when I got sick, but I just couldn't be bothered. And I've bought enough material goods for ten lifetimes.'

'That doesn't matter.'

'How can you say that?'

Father Dwyer looked taken aback. 'It's between you and the Lord.'

'Well, according to the Gospels, it would matter to him. Jesus is much more of a zealot than I remembered. It's heaven or hell, if you do this or that, and that's it.'

Father Dwyer honked with laughter. He had teeth like Brian's — black, missing — and for a second Marie felt Brian's absence so keenly that she wanted to mention him.

'Jesus is no pushover, that's for sure. He's on a mission. He knows what he has to do and nobody's going to stop him.' Father Dwyer picked up the little book and flicked through it. 'You'd enjoy Peter Levi's translations. They're very conversational. You really feel that you're *there*.'

'I doubt I'll have the time, Father.'

'No. You probably don't need me saying things like that.'

'My son brought me in a James Ellroy. I'm sticking with that.'

Marie's mouth felt dry. She hadn't spoken this much since Brian. With her children, so much was relayed without words. She asked the priest for a glass of water and he complied. Then he unzipped the black leather square he was holding and brought out a Bible, a piece of Irish lace and some rosary beads. 'Would you like to pray now?'

'You've been sent to give me my Last Rites, haven't you.'

'I can certainly do that.'

'No.'

Father Dwyer's hands became still. He looked at Marie with polite concern.

'No, Father. I haven't done my confession, or communion —'

'I can give you those as well, if you like. But they're not strictly necessary.'

'*No*.' Marie's tumours began to pulse. 'I'm lapsed, Father. For very good reasons. I don't believe in the Sacraments.'

'Marie,' he said softly. 'That doesn't matter. The mistakes you've made don't matter now. Your heart is open to the Lord, and I can give you His blessing.'

'My heart isn't open to the Lord, Father. It's open to the Bible. It's not the same thing.' She sat back against the pillows, churning. 'I don't believe in God,' she said again. 'I don't believe in heaven or hell. I only believe in the Sacraments as sentimental ritual. And I don't think my disbelief is a mistake. So if I took the Sacraments from you now it would just be hypocrisy. Deathbed comforts.' She rested her gaze on him. '*Bullshit*.'

Father Dwyer was silent. Marie stared at the ceiling, trying to calm down. When her heart rate rose, the pain increased, emotions lighting the tumours like neon. She looked on the bedside table for morphine tablets, but there were none. She remembered that she didn't know what day it was and whether or not she was being picked up.

'My children might walk in any minute now.' *My children*. She liked saying that; she loved her children.

'I can leave if you want.'

'I was enjoying your company, Father.'

'So was I.'

'I didn't bring my children up Catholic, you know. My husband was an atheist. But I made the choice myself. I didn't want my children being told that they were born bad, that sex was bad, that their thoughts were being policed. They aren't perfect, but I don't think they'd be better people if they'd been brought up Catholic. I didn't like what the Church was doing and I still don't.'

'The Church has made a lot of mistakes.' Father Dwyer nodded.

'It doesn't say so, though, does it? Listen to the Pope now, traipsing through Africa telling them from the safety of his cortège not to wear condoms. Just like the one before him. Stupid old men telling women about child-bearing!' she spat. 'Yes, the Bible's beautiful, but it's all men in there. What does that say to me?'

'But Mary Magdalene is at Jesus' right hand. And Jesus' mother, Mary, is one of the most important people in the Bible!'

'For getting pregnant without having sex, for being a chaste mother!'

'That's just allegory.'

'Of what? Women going without?'

'The Bible is the tip of the iceberg, Marie.' Father Dwyer leant forward eagerly. 'There are so many fascinating things still coming to light, especially about Mary Magdalene.'

'This Church taught me to be ashamed of my gay son, and I passed that on to him,' she said despairingly. 'It never stops.'

Father Dwyer wrapped the rosary around his fingers until they disappeared beneath the beads. 'Marie, we have to remember that we're all human and all make mistakes. I'm not making light of this. Some of those mistakes are catastrophic, with lifelong consequences. In the end, we have to form our own relationship with the Lord.'

'Well, what's the point of the Church, then? Why do you wear the collar?'

'Because I believe this is the best way I can live my life. I'm committed to the Lord, and for all its faults I'm committed to this Church.' Father Dwyer changed his tone. He said brightly, 'How many children do you have, Marie?'

'Three.' Marie shut her eyes but it did not stop the tears from trickling out across her cheeks. 'This bloody religion has cast a shadow over my entire life.'

Father Dwyer began to pray.

The next knock on the door came from Rhys, who let herself in as the priest was leaving. Carla arrived as well and there was a moment of chaos. After the greetings and the priest's departure, Carla checked Marie's blood pressure and pulse. 'You've picked up nicely. I think we can let you go home now.'

So, Marie thought, it *was* the next day. 'What's the time?'

'Almost three-thirty. I'm going to give you an Endone as well. It's a suppository. As long as you don't mind, it's a better way to medicate you because it doesn't pass through your stomach.'

Marie rolled over. Carla drew the curtain to insert the small white egg. 'It comes on pretty quickly.'

When the curtain was opened, Rhys offered to help pack her things. Her eyes were shining. 'We just had a hailstorm. Was it hailing over here?'

'I'm not sure.'

'Hat looks great, Marie. Matches your eyes.'

'Susan made it.' Marie's memory perked at the mention of her. She wondered if she was due to visit today as well.

'Is your son coming to pick you up?' said Carla.

'I don't know.' Marie couldn't find her phone. She didn't seem to have brought her address book either.

'And, um, how did you like Father Dwyer?'

'He was nice.' So it was Carla who had arranged that. She was forgiven.

Up out of bed, pulling things from drawers, Marie felt weaker. Rhys was packing her toiletries. 'I can take you home if you like, Marie.'

'Are you sure? What about Travis?'

'He's with his father.'

'I'm going to give you some fentanyl patches and morphine to take with you,' said Carla. 'And I'll be over in a couple of days.'

They took the lift to the ground floor and walked along the corridor towards daylight. Marie could see a woman illuminated in the doorway, huddled, expectant. Then she was coming towards her, calling her name. It was Susan.

Marie introduced her to Rhys. Susan looked Rhys up and down, then extended her hand. Rhys put down Marie's bag and extended hers. 'I really like the cap you knitted.'

Susan started in surprise. 'Thank you. You're going home,' she said to Marie.

'Yes. Time's up.'

'Can I give you a lift?'

'We're fine. Oh Susan, I'm sorry you drove all this way.'

'It's alright. I went to lunch at Rose Bay with Gina. She wants to come and visit you.'

'Any time.' A wave of exhaustion came over Marie. She would

have happily sat on the ground right here. She mustered the last of her energy. 'Come back to Sirius now, if you want.'

A man walked past with a face like crumpled, pale blue tissue paper, a cigarette between his lips. He lit it just before exiting, the smoke drifting back behind him.

By the time Marie got in the car, she was trembling. It took a lot of effort to clip the seatbelt in and put on her sunglasses. The arms dug into the side of her head and she wondered if it was possible to lose weight from one's scalp, or if it was just that the pain had spread there as well. Rhys's car smelt new. A water bottle and a toy clattered around her feet. Marie remarked on the car.

'Yeah, it's a hire car.'

'Why are you driving a hire car?'

Rhys seemed to be driving east rather than north. 'Bikies smashed my windscreen. Same ones that petrol-bombed the shop.'

'Why?'

'I'm not supposed to be talking about this.'

'I'm hardly in a position to be passing things on.'

Rhys looked over. 'Marie, the bikies run just about every tattoo outlet in this town. They avoided Darlinghurst and Surro a long time cos of the poofter factor, but now they want in. Tattooing is so popular now you can imagine how much the cunts're rolling in it. Rob won't pay them and I don't blame him. But I think he doesn't want to pay them for the same reason he doesn't want to pay tax. So we're getting full-on attacked cos Rob's tight.'

'So that's what the scorch mark on the footpath was. It's criminal.'

'I don't care about the law, I'm outside it too. I care about violence and standover. They think they're such outlaws but they're just fascists. Suits in leather clothing. They threatened Travis. I hate them. They *touch* my son —'

'You don't want to go to the police?'

'I don't run the business. I'm just the artist. God, listen to me. I'm sorry. Like you don't have other more important things on your mind.'

'Don't apologise. I asked. I'm actually glad for the distraction.

How's Natasha?'

'She's going to live in London.'

'Really?'

'Her father bought her a house and she's taken off on the First Home Owner's Grant. I knew she wanted to leave Sydney, there was even talk of me going too, but I didn't know she had a house coming to her. She was looking at real estate the whole time we were together but always said it was just a fantasy.' Rhys slouched over the wheel, glum, angry. 'Nowhere but Sydney, eh.' She changed the subject. 'I'm taking the scenic route. I want to show you something.'

As Rhys turned onto South Dowling Street, it began to hail lightly. All along the edge of the park, Gymea lilies like giant matchsticks poked from their beds of long green blades. The lawns were white with hail, like a fairytale winter. Marie wound down the window a crack. There was a cool nip in the air, her fentanyl patch was wearing off, and she felt a bittersweet awareness. She was back in the real world of working lives and argument and weather on your skin. She watched the city pass by, and every car, every building, every crane and cloud seemed to hold a perfect symmetry, as though they had all come together in this one choreographed moment. When they reached William Street, Rhys slowed alongside a dilapidated shopfront. The flash above the windows was still there, the interior empty except for some refuse across the floor.

'The tattoo parlour,' said Marie. 'It's gone.'

'It was there for nearly thirty years, y'know. There was probably a tattooist working this street continuously throughout the whole twentieth century. And now there's none. I think of the old places every time I drive down here. All those spirits of the skin, floating above the traffic.'

'So I'm carrying a bit of history on my body.'

'You could say that.'

'I was drunk when I got those first tattoos.'

'Really?'

'As a skunk.'

Rhys laughed. 'How old-fashioned of you.'

'Did you know Neil?'

'Vaguely. He's a good tattooist in an old-school kinda way. I like old school.'

'He's a bikie, isn't he?'

Rhys smirked. 'Neil is a *motorcycle enthusiast*.'

At the lights she pointed down to Woolloomooloo. 'And that's where I was living when I first started tattooing. In a squat. Great place. We were there for years. It's a freeway now. You'll have to direct me, Marie. We're *just* gonna beat peak hour.'

'The bridge, so I can see.'

The car crawled up the hill towards the sunset. A bleating began at Marie's feet.

'Is that my phone?' said Rhys. 'No, mine's here.' She patted her pocket.

It was bleating in Marie's bag, but the effort of bending down to get it was too much. She let it ring out. 'I'm down to four months,' she announced.

'What do you want to do?'

'Go for a bushwalk. See Nell. You know I wanted to get gauntlets, and we never finished the angophora. I feel incomplete.'

'Maybe I can paint the gauntlets on.'

'You never would have tattooed them, would you.'

'Actually, yes. I just felt you needed to wait a bit longer. More people are getting their hands done now; it's not such a big deal.'

'I think I just want to make the most of this last fortnight in my house and garden.'

'That sounds good. Then you move?'

'Yes.' Marie groaned. 'I'm dreading it.'

Rhys turned onto the Cahill Expressway. The sun was low and she pushed down the visors.

'I was cruel to Blanche.'

'You're very different from each other,' Rhys said diplomatically.

'Are you going to have another child, Rhys?'

'Probably not. Why?'

'You can't love all your children equally, you know. They tell you that you can, that you *have* to, but you can't. And you end up feeling guilty about it for the rest of your life.'

Marie's little speech exhausted her. Her mouth was completely dry. The water bottle at her feet was empty. She could sense the familiar marching band of pain start up in the pit of her stomach. She looked at the girders of the bridge flicking by, the ribbed sky stretching either side. She found herself smiling a greeting or a farewell to the impervious, beautiful scenery. 'Oh, Rhys. We had so much fun, didn't we?'

'We sure did.'

Clark spent the morning catching up on chores. He cooked the chick peas he had soaked the night before, did some washing then from eight-thirty onwards made a list of overdue phone calls, including one to Nell's child care to check on her progress. Rachel, the manager, thought Nell was *so precocious and one of the most on-to-it kids I've ever had here*. Clark hung up feeling proud and satisfied. He wrote up his Progress Report for first semester, transferred Nell's child allowance, read the backlog of emails from his department and paid all his bills. He wrote an email to Janice about Nell, so as to avoid talking to her directly. The chores he enjoyed the most were the administrative ones, the completion of each giving him a satisfaction he hadn't felt since he'd stopped working in an office. The crispness of the morning had lasted into the heart of the day; he was tingling with energy when he finished. He thought that he might go back to an administrative job when he finished his thesis; it seemed to make him happier than writing. He would never be a writer, he realised that now, but it came to him more with relief than disappointment.

At midday he made hommus and a tuna salad. Sylvia's car was being serviced so he went to pick her up from Bondi Junction. Beachside trysts were so rare. They had three hours together and Clark couldn't wait to get her home.

Inside the car, she moved immediately into his embrace. 'Franco confronted me today. He's started to suspect something.'

'Don't you think it might be better just to tell him?'

'I *can't.*'

Clark headed down the hill. The sky in the east had turned pale grey. He drove with one hand, holding Sylvia's with the other, surprised to find a spark of empathy for his rival glowing in his heart. It flamed to mistrust and again he considered that if Sylvia was deceiving her husband, she was also capable of deceiving him. 'I have to pick up my mother at three-thirty. We've got three hours together, cheaptart.'

Sylvia squeezed his hand. Sunlight shafted through the light cloud cover then suddenly it began to hail. In seconds the patter became a violent, copious downpour. Clark moved into second gear and crawled to a stop below his building. Onto the roof, inches above their heads, the hail thundered. Sylvia was laughing in the mayhem.

Clark looked in wonder at it falling through sunlight, piling up on the windscreen. 'It's incredible!'

Sylvia was grinning from ear to ear. 'Isn't the apocalypse beautiful?'

Clark touched her face. 'You'll be alright, Sylvia. So will we.' He got out his cigarettes, and they smoked holding hands beneath the harsh drumming of ice on metal.

'I spoke to Maurice,' Sylvia said. 'He's seeing Leon tomorrow.'

'Thank you so much for that.'

'No worries. Maurice is a really good barrister and a nice guy.'

'Leon said he hardly had anything on him. I can't understand why this has to go to court.'

'Poor bastard.'

'And I can't understand why he's carrying drugs around at a time like this.'

'Maybe he wanted an escape. Have some fun.'

'He was taking *ice.*'

Sylvia looked out the window. Again Clark sensed her strain. Getting out of the car was not an option. The hail poured down, enclosing them in a white pod.

'Clark, he doesn't deserve this. He's being charged with indecent exposure and resisting arrest as well. They got him at a beat. That's just between you and me.'

'A *beat*. Where?'

'Moore Park.'

Clark was silent. He couldn't believe his lover, who had never met his brother, knew more than he did. He felt a twinge of embarrassment about the beat. Sylvia seemed to be hearing his thoughts. 'The law is an ass, Clark.'

'Well, why did you become one then?'

'I don't know. I thought I could make a difference. One day soon we'll be getting arrested for having pictures of fags on our hard drives.'

'So that's why he said the cops were homophobic.'

'No doubt they were.'

Clark tightened. 'I don't agree with gay guys doing that in public. Call me homophobic too, if you like. It's a park, for god's sake. What if a kid comes across that.'

'Who takes their kids to the park at midnight?'

'They do it in the day too. They're everywhere.'

Sylvia pulled another cigarette out of the packet. 'We're living in a police state.'

'Oh, come on, look at the rest of the world. It's a fucking picnic here.'

'The anti-terrorism laws might as well have no sunset clause and the sniffer dogs are a prime example of them being used against citizens for no better reason than good old oppression. The operation that got Leon would have cost thousands of dollars. For what? Shaming and intimidating, a couple of petty fines. It's just revenue-raising and fear-mongering.' Sylvia grew vehement. 'And I'm sick of people pointing to worse places as an excuse for not opposing the creeping tyranny here.'

'I'm way better informed than the average person and I care, you know that,' Clark replied with equal vehemence. But he knew they weren't fighting about issues, they were fighting against each other pure and simple. He tried to calm down. 'I didn't know there was no sunset clause.'

'Hardly anybody knows anything. Hardly anybody cares. The

federal government has enclosed us in legislation so constrictive that the state government is forgotten. They pass these laws and nobody says anything. We haven't even got a bill of rights in this stupid country.'

She was getting that awful shrewish tone. The thrumming of hail was now muffled by a thick coat of ice all around them, and their voices boomed inside the small car. Clark was surprised to find himself implicated, even defensive. He said, 'Do you do anything?'

'I screech away in a lecture theatre and write papers on law reform for musty old journals with a readership of one legal-aid lawyer and his dog. What do you reckon?' Sylvia began to laugh. 'I meant cigarette fags, by the way. Not men.' She stubbed her cigarette out and ran her hand through his hair. 'How's your mother?'

'Taking painkillers by the bucketload.'

As suddenly as it began, the hail stopped. Clark went to open the door, but Sylvia put a hand on his arm. 'Let's go down to the ocean.'

Clark drove slowly, the tyres crunching and slipping on ice. His neighbours were emerging, dazed and smiling, taking photographs, checking their cars for damage. It was surreal: Bondi icy in the sun, every street completely white. They drove onto Campbell Parade and the grassy slopes that ran down to the ocean glittered like snowfields. The waves moved in, one after another, huge, angry, relentless. He was elated by the day's extreme weather yet scared of the tension emanating from Sylvia. He was sick of his single life in his little flat, his solo dinners, his paltry fortnightly meetings with his daughter. He wanted more. He thought of Sylvia's body with its history and strength and private concerns. It seemed a cathedral, and a fortress. He pulled up in the car park facing the ocean and cut the ignition. On the path below, kids were throwing ice balls at each other. Everywhere were drifts of it. 'I made us lunch,' he said hopefully.

'I don't have time to stay for lunch, Clark. I have to go home.'

'Is Franco there?'

'Yes. Right now, he thinks I'm at a staff meeting.'

Clark began to simmer. 'It won't be like that when we're together, Sylvia. We're going to be honest. We're going to be monogamous. And you're not going to do any sex work.'

Sylvia swung around, her eyes wide. 'Why do you *always* bring that up?'

'I'm just jealous,' Clark almost shouted. 'It's awful, I hate it, I'm sorry, but I can't help it!'

'I *trusted* you when I told you that. God! The last thing I need is *your* moralism.'

His heart shrivelled as though it had been thrown into a hot pan. 'I'm sorry, I'm really sorry. I had no right —'

She began to talk urgently. 'Alright. You want honesty? I fell in love with you because I'm not fully satisfied where I am now. You *know* stuff, you tell me stuff. Franco isn't much of an intellectual and he doesn't make me laugh like you do, and like any long-term couple we don't have much sex anymore.' She was rearing back against the window staring at Clark with tears in her eyes. '*I'm* sorry.'

'No, *I am*. We're both really stressed out and taking it out on each other which is counterproductive.' He put his hand on her thigh. It felt like a glove on a block of wood. '*I'm* sorry, cheaptart. Okay? Forgive me?'

The pet name sounded lame and tawdry. Sylvia looked exhausted. 'Let's get into the back so we can cuddle.'

They climbed through the gap between the seats. She lay her head on his chest and he stroked her hair, its apple scent rising through his nicotine fingers. Sylvia touched his face. 'I fell in love with you, Clark, and I've been on the verge of leaving Franco for you. But as much as we get on, we're really different in some fundamental ways.'

Clark swallowed. He was terrified she would mention what he had done — nearly done — the night she had stayed. He was still carrying guilt about it, and it was unbearable. He wanted to pull his jumper over his head. He wanted to cut off his dick. He kept his face averted and his hand in Sylvia's hair while she said what he had been afraid of her saying for a while, what he had been driving her towards, out along the bending branch, further and further to the thin end till the final snap came as a relief.

'I can't do this anymore, Clark. You know I love you, but we're just too different. We're beginning to really hurt each other and we have to stop.' She sat up when she had finished speaking, her face hidden behind a curtain of hair.

'I love you,' said Clark.

'I love you too.' She held him for a long time.

Then she took his hand. 'Listen, I wouldn't mind having a bit of a walk alone on the beach, okay? Then I'm going to get the bus home. I feel pretty drained and I need to zone out for a bit.'

'Sure.' He got out of the car, walked around to her side, and opened the door for her.

The wind whipped her hair about her face. 'You hang in there with your mother, okay?'

He didn't watch her walk away. He went down to a bench on the esplanade facing the beach. The clouds had peeled away and the sky resumed its rinsed, fresh autumn blue of the morning. The swell was huge. Nobody was in the surf. You could die in a surf as big and wild as that. He had been swimming less as the weather turned even though the ocean was still twenty degrees. He must get back to it. Looking at the churning surf he thought, as he had so often before, that it was a miracle to have this on his doorstep. It was the most beautiful place in the world.

But nothing could lessen his desolation.

Half an hour later, Clark drove home. He had left all the windows of his flat open and it was chilly inside. Hailstones and water were strewn across the table, on the floor. His stomach felt like a screwed-up rag so he put the lunch in the fridge. He shut the windows, cleaned up, then switched on the computer and checked his email. He realised at some stage that he had a raging thirst and drank some water. Then he realised that he was late to pick up his mother. He ran down to the car and drove as fast as he could into town. At Centennial Park the traffic stalled. The hail was still banked in drifts around bushes. He switched on the radio. *We're all compulsive home renovators*, said an announcer in a crisp white voice. Clark moved the dial. *Sydney Afri-can community*, said a fruity black voice, *is goin' dance this weekend, oooh yeah*. Seun Kuti poured into the car, the music running over him like sunlight on stone.

He ran into Susan at the hospital entrance. 'She's gone,' Susan said, flustered.

'How? Who with?' Clark didn't know Susan was coming today. 'Blanche? I thought she was working.' Maybe Blanche had handed in her resignation today. He felt excited for her.

'No, that tattoo woman.' Susan touched her wrists.

'Rhys,' Clark affirmed. Although he had never met her, he had heard enough; and he had resented her so strongly he felt like he had met her. Susan looked around as though she were expecting someone, and Clark felt sorry for her. For better or worse, she was his mother's oldest friend and she was still here, still looking in on her. He asked her the time and realised he was a whole hour late. He was glad that Rhys had been on hand and he found himself wanting to defend the tattoo artist against Susan. That this feeling was also an attack on his own previous animosity did not escape him. He took out his mobile. 'How is she?'

'I barely recognised her, she looked so small and frail. I'm finding it all *extremely* difficult.'

Clark pressed his mother's number. 'Yeah.' He held the phone to his ear, not expecting anyone to pick up. 'Where're you parked, Susan?'

'Over there. No. Bloody hell. I don't know. I hate it around here.'

'I'm that way. Why don't you walk with me? You might remember.'

They set out across the road. 'I hear Blanche is expecting. That's exciting news. Louise said she'd been sick.'

'Yeah, but she's better now, her first trimester's nearly over. The hormones'll start kicking in soon.'

'That's wonderful news for Marie too, isn't it. Grandchildren are such a delight.'

They entered the maze of laneways on the other side of

Missenden Road. 'God,' said Clark. 'We just had the most incredible hailstorm in Bondi. And nothing here.'

'Oh, it hit Mosman. Bloody well damaged my car, actually. Leon's still there trying to save the garden.'

Clark was wondering whether or not to invite Susan home. She might just come anyway. She had left a pot of vichyssoise on the patio a week ago. She was carrying a box of mints with her now: she never arrived without some sort of gift. And the cap — colourful, jaunty, almost a collusion with Marie's latter-day self. Yes, invite her home, she's been kind. A text came through and Clark whipped his phone open, but it wasn't his mother, it was Sylvia. *I had such a great time with you, Clark cheaptart. Thank you for everything, and sorry for everything too. Much love. xxo.* Clark wanted to throw his phone on the ground and jump up and down on it.

'Do you want to give these to your mother? Or should I come over?'

'I, um, yeah! Come over. If she wants to go to bed, she'll just go to bed.'

They arrived at a sleek new Peugeot with a pockmarked bonnet. 'Oh, my car. Thank you, Clark.'

'No worries.'

Susan fished into her bag for keys. 'So I've finally seen Rhys,' she mused. 'She's quite pretty underneath all that nonsense, isn't she.'

Rhys didn't stay long when they arrived at Sirius Cove. Marie was too tired and they knew the others would arrive soon. She took Marie's bags up to her bedroom and they said goodbye. Marie was glad for the time alone.

Her house was like a palace, her bedroom a luxury suite. She sat on the bed and gathered strength, then slowly began to undress. Her body was tiny, the flesh drooping around her hips. The bones of her chest emerged and her breasts lolled, empty. She went into the ensuite. She took off Susan's cap and moved closer to her looming head, the yellowing skin like an old cloth dropped onto the bones of her face, the irises like beacons around diminished pupils. The tattoos were wrinkling but still looked beautiful, like crushed silk.

She smelt of the hospital. Of medication, antiseptic, piss, shit, bile. She could taste her foul breath. She was like a moonwalker, weightless in this wondrous alien world, crossing through the ensuite past the texture of clothes, gargling Listerine, moving to the shower, claw hands clutching a towel. She couldn't remember the last time she'd had a proper shower. Trembling, she twisted the taps, and slowly adjusted them till water poured forth at the right temperature. The stench of chlorine filled the cubicle. They must be flushing germs from the low dams. She stepped beneath the shower, soaping herself carefully. She emerged glistening and triumphant as an athlete. I'm here, she thought. I'm *still here*.

She rubbed cream on the old bag of her body, struggling to reach her spine. Fatima had even left fresh pyjamas out. Bed, clean sheets, smell of white cotton. She had a day's supply of painkillers until Carla arrived. She drank a dose of liquid morphine, unpeeled a fentanyl patch and stuck it on her thigh. She climbed beneath the covers and sank into darkness. Goodnight, goodnight. Outside, the sun was drawing below the horizon. Little patches of white glinting here and there in the garden were all that was left of the hailstorm. And the creaking of bark on deck, water slapping stone, and the screeching, screeching cockatoos.

She dozed, aware of someone looking in on her, people at the door, then the clock's hands moving past midnight. These were the hours of creeping fear. So little flesh left that her knees scraped against one another like rocks. All night shifting a pillow between her legs, longing for her cat, longing for Brian. She sat up at one stage to take more morphine. Her neck hurt, her back hurt, her knees hurt, and her belly screamed over everything the loudest hurt of all.

She woke to the light thud of a cat jumping on the bed. Footsteps delicate up the covers towards her, but she couldn't move. She lay trapped and distraught in the dark. Then a last desperate lunge and breaking through the weight she found herself alone in reality. She took two more tablets and drifted back into her memories.

Leon went to George's to borrow a suit for his appointment with the barrister. He was surprised when the door was opened by George's boyfriend. Linus was Dutch or something but had been here since he was a teenager and spoke without an accent. He was a couple of years younger than George but almost bald, not particularly fit. He had a homely look about him.

He shook Leon's hand. 'Hey, what a bummer.'

'Yeah, it's pretty surreal.' Leon entered the apartment shyly.

'George is in the bedroom.'

Leon walked down the hall. Bruce was slumped against the wall halfway to the bedroom. 'Bruce!' The cat thumped his tail and Leon stooped to rub his knuckles along Bruce's throat to receive the soothing vibrations.

George greeted him with a hearty hug and back slap. 'Fucking bummer, mate.'

'Yeah. Back to the 1950s.'

'Like, full-*on*.' George smelt of garlic. He was dressed for work. He had his wardrobe open and a few items of clothing laid out on the bed. 'You're actually more Linus's size — you're both a bit bigger than me. But I got these out anyway.'

'Thanks, mate. I really appreciate it.'

'You okay? You look a bit whacked.'

'I'm not sleeping that well.'

'I feel a bit guilty, to be honest.'

'No. Why?'

'Cos I kind of kicked you out.'

'I kind of instigated that turn of events.'

'Yeah, but, the drugs.'

'It's okay.'

More than the possession charge, Leon was worried about the one of indecent exposure. He didn't want to talk to George about it: George's sympathy was enough. In daylight, Leon could see the details of the room: shoes that obviously belonged to Linus in the corner, a photo of the two of them on the dresser. He was glad he hadn't had sex with George in this room. Anywhere in the house, come to think of it.

'You really need a suit for your appointment?' said George.

'No. But I can't wear these jeans. And I'll need a suit for court.'

'Okay, go for it.'

Leon held the trousers against his body. They were probably too short. The suit looked intimidating, funereal or corporate, and he left it. He didn't even have a suit in Brisbane but he did have a pair of black trousers and black leather shoes. Still, even if he had brought everything down to Sydney, he knew that almost his entire wardrobe was composed of scungy gardening clothes, or casual clothes. It made him feel insubstantial, an amoeba in the serious world of men and careers.

'It's the sort of thing I should own, isn't it. I mean I'm going to need a suit for Mum's funeral.'

'I like getting into a suit now and then. Makes a man feel sharp.'

'These brogues look spiffy.'

'They'd fit you.'

Leon slipped off his jeans and trainers, angling himself away from George. The shy, chaste feeling that coated him on entry to the apartment lingered; he kept it on as protection. George, as though in tacit agreement, rifled through a drawer up the other end of the wardrobe. Leon put on the trousers and found that if he slung them low they were fine. The shoes fitted perfectly.

Linus came down the hall to use the bathroom and stuck his head in the door. 'Smart!'

'A fine upstanding citizen, if ever I saw one,' George agreed.

Leon turned in the mirror. 'D'you reckon I should shave? I really don't want to.'

George walked him to the door. Leon described Carla, and George seemed to think it was the same nurse he had worked with in Ward 17. 'She's great. Can't get better, really.'

'That's good to hear.'

'Will you keep me posted?'

'Sure.'

George watched Leon walk out of the building. 'Hey, are you moving back or what? Have you decided?'

Leon turned. 'I guess so. I guess I'm here now.'

'Well, that's great.'

'I have to get a job.'

'What about your business?'

'I don't know. Maybe I'll wind it up. Hey, you know what my fees with this barrister are? Fifty a phone call, three-fifty a meeting, and three and a half thou for a day in court. Even if the hearing only takes ten minutes and the charges are dismissed, I still have to hire him for the day.'

'Yep, barristers' fees are like that.'

Leon shook his head. 'Why can't I charge that for a day in someone's garden?'

'Ditto, mate. But that's what they cost.'

'You need to tell me everything,' Maurice Parker said. He looked like a guy called Rosten that Leon had gone to school with. Nut-brown eyes, skin of a rich paleness that would tan if given a chance; a suggestion of voluptuousness although he wasn't overweight. His manner was unperturbed. 'You never know what they can bring up in court, so we need to bring it up first if it needs to be brought up.'

'What sort of things? I don't have a record.'

'Good.' Maurice was taking notes. 'Speeding fines? Parking fines?'

'Um. Yeah.'

'Paid up?'

'I got a parking fine the same night, actually. Because I was in lock-up. I should send it to NSW Police.'

Maurice didn't catch the joke. 'Paid it?'

'No.'

'Pay it.'

'Okay.'

Suddenly Maurice smiled. 'When you get home.'

'Okay. Sure.'

'Habit of not paying your fines in general?'

Leon stroked his beard. He was pretty sure he'd skipped out on fines when leaving New South Wales. He sometimes visualised late-payment penalties floating into his old letterbox. Somehow, a glitch in the switch to a Queensland licence had let the fines fall through the net. But, from time to time, he remembered them and wondered if they would catch up with him. Now they assumed monstrous proportions. He began to sweat.

Maurice read his mind. 'You can find out online if you have any outstandings. So what happened on the night. Let's go through it step by step.'

'I went to a mate's for a drink. We had a few beers and, um, indulged a bit — my mate was celebrating the end of exams, you know; it was a completely spur-of-the-moment one-off thing when he suggested to me that we indulge. I had no idea, really; I wasn't expecting it.'

Maurice waited politely.

'Anyway, George didn't want to go out and he told me there was a party on, so I walked there cos I didn't want to drive because I was over the limit.' Leon hoped the responsibility in this decision shone through. 'And it was across the park so that's why they got me there.'

'So the drugs were yours.'

'*No*. George gave them to me —'

'They had come into your possession. They were on your person.'

'But I wasn't even thinking about it, and George has nothing to do with this.'

Maurice listened, twiddling his pen while Leon talked about his innocence, the paltry amount, how stupid it all was. 'Leon, we're going to have to plead guilty to the possession charge. The drugs were in your pockets. Pleading guilty can make you look better in some circumstances. Section 10 — good citizen with no priors — you'll have to get some character references. Can you think of anyone who can give you one?'

'Um. I know the head of Triage at St Vincent's.'

'Great. What's his name?'

'George Shehadie.' Leon smiled. 'The guy who gave me the crystal.'

'Leon, when I said, *Tell me everything*,' Maurice said drily, 'I didn't mean everything.'

Leon's eyes travelled across the law books on Maurice's shelves. There must have been hundreds, probably all in small print. It was like looking at an enormous factory from the outside, hearing the grind of machinery through the walls, knowing you were about to be pushed in like meat into a mincer. Here he was, the son of a rich businessman, with the best education money could buy, almost halfway through his life, and he knew nothing about the system that governed him. There were no shackles on his limbs: he could get up and walk out of here right now if he wanted. But there was a shadow. And it had changed everything.

'The fact that you were going from A to B is in your favour,' Maurice was saying. 'But if you were having sex with this man —'

'I wasn't.'

'You're being charged with indecent exposure.'

'I was fully clothed.'

'Did you have your penis out?'

Leon cringed. 'I wasn't doing anything!' He remembered the man's chest hair beneath his palm, his beautiful eyes. How pathetic he had seemed as soon as they got caught, a total turn-off. A lot of what Maurice said was jargon or else it was Leon's inability to concentrate. The photos on the desk were tilted so both Maurice and his clients could see his family. A woman holding a baby. Maurice standing on a rocky coastline, holding a child's hand, a fishing rod in the other. How alien it seemed and yet Maurice could have been Joel Rosten from Shore, chewing his pen at the desk adjacent during the HSC. Every night and every day since the bust, Leon had thought of worst-case scenarios. That everyone would find out, and he would be shunned, unable to work. That he would go to gaol.

But Maurice was saying something completely different. 'You're free.'

'What do you mean?'

'You have no dependants. You said you were living between cities, didn't you?' Maurice capped his pen and straightened the papers on his desk.

'Yes.' Leon realised that the appointment was winding up.

'I envy you that flexibility. Horticulture. That must be a *great* job. Have you always wanted to be a horticulturalist? What got you into it?'

'My mother, I suppose. I grew up in a beautiful garden next to the bush. Plants were always kinda fundamental.'

'So grounding, having your hands in the earth every day. I nearly became a horticulturalist, you know. It's my fantasy job.'

'Really? Why didn't you?'

Maurice led Leon to the door. 'Oh, you know, pressure from Dad to study law. Not that I don't enjoy it. But if we have a recession here and my work dries up, I'm going back to the garden.'

'You won't earn as much.'

Maurice smiled quizzically. 'I'm not motivated by money, Leon.'

Marie started to get dressed when Fatima came upstairs to clean. The vacuum approached as she pulled on a clean bra. When Fatima knocked, Marie called out, 'It's alright, you don't have to do my room today.' The vacuum receded down the hall. Marie was unable to close the clasp of her bra. Every time she reached behind, her hands lost strength and dropped by her sides. A colossal weakness overtook her and when the bedroom door swung open in the breeze, all she could do was stay where she was sitting on the bed, trying in vain to pull a shirt over herself before Fatima noticed her.

Fatima switched off the vacuum cleaner and came up the hall. 'Can I help you, Mrs King?'

'I can't.' Marie shrugged. Half naked, helpless and humiliated, she plucked at her bra.

Fatima's expression was clear and unafraid. She stood behind Marie and fastened her bra, then held the shirt open and Marie put her quivering arms into the sleeves. Looking down at her wrinkled tattoos and emaciated thighs, Marie didn't care anymore abut her state. She was sick: this was how she looked, and that was that.

'Do you like pants? Something from the cupboard? A skirt?'

'There's a wraparound skirt in there that I could put on.'

'Yes, I know.' Fatima fetched it from the ensuite, bringing out the cashmere hat as well. Marie stood up and let Fatima help her put the skirt on. She bowed her head to receive the cap.

She descended the stairs with Fatima at her elbow. Something funny in her left knee, so that when she bent it the knee wouldn't straighten again properly. At the bottom, Marie turned to Fatima. 'Thank you, I'll be alright now.'

It was snowing in the mountains and an icy wind had swept over the plains into the city. Marie walked down the side path into the bottom garden. The mulch she had piled around plants before the sale was still high. The blackboy, as Leon had pointed out, was dark with scale.

She drifted beneath a low, glowering sky. Along the northern fence, the wattle was in bloom. She attempted to pick some and it sprang out of her hand. She tried again, some yellow fluff remaining in her palm. She walked across the lawn to where the view was open and gazed at the bush along the headland opposite. Beneath the lime tree she found Blanche's fossil-fern headstone. She released her handful of wattle over the grave, wondering about Mopoke's death. Most animals hid themselves to give birth or die. Were they ashamed of their pain? In their vulnerability did they expect attack rather than comfort from the pack? Did animals understand what humans so often denied: that all life was dispensable? We humans with our drama and ceremony and paraphernalia. Marie thought of Mopoke's difficult last months: she must have been relieved to die. 'Well, Moey,' she said to the grave, 'I don't think I'm going to make it back to the bush after all. I'm just too tired. I'll just have to look at it.'

She wasn't afraid of dying now. But she was afraid of that fast-approaching threshold beyond which lay intolerable pain or helplessness or self-disgust. And although she had listed the furniture she wanted taken to Neutral Bay, she still could not countenance the move.

She continued to the bottom of the garden. Asparagus fern was creeping over from the Hendersons'. She wanted to pull it out, but it remained a thought, her body unable to carry out what her head directed. Then the squall came in.

There was ice in the rain. It sliced against her cheek like flint. She shuffled back up to the house enjoying the violence of the weather, watching the garden whip and lash. A squawking rose from the reserve. Two cockatoos flipped out beneath the crown of a phoenix palm, their wings flapping as they dangled upside-down, screaming deliriously in the rain.

Leon was in the kitchen when Marie came back inside. He had returned from his appointment with the barrister and was drinking cordial. 'You're drenched.'

'It's lovely out there. You look smart in those clothes.' Marie removed her wet cap, and Leon fetched her a towel and jumper. 'How did you go?'

Leon hadn't told his mother about the indecent-exposure charge either. The only people who knew were George and Maurice. 'The barrister was really nice. A wannabe gardener. He said it mostly depends on the magistrate.'

'Let's have a joint. I still have Brian's pot in my handbag.'

'Well, who'd've thought I'd be getting stoned with my mother right when I've got drugs charges.'

'It helps me eat. It helps with the pain.'

Leon didn't like smoking much and wasn't a very good roller, but his mother liked the company. He settled her on the couch with an ashtray and went into the kitchen to finish preparing pumpkin and sweet potato soup. He noticed no difference in his mother when she was stoned. He supposed she was stoned all the time on painkillers anyway. The sheer effort of carrying the disease must be enough to make a person vague, he thought. He laid the table and brought out the meal. 'Remember the hissy fit Dad had when I got busted for smoking pot at school?'

'He wasn't above smoking when he was young. We both had the occasional puff.'

'Why did you give up?'

'I think we just forgot about it. Maybe we thought we were above it … It was considered more classy getting drunk on expensive alcohol.' Marie began to cough, and Leon rubbed her back. He could feel her bones through the clothes.

'The barrister asked why I became a gardener and I told him it was because of you.'

Marie fixed him with her fierce blue eyes. 'You're good at it, Leon.'

'I'm good with plants but I'm crap at running a business.'

'You'll have to sort that out then, won't you.'

Leon picked up a cushion she had knocked to the floor during her coughing fit. He stood there twisting it in his hands. 'Yep.'

'Where did you get those clothes?'

'George.'

'Is he well?'

'He's great.'

'That's better.' Marie handed him the joint, then settled into its fog. 'I could try eating some soup now.'

Leon moved the heater around to face her. Marie had trouble controlling the spoon. Her hands felt like twigs slithering around the handle. She took a breath and tried again, the creamy relief of lentils finally sliding into her mouth. She concentrated on the food, aware of Leon watching her. 'When are you moving back to Sydney?'

'I don't know.'

He was so quiet, tearing his bread, sloped over his bowl, checking her face every so often. 'Stop dithering, Leon. Forget about your father, forget about George, and move back to where you belong.'

'It's just the huge cost of this court case —'

'Forget about money. You'll be inheriting. *Do* your horticulture' — she banged a bony fist onto the table — 'in *your* city.'

The clouds had thinned to messy white skeins and the gutters dripped in the sunlight. 'I might look for a job with National Parks. Go and do arboriculture at TAFE, get a licence for big vehicles and away I go,' Leon replied. 'I'm not sure I want to go back to doing the books, let alone the gardens of north shore ladies. No offence, Mum.'

'No offence taken. God knows they wouldn't hire me. We did a good job with the garden here, Leon.'

'*You* did.'

'Yes. I'm proud of it.' Marie put down her spoon and gave her plate a push. She had finished the entire bowl. She drank some water and felt immediately better. 'This is what's keeping me alive.' She held up the glass. Leon didn't understand. 'I know the garden can't be saved,' she went on. She could feel rumbles begin in her stomach; soon they would be embarrassingly loud, then issue as farts. 'Now, while it's damp out there, let's go and burn the blackboy.'

The trunk of the blackboy was barely visible beneath the fountain of wiry stems. Standing close enough to be spiked by them, Leon could see into the heart of the plant where the scale was most copious. It extended a good foot up the stems in a suffocating black cloud. 'This is the plant I missed the most in the tropics. It could put a blossom stem out after this, you know? Maybe next year? Did you know the flowers are bisexual? Did you know blackboys live up to six hundred years?'

'I always found that so comforting.'

Leon parted the stems to inspect the infestation. He checked the direction of the breeze with a wet finger. Below them the toothpicks of masts bobbed about; a hydrofoil streaked across the distance. Leon lit the blowtorch and held it at arm's length as it heated, the flame invisible in the sun. Then standing upwind he aimed it at the plant's extremities. *Vooomph*, the stems ignited, releasing pungent oil scent. The air above quivered, ash began to drop in a circle and, as the flames poured into the heart of the plant, Marie and Leon cheered. Marie held her sleeve over her face as the wind changed and the smoke billowed towards her. The stump emerged, coated in embers.

'How many creatures did we just kill, do you think, Leon?'

'I don't know. Millions?' He watched the dying fire with satisfaction. 'I won't leave it here, Mum. I'm going to take it with me when we move.'

When Blanche got to work, she realised she had forgotten her BlackBerry and brought the wrong mobile phone in. It was a measure of the stress she was under that the night before she had put her mobile into the phone drawer and this morning had accidentally taken out an old one, uncharged, with no sim card in it. The phone drawer collected a new tenant every six months or so, when Blanche or Hugh upgraded, or Blanche was given a sample. She rang Hugh from her landline and told him not to contact her on her mobile.

'We have to get rid of those bloody phones,' he said.

'I don't want to throw them out. It would be a waste.'

'Have you seen Terry yet?'

'No. I'm going to do it at the end of the day.' Blanche felt light-headed with fear and excitement. She felt so powerful: the proverbial bolt from the blue.

'Fair enough. Then we're having champagne.'

'Then I'm going to Mum's, actually. Sorry, Hugh. We have to finalise the furniture.'

The office was unusually quiet. Nobody had replaced Lim. Kate was on facebook when Blanche walked past, just sitting there with the screen fully visible. Blanche hadn't completely decided whether it would be better to hand in her resignation now or wait until the end of the day. Passing the open plan, seeing the way the light came in, hearing the amiable chatter, she felt sad. She had been here for ten years. She was bloody good at her job. How would she cope without it? On her way back from the bathroom, Kate beckoned to her and Blanche went over. Kate offered her a cashew and Blanche accepted. Her appetite had doubled; every day she became more aware of how much of her energy was channelling to the baby. She could almost visualise the food she ate pouring down a tube straight into the foetus. A *baby*, she had thought, in wonder that morning driving into work. *There are two people in this car!* And her entire body seemed to fold protectively around her belly.

'Can I see you for a minute?' Kate asked.

'Sure.' Blanche led the way back to her office. She could feel a smile pushing through her lips: she was dying to tell Kate about her pregnancy. She didn't care about facebook, or solitaire, or having to organise her mother's things tonight. She didn't care about

Kate taking her place: let her take everything. For a moment, she didn't even care about her mother's impending death; a supreme acceptance of everything and everyone exactly as they were flowed through her.

'I've got something to tell you,' Kate said when they were sitting in Blanche's office.

'What?'

'I'm leaving.'

Blanche stared.

'I'm going to work with Lim. I gave Terry my resignation letter this morning.'

'Wow,' Blanche managed.

Kate began to console her. 'Oh, I'm sorry. I really like *you*. It's just too good an opportunity, you know. I'll be head of the art department. Oh, Blanche, it's a tough time for you, isn't it, with your mum and all. I'm sorry.'

Blanche could see how pleased Kate was with the crushing effect of her announcement. She had always considered Kate's confidence a supreme quality. Her mind began to run from corner to corner. Should she tell Kate she was going to leave too? Should she tell her she was pregnant? She looked at Kate in her cowboy boots and bright red skirt across which ran a hare and tortoise. She suddenly saw her as a companion, someone to have fun with on a Friday night. A younger-sister sort of thing. How she would have loved to have had a sister! And that skin, that accent. She burst out laughing. 'God, I'm just so shocked. I mean *I'm* leaving. I've got my resignation letter too!'

Kate drummed her heels on the floor and squealed. She jumped up to shut the door. 'Fookin' Terry!' She eyed Blanche's fridge. 'Let's have a drink! Now!'

'Hang on, hang on.' Blanche couldn't stop grinning. She moved the papers on her desk. 'I do actually have to do some work today, Kate. Like I'm not leaving for another month. And I'm still not up for drinking much.'

'Oh come on. Just one shot.'

Blanche realised that she'd nearly given her pregnancy away.

Fuck. Which then made her realise that she still wasn't ready to bond with Kate and mention it. 'Okay then, one shot.' She had a bottle of Polish bison vodka with an unpronounceable name in her freezer, a luminous pale green with a strip of grass in it. She poured two shots and they knocked them back. 'Right, my turn now.'

'You go, girl.'

Blanche walked down to Terry's office breathing fire.

Terry had his glasses on and was writing on his computer. He looked up at Blanche's knock and motioned her in. His fingers flew across the keyboard as she sat down. Blanche rarely saw him like this. Terry preferred to be seen as perennially casual: all the better to sneak up on someone when they least expected it. But diligence became him, maybe because the customary savagery was channelled into the keyboard instead of the conversation. He finished and pushed his chair away then propped his foot onto his knee. Those bloody winklepickers. Blanche didn't feel the slightest bit intimidated today.

'So,' said Terry. 'Kate. What a shame.'

'Damn straight.'

'Could you see it coming?'

'Not at all. I knew she was really ambitious, but I just assumed that would play out here.'

Terry grinned, surprising Blanche. 'So it's just you 'n' me, kid,' he said, cavalier.

Blanche knew he was quoting someone from a movie; Clark would have remembered who. Terry was looking at her with shrewd challenge. There was a whole office of staff out there, but she knew what he meant and she agreed: none of them suited her like Lim and Kate had. She saw a kernel of playfulness in Terry's eyes too. Yes, this was how men operated all the time with each other. They were in perpetual competition. Hadn't Ross and Jonesy thrived on that, isn't that why their friendship survived the break-up of their business? A surge of strength ran up Blanche's spine. She could have picked up that stupid Marc Newson couch and thrown it out the window.

She met Terry's gaze. 'Yep, back to basics. We'll have the edge when they pitch for the same stuff.'

'So will they.' Terry's eyes twinkled. 'I'm not worried.' He patted a stack of papers on his desk. 'You should see the applications for Lim's position. Crème de la crème, baby. Three from agencies in the US, two from Europe.'

'Why are people applying from overseas?'

'They're losing their jobs. There's a flood of labour coming home. I've got thirty-five applications here altogether. We're going to have a *feast*. And a bloody pain in the arse. Meeting at four? I'll have culled them by then.'

'Sure.'

Blanche walked back across the open plan. Kate was motioning to her, but Blanche kept walking with her eyes down, pretending to be vagued out, then went into her office and shut the door.

When she arrived at Sirius Cove that evening, she found Rhys in the kitchen. She was looking inside the fridge. She started guiltily at the sound of Blanche, but Blanche was expecting her: Leon had said she was due.

'Thank you for bringing Mum home last week.'

'She said she thought she could manage a bit of dinner.'

'That's a good idea. There's probably some soup in the freezer.'

Blanche went through to her mother, who was dozing on the couch. She crouched before her. Marie looked peaceful, her skin smooth and tanned in the twilight. The news was on, a member of the Taliban saying, *We don't just want to impose Sharia law on Afghanistan, we want to impose it on the whole world*. Blanche turned it down. She touched her mother's hand, and Marie's eyes flew open.

'Rhys has come to paint the gauntlets,' Marie said.

Blanche didn't know what her mother meant. She seemed a bit delirious lately. 'Can I get you anything?'

'Water.'

Marie was dozing again when she put it before her so Blanche left the room. In the kitchen Rhys was removing clingwrap from a tureen. 'I found this. It looks like something she could eat, but I don't know how to work the microwave.'

'It's from Susan. Here. I'll do it.'

'I met Susan. She seems pretty upset.'

'Mum was too out of it for a visit last time she came over. This looks good. Of all things, I've got a craving for Redskins.'

'How far gone are you?'

'Eighteen weeks.'

'It must be getting better now. You'll have some good months before it gets difficult.'

'I do feel good but I'm still scared.' Blanche put the tureen in the microwave and pressed some buttons. 'Especially of the birth.'

'Don't be. Hormones are the best painkillers.'

'I'm also scared of becoming a hausfrau.'

'That's inevitable for a while.'

Blanche tried to concentrate on Rhys's face and avoid her hands. One of those naturally slim women, no doubt. Blanche always wondered how they carried pregnancies. She was wearing lipstick today; she looked quite nice.

Rhys turned to find Blanche examining her. 'You'll miss your job, eh.'

'Actually, I've decided to stay.'

'Really? Are they going to give you maternity leave?'

'No.'

'I guess you can afford to stop working.'

Blanche wondered if Rhys was like her brothers, making presumptions about her wealth. She thought of her debts and the reduction of her inheritance. She could afford to stop working but she could no longer afford the lifestyle she wanted: none of them cared about that, in fact they were probably happy. 'Yes and no. I was going to resign today but I've decided to stay as long as I can, and get back to work as soon as I can. There's a top female creative who worked right up until two days before she gave birth and was back at work full-time soon after.'

'That's impressive,' Rhys said dubiously. 'She mustn't have been breastfeeding.'

'You had your child on your own, didn't you?'

'Pretty much. But Travis's father helped out, as well as my business partner Rob.'

'So not really on your own. Did you stop working for long?'

'Almost a year. I let everything go. I went into debt. I built back up slowly.'

'But you're really successful now, aren't you? So you didn't lose out, at the end of the day.'

'Well, I was planning an exhibition when I fell pregnant. I had to write it off. But I'm back onto it now.'

'You're going to have an exhibition? I didn't know you were an artist!'

Rhys smiled as though at a private joke. The microwave pinged and she popped the door then removed the tureen with a tea towel. Blanche was aware of a shield being held up against her. She felt bad about her tone at Rhys's place a few weeks ago. 'Where are you showing?' she persisted.

'Fussel and Warhaft?'

'Really?' Blanche was impressed and a little envious. 'What sort of work?'

'Paintings.'

'So you'll give away the day job if your show sells out?' Blanche said eagerly.

'God, no. Tattooing is still the top of my pyramid. Marie told me you were a great drawer when you were a kid.'

'Did she?' Blanche stopped, soup plates in her hands.

'She said you went to art school.'

'Yeah, then I sold out.'

'You could draw when you stop working. I drew when I was pregnant and breastfeeding. Crap mostly, but it felt good. Do you ever get ideas?'

'I bought a whole lot of charcoal and paper a while back, around the time I fell pregnant. I got obsessed with tunnels and alleys. Freud would have a lot to say about that I'm sure.'

'Or the road builders of Sydney.'

Blanche moved cutlery around on the table. She was trying

to remember what she had done with the drawings. She couldn't even remember what she had done with the unused paper and charcoal. It bothered her. 'They were in a sort of abstract expressionist style. Kind of obsessive.'

'That sounds great.'

'My graphic designer loved them.'

Rhys looked at her with interest. 'And what else?'

'Oh god, I don't know. I ran out of time.' Blanche placed some soup on a tray for her mother. 'It must be strange, working on people's bodies.'

'It's kind of an honour. On the good people.' Rhys smiled. 'Like your mother.'

'My mother was never a body-conscious person, you know. She really took us all by surprise.'

'It's not just about the body. The body contains everything else.'

Marie could hear Blanche and Rhys speaking in the kitchen. A hushed, even exchange, broken at one stage by an exclamation, couldn't tell if it was a bark or a laugh. Exhaustion had hit early today. She couldn't tell in what order things happened. The touch of Blanche on her shoulder, living room visible one moment, swathed in darkness the next. The television glimmering, then lights on low and a candle on the coffee table. A sudden silence making her struggle to sit upright, thinking she was alone in the house. Then she heard them again. Soup steaming on a tray before her, Blanche saying, 'Do you want to sit up at the table with us, Mum? Or do you want to eat it there?' Marie looked at the soup. Her mind devoured it, but her body felt distant, a shrivelling ball of pain that wanted no interference. Maybe if she rested a bit more. She lay back against the cushions, listening to Blanche and Rhys talking quietly at the table. *Children, work,* she made out a few words. She fell back to sleep.

She had begun to secrete the fentanyl patches and morphine days ago. The idea had come to her when Carla accidentally dropped a vial. It plopped under the bed without her noticing, and when she left, Marie rescued it. She put the vials and patches in the bottom drawer of her bedside table, beneath a scarf, alongside a syringe Carla had discarded after one use.

They knew the cancer had reached her liver, but nobody knew why she was so distended. As the rest of her shrank, her stomach grew. She was monstrous. Jaundice stained her skin and eyes. Fluid collected in her feet, Carla massaging them each visit. Marie still managed to brush her teeth every night.

She seemed so often to be surrounded. She felt as though she were at a party and the lights had been dimmed, an expectant hubbub like a speech in the wings. Noise, muted; heat, light, movement. Susan, Rob, Stew, Nell, her children, her children. So many things to be done, so little time. Did she say it? Or think it? Was that Blanche? Or Judy. In the car with Judy in Tasmania, driving towards their mother's birthplace in Liffey. And all along the horizon, the smoky blue line of the Western Tiers.

They were in Avalon, in the backyard filling trumpet flowers with water to squirt through the fence at the goats next door. Win's market garden. Imagine that, Leon. It was twenty years before I learnt that trumpet flowers were Honolulu lilies and a noxious weed. Smell of Chinese food, Win's silent wife. Win beheading the chooks, blood pulsing, passionfruit along the fence, those flowers seemed to have been designed by God ... Don't go back there, it's all changed. It's all big houses now. *Drug-dealer mansions at Whale Beach*, Ross used to say, *ha-ha*. My mother was quite cold, Blanche, she was a mystery to me. My father was in Changi. We could never complain. He'd say, *Well, it isn't Changi*. My parents told me so little. It was as if I was born in a cabbage patch in that market garden on the northern beaches.

Tickle of contact. A liquid chink, chair squeaking. Marie opened her eyes. Rhys was seated before her with paints and a brush.

Marie splayed her hand on the cloth that Rhys put down.

'Any requests? Colours? Plants?'

She tried to think. A jumble of images. 'Birds of paradise?' Her mouth felt like cottonwool. 'The ocean, waves?'

'Yeah. And I was thinking palms. Something long and slender.'

'The Gymea lily is shooting, Mum.' It was Blanche's voice.

She was sitting on the other couch. 'Leon said it's because of the drought.'

'Yes. They flower when traumatised.' Marie thought: I must go into the garden tomorrow to see that.

'That's a good idea,' said Rhys. 'Gymea lily.'

'Can I get you anything?' Blanche addressed both of them.

'Maybe another rag? Thanks.'

Marie felt her eyelids drooping. Again the chink of Rhys dipping her brush into the jar of water. The cool lick of sable along her wrist. It travelled her nerve endings and she managed to sit up to watch the gauntlets forming. This brilliant, wide-awake reality, sweet and tangy as citrus. Rhys worked fast. Wavy dark blues appeared around her wrists; along her tendons burnt orange lines with little hooks at the end. Green jags for palm fronds. The narrow sable tongue insinuating itself along the corrugations of her hands.

'Can you hold them still for a few minutes so they dry?'

Marie tried to stop her hands trembling. They looked so beautiful. She felt like a queen. Here on her throne, waiting, waiting.

Blanche had left them alone for most of the work, then returned as Rhys finished. Marie met her eyes, troubled and brimming. They smiled at one another.

'Thank you,' said Blanche to Rhys in the kitchen afterwards. She covered her eyes. 'I was always trying to make her love me more. I'm just like Dad. More, more, more.'

Marie left the balcony door open and night filled the house. There was the rustle of an animal in the foliage outside her window, then the scatter of kentia palm nuts on flagging. Somewhere on the harbour someone was having a party and rap music pumped across the water, its urgent macho voice crystal clear.

She switched on the light and went to the bathroom to clean herself with a washer. Poured a glass of water and took it back to bed. She sat propped against the pillows with the fentanyl patches on the covers beside her, opened her nightgown and laboriously unpeeled a patch from its protective backing then placed it on her thigh. She unwrapped the next. She hadn't counted on it being such an effort, the stubborn adhesive taking all her energy. She dropped it and it stuck to the bedcovers and she cursed. Paused to catch her breath. She worked her way through the box, calmly, efficiently, as though in a dream. The patches were irritating, the glue sharp against her skin. She fought the urge to scratch them off.

She hadn't eaten for almost three days now; she hoped it would help the chemicals absorb quicker. She unscrewed the bottle of morphine and drank it down. Too ambitious. She lurched forward gagging, pressed her lips together and swallowed. She followed it with water, willing the mixture down. She finished them in alternation. Sweet thick morphia, cool water, cool water. She burped so loudly she worried she would wake Leon. She began to feel dizzy.

Last of all, she filled the syringe with as many ampoules of morphine as would fit. She lay on her side, introduced it into her rectum and depressed the plunger with shaking hands. She slipped, cursed, and persisted. She did this a second time, proud of her strength and will, and when she had finished, lay there catching her breath. She hoped it was enough.

She pushed away the debris of wrappings and bottles, wishing vaguely she could clean them up to save someone the trouble. She was hot. Itchy. She fumbled to remove her socks then stretched on her back, listening to the night. She remembered Nell watching television the last time she was here, her rapt face in the screen's blue light. She stepped into the memory and held her against her hip, played with her hair. And all across the night the *chink-chink* of crickets, tiny, random, like city lights.

Leon overslept and dressed without showering so as not to be late. Not wanting to wake his mother, he rushed out the door and drove to Neutral Bay.

He always loved the descent to the harbour, how the opposite shore pressed flat and close. The address was several blocks above the foreshore and the building had no view, but you could see the water from the corner. Clark was walking down the street as Leon parked; Blanche was already in the flat.

The tenants had moved out only the day before, and the place still felt warm with habitation. Leon followed his siblings from room to room, admiring the floorboards and layout. The light was good, except in the smaller bedroom where he would be. He needed to have a discussion with Clark and Blanche about how long they expected him to live with his mother. What if she lasted another six months? It would be like home nursing in a way. Then again, he wouldn't be paying rent. He had an urge, as he lingered in this room, to begin looking for a place to buy. With the First Home Owner Grant and his inheritance, he could get a little flat in Maroubra or somewhere. He would even have enough left over to have a holiday. He smiled at the thought. His future seemed full of ease and possibility.

The main bedroom was big and light. Over the mantlepiece was the clear white imprint of a robe on the wall, the sleeves flared like a person in flight or a child's impression of an angel. 'Wow, how freaky,' said Leon. 'What's *that*?'

Blanche touched the wall then looked at her fingertips. 'They've had a candle here, that's all. It's the shape of a kimono. They must have hung a kimono on the wall. We'll have to dock their bond.'

There were hooks on the picture rails, a washer in the corner. The outline of dust describing a wardrobe, another narrower one that could have been a bookshelf. There was a used bus ticket on the bathroom shelf and a packet of castor sugar in the otherwise empty kitchen cupboards.

They walked into the backyard and Blanche turned to her brothers, eyes shining with pride. 'It's good isn't it? It's perfect.'

'Yeah.' Clark nodded. 'It's exactly what she needs. So what's the plan?'

'Fatima's going to Sirius today to clean. Tomorrow morning the removalists pack.'

'I'll be helping with that, then come here with the removalists to unload the furniture,' said Leon. 'I'll arrange the living room straightaway.'

'I'll come at lunch and help you out,' said Blanche.

'I'll stay with Mum,' said Clark.

'Give her her lunch in her room,' said Leon. 'Hopefully it won't be too disturbing up there.'

'Yeah, and I'll pack her clothes beforehand,' said Blanche. 'God, it's exhausting just to *think* about it.'

'I'll get her comfy on the couch while you set up her bedroom, and I've arranged for Carla to come at five o'clock.'

'Good on you, Leon,' said Blanche.

Leon smiled. He toed the bull grass. 'You could run a vegie garden down the side of this yard.'

'Nice idea, but there are seven other tenants here.'

Leon pictured the blackboy down in the corner, but there was no way he'd be able to move it. He'd just said that to make his mother feel good. It saddened him to lose that plant. He looked at the Deco building. He was surprised at how nice it was. 'How much is a flat like this worth?'

'Hmm. Four or five hundred?'

'Jesus.'

'Is that all?' said Clark.

'The market's gone down. It's cheaper than Potts Point and places like that.'

'Is it?' Leon said in surprise. 'I could almost afford a little place like this with my share of the estate.'

'Of course you could, if you get a job.' Blanche nodded encouragingly. 'Easily.'

Clark said something but an electrical whine began over their heads, drowning him out. They looked at one another in consternation. The noise was coming from the flat above.

'It's a bloody circular saw,' Leon said. 'They're renovating.'

Clark could see the silhouette of someone in the kitchen, a couple of panels propped up next to them. 'It's Sunday!'

'They can't do that,' said Blanche. 'We'll have to get onto the council.'

'I'm going to the toilet,' said Leon.

Clark looked Blanche up and down.

'Your pregnancy's beginning to show. You look great.'

'Really? God, I haven't said anything at work. Maybe it just shows to people who know about it.'

'Janice used to say the best time to be pregnant is seven months. She used to come home and talk about pregnancy esteem, how well people treated her. Why are you worried about them seeing at work?'

'Because a pregnant woman is a retrenched woman?'

'I thought you were leaving.'

'I will to give birth.' She read his disappointment immediately. 'Don't give me a hard time, Clark, okay? It's my decision.'

After all that, thought Clark, she doesn't want to change. Unbelievable. His phone began to ring. 'Sorry.' He fished it out of his pocket and saw Sylvia's name flashing on the screen. The circular saw started up again. 'I have to take this,' he said, and walked to the end of the yard. 'Hallo?'

'Hi. I was just ringing to see how you were, how everything was going.'

Her voice was very faint. Clark leant against the paling fence, trying to hear. There had been no contact since the split at the beach. He scanned the rest of his day: nothing that couldn't be put off, in case Sylvia wanted to see him. 'I'm okay. Just rolling along. You?'

'Yeah.'

He thought he could hear her sniffing over the whine of the saw. Another phone was ringing somewhere. He pressed his to one ear, blocking the other with his finger. He rose on his toes to look through the paling, found a chink of harbour. He still couldn't hear what Sylvia was saying.

Blanche was waving at him. She approached across the grass, her phone pressed against her thigh. 'I have to go, Clark. Fatima's at the house and she can't get in.'

'Okay, okay. Can you hold on a sec?' he said to Sylvia.

'Do you know where there's a spare set of keys?' Blanche asked him.

'Doesn't Fatima have her own set?'

'She forgot to bring them. She thought someone would be there to let her in.'

'Leon would know.'

'Leon!' Blanche shouted back at the building. 'I'm coming now, okay, Fatima?' she said into her phone.

Clark watched his sister walk away. 'Sorry,' he said to Sylvia. 'What did you say?'

At last, her voice came to him.

'I said, I miss you.'